This is a work of fiction. Names, characters, places, and incidents either are the product of the author's imagination or are used fictitiously. Any resemblance to actual persons, living or dead, events, or locales is entirely coincidental.

NORTHLAND
Dark seas, dark fate, dark seas
To the ocean we go
With a heart full of vengeance
And a tale full of woe
We'll hunt the sirens
Till the end of days
Dark seas, dark fate, dark seas.
PORT DEVLIN
BROKEN PROMISES
AISLE OF THE BLACK WATER
DAUGHTER'S PASS
BAY OF THE RED SAND
GRAYMONT
DAGGER TOOTH
GRISOM ISLAND
THE BLEEDING CHANNEL
ABEL'S POINT
TRESON HARBOR

In the dark of the night, on the restless sea
Dark seas, dark fate, dark seas.
A pirate's son with his father bold
Dark seas, dark fate, dark seas.

Chorus
Dark seas, dark fate, to the ocean we go
With a heart full of vengeance and a tale of woe
We'll hunt the sirens with the end of days
Dark seas, dark fate, dark seas.
Chorus

The sirens came with their haunting song
Dark seas, dark fate, dark seas
They took the crew and his father strong
Dark seas, dark fate, dark seas
- Chorus -
The boy grew up with a fire inside
Dark seas, dark fate, dark seas.
A hunter now with a crew of pride
Dark seas, dark fate, dark seas.
- Chorus -
With a ship so grand and a crew so brave
Dark seas, dark fate, dark seas
He'll find the sirens and send them to their grave
Dark seas, dark fate, dark seas.
- Chorus -

4

This is a dark fantasy romance and contains instances that may trigger some readers such as:
- Violence
- Sirens eating humans
- Graphic sexual situations
- Violence against women
- Breath play
- Suicide (off page)
- Thoughts of suicide
- Human trafficking
- Attempted rape and references to past rape
- Rape (in a dream setting)
- Bondage
- Torture
- PTSD
- Blood play

To the man who pushed me to publish my very first book when I didn't think I was good enough and who continues to believe in me even when I don't believe in myself.

I love you, Alex.

We are debris on a monstrous tide.
Leaves in a violent storm.
~The Acts of Man

A man who seeks to control the sea is a fool.

No ship is big enough. No man is strong enough. The ocean is the mother of all destruction and to sail on her raging waters means a thousand lucky moments or one unlucky death. It is a gamble I relish.

But today is not my day and I smiled into the brutal wind knowing it.

The skies were gray and the rain beat down on my sun-chapped cheeks, chilling me to my bones. But the weather didn't know that I could not be swayed by the grip of an icy tempest. I held onto the shroud with one hand, watching as the Burning Rose rocked and stooped over undulating waves. Her crimson sails were rolled up tight as the storm pelted the deck. Men were shouting frantically, holding on to whatever they could as the ocean reminded us all of her unyielding power.

But she would never get fear out of me. Never again.

A smile and a maniacal laugh? Perhaps.

My lips stretched, ignoring the salt water spray coating my tongue, and I laughed in the face of death and all that aided him in making the last moments of a man's life a terrifying ride. I mused over the threat of oblivion and raised my free hand to challenge the heavens.

Do better, I thought. *Do fucking better.*

"Vidar!" someone shouted. Only one man could yell louder than an ocean storm. I whipped my head around, still guffawing at the ocean's attempt to sink us, and saw Gus gripping the foremast as the ship rocked hard to one side. "You crazy fuck!"

"What?" I barked. "Never seen the bridge to hell?"

"This isn't the bridge to hell!" He lunged for the shroud beside me and wound his arms through the thick ropes. "This *is* hell!"

The Burning Rose gave one more heave before the skies opened, allowing a beam of red twilight through its thick, clouded veil. The ocean turned a violent cerise as it reflected the sun's rays. While the water still rocked us back and forth, the wind had all but completely died as we reached the edge of the bellowing gale.

I swept my tangled, sandy blonde locks back from my face. My coat was pounds heavier and filled with water and my boots sloshed, but those were all minor discomforts. Gus shook out his white beard, but his head was but a naked orb now. We locked eyes and for a moment we just took it all in. Then we both laughed at the stupidity of it all. Risking our lives on the seas. Surviving storms.

Hauling barrels of heads packed in salt through the chaos.

This time, we had only two. It had been a slow couple of months. The wicked monsters of the sea had been staying inconspicuous and they'd changed their feeding habits. They never took to land in the same places and they rarely took on entire crews anymore. It had made them harder to track over the years.

But I would always learn their ways. And I would always break their patterns. I would make the ocean as terrifying to them as it was to most humans who sailed its vicious waters.

"This isn't hell," I said, catching my breath while I could. "I've seen hell."

I turned to face the painted waters, eyeing the wall of clouds toward which we were sailing. We were a day from the port. Perhaps more if we drifted further off course.

"Aye," Gus nodded. "You've seen worse than hell, my boy." He slapped my shoulder. "But ye be the devil to the spawn of hell, now. I think there may be a throne down there for you."

"Aye," I groaned, stooping to pick my hat up off the floor by my feet. The leather tricorn was soaked through like everything else on deck. I lifted it and dropped it on my head, tipping the front of it at Gus. "I'm the devil. And we're almost home." I took in a deep breath of the chilled air and roared, "Off your asses, dogs, and drop the sails!"

"Dark seas, cap'n!"

"Dark fate!" I laughed.

I strode to the foredeck, staring out at the red horizon as the equally red sails untethered and caught the wind.

Red sails. The Burning Rose was known for them.

And every siren in the south sea could see them coming from a mile away. I wanted them to. For when my red sails were in view, they knew they were already dead.

We arrived in Treson Harbor with empty stomachs and soggy boots. Mullins was quick to help me unload the barrel of salt. We pulled two heads out of what was now more like a brine and stuffed them in a potato sack.

The public wasn't fond of people carrying heads through town right in the open.

"How much do you think we'll get for two?" Mullins asked.

Sunlight reflected off his dark skin, the glint on his bald head nearly blinding me as I tied off the sack.

"For the young one? Enough. The matron, though." I let out a small chuckle and shrugged. "More than enough."

"If you just sell 'em to the damn establishments," Uther, one of my other crewmen, started, "We could make more than—"

"We are selling them," I grinned, raising a brow sarcastically and kicking the barrel. "Well, a bit of them."

"Forty years of this shit," Gus mumbled, unloading more cargo with the others, despite the state of his creaky back.

"Get what you can for the other loot," I told him, handing the sack to Mullins. "I'll be back tonight with our bounty."

He tossed the sack over his shoulder and we started walking through the bustling streets inland toward the governor's house. It was a long trek, but it would do me good after being on a ship for weeks.

The rain made the streets a muddy mess, but a bath was waiting somewhere in a sweaty brothel. Business needed to be taken care of, though. The coin came first, then the luxuries.

"I heard Paxton Smith is doubling the price he pays for tongues these days," Mullin's said as we hauled our loot across town. "And Madam Letty is doubling the price she pays for the ones without. She comes through once a month now, you know."

I scoffed. "I don't trade tongues and I don't trade sirens with their heads attached. That dirty business is for pirates and scum."

"Some of the men might disagree. I been listening to the chatter." He leaned closer as if part of my crew was in earshot. "Not many hunters are coming in with anything to show for it. 'Cept us. Word is, they think you're picking the market clean. Leaving none for the rest of 'em."

"It's not a market, Mullins. They're wicked beasts and a hunter's job is to kill them. Not sell their tongues and sell their bodies into slavery. The only good siren is one without her head."

"Right. Right."

His shutting up didn't make me think he'd dropped the subject. I groaned and rolled my eyes.

"Out with it."

"Well, it's just that we're the best hunting ship on the waters. Why not capitalize a bit more, you know? More coin means happier crewmen."

"You think my crew's unhappy?" I said jokingly.

"Nah, captain. Not at all. You treat us right and all. But there's a whole ocean of wealth out there we're not tapping into. We bring the governor heads and we collect the bounties. But we could do more, don't you think?"

"I think wealth looks different to you and me." I stopped, turning to Mullins and poking him in the chest with my finger. "See, you want to kill for the coin and you're perfectly fine risking your life for that. For a piece of silver or two." I backed up a step, raising my palms up and grinning. "I kill because I like killing, mate."

I continued walking down the muddy street. He watched me with narrowed eyes and then a smile tugged at his full lips and he shook his head.

"You are a crazy man, Vidar. Maybe too crazy for me."

"Ahh, you say that every time we get back into town," I laughed. "But we both know you'd be bored with any other captain."

Vidar

He swept his blade across her knee
And down she fell, a slayer was he
~A Sea Shanty

I stood before Governor Whitton as he fattened himself on a pork thigh. The dining room of his pristine mansion was quiet save for the sound of his chewing and the slow rhythm of water dripping off the hem of my still-soaked coat onto the stone floor. I'd tracked a muddy trail into his home. Not that he cared. Two servant girls were cleaning behind me, making sure traces of my presence were erased.

Whitton was fully focused on his meal, his plump cheeks bouncing with every bite of greasy meat. He smacked his food and internally, I was wincing at the irritating sound.

Gnawing. The ripping of flesh. The slurping of fresh blood and pleasured moans of hungry mouths. Teeth scraping on bone. Tendons snapping.

I cleared my throat, hoping the governor would get on with things.

At my feet sat the sack with two heads stuffed inside. I was eager to pass them off. Burn them. Burry them. Whatever I was asked to do with them after I was paid.

"How many did you say?" Whitton asked with a full mouth.

He slapped his half-eaten leg of pig onto his silver plate, splashing melted butter onto the ivory tablecloth. With greasy fingers, he picked up a crystal glass of wine and slurped its contents. His wooden chair creaked under his weight as he leaned back to regard me and my bag.

"Two," I said simply. "One of them a matron."

"Oh?" he said with boredom. "Which matron?"

"Matron Ethrelia."

"Hmm." He took another drink, waving a hand at one of his other servants.

He had no idea what any of their names were. He knew very little about anything, especially sirens.

The servant walked to the sack and picked it up, setting it on the table next to Whitton. He untied the ropes, pulling it open to peer inside. I could have warned him, but I didn't. Instead, I watched as the young man reared back with disgust at the macabre sight and the wall of sour stench that hit him in the face. He went pale, his eyes glazing over, and I knew he was trying not to retch.

"New kid?" I said, lifting a brow toward Whitton.

He shrugged with disinterest.

"I'll give you fifty," he sighed.

I stilled, eyes narrowing at the pampered fuck. "Fifty. For one?"

"For both."

Chuckling, I said, "That won't go over well with my crew."

"I'm not responsible for your crew."

"A matron alone is worth—"

"They're worth what I say they're worth." He picked up his pork leg again and continued gnawing on the meat. "The Ginger James' crew brought two of the singers to shore last month. Madam Letty put them up in her brothel and I swear half of Dawn was here paying just to see them and paying more to touch them."

Which meant Madam Letty was paying twice as much in taxes. I ground my teeth at his greed, but I wasn't surprised by it.

"And?"

"And the butcher in White Crown has been asking about tongues. Says his governor got a taste for them and is willing to pay hundreds."

"Wonderful for him," I said with a sarcastic smile.

Finally, Whitton's eyes met mine, partially yellowed and droopy. He had the face of a bulldog without any of the cute-ugly appeal.

"So, killing them is outdated. No one cares about their heads anymore. They care whether or not they can eat their tongues or fuck them."

Disgust roiled through me like turned milk in my stomach. I hung my thumbs on my leather belts, transferring my weight to one leg.

"The only good siren is a dead one," I muttered to myself, repeating words my father fed me over and over as a child.

"What was that?"

"Cutting out their voice and selling their bodies is wrong."

Whitton leaned back again, resting his hands on his round belly.

"Sympathizing, are we?"

Never. "Keeping them on land around all these people will turn bloody someday, and not for them. For us."

"The fact is, Treson Harbor is the biggest town on this coast. People inland want exotic things. Excitement. We can give that to them. In a year's time, this will be the richest town this side of the country because we have what no one else has. We have creatures of the deep. Creatures some people still think are just myths. That's a lot of coin I could be putting in your pocket if you'd just bring me some damn live ones instead of this shit."

He knocked the sack off the table, letting the heads roll across the floor with a wet thump. Gray, clammy faces with mouths agape peered up at the ceiling, long tresses of black hair like an ink spill on the floor.

I wasn't buying it and Whitton could see it. He leaned forward, elbows on the table, and grumbled against the fat of his abdomen pushing on his lungs.

"Times have changed, Woelfson. Those creatures aren't feared anymore. Merchants don't go missing like they used to. The ocean's safer and people don't want heads, they want product."

Disgusting.

He waved his hand at the same servant that nearly expelled his last meal all over the dining room and the boy walked stiffly out of the room.

"The oceans are safer because I've hunted every damn singing temptress under its waves and those that are left have fled," I argued. "Our merchants wouldn't be sailing with as much confidence if I wasn't out there hunting. Our fishermen would be too scared to go out. I've killed the most and if I hadn't, children would still be lying awake at night afraid of what's out there. We wouldn't have bronze bells hanging over every chapel and on every dock"

Whitton still seemed bored as the boy servant returned with a platter covered by a silver dome. He set it down in front of the governor and backed away.

"If I was focused on tongues, I'd have never cleaned the tides of those wicked monsters and we'd be a fucking ghost town. But because of me, rats like Collin Jones and Peter Michaels can hunt for tongues instead of heads. Merchant ships like the Camdon and Cornwallis leave and come back. That's how you make your town rich. With successful trade. Export."

"Hmf. The Cornwallis has been gone two weeks longer than expected. I wouldn't use them as an example."

Tucking a fresh napkin in the collar of his shirt, Whitton lifted the silver dome from his plate to reveal a small strip of red meat atop a bed of pickled watermelon rinds. I furrowed my brows at the odd delicacy, somewhat in denial. When Whitton's knife cut into the meat and the rare insides glistened pink, my nose twitched with revulsion.

Whitton sliced off a bite-sized piece of the tongue and slid it between his teeth with a pleasured sigh. He made a show of chewing the bite slowly and then pointed his fork at me.

"You're about to have some trouble, Woelfson. If you don't evolve with the times, people like Collin Jones and Peter Michaels will try to take you out of the picture. And I won't be able to stop them. See, they've adopted the skin trade and if you keep killing their product and leaving nothing to be scavenged, you'll have a war on your hands with the other hunters."

"Hunters," I scoffed. "What's a hunter that doesn't kill his prey?"

"Still a hunter. Just one who values coin over his own personal vendettas."

"What you're doing here is dangerous. Keeping sirens on land. It won't end like you want. Their voices grow back. Their tongues grow back. You silence them and they'll find a way to whisper in your ear."

He took another bite, unbothered. "Which is why I can think of no better person to make sure they're maintained."

"Maintained?"

"The ones we already have in Treson Harbor need regular… trimming. Not everyone can afford one of those…" He paused, staring at my chest and circling his fork in the air toward me. "One of those… things."

"A silentium," I said flatly.

"Yes, that. Common folk can't afford nor do they want to wear one of those things. So," he shrugged. "We keep them trimmed and quiet and leashed and the money flows."

"I'm not 'trimming' your stock."

He smiled, still chewing, and raised his hands out to the sides proudly. I stared at him, trying my best to mask the utter disgust I was feeling at his proposal. But if he wasn't going to pay me anymore for the heads of defeated beasts, I wasn't going to keep my crew for much longer.

My father would be sickened by the way things had evolved. Or perhaps he'd be proud. Almost single-handedly, I'd thinned the numbers of those damned sea creatures so much that townspeople barely considered them a threat anymore. At the very least, I'd driven them back from our shores and into rougher waters where most ships didn't even venture.

But with the lack of threat came ignorance. Comfort.

One day it would lead to violence, but I seemed to be the only one who knew it.

"So?" Whitton said, slurping his wine. "Do you consent to our new deal?"

"What deal is that?" I sighed.

"You, the best hunter, son of the great Ethelwoelf, remakes his name. You bring in the women. You collect the reward."

"Hmf. You mean you collect the reward."

"If I get rich, you get rich. It's time you realized the way of things. I'll even give you an advance because I'm that confident in your skills, captain. I'll double my offer for those rotting heads if you agree to bring back the spoils of your next hunt alive and intact. Come now. You have a crew to pay and a woman and child to support."

Nothing about the governor's offer sat well with me, but my thoughts wandered to my crew. Almost every one of them was plucked off the streets and they relied on me and our hunts. Some of them relied on them to feed their families. Perhaps Mullins was right. Perhaps Uther was right.

Fuck, who was I kidding? They were all goddamn fools…

Agony makes a dead man or a dreaded man.
The dreaded man knows the devil and the devil fears him.
~Unknown

A man could not appreciate a hot bath the way a hunter fresh off the stormy sea could. I had gotten a room to myself for the night and most of my men were quick to take what they were owed so they could throw it away on good rum and women. I had plans to pamper myself in a tub with a platter of bread and grapes to keep me company.

I tossed my salt-crusted clothes over a chair, leaning my cutlass against the bedpost. Just before stepping into the tub, I unbuckled the leather vambrace on my right forearm and slid it off. The thing took two wooden fingers covered in leather with it. I'd gotten used to not having a pinky and ring finger on my right hand since they'd been bitten clean off at the second knuckle. And Gus was good enough to engineer multiple gloves to fit my hand over the years. He was a good man. Sometimes too good. He'd been trying his best to look after me since I was a boy, even if it had almost killed him more than once.

I sunk into the warm water with a relieved groan, letting the heat blanket my tired limbs. Downstairs, the tavern was bustling. My ship wasn't the only one recently returned from the savage seas and there were plenty of men seeking the company of women and drink. I needed neither. My mind was full of conflict. The governor's words rang in my head and it was a sour tone. Imagining myself joining the ranks of those filthy skin traders made my teeth grind.

Before I could fall too far into that sickening train of thought, there was an insistent knock on my door followed by someone barging in. I rolled my eyes toward the intruder to see a short, busty woman in a cream-colored dress sliding into the room. Her red curls were piled on her head and held up with a thin scarf. Her eyes scanned the room for a second before catching me by the fire soaking in the tub.

"Vidar," she huffed, stomping further into the room and closing the door behind her.

She was quick to start picking up my clothes and draping each item over one arm.

"I had to hear the Burning Rose had docked from Janessa," she complained. "You can't even be bothered to come home?"

"It's not my home, Agnes," I sighed, splashing my face. "I gave it to you."

"It *is* your home. You can't just live in taverns and brothels."

"It seems to be working out quite well, actually."

She dragged a chair near my tub, letting the legs scrape obnoxiously on the floor, and dropped the bundle of my clothes in her lap with a sigh.

"David is asking about you. Says he's anxious to be part of your crew."

"We've talked about this."

"If he doesn't start working on the Burning Rose, he'll enlist with one of the other crews and you know it. I'd rather he go out there with you than one of those scum crews that brings back those witches alive."

I turned to look at her, leaning my head back against the edge of my bath.

"Suppose it's a bad time to tell you that Whitton is demanding I start farming them rather than hunting them."

Her already pale, freckled face went paler. "What?"

"Says he won't pay for dead ones anymore."

"But… bring them here? To Treson?"

"Here. Inland. Doesn't matter. He has a plan to make Treson Harbor rich off them."

Saying it out loud made my skin crawl.

"Well… that's just ridiculous."

"Ridiculous," I lifted my head to look at her, brows raised. "And it means David isn't joining my crew. Have Sean take him under his wing. Blacksmithing is a good trade."

"He wants to be on the sea," she sighed, dipping one of my scarves into the water to begin scrubbing my shoulders. "Like his father."

"His father died on the sea."

"He knows. But you didn't. You're his hero and I curse you for it." She moved her hand slowly along the side of my neck, nudging tendrils of dark-blond dreadlocks out of the way. "You've taken good care of us. Too good. And I know you spared me too many details of what happened that day. To you and to my Jack."

"Jack was my father's best friend."

She went silent, her fingers caressing the back of my ear. The soft crackling of the fire and the muffled noise of the tavern were all that filled the space. I stared across the room at the wall, watching the firelight and shadows mingle on the wood.

Agnes was a sorrowful woman. Her husband was dead… and I'd been the one to carve up his corpse for the bitches that ate him. He had left her in Treson Harbor with a round belly. When my mother could not stand my need for vengeance and the general cloudy, gloomy town where she once lived with my father, she left. The last I heard, she lived with my aunt in Nelson drinking tea and spending my father's money.

I should have been bitter about that, but I wasn't. I didn't enjoy the thought of my mother seeing my dad in my face or the torture of my actions in my eyes. When I came back from that hunt, I was not the son that had left. Perhaps she left because she realized her husband wasn't the only man who had died at sea. Her son, too, had become little more than a ghost of the one she knew.

When Agnes' hand began to slide over my arm, I knew the mood she was in. I saw it from time to time, usually when I was gone a long while. Her touch traced over the hardened muscle of my shoulder and bicep and all the way down to the severed fingers.

"You are such a wounded man," she whispered. I kept my eyes on the wall, listening to her talk. "Those awful creatures took everything from us and you've given so much to hunt them down." Leaning forward, she rested her cheek on the top of my head, her fingers continuing to trace across my skin. "What can I give you, Vidar? You've been so long at sea."

When her hand started to descend into the water and wander south, I calmly took her wrist to stop her and lifted her knuckles to my lips. Craning my head back, I caught the look on her face. She was such a lonely woman. Despite giving her my house to raise her son, I knew she needed much more than lodging. I was fourteen the day I came back with two fewer fingers and a figurative sword through my heart. She was a mother… she wanted to nurture me. Make me feel better. She wanted to help me heal.

When I turned twenty, she stopped seeing me as a boy and realized she needed healing, too.

So, two broken people found themselves in bed together seeking something different than anger, sorrow, and grief. For her, it was fleeting bliss. For me… it was wrong. I couldn't be that man for her. I couldn't be a father to her son. I couldn't be the man of a house I didn't want. My place was on the sea, the place where I would live and die. The place where I would become a killer.

Killers couldn't be husbands and fathers. My own father had proven that.

"Agnes," I said softly, lifting my hand up to cup her cheek. "Take my clothes and wash them. I will come to the house tomorrow morning."

"Will you stay?"

"For a night. In the pocket of my coat, there is coin. Take enough to make a dinner for the three of us."

Though a bit let down, Agnes smiled with partial satisfaction and nodded.

"It will do David some good to see you."

It didn't do anyone good to see me.

"Now, leave me to my bath. The seas were rough."

Her shoulder slumped a bit, but there was little to be done about it. She had a roof over her head and that was the best I could do. At best, one day she'd leave Treson Harbor, find a man who thought those rosy, freckled cheeks were the most beautiful thing in the world, and take her away. At worst, she'd die waiting for me because losing Jack had taken too much of her for anyone to repair.

My bath water cooled soon after Agnes left. I rose from the tub and threw on a fresh shirt and trousers, tying my hair into a thick bun. I'd grown rather scruffy since being at sea. Rather than shave completely, I trimmed up my newly formed facial hair and then made my way down into the tavern to join my men.

The music was loud and the people were even louder. The whole place smelled like stew and ale. Toward a back corner, I spotted Mullins, Gus, Harlow, and James. Each of them was holding a wooden mug and boisterously talking and laughing while they shared a platter of salted fish and bread. I made my way through the crowds, nudging a drunk Harlow out of his seat to sit down and prop my feet on the table.

Immediately, one of the barmaids leaned over me, giving me an ample view of her plump breasts as she filled a wooden mug with ale. Gus raised his cup to me with a wink and took a big swig. Just as the woman was walking away with her pitcher, I coiled my arm around her waist and hoisted her into my lap. She giggled, trying not to spill. Coils of blonde hair hung over her bare shoulders and she smelled like rum and baked bread.

"Anastasia," I greeted.

"Vidar," she returned in that delicious accent of hers. "Back so soon. But for how long?"

My eyes skimmed my men's. "Not long."

Stabbed too many times in the heart,
a man's soul splits in two…
and he is the space between.
~Father Eldrich III

"Truly?" James said, a mix of excitement and nervousness in his voice. "Whitton *wants* us to bring 'em back alive?"

Gus chuckled before filling his mouth with another big gulp of ale. Not much bothered him at his age. Nor did much surprise him. Not with all the tales he could tell.

The rest of the men at the table had stopped drinking like they were expecting me to have a fit over the matter. I skimmed their eyes and brought my mug to my lips, taking two big drinks.

I would need a lot if I was going to go along with Whitton's request.

"Drink up," I said, wiping my mouth with the back of my hand. "You earned it, boys."

Anastasia slid to her feet as I stood and attempted to follow me out. Most days, I would have welcomed her company. She was a gorgeous woman. Foreign and sweet. Easy on the eyes and good with her hands. But my mind was a mess and unless I had a few more mugs full of ale, I wasn't going to be able to enjoy her company. I turned and kissed her on the forehead before giving her a gentle shove to tell her to stay while I headed out to the porch.

Outside, the sound of music was muffled behind the wooden walls and all I could hear were the waves at the docks and some faint giggling whores as men chased them down the muddy streets. I took in the stale sea air mixed with the scent of mud and fish. The only damn smells I knew and they weren't even pleasant. But they were home… and Whitton wanted to stain the place with those she-demons from the deep. Imagining our brothels filled with tongueless sirens dressed in pretty costumes with powdered cheeks sickened me.

Sitting like a sleeping giant on the waves was the Burning Rose, waiting to set sail again and dye the waters red in the hunt. Only I would have to tell her there was no killing to be done. Only harvesting… like a damn, greedy fool.

I felt the particular rhythm of Gus's limp before he announced his presence.

"Crew's excited," he grunted, leaning on a wooden post beside me with a mug in hand. "A bit scared to show you, though."

I sighed sharply. "I won't fault them for being interested in money. Half of them don't even have a bed to sleep in."

"And half of them don't care. Those men live on the sea, same as you. Boys like Mullins and Billy would follow you to the bottom of the ocean if you asked. Why? Because you gave them a life better than they had."

"What's your point, old man?"

"Point is, if you want to refuse whatever deal you may or may not have made with that cunt, Whitton, say so. The Burning Rose will be a pirate ship again and we'll sail the water for different coin."

I laughed at the simplicity of it. And the sarcasm.

"I took her from pirates," I said. "I'm not putting that stain on the Rose again. Besides, she likes hunting more than she likes plundering."

"You talk about the bitch like she's your wife."

"She's pretty enough with an attitude that makes her as wild as any woman," I laughed again.

"Well, I suppose I didn't survive that night to throw you in a loony bin. You know I'll be behind you, no matter your decision. Just like I stood by your dad."

I nodded, glancing down at my gloved hand. It was a harsh and grotesque reminder of why I did what I did.

"So?" Gus asked. "You reluctant to bring 'em ashore because they're dangerous or you just can't stand not killing 'em?"

"Both," I sighed. "And neither. They're only good when they're not breathing." I turned to look at him. "And I won't be part of a slave trade, no matter who I'm trading."

"Is that your morals or your caution speaking?"

I shrugged. "I don't know anymore, Gus. I just know this whole thing is wrong. Bringing them on land for people to play with, with or without tongues, will end in a lot of blood and I doubt it will be theirs. Maybe not today. Maybe not tomorrow. But when you play with fire, eventually it catches something you don't intend and by then, it's out of control."

His eyes fell on my gloved hand as he took a drink from his mug.

"You know what I think?" he said, nodding toward my missing fingers. "I think you're terrified *she'll* show up one day and tear this whole damn world apart trying to get to you."

A slow chill rolled down my spine and I straightened, rolling my shoulders back.

"I haven't been scared of a siren since the day they ate the crew."

"Nah, I'm not talking about being afraid of what they'll do to you. I think you're afraid of what they'll do to *us*. What *she'll* do to us. Don't think I haven't seen it, boy."

"Seen what?" I asked though I knew what he was going to say.

"You check the face of every damn bitch we behead." He ran his fingers along his cheek from his ear to his mouth and raised his brows.

"You're looking for the thing you left. So? Would you be relieved if one of them was her? Or would you be—"

"Overjoyed. Maybe I can cut what she took from me out of her stomach," I joked, holding up my hand.

We both shared in laughter, shaking our heads at the stupidity of it.

"Aye," he said, pointing at his eye. "I'd do the same, but you already killed the one that took my eye."

Nothing about it was amusing, but over time, all we could do was laugh about it.

When we started to wind down, I found myself leaning on the railing and staring down the long street to the pier. The Rose was out there, waiting. My enthusiasm was waning, though. Perhaps I'd do what Whitton wanted for the sake of my crew and their pockets. Perhaps, once I was sailing in the black water again, I'd change my mind and we'd hunt like we normally did, with nets and harpoons. I wouldn't know until I was out at sea again.

All I knew was that things were changing and not for the better. Things were going to get darker than they'd ever been.

"I'm going to visit Agnes and her son for a day or two," I said, straightening off the railing. "I need to have a talk with David."

"Ahh, how's the young boy now?"

"Not a boy anymore. He's getting eager."

"Going to talk him out of sailing with us, then?"

"How'd you know?" I smirked.

"Because you tried to talk all of us out of it," he said, a solemn tone to his words.

"Yeah, well…"

Gnawing. The ripping of flesh. The slurping of fresh blood and pleasured moans of hungry mouths. Teeth scraping on bone. Tendons snapping.

"Go, then," Gus said, slapping me on my back. "Take a few days. We all need it."

I nodded, heading back inside. "We leave in a week. Tell the men to start restocking the food supply and to get more hemsbane oil to clean our blades."

"And nets?"

I hesitated, biting the inside of my lip. "And nets."

•   •   •

Sitting at the dinner table across from Agnes was a bit torturous with the way she kept eyeing me. The lonely woman wasn't in her right mind. She needed a husband. An old man with money who would stay home and be with her. Not me.

But she wouldn't see that. I'd have to fight my way back to my ship like I always did and we'd end up parting ways in anger. But then I'd return and she'd cling to me, quietly begging with those sad eyes of hers for me to stay and be with her. Touch her. Care for her like a husband should.

But I wasn't a husband. I wasn't a father. I never had been. I was just a fourteen-year-old boy who felt guilty and lonely enough to take her and her unborn child under my care.

That didn't change the fact that I was all David had ever known.

He sat to my left, scooping up spoonful after spoonful of leftover stew only to dump it back into his bowl. The silence between us was agonizing. As much as Agnes tried to make us a family, we were both too twisted inside to ever feel something more than fleeting desperation toward each other. I'd only come to realize that much sooner than her.

"He's getting quite strong, you know," Agnes said, feigning a smile. "May not look it, but he can lift grain bags by himself now."

"I don't doubt it," I said with a nod.

"He butchers the animals himself now, too. Handles—"

"It's good you have him around, then," I cut her off, eyeing her carefully.

I knew where she was going with the conversation. She wanted me to know how useful he was so I would reconsider bringing him with me, but my mind was set.

Finally, Agnes stood and began clearing the table of dishes. The candles were nearly burned to the holder and there was dust on the shelves. She hadn't been taking care of the place and it showed. I looked around as she removed my empty bowl from the table and sighed at the obvious neglect, leaning back in my chair. When one of the candle wicks finally burnt out in its own wax, I raised a brow.

"There's money enough to get new candles," I said.

Agnes emptied what food scraps were left into a bucket for the pigs and set the bowls into a wash bin. I knew she heard me even if she didn't acknowledge it. The woman was forgetful. She began scrubbing dishes and I glanced at David, who looked distracted by his thoughts. The scrawny young man had a head of red, curly hair like his mother and skin too fair to survive the sun on the open sea. I suspected the look on his face was because his mother had told him about my refusal to bring him onto the Burning Rose, but it couldn't be helped. I wasn't going to put him in the same position I had once been in. It was no place for a young man.

Finally, I stood and walked into the kitchen to help Agnes wash the dishes, drying the ones she'd set aside and stacking them on the cutting table.

"There's no need to help. Your hands will probably get them dirtier," she chuckled.

I chuckled back and shrugged. Even after a bath, my hands were calloused and my nails seemed permanently stained.

"If I'm around, I won't have you doing the work yourself," I said.

"But you're never around," David finally spoke up, talking under his breath like a pouting child.

I glanced back at him, but I didn't respond. I'd been like him before. My father took me on the Mother's Fang because I begged and it turned me into a broken man far too soon. I wouldn't bring David into that nightmare. Few men could walk that line and none of them were untouched by some level of madness.

"He's upset," Agnes muttered. "Don't mind him."

"I'm not upset," David argued. "I expected him to refuse me. I'm not his son. Not really. So why would he want me around?"

"David," Agnes turned chidingly. "Vidar loves you."

He threw his chair back, letting the wood scrape loudly against the floor, and stood.

"If he loved me—if he loved *us*—he'd come around, but even when he's anchored here, he stays in brothels, fucking every woman but you."

"David!"

"And for some reason, you crawl back to him every time he docks. You're pathetic."

I spun around and took two strides toward the scrawny young man, smacking him across the face with the flat of my palm. Agnes gasped but didn't intervene. David was too old for spanking, but clearly, his mother hadn't been disciplining him. His head snapped to the side, but instead of cowering, he just clenched his jaw. Maybe he was growing up after all. He certainly took the pain like a man.

"Don't speak to your mother that way," I said, grabbing the boy's chin and forcing him to look at me. "She is your mother and you'll respect her."

"What about you?" he snapped back. "Do I have to respect you?"

"I don't give a damn what you think of me, boy." I released him and stepped back, straightening my shoulders. "You're right. I'm not your father. And I'm not around enough for you to see me as one, but she's your mother and she needs you."

"She needs *you*," he spit, his eyes reddening.

For some reason, that threw a pick in my heart. I swallowed and took a deep, centering breath. I didn't have words. Not ones I wanted to say at that exact moment, anyway. Not with Agnes standing right behind me. I half-glanced back at her and then stepped over to continue drying dishes.

"Take the leftovers out to the animals," I said to David.

He walked stiffly over to the bucket full of scraps and left out the back door toward the animal pens. Agnes turned and continued scrubbing dishes and rinsing them, her shoulders tight.

"You didn't have to hit him," she said softly.

I slammed a bowl down on the table and sighed sharply.

"I cannot take him with me," I reiterated.

"You have a cabin boy younger than him on your crew."

I scoffed. "Whose father whipped and raped him until he was ten and old enough to drive a kitchen knife through his gut. That boy's already ruined and if he's not on my ship, he's off to the gallows. David has a chance. And I cannot believe that is the life you'd want for him. Not after what happened."

"I don't know everything that happened. You never told me."

"You don't want to know what happened!"

She snapped her head toward me, sorrow making her eyes swell. We stood for a while just staring at each other and letting our thoughts spill into the silence between us. Finally, I spoke.

"Maybe you should sell the house," I said. "Move inland. David can join a good trade. Perhaps you can find a man who will look after you the way you deserve."

"Leave Treson? This… this is our home."

"And it's about to become much more dangerous. Whitton is promoting the trade of sirens, alive and well, in Treson Harbor and in neighboring towns."

"That's ridiculous. You cannot allow it."

"But it's true and I have no power over the matter. This next run, I'm to bring him live ones."

"You're helping him?"

"What I bring back combined with what you get for the house will be enough for you to leave Treson."

"You can't do that." Her eyes began to glisten with tears.

"David can't be out there with the way things are turning. He needs to understand that. You need to understand that."

Agnes stepped forward and shoved me, her tiny hands barely pushing me off balance.

"Those creatures killed my husband," she said. "They killed your father. How could you think to ever leave any alive."

"I'm not discussing this with you any further."

"You swore you'd kill every last one!" she screamed, pounding my chest with her fists. "Every one, Vidar. You promised me!"

Again and again she hit me and I let her until her hand connected with my jaw. I grabbed both of her wrists and she began to thrash, emotional and crazed. I shoved her back onto the tabletop, pinning her wrists on either side of her head. She was heated, tears wetting on her cheeks. Our eyes met and for a split second, her pain became mine. I promised her I'd kill every last daughter of the sea, but that was a young boy's promise. A foolish one. I was about to say so when Agnes raised her head and pressed her lips to mine. For a moment, I started to kiss her back. Chasing a bit of pleasure would give me a fleeting bout of relief from the shit that filled my head, but I quickly came to my senses.

I pulled back, shaking my head as I released her and stepped back. She sat up and tried to reach for me, desperate for affection. For touch. I gently kept her at a distance.

"I am not the person to fill the role you need filled," I said.

She sniveled, brows knitted. "I don't need you to fill a role. I just want to feel your warmth before you leave again. I need your arms around me."

"Agnes, stop." I gathered both her wrists in one hand and cupped her face with my other, wiping her tears with my thumb. "Do as I say. Leave Treson. Use this beautiful face on a rich man who will love you."

She stopped pushing toward me, her face relaxing into a blank stare for a while like my words had cut her too deep and made her numb.

"Then it's true what David says," she whispered. "You don't love us. We were just the burden you inherited when Jack was taken by the sea. Your guilt incarnate." She paused as if waiting for me to deny it, but I couldn't even do that for her. Slowly, she pulled away from me, shoulders hunched with defeat. "Then consider yourself relieved of us when you set sail next. The next time you dock, whenever that may be, I pray we are gone."

Her voice was monotone and empty which was more painful than it would have been if she'd yelled at me. But I still made no attempt to dissuade her. In truth, I did love her. I loved David. I would do anything to see them safe, but safety was not all they needed. If my coldness finally convinced Agnes to move on, then so be it. It was the best I could do.

As she walked quietly to her bedroom, I glanced at the back door. I wasn't staying in that house for a week. Not after the words we'd just exchanged.

I walked to the door and pulled it open to find David leaning against a wooden post just outside, the empty bucket in his hand. He looked up at me, his face as solemn as his mother's without as much pain. The look in his eyes said he heard everything. I stepped out and shut the door behind me. Leaning against the opposite post and crossing my arms, I waited for him to speak his mind now that we were alone.

"She cries into her pillow at night all the time, you know," he admitted. I wasn't surprised. "She misses you."

"She misses your father. She misses a man in her bed. But that can't be me. I regret that I made her think it could be."

He hesitated for a long moment, letting his eyes wander. "Are we really just your guilty burden?"

I looked him straight in the eyes and took a step toward him, grabbing him by the back of the neck.

"You listen to me," I said, pointing a finger at his face. "Never once have I ever thought of you two as a burden. Did I care for you and your mother out of guilt? Yes. But also, because I wanted to. Because I loved your father. But you're a man now. And a man takes care of his mother, you hear me? And you can't take care of her from my ship." I straightened and grabbed his shoulders, squeezing his slowly developing muscles. "Use these muscles and pick up a trade."

I looked him in the eyes again and raised my brows, waiting for a response that would put me at ease. It took him a while, but he finally answered.

"Yes, sir."

I patted his cheek and stepped back, leaning against the post again. "Good man. Besides," I looked up at the full, reddish moon behind the parted clouds. "You don't want to be like me. Men like me are empty and empty men can't take care of their loved ones like they should. I pray that you never become this."

Dahlia

Beware, beware, the beasts atop the waves
They're quick with nets and quicker with their blades
~ A Siren's Lullaby

The moon was full and bright that night, peeking momentarily from the parting clouds like a baby crowning, blood-red tinge and all.

Birth was an ugly thing, but it was everywhere. I remembered my birth all too well and it was one of my many curses. The first thing I heard was screaming. The water carries sound so much farther than the air. All of Theloch would have heard my mother's suffering cries. I came into this world from cruel agony. It was one of the hardest births my people had witnessed in years.

And somehow, she loved me for it. In her own way, at least.

Pain was one of our many languages. We endured it. We inflicted it. We welcomed it.

But nothing had prepared me for the day she was killed. That was a pain I did not think I could endure. She was Reyna. A matron. The mother of waves. A terror to our enemies.

I was a stupid, skinny child of the deep to think her invincible.

I paid the price.

Traitor. Leech. Coward. Soft-hearted. Spineless. I'd heard so many whispers since that day, that it was hard to remember my real name. Dahlia. The bitch daughter of Reyna. I was unworthy scum to the Kroan and I deserved to be treated as such.

No sacrifice was enough. No act was enough. No kill sufficed. I would never forgive myself and neither would my people.

I was leaning back against a rather uncomfortable incline of black rocks inside a cave that night, staring at a pool where the tide had left water behind. Above me was a gaping hole in the cave ceiling where the moon cast rouge light on the placid pool. Lune bled that night and that meant violence. She would bring the tide soon and my cave would be buried beneath the waves. But it didn't matter. Though torturous, my patience was an art. I had needed to practice it over the years since my sister slit my throat and left me to the currents beneath the waves.

I believe she expected the sharks to tear me apart.

Lune knew they tried and left the scars to prove it.

But my flawed skin had become my identity. I did not grow up to be the beauty that was my sister and I never really reflected my mother's grace in song.

I was an ugly, wicked thing filled with anger and hatred.

"We found a ship," a voice said.

I didn't have to look to know whose it was. Meridan was soft-spoken. She was fierce with a blade but gentle with her tone. And she was loyal to me. They all were. It was not that I was a convincing leader or a well-spoken woman by any means. It was simply because I was angrier than all of them. Driven.

Especially now.

"How far?" I asked.

Meridan uncurled from the waves, her long limbs slick with salt water. Her serpentine body turned instantly to slender legs as she walked toward the pool and stood across from me.

"Near Dagger Tooth."

Her eyes were a bright white in the darkness, colorless and glassy. All the Naros looked that way. They were from the dark depths. Freckles of glowing specks scattered her face in subtle patterns and silver-white hair hung past her hips in rope-like tendrils. They had no song. Only a face that could lure a man in like gold could lure a greedy king. Their skin was often so pale, it was nearly translucent. In the right light, her bones and veins could be seen beneath it.

I slowly stood, coming to my full height nearly a hand taller than she was with muscle tone that set me apart from her peculiar-looking kind. I wasn't the ideal temptress by any means with my hard edges and battle-torn skin.

And the long, prominent scar that stretched from my left ear nearly to the corner of my mouth.

"Where are the others?" I asked, picking up a small armband from the ground.

I wrapped the thing around my bicep and sheathed my bone dagger in the binds.

"Already scouting ahead for… *them*," Meridan answered. "Nothing yet."

"Good."

I headed toward the frigid water. It was the season of the storms. Not many ships hunted the seas that time of year… unless their goals were more sinister than exporting goods.

I walked down a slick incline of stone toward the lapping waves and let the water grab at my legs. The reentry into the sea was always jarring, no matter how many times I'd done it. The water stripped away all that I was on land and land stripped away all that I was in the water like I was wearing two different skins. Each transformation was like being turned inside out. My legs fused together into a long, eel-like appendage and I sunk to the stone, pulling myself deeper into the water. Small, barbed fins ran down the length of my slick lower half with a main fin at the very end that cut through the water like a blade.

But it was askew, part of the left half gnawed off by the only other thing sirens feared besides humans. Creatures from the trenches far beneath the depths, further down than any of us could swim. Even the Naros.

They hadn't come up to the surface in a hundred years. It had been long enough for many of my kind to stop believing in them. Blasphemers, the Kroan called them. Of course, I was a blasphemer, too, for praying to Lune over the deep ones, but praying to Akareth had gotten me nowhere and given me nothing.

Neither had my former clan since my mother had been slain.

Meridan and I darted into the water toward Dagger Tooth, a small island that used to be frequented by sirens until that dreaded ship with red sails and others like it started swarming our waters. Hunting had become more brutal than ever and yet the clans hadn't unified against them yet. Infighting was going to destroy us faster than the men on their giant, wooden ships. Less territory meant shorter tempers, territorial wars, and general unrest.

And even the Naros were feeling the tension. As separated as they were, the effects of it all were leaking into all corners of our world.

All of it filled me with a rage I could only douse when I was killing.

Humans. The word made my mouth sour. The sight of one turned my vision red. I ducked under the waves and sliced through the water toward the island, my nails biting into my palms. In the water, everything was clear. The cold embraced me like a hateful mother, nurturing my resolve. She was as angry as I was. Every ship she could not crush under her waves made her a little bit less tolerant.

I was going to kill for her again. I was going to feed her frigid waters with blood and watch her tides swallow every bit.

The moon was high, but the clouds were rolling in. They'd cover our approach. As we neared the island, I let out a small chirp, letting the ripples of sound skim the water. They reverberated back, telling me exactly where the wooden belly of a big ship was sitting on the water above before I could even see it. I veered toward it with Meridan close in tow.

The ship was anchored off the coast. I wasn't sure why anyone would anchor near Dagger Tooth. It was an island known for its shark-infested waters, jagged reefs, and rough shores. No normal ship would be so stupid to corner itself like that, even with a storm coming.

When we got closer to the ship, I saw Voel and Kea circling the belly. A flash of lightning from above lit up the undulating waves, showing the true size of the thing. I'd seen larger ships on the seas, but this one was considerable. A merchant ship, no doubt.

Taking merchant ships prevented goods from being transported and anything we could do to disrupt the filthy humans made a difference.

Plus, my sisters were hungry.

The four of us surfaced close to the ship where lookouts would not see us. On the side of the vessel were nets that were hanging toward the water. It seemed a stupid idea to give us such an easy way to board, but it was their mistake. The ship rocked against the waves and as the weather picked up, a harsh mist of rain gave us an additional bit of cover.

I came to the edge of the ship first and peeked over onto the deck. I saw only a couple of men braving the abusive wind to tie down cargo. I rolled over the railing into a crouch, pulling my knife from my armband. The others crept onto the ship behind me and scattered in two directions.

There was no singing in the midst of a storm, but it did not matter. These men would die fully aware before they were devoured.

I saw my corpse and from its
mouth came the hate of a thousand dead
~Ghosts of War

The storm seethed. The ship rocked. Men were screaming as we painted the deck with their hot blood. One by one, we cut them open, spilling their soft insides on the floor. The two on deck were first. I opened one's throat with my knife, silencing him forever before he knew we were even there. Meridan finished the other one quickly, covering his mouth with one hand to muffle his screams as her teeth tore a hole in his jugular.

She favored the taste of the freshest blood.

She looked up at me with blood-smeared lips. "The taste of hemsbane is faint. We can feed on them."

I noded before I forced my way into the captain's quarters and butchered the man sleeping there. I did not even stop to see what he looked like.

Kea and Voel were already slithering down into the bowels of the ship and soon, Meridan and I followed, picking off anyone we found on the way to the forecastle. We killed as quietly as we could, certain we'd find a majority of the crew below deck. Waking them all at once would be a chaotic bloodbath. The bloodbath part I could deal with. The chaos I could do without.

I didn't want anyone getting hurt.

On the way, we passed stacks and stacks of cargo tied down with rope nets. Wooden boxes, barrels, and large rolls of furs, leather, and cloth were piled to the ceiling. Sinking the ship after the slaughter would deprive the coastal towns of large amounts of trade goods. A hint of something resembling happiness teased my thoughts.

We searched every room we passed, getting a feel for the kind of ship we were about to sabotage, but we couldn't find anything important enough for a ship to be braving a storm and rocky shores to transport.

Up ahead, the cabin was filled with at least twenty men. I could smell their filth and hear their deep breathing. They were fast asleep and perfect for the killing. I turned my knife backward in my hand, preparing to stab each man in the heart, whether he was awake or not.

"Dahl," Meridan whispered, grabbing my attention.

She was standing in the doorway of a dark room, her white eyes blinking with confusion.

"Should we…" she paused a moment. "Should we kill these ones, too?"

I furrowed my brows and peeked past her into the dark chamber. Stepping forward, I could smell a plethora of other bodies, but ale and foul breath weren't prominent on the ones in the other room like they were on the crew.

I let my eyes adjust to the darkness and found two holding cells with wooden, barred gates. Inside, I could see six forms. Two of them were young women, their round faces filled with innocence and youth. Perhaps teenagers. The other four were children. Young children. They'd all been stripped of any real clothing and I knew well enough that humans weren't as tolerant of the frigid, harsh temperatures at sea. In the back corners of the cells were thin blankets, all damp and filthy, for the girls to sleep on.

The group was huddled up close in a cluster as far from the bars as they could get. I knew they couldn't see us in the dark like I could see them. Perhaps they saw Meridan's glowing freckles and silvery hair, but me? I was dull in the night with inky hair and dark eyes. I could look upon them and know they weren't looking back.

But that made it easy to see their fear. Their fatigue and sadness. The bruises on their skin and the cracks in their dry lips.

"Well?" Meridan asked.

Empathy for humans was hard to come by among my kind. They weren't worth a thought, especially in my experience.

But they were kids. Young kids. I stared at them, finding it hard to imagine my blade sinking into their malnourished, weakened bodies.

Looking back, all three of my sisters were watching me, waiting for my decision. The fact they had to ask me what to do made it obvious that they had reservations as well.

But the last time I trusted my sympathies, it destroyed my life… and the lives of others.

I glanced back at the kids and watched their skinny limbs tremble in the dark.

I was a killer. I enjoyed killing men. Pirates. Hunters.

Children were different. At least, I wanted them to be.

Kea stepped up beside me, the glow of her deepwater skin illuminating one side of my face. She was the same as Meridan and was easy to see in the dark. One of the girls gasped, speaking in a language I didn't understand. The look of fascination on her girlish face was not what I expected to see at all. She pointed a shaking finger.

"Pasaio," she said.

I cocked my head to the side with confusion, watching the other girls duck their heads and huddle closer together, whimpering softly.

"They're from the ice," Kea said. "Much further north. There's a clan there."

"The Maruhk," I muttered. "I know."

"They sometimes deliver fish and seal carcasses to the locals and the locals sacrifice willing villagers once a year in thanks. At least, that's what I've heard."

I scoffed. "Cooperation? Between humans and us? Another rumor spread by hopeful lips."

Kea shrugged. "They're only rumors. But she just called us sea angels, so perhaps they're based on something true. Not that we can ask those coldfins about it. They never show their face outside the frozen waters."

"How do you know what she's saying?"

"There was a sister in my clan who was a northerner. Those frigid waters aren't much different from deephome."

No one ventured far enough north to see the Maruhk. Some clans didn't even think they existed anymore, but hearing Kea confirm it piqued my curiosity. To live in waters so cold and covered in ice seemed impossible, but the furs and leather stacked on that ship suggested the crew was coming from somewhere where fur and leather were abundant. A northern tribe that relied on it to survive the cold seemed logical. Believing sirens could have any sort of honest relationship with humans, however, seemed too strange.

"Well, we can't kill them," Meridan said. All eyes fell on her. She looked almost ashamed to have spoken up. "They're just children. Cold, frightened children."

Her words strengthened my resolve. I needed her there to say what I wanted to.

"They're *human*," Voel said. Her gaze snapped toward me. "I'll do it if no one else wants to."

"We're not killing them," I said.

"Dahlia—"

"We're not killing children," I repeated, staring at Meridan's face where my own naivety reflected back like I was staring at myself eighteen years ago.

But maybe I liked it. Maybe I missed her.

Those girls reminded me of the thing I could have been, but I never got the chance. I was born, and innocence ran away screaming.

"So? What do we do with them?" Voel asked.

I slowly walked toward the bars and crouched down in front of the girls. They could see me now. Barely, but it was enough. I wasn't even sure they would understand my next words, but perhaps I was saying it for me more than them.

I held a finger to my lips and smiled softly.

"Cover your ears now, darlings," I whispered. "It will be over so much sooner than I'd like."

It took a moment for the girls to understand. It wasn't until I lifted my palms to my ears to demonstrate that they knew what I was saying. It was one of the older girls that got it first and she started to help the younger ones so each of them was cupping their hands over their ears.

Kea was already gone. Voel was close behind her. I turned and looked over my shoulder, my smile turning into a grimace. Meridan had a disgusted look about her and turned to join her sisters. I let the vision of the children in the cell fuel me when I heard the first blood-curdling scream from the sleeping quarters.

I marched after my sisters and found Kea straddling a man in his hammock, driving her knife into his chest over and over again until she was painted red. Voel was dragging a man back by his ankle after he'd tried to run away. Meridan was just leaping onto a man as he was sitting up, her teeth gnawing a large chunk of flesh right off his face. His teeth were uncovered once his cheek was torn away and he let out a gurgling shriek. The coppery scent of blood filled the room and the beautiful song of death vibrated in my bones. I took a deep breath and clutched the handle of my dagger, cutting off a man's escape as he tried to flee the room. My knife swept across his throat faster than he could figure out I had one. Hot blood sprayed my face tand I reached out with my other hand to grasp his wiry hair, keeping him upright as he bled. He looked at me with wide eyes, clutching at his open throat as I licked my tongue over my bloodied lips.

He tasted foul. Sour. Full of drink and rancid food. And the hint of old hemsbane was bitter.

His eyes glazed over with shock and then slowly lost their luster entirely as death gripped him.

When he fell, his shirt stretched to the side, revealing a barely healed mark on his left pectoral where I expected to see a bronze pendant. It was sloppy but recognizable. I'd seen the same crescent symbol with a slash through it a thousand times before.

"What are you looking at?" Voel asked, striding toward me, a strip of torn flesh in one hand.

"I don't think we're the first sisters to have visited this ship," I said.

Their voice alone, you may not hear
But when bronze bells hum,
you know they're near.
~A Bronze Bell Engraving

"Move your asses, boys! We don't have all day!" I shouted.

My crew chuckled as they hauled supplies onto the boats to be taken to the ship. Sacks of beans. Jars of pickled vegetables. A fresh stock of hens and a few goats. The list was standard and therefore easy.

Gus stood leaned up against the dock's wooden post where a small bronze bell hung over his head, lightly swinging as the foot traffic vibrated the flooring around it. He had one hand tucked into his belt while his other held a pipe to his mouth. Streams of white smoke puffed from his nostrils as he let his gaze roam over the docks, watching every person tying nets, gathering gear, or knotting their boats.

I followed the direction of his gaze to a boat packed with a dozen men rowing to shore from around the bend. I recognized the obnoxious purple color of Collin's hat before I could recognize his face.

"Prick," I said, taking a lean on the post next to Gus.

"Oy, would you look at that," someone said. To my left was a fisherman holding a bundle of torn nets. He was missing teeth and his hair wasn't far behind, but the drink was so potent on his breath that I doubted he cared about any of it. "Cap'n Collin is back."

"Wonder if he's seen any of them weird fish," someone else said in passing, dragging barrels of crabs across the mud.

"Weird fish?" I spoke up.

"Aye," the man with the nets replied. "Thought they was sirens at first. But I've never seen sirens move like they did. Almost thought they'd sink me boat the way they kept bumping 'er hull."

"You get a good look at one or are you just talking about your drunken stupor?" Gus asked.

The man laughed. "Who knows anymore? Ocean's full of things my head will never be able to wrap around. I saw what I saw or I didn't see what I saw, but in the moment, it sure felt real enough."

He staggered away with his damaged netting and I took note of how the fibers of the ropes were shredded in multiple places like someone had taken a knife to it. Could have been sirens. Could have been rocks. Could have been anything, but it was enough for me to spare a thought.

"Madman, he is," Gus said under his breath.

"Around here, madmen are mad until they're not," I said.

We both let out a mild chortle before turning our attention back on Collin.

An eerie silence passed between us as we watched the man and a fraction of his crew float up to the docks. It was then that I noticed why Gus was on edge when he was usually relaxed.

Crammed between two men sat a woman in a poorly fitted dress made of stained cotton. Long auburn hair was a stark contrast to her pale, almost bluish skin.

She wasn't human.

And she was very much alive.

The woman's body was as voluptuous as a Greek statue. Her clothes were loose and clearly not her own. Tiny wrists were bound with irons that had already made her bleed and around her face was a leather strap that covered her mouth and buckled in three places behind her head.

I glared, the pit of my stomach twisting with warning. The woman sat stiffly, but when the men started to stand and shuffle off the boat, her head turned, eyes quietly observing. She was absent worry or fear. I'd never met a siren who showed either of those emotions. Collin himself with his expensive coat and embroidered hat with the stupid feather in the band, grabbed the woman by her arm and hauled her to her feet, forcing her off the boat. She didn't struggle or protest but rather kept her eyes blankly forward.

"What the fuck," I muttered to myself, scrubbing a hand over my face.

"A living one on our shores," Gus sighed a breath of smoke. "And to think I been tellin' myself this whole time it would never stick."

"We'll be seeing a lot more of it pretty soon."

"Don't feel right."

"No. No, it doesn't."

Collin walked toward us with the siren in tow, a smug look on his sun-chapped face. He took off his hat and tucked it under his arm, revealing brown hair tied into a low ponytail.

"Gentlemen," he greeted, looking down his nose at a couple of my men as they carried a crate across his path.

Gus was better at pretending he liked someone when he didn't and inclined his head at the man, taking another puff from his pipe.

"Collin," he said, ignoring the siren he had by his side.

She looked obedient. Docile. But I knew better than to think a siren could be tamed or even beaten into submission. They feared nothing. Not even pain. I eyed her cautiously, but she continued to ignore everything and everyone around her.

"Getting ready for a hunt?" Collin said.

"Looks that way," I returned, unable to take my eyes off the prisoner.

"Pretty, isn't she?" Collin said, stroking a finger across her smooth cheek. Still, she was like a doll.

"I wouldn't use that word, but she's definitely eye-catching."

"Never seen one like her before," he continued, taking a strand of her unusually reddish hair between his fingers. "Thought she'd pull in a lot of coin."

At that, I saw the faintest flare in her nostrils. She was hearing everything Collin was saying. She was feeling it. She wasn't scared, though. The look in her inky eyes was enraged. She was a mountain, quiet and still, with a fountain of molten lava beneath. I narrowed my eyes at her, glimpsing her bound hands to see her clenching her fists so hard she was drawing blood.

"I wish you luck," Collin said. "The waters are growing sparse and yet somehow more dangerous." He looked at me with a lazy sense of mocking. "But we all know how you like the storms, Bone Heart."

I felt the woman's gaze on me before I saw it. The moment Collin said my name, something in her shifted. Her eyes flicked toward me, dark as night and yet blazing with hate. She knew my name. I smiled internally at the thought. My name had spread far and wide throughout the deep and I enjoyed how it shook the spirits of her kind. I glanced her way and for a second, our eyes met like a hammer against reddened steel. There was the subtlest twitch in her jaw when she glimpsed my chest, which was absent of any jewelry save for a necklace with a few teeth hanging on it.

I sensed it.

Gus sensed it.

The only one too stupid to sense it was Collin.

The woman's eyes widened like all the rage and hunger had burst inside her. She shoved Collin away, her nails scraping into the fabric of his fancy coat. He stumbled back and she reached up, snapping the leather gag off her face so quickly that no one could stop her. Her focus zeroed in on me as she spoke in a tone that pierced straight to my soul.

Whether our language or theirs, any man could understand. The voice was one and many all at once. Whispers and seductive tones coiled together to sound as otherworldly as most sirens looked.

Kill them all, the voice said, doing its best to wrap me in its barbed embrace.

I could hear the tones. I could hear what they were trying to do to me, but they would fail. I didn't wear a silentium like my crew, or any man who hunted the seas as I did. No, I learned long ago that a simple trinket could be snatched right off your neck.

The bronze bell hanging above my head started to hum, the undertones of that terrible voice of hers vibrating through the metal until the air was filled with a haunting moan akin to when the wind caught a groove in a cliff just right. And at that very moment, my chest began to flutter with that same subtle vibration.

All eyes went to the bell when the hum began and then swept quickly back to the siren. In a matter of seconds, my hand was on my blade. I ripped it from my belt and took a wide step toward the woman as her words pounded against my ears. My hand jutted out and clutched her slender neck, squeezing until her voice was cut off. It took three steps for me to have her pinned against another post where I could run her through. I held the tip of the sword to her chest, but before I could thrust it into her heart, I heard the hammer of a pistol cock. I stopped, my eyes catching the metallic barrel only inches from my head.

Fucking Collin.

"Now, I went through a lot of trouble to get this one. You kill her and I kill you."

I turned my glare on him, baring my teeth when I heard several other guns cock and blades unsheathe behind me. I didn't have to look back to know it was my crew. The sound of them loading the boats had ceased altogether. I half glanced over my shoulder to confirm and saw Mullins right beside me, jaw muscles pulsing as he pointed his pistol at the fancy cunt, Collin.

Collin's throat bobbed as he swallowed and then he masked that nervousness with a sly smile.

"You break it, you buy it," he said with a shrug.

"She still has a tongue," I hissed.

"Of course, she does. Keeps it fresh."

Collin slid his pistol into his belt and then replaced the gag over the woman's mouth, shoving me away from her as soon as the buckles were secured again. Then he gestured to one of his men with a rope. The man—or boy—was too young to be on a hunting ship. He hobbled forward with a limp and started wrapping the woman tightly in additional binds until she could no longer lift her arms. Then two other men took her by the shoulders and started forcefully leading her away from the docks.

"Happy hunting, boys," he said, putting his hat back and tipping it mockingly.

I watched Collin go with his unenthused crew and siren prisoner, clutching the hilt of my cutlass so tight, my knuckles cramped. Slowly, I heard my men putting their weapons away and turned to face them. All eyes were on me, quietly asking how the fuck we were going to deliver living sirens if I couldn't even hold myself back from killing someone else's captive.

I was asking myself that question, too.

Gus was still leaning against the post puffing on his pipe only now his hand was resting on the butt of his pistol instead of in his belt.

Taking a deep breath, I brushed my hand over my hair and slid my cutlass into its sheath.

"Back to work," I ordered.

Vidar

A survivor was he of a nightmare at sea.
A wolf cub from the Mother's Fang.
~A Sea Shanty

The ocean reminded me of so many dark things. Horrible things. It took the spirit of the Mother's Fang and the creatures within took her crew. I'd done nothing but kill monsters or watch people die on the ocean and yet it felt more natural to feel the floor swaying beneath me than it did to stand on solid ground.

It was two days into our travels. I was going to follow the merchant routes, but we had a particular path that was much less direct and much less obvious. Sirens stalked the merchant routes and following them exactly was too conspicuous. Too expected. Daughter's Pass was too rough that time of year, even for the Rose. So we sailed in between.

I stayed on the stern for some time the next morning, sitting on a stool with my feet up on the helm's railing. In my lap was my book of smeared charcoal sketches and blotted ink writing.

The sea air really didn't do paper any good. Even with the leather binding, nearly all of my sketches had been tarnished in some way.

I'd started a new sketch, trying my best to remember the siren Collin had in cuffs before we left. She was different and a different siren was something I didn't like. I always tried to record all of the information I could gather on our hunts. Their weaknesses. Their appearance. Their strengths. I'd come to find they were all different and I wrote every detail in that damn journal. When I could no longer stand thinking of that woman's face, I tucked my charcoal into the folds of the paper and closed the book, setting it aside.

I stared out at the undulating expanse wondering how much I still didn't know about it. My heart still wasn't completely set on taking Whitton up on his deal. It could hardly even be called a deal at all. It wouldn't be long before every man-eating bitch from the sea decided to come ashore and wreak havoc on everyone, not just hunters and fishermen. What Whitton didn't understand was that we were at war, even if he never rolled his fat belly onto a ship himself to see it. He was safe in his mansion eating the spoils of every hunter's sacrifices.

The weather was calm and the sky was sunny all morning until a thin fog rolled in. The rain was soon to follow, but I had some time to think. Not that thinking ever brought me much comfort.

Below me, a few men had gathered on deck with an overturned barrel and some dice. The sound of the dice rolling soothed me a bit. I'd listened to that sound over and over on the Mother's Fang though I'd never participated. I was always too distracted by the sea and the way she moved like a temptress only to strike down anything that wasn't ready for her violent tempers.

A few other men sat up against the rail talking. And then there was Gus with a bottle of rum in his hand and a foot propped up on a crate. The wind was soft, fluttering the sails and allowing us some time to just drift. I enjoyed the silence, but Gus never did. He told me many times that the noise of a busy tavern or a booming town was where his soul was at peace and I couldn't blame him. The laughter and boisterousness of a crowd kept his thoughts in line.

For me, the absence of sound was bliss.

"Join us, Cap'n," someone said. I glanced down to see James trekking up from below with another barrel to sit on.

"Cap'n don't join in games," Mullins chuckled, tossing his dice out.

"Fine where I am, James," I nodded.

"Well, it's too damn quiet on this deck," Gus rasped loudly, clearly getting a bit agitated.

"Not our fault the weather's agreeable," Mullins replied.

"Sing a song, Gus," someone added.

"Aye, I'll sing a song," he grumbled, staggering toward the railing and leaning forward on his elbows.

There was a moment of silence as the men rolled their dice again and made some disappointed sounds. Then Gus started tapping the bottom of his rum bottle on the wood. One. Two. Three. He kept tapping it and tapping it and then started to sing to it. He was a great singer, his voice deep and rough like the sea in a storm.

In the dark of night, on a restless sea
Dark seas, dark fate, dark seas.
A pirate's son with his father bold,
Dark seas, dark fate, dark seas.

Dark seas, dark fate, to the ocean we go
With a heart full of vengeance and a tale full of woe
We'll hunt the sirens till the end of days
Dark seas, dark fate, dark seas.

The sirens came with their haunting song
Dark seas, dark fate, dark seas.
They took the crew and his father strong
Dark seas, dark fate, dark seas.

Dark seas, dark fate, to the ocean we go
With a heart full of vengeance and a tale full of woe

We'll hunt the sirens till the end of days
Dark seas, dark fate, dark seas.

"Gus!" Mullins called out. "Really? Are you singing that on this ship while we're in the middle of the sea hunting sirens?"

Gus took a swig of his rum. "Don't forget it," he said, pointing a finger at the men playing their game. "Crew don't always win. You all signed up for it."

"You don't have to make us regret it," someone said.

"Nah, it's too late to regret it." His eyes flicked up to meet mine where I was standing unphased above them. "Any minute, we could be torn to bits. He knows it. We all know it."

"What are you going on about, Gus?" I sighed.

"This deal with Whitton. It don't sit right with me. You saw that woman in town. She alone could kill twenty men before someone could restrain her again. It isn't worth it."

I sighed again, shaking my head at the fact that I couldn't agree more. But I didn't like seeing a strong drink take away Gus' collected demeanor. It reminded me that the waters under the surface of those stoic eyes were just as squally as mine.

"What are you saying, Gus?" James asked.

"I'm saying this is wrong, sailing out here looking for sirens to enslave. Fuck the money." He pointed up at me. "That's our captain. That's Vidar Bone Heart, but the wolf cub of the Mother's Fang first. He knows these creatures better than anyone and I've been seeing it in his eyes since we left. This shit's going to get us all killed and for what? A pocket full of coin?"

"One good run could fill our pockets for months," Uther said. The man was fairly new to my crew and he hadn't grown up on the coast like most of us.

"Yeah, and it'll fill that town with things that will eat your kids alive," Gus said.

"Don't got no kids."

"Good."

I pinched the bridge of my nose and took a scan of the waters surrounding us. Black waters. Water I couldn't see through. It was a time when we had to be more vigilant.

"Gus," I said, waving my hand at him. "A word."

He groaned, taking one more swig of his drink before corking the bottle and setting it down on the barrel in front of the men. He swayed as he walked up the steps toward me, but I knew his sway wasn't just from his drink. It was the weakness in his left leg that worsened the longer we were at sea. He was getting old and his injuries were catching up to him.

Meeting me at the top of the steps, he leaned forward on the railing with a sigh. I stood next to him, perching my elbows on the carved wood.

"Something on your mind?" I asked.

Below, the men watched us for a bit before continuing with their games. But they had quieted. Their ears would seek out our conversation and I usually let them. There weren't many secrets on my ship.

"The waters are changing," Gus said. "Been feeling it for a long time. I know you have, too. Every time we sail out, I feel like we know the waters less and less."

I nodded, staring off toward the clouds gathering in the west.

"Something is definitely different," I admitted.

"You know, me and your dad had this same kind of conversation just before that wretched island."

I turned and met Gus's cloudy eye. "Did you, now?"

"He told me the tides were shifting. I agreed. We went on anyway. See, the ocean doesn't bend to us. You know that better than anyone. We push hard enough, she'll figure out our tricks and she'll push back."

"You think we've been pushing too hard?"

"I think this whole idea of Whitton's to bring business by offering exotic captures is going to change everything and not in a good way."

"So? Tell me your thoughts, old man. You think we should all retire? Let the bitches kill merchants. Fishermen?"

"Maybe man wasn't meant to live on the coast in the first place," he grumbled. "Maybe man should stick to land. Bad as it all is, the sirens stick to the sea. We bring 'em into towns, that won't be the case anymore. And it's not like we get thanked for all we do. If we were gettin' proper thanks, we wouldn't be living like dogs half the time."

Something in me had considered that before. I couldn't see an end to the conflict between man and sirens. I was simply going through the steps, letting vengeance guide me. But in truth, it was a path that I knew would end in death and likely long before I reached old age. Looking down at my men, I wondered if any of them saw it that way or if it was just a job to them.

Mullins, a man I purchased with coin (and a side of violence) from a man with no regard for life and an affinity for pain. James, a man who was once a boy with no shoes looking for work on the muddy streets of Boralis. Any work. Boil was a cook with too many gnarly features on his burned-up face to get a job anywhere in the eye of the public. Kole, Barney, Uther, Ben, Laurence, Jesse. They didn't join my crew because hunting was their passion. They joined because they had nowhere else to go. Whether I earned their loyalty or not, it was a job. When they got enough coin, they'd stop. But me? It was my life.

"I know what you're thinking," Gus said. "You're thinking that if you stopped, they'd win."

I can't stop.

But I didn't say that. I didn't say anything. My motives had always been and would always be different from my crew's. For me, there was never going to be an end.

"Captain!" Jesse called from the crow's nest.

My eyes flicked upward to see him pointing his finger westward. Following it, I saw a distinct shape floating on the water. A ship. I narrowed my eyes at the fact that no one ever took our route due to the moody waters and the shallows, which my crew knew very well. Other ships would be stupid to risk their cargo.

"Bit far from the usual pathing," Gus pointed out.

I pulled a spyglass from my belt and aimed it at the drifting ship.

"Sails are up," I said. "They're anchored."

"Out in these waters?"

Handing the spyglass to Gus, I said, "Whitton said the Cornwallis was behind schedule. They've been missing for a bit."

I marched over to the helm and immediately started barking demands at the men. Whether the ship was the Cornwallis or not, a familiar itch coiled around my spine. Something was off about it and I was going to find out what it was.

9
Dahlia

*Wronged by a man upon the sea
now sharp as a knife and vengeful is she.*
~ The Broken

With a sharpened blade, I made a clean cut across the red meat of a freshly caught tuna. A thin piece separated from the body and I held it up, smiling as I sucked it into my mouth. The fresh fish melted between my teeth.

The young girl sitting in front of me was bundled in one of the furs from the storage and smiled at me as I exaggerated my enjoyment of the food. We were sitting on two small crates on the deck with a third crate between us where I continued cleaning fish and showing the girl how to carefully strip the meat. We couldn't speak the same language, but she was observant, watching every bit of the process. She even tried a piece of the raw fish and the way she ate it made me think she was no stranger to the taste.

"Ahnah," she said once she swallowed. Then she followed that with more words I couldn't understand.

"I wish I knew what you were saying, otessi," I said.

Her little hand reached out, surprising me when she pressed two little fingers to my chest.

"Mm," she said before pressing her hand to her own chest. "Ahnah."

"Your name? Ahnah?" She smiled, showing off her two missing front teeth. "Ahnah," I repeated, pointing at her with the tip of my knife. Then I pointed it toward myself. "Dahlia."

"Da'ya," she said, unable to form the sound properly without teeth. She pointed at herself once more saying, "Ahnah," and then gestured to me. "Da'ya."

Language barriers were thick, but somehow, knowing her name had cracked a hole in it. It excited me. Smiling had become foreign to me, but I felt my lips wanting to do it before I started carving the fish again. Ahnah began talking, her tempo sped up with excitement, but I understood none of it.

"Getting comfortable?" Voel asked, her tone a bit accusatory. I turned to find her standing at the railing as if eager to get off that ship.

None of us liked ships. They brought death and torment, but I couldn't leave the girls to drift into the ocean. I was still unsure what to do with them, but my damn conscience hadn't learned its lesson yet.

"Not getting comfortable, Voel," I sighed, setting strips of tuna to the side.

Ahnah took a handful and ran off, likely to distribute them amongst the others while Voel moved into my space.

"How long are you going to take care of these girls?" she asked.

"I don't know."

"You know what they are, right?"

"I don't, actually. Kea knows *of* them, but she doesn't know much else. None of us do."

"I'm not talking about that. No matter what, they're human and they'll be just like the others one day."

"They're young girls," I said, slicing through another piece of tuna.

"Young or not, you know what happened last time you took pity on a young human with sad eyes."

I slammed the tip of my knife into the wooden crate and stood to face Voel. Despite her smaller frame, she never cowered in my presence when I was agitated. I never wanted her to. We were equals, but I wanted her to know she'd ventured somewhere she shouldn't have. We all had our boundaries. I ground my teeth and stared at her, waiting for her to realize her mistake. Voel was defiant, though. She was like me. She'd endured plenty of torment from humans and her own kind just like I had. It took her a moment, but eventually, she bent. Whether disappointed or not, we'd always respected each other.

"I shouldn't criticize your decisions," she said.

"You can leave anytime you'd like," I clarified. "Any of you can."

"I know."

"Then why haven't you?"

"Because we are stronger together."

"Then help me figure out how to get these girls off the waters."

"We'd have to sail them home, but we don't know how to sail and every second we stay on this ship puts us in more danger."

"I know," I admitted.

If only the girls knew how to man a ship. Talk of the Maruhk had been filling my head for days. I couldn't shake the interest I had in the idea of sirens and humans coexisting. I wanted to see their home… but I knew that it was more likely I never would. I couldn't very well ask where they were from or drag them through the water to get them there. All I knew was they were from the north. Further north than I'd ever ventured.

My eyes wandered as I tried desperately to come up with more options and when they did, something grabbed my attention. On that foggy day, it was hard to see great distances, but there was one set of sails that flaunted their presence like no other dared.

I paused, staring over Voel's shoulder at what I almost thought was an illusion. But the longer I looked, the more I realized it was real. Crimson sails. Voel turned to discover my distraction and bristled.

"Father below," she muttered. "That's the Burning Rose."

I glanced around the deck at the girls as they snacked on the fish. The Burning Rose was a cruel vessel filled with ruthless cutthroats. I wanted them all dead. And if they were headed for us, I had little faith they'd treat the girls with any less cruelty than the men before.

Voel spun to face me, eyes wide with alarm.

"Dahl!" Meridan's voice called out from below. I stepped over to the railing and peered overboard to see her and Kea in the water. "Red sails! Coming this way fast!"

I glanced at the ship again with disdain and then at Voel, making quick decisions. There was no time to think and plan.

"If you must go, go," I said.

"What are you doing? You're not staying here." When I didn't respond, her brows knitted angrily. "You cannot stay here for the girls. It cannot be worth it."

"We need to go!" Kea called out.

"I'm not leaving these girls to cruel men. That is my choice to make."

"If they find you—"

"They won't. And if they do, I'd never think of blaming you for running, Voel. You know that."

"This is *Bone Heart*," she emphasized. "If he does catch you, your head will be on a spike. Your body will be left for the sharks. No questions."

"I know."

I nudged Voel toward the railing and felt my blood starting to rush with excitement. She didn't understand it, but my anger ran more deeply than I had ever let on. I wanted to see the girls unharmed, but if I could find a window to slit the captain's throat in the process, I'd relish it. I'd die for that chance. The Burning Rose had taken many sisters and I despised its captain almost as much as I despised the boy who'd planted that hate in me all those years ago.

Voel grumbled and then ran toward the railing, leaping over into the waters below. I saw Meridan staring up at me expectantly from the waves. I just shook my head at her. We both knew that she and the others stuck out like candle flames in the dark. They were meant for the darkness of the deep. When it was clear to her that I was staying, she ducked under the waves and out of sight.

Looking up, the red sails were getting closer. I glanced back at the girls, who were only just realizing something was amiss. I pointed them toward the stairs leading below deck.

"Get out of sight," I ordered, knowing they didn't understand me. But I needed to convey something and my tone seemed to do that just fine.

The oldest girl started to gather everyone up and lead them all below, yanking the fish knife I'd been using from the crate as she went. I took a few moments to watch those red sails before I started to strip out of my clothing. Once I was naked, I ventured below deck behind them and found myself a corner filled with empty crates and broken furniture. I pressed myself against the wall and let my body adapt to the colors and textures of the wood and supplies until I was nearly indistinguishable. From my position, I could see the stairs leading down. The girls had split into pairs and scattered throughout the lower level. It made me nervous to know I couldn't see all of them, but there was no time to organize a better plan.

On my arm, my bone knife was strapped tightly. While I still had time, I slid it from its leather sheath and held it at my side, hiding it behind my forearm. Gradually, I slowed my breath, bringing my heart rate down so I could listen. Around me, the girls were silent. They knew how to hide. They were smart and brave, which made me more inclined to stay and see them safe. I didn't know how I was going to do it, but I had proven to myself time and time again that I could do impossible things. Perhaps I could take out the crewmen one by one somehow and wipe that red stain off the tides for good.

It was a ridiculous idea. A dream.

The eerie sound of a heavy ship cutting through the water got my heart pumping again and I had to force it back into submission. I heard distant voices yelling at each other and shouting demands. They were close and they were going to board. They called out for an answer, likely expecting the ship's crew to call back, but they were sitting in our bellies. What remained of them had been tossed into the water save for their blood, which had soaked into the wood.

When no one answered their calls, I heard the slamming of boards and the stressing of ropes as they began to move onto the ship. More muffled conversation took over the deck. Multiple pairs of boots began tromping above me. I had to stay calm. I had to stay hidden. I was one woman with teeth and a blade, but I knew how to use both. If they found me, at the very least, I could take a few body parts with me into death.

When boots finally started to move downstairs, I sunk a bit further into the shadows, watching as men began to slip into view.

I had never been so close to the Burning Rose or her crew. I'd heard many stories. Horrifying stories. I'd seen the sails. Heard the wailing of her victims. I had hated the damn vessel for a long time but never had such a clear chance to do damage to the men who sailed her. My mouth was watering at the thought. The abhorrence I kept wrapped so tightly inside was starting to get restless at the scent of their bodies as they filled the space. Sweat. Rum. Leather. Blood. Metal.

I saw a man with dark skin and a shiny bald head walking with his blade drawn, looking in corners. Behind boxes. When he caught a whiff of the old blood in the sleeping quarters, he let out a huff of air and covered his nose with his sleeve. There was a man behind him who mimicked his gesture and the two of them walked deeper into the cabin to investigate.

"Captain!" one man called. "Got a bit of a problem."

More boots started to descend the steps. I watched as a big, burly man with a white beard and an old, worn coat ducked into the lower level.

Something about him…

Behind him was another man whose golden, sun-bleached dreadlocks hung over his broad shoulders. He wore an aged, red coat with thick cuffs. I only caught a glimpse of him before he passed my hiding space. He smelled of the oak that made his ship, but he smelled more of the salty water that carried it. It wasn't surprising. His ship hunted in all seasons. In all weather. It was navigating the tides and killing more often than any other vessel.

Bone heart.

His steps were accompanied by the faint jingle of buckles, beads, and whatever weaponry he kept on his person. He was big, having to duck into the sleeping quarters to see the remains of the massacre my sisters and I had wrought on the late crew. Part of me was excited to watch them discover our slaughter because I knew one day it would be their crew painting the decks of their cursed ship.

"Fuck," the captain muttered, hanging his thumbs on his belt.

I stayed so perfectly still, barely breathing as I watched the men. The captain especially. When he moved aside, I caught another glimpse of the older man with the beard and narrowed my eyes. I knew him. I did. I felt it in my bones. But I'd never seen the crew of the Burning Rose before.

And then it clicked.

As the old man wandered to a pile of bins and boxes near the wall, I glimpsed an eye patch. Then I saw it. A black sand beach. Men screaming. My mother's taunting words. The violence and excitement came back like a blow to the gut and I saw him there. The old man had been on the beach that day when my mother and her closest sisters were killed. The day when the crew of the Mother's Fang was tortured and slaughtered.

The day when I foolishly freed a boy from a tiny cage.

I was distracted from the jarring memory when one of the littlest girls emerged from behind the pile of bins and took off toward the steps in a panic. The old man had found her. The captain moved to intercept her and I nearly pounced from my hiding place to jam my knife into his head when his men followed, all of them with their blades out. I stood my ground, tonguing my throbbing teeth as the captain grabbed the girl and spun her to face him. She screamed and cried as an older girl came running out from the same pile of cargo to help her. The old man reached out an arm to stop her and I felt my muscles burn to cut him open.

"Hey!" the captain said, trying to restrain the young screaming girl. "I'm not going to hurt you."

Lies.

The old man looked around at the rest of the cargo, his thick brows furrowing. Then he looked at the girls again.

"What are two girls doing on the Cornwallis?" the dark-skinned man asked.

"What kind of cargo is this?" the old man added. "White furs? We don't get this shit from any of the regular routes."

"North?" another man said. "They hunt great white bears up there. I've heard it before. These are worth a lot of money."

"What's your name?" the captain asked the girl.

She started to babble in her language and the old man seemed to perk up. When he spoke back in a slow and calculated sentence in the same language, the girl's struggles stopped and she sniveled, caught off guard. She nodded at him, wiping her eyes.

"She was taken by men," the old man said. "Seems like the Cornwallis was smuggling some rather exotic goods since we've been cleaning the waters of threats."

The captain groaned and stood up straight, rolling his shoulders back with aggravation.

"Fuck," he growled.

"You think what happened in there was sirens?" someone asked.

The old man slapped the crewman over the head. "You think these girls did that?"

"Why are the girls alive, then? Last I checked, sirens don't discriminate."

"Ask if there are more," the captain said, prompting the old man to construct another slow sentence in the girl's language.

The two girls met each other's gazes as if silently asking if they should answer. They opted out of doing so.

Good girls.

Sighing, the captain handed the smaller girl to his men. "Take them to the Rose. We'll keep searching."

"And the cargo?" the dark one asked.

"Take it all. The men of the Cornwallis have no use for it and I think Whitton owes us whatever we find on these cursed waters."

The two crewmen took the girls up the stairs and I watched as the captain and the old man met just at the bottom of the steps to talk. The captain scrubbed his face with his hands as if he was tired and shook his head.

"Blood's old," he said. "Sirens don't leave survivors. They could be back. For all we know, they're keeping these girls alive just to slaughter later. We'll check the rest of the ship, move everything, and then I'll stay aboard."

"Stay?"

"Me and a few others. We'll stay. If anyone is coming back for these girls, they'll meet our blades instead."

"It's as good a plan as any. One your father would have made."

The captain groaned and headed deeper into the lower levels. I knew he'd find more girls down there. If no one else followed, I'd have a chance to stalk him into solitude and take him.

"Relay my orders, Gus," he said as he walked.

"Blade out, Vidar," the old man called after him. "You're not invincible."

My heart thumped painfully, my breath catching like a weave of thorns in my throat.

Vidar.

I felt myself beginning to shake as the two men went opposite ways.

Vidar.

I listened to the captain's boots venturing further into the ship and the long scar on my cheek burned at the sound of his name like the wound had reopened.

"Vidar. My name's Vidar," the boy said.

I swore to Lune I would never forget the name.

Vidar was Bone Heart. Vidar was the terror of the sea. The captain of the Burning Rose.

Vidar was that little boy I freed. The boy who accepted my mercy and then uprooted my entire life.

The man I'd been waiting to kill for eighteen years was only steps away and oblivious to my presence.

*She was made to hate and hate would
drive her mad.*
~Unknown

I froze when I realized Vidar was there. For the first time in nearly two decades, I could almost touch him. I wanted nothing more than to paint my ashen skin with his hot blood, but instead, I watched his crew scour the ship. They found every last girl and I watched as they were taken off the merchant ship and transferred to the Burning Rose. I knew I could have taken a chance and gone after Vidar in the process, but my gut told me to wait. It told me to catch him unawares. So far, the men didn't seem inclined to harm the girls and after I got the flesh I was owed, I'd return to see that they were taken care of.

Somehow…

If I killed the crew of the Burning Rose, I would be in the same predicament, though. I couldn't sail. I couldn't bring the girls home.

I would figure all of that out later. My priority was Vidar. No matter what, I'd have his heart.

But I had to wait. I couldn't just slaughter him, now. No, Vidar was special. He deserved something more memorable. *I* deserved something memorable.

I waited in that corner for some time after the men had loaded all of the supplies and all of the girls on the other ship. Until the sun retreated from the sky and storm clouds began to roll in. The Rose sailed some ways from the stagnant merchant ship, likely to get out of sight. Vidar and his men assumed sirens were returning to finish the girls off. They knew the red sails would scare them off if that was the case. I was left to think on that vessel for a while as Vidar and three other men stayed aboard, quietly patrolling before they settled in for the night. I was growing stiff and eager in my hiding place, itching to feel his blood between my fingers. I gathered my hate and rage and emerged from my corner as soon as the men went silent.

The night was on my side and the clouds blocked any light the moon could shed across the deck. Rain was pelting the ship, but there was no wind, which meant the ship was steady and easy to navigate.

My insides fractured with more pent-up anger to think that Bone Heart was Vidar himself. Those red sails had haunted my kind for years and to finally know that the captain of that ship was Vidar, the boy who lied to me, burned worse than any flame could mar my skin. He slaughtered my mother and left me with the only scar that really mattered. As I emerged from below deck, I brushed my fingers over the raised line across my cheek, remembering how his bronze blade cut so easily through my flesh.

I kept my dagger tucked against my forearm as I crept around the corner at the top of the steps. Every inch I moved was an inch closer to the vengeance I'd craved for eighteen years. I'd dreamed of sinking my nails into his eyes. Of scraping the meat off his bones. Of tasting the sweet tang of satisfaction on my tongue as I drank his blood.

I peered across the deck searching for a lookout. Any smart man would have one or two. Someone in the crow's nest perhaps. Every known ship had a bronze bell that would hum if any siren tried to use her voice nearby and sirens knew they had them. Our voices were near obsolete to men like Vidar and his crew. But like men had adapted, so had we. So, smart hunters never took their eyes off the sea, even at night.

And I knew very well that Vidar was a smart hunter.

I let my eyes climb to the crow's nest to see a skinny young man standing watch. But I could surpass him.

Quietly, I crept around the corner, immediately getting drenched in the cold rain. The doors to the captain's quarters weren't far. A sliver of light peaked through the cracks in the wood telling me someone had claimed the space for the night. Likely Vidar. Taking in a deep breath of air, I could smell the wax of a burning candle. The scent of oak and rum. Leather and sweat. All the human scents mingled in my nose to feed my drive.

I started toward the cabin, staying low. When I reached the doors, I pressed myself against the wall beside them, listening. I heard nothing aside from some deep, slow breathing from within the chamber. Even his heartbeat was sluggish. He was sleeping.

My teeth ached to take a bite out of his throat knowing he was just beyond those doors, unaware. Bone Heart. The captain so many of us feared was that pathetic little boy with the treacherous pleas. And he was just. Beyond. Those. Doors.

I took my knife into my hand and slowly stalked toward the ringed metal handle, pulling lightly at it until there was enough of a crack to see inside. I saw a table. Maps and trinkets were scattered atop it. Among them was the single candle burned nearly to its base.

I glanced back up at the crow's nest one last time to make sure I hadn't captured any attention. The man was looking entirely in the wrong direction so I carefully slipped inside the cabin, staying so low to the ground that my breasts nearly touched the wood. Inside, I took up a place in the corner behind the table, letting my skin adapt to the colors, tones, and textures of the room. A pile of old sheets covered in the former captain's blood sat in a corner.

Peeking through the space between the table and the wall, I could see Vidar's bare feet on top of the narrow bed. I trailed upward along cotton-bound legs to his waist and a hand hanging over the edge of the bed.

My breath paused upon counting only three fingers. His last two were severed at the knuckle.

I could still taste his blood on my tongue and feel the crunch of his marrow between my molars. I had found him. He'd been under my nose the whole time, sailing our waters and killing more of my kind than any hunter before him. It was Vidar all along. My own personal demon.

I took a breath of his particular scent again, letting the smell of his flesh, his leathers, and the subtle trace of rum on his breath fuel me. Then I uncurled from my corner, fingers clutching my bone dagger with breaking force. Oh, how I'd longed to sink that dagger into his gut and watch him squirm.

My eyes crept up the length of his body, over scarred and sun-licked skin. Corded muscle meant for slaughter and pain. Tattoos. His thin cotton shirt did little to cover him. My eyes paused on the scar over his sternum. It was short but rigid with the faint remnant marks of stitches.

But no silentium. No necklace to warp my voice and render it useless. If I used my voice on him, it could work. Unless he wasn't that stupid. Recalling his deceit and his actions when we were children, I couldn't say that he was. No, he was smart and he knew exactly what dangers lurked beneath the waves.

I turned my knife in my hand as I inched closer to the bed, watching his chest slowly rise and fall with every breath. Finally, my eyes came upon his face and I saw nothing of the child I met nearly two decades ago. His features were chiseled and strong. A layer of stubble framed his mouth and traced his jaw and long, sun-bleached dreadlocks fanned out around his head. The boy I knew was soft. Too pale for the sea. Scrawny. This man was built to overpower. To kill. To *hunt* and slaughter my kind.

I tasted blood in my mouth and realized I was clenching my teeth so hard I could break them. I eased the muscles in my jaw and took a silent step forward. Then another. Slowly, I let the colors of the room melt off my skin until I was myself. Pale, scarred, and ravenous. My shadow loomed over his bed, slithering like an ink spill across his body. I raised the dagger, my pulse picking up until my skin was warm with anticipation.

I wanted it to be slow and painful. I wanted to see his eyes. For him to know it was me. But I would slaughter him in his sleep if it was the best I was going to get. If it could clean him from my nightmares and let me sleep at night.

I leaned over him, wet tendrils of my black hair hanging over my shoulder. My shadow devoured him, finally finding his face. He was so close. His heart was right there, ready to be pierced. I could hear his pulse and see the movement of blood pumping through the vein in his neck. I breathed him in, wishing to see his eyes. To see the shock on his face.

Just then, a single drop of cold water slid down a tress of my hair and landed on his cheek. His brows twitched at the sensation. I could have stabbed him then. I could have driven my dagger right into his chest and watched him drown in his blood. I could have slit his throat so he couldn't scream. Any number of things would have brought me pleasure.

But I didn't do any of those things. Instead, I watched as his eyes slowly fluttered open and focused on me leaning over him. Earthy brown. They were the only thing resembling the boy I met so long ago.

Something about the slow realization that washed across his face excited me. Our eyes connected and my heart leaped into my throat. Vidar, son of the wolf, only inches from my face and the tip of my blade.

He was mine. Finally, mine.

"You," he whispered.

I showed my sharpened teeth before I spoke. "Me," I snarled.

I thrust the knife toward his throat only to stab the pillow beneath his head as he rolled to the side. His knee connected with my ribs hard enough to make me stumble back and in that time, Vidar jumped to his feet, awash in the dim candlelight. He was big, but large prey thrilled me.

He looked at me with a sense of wonder like he hadn't quite registered whether he was awake or sleeping yet. I glared from beneath the shadows of my brows and took a step back, flipping the dagger in my hand while my other palm slammed down on the candle, extinguishing the flame. The room fell dark, but he was perfectly clear to me. His heartbeat sent ripples of visual sound through the room. His blood practically glowed beneath his skin. But the moment the lights went out, he sprang into action.

I wanted there to be panic, but I should have known better. Vidar knew exactly where to find a weapon and precisely two steps later, he was pulling his cutlass out of his belt, which was draped across a chair near the door.

I should have been smarter. Were I less eager, I would have hidden it before he woke. But no matter. He couldn't see me… but I could see him.

I stalked forward, silent as death. Vidar moved for the door and I lunged, pushing him into the wall hard enough to knock whatever was hanging on it to the floor. He reached around, fisting a clump of my wet hair and tugging my head back with a sharp snap just when my knife was going for his stomach. I choked back a scream and turned my head, biting down on the inside of his wrist. He growled in pain and shoved me away from him.

He was holding back. He could have used his blade and he didn't. What foul plan did he have for me and had he been perfecting it all these years like I'd been modifying mine?

I licked his blood off my lips and couldn't help the moan that slipped off my tongue at the sweet and salty taste. I swallowed it down and slipped into the darkest shadows, silencing my breath completely so Vidar was forced to still himself and listen. But his human ears would never hear me unless I wanted him to.

"You taste like lies and death," I whispered into the silence.

I could hear the soft *drip, drip* of his blood as it slid down his fingers from the crescent bite. I could smell his scent permeating the room even further.

A smirk tugged on the edges of Vidar's mouth and he shrugged, fire behind his blind eyes.

"So, you have been looking for me," he spoke, his voice deep and calm despite the danger he was in.

I stalked to another corner of the room. "Did you think I wouldn't?"

"Oh, I knew you would." He turned toward my voice, his cutlass hanging loosely in his hand. "It's in your nature, right? To hunt. Just like me."

I cocked my head at those words. "We're not alike."

"Aren't we? I've been looking for you, too. On every face of every bitch I've beheaded."

Suddenly he swung directly toward me. I ducked out of his reach, watching the blade cut right into the wood where my head had been.

"I'm rather distinguishable, aren't I?" I hissed, standing up behind him.

Vidar spun around and swept his blade toward my neck. I leaned away from it and then dropped to the floor in a low crouch, creeping into another corner.

"You killed the men on this ship," he said.

"Gruesomely."

"And why are the kids still alive?"

"Dessert."

I chuckled, my voice carrying through the room like a rippling whisper. A mere taste of my abilities, but I couldn't help it. He brought out the predator in me like blood attracted a shark. I could hear the hum of a silentium in the room and my ears followed it right to his chest where that gnarly scar sat on his sternum.

The man had cut himself open and placed the damn thing under his skin.

As if that would make it harder for me to snatch it off of him if I tried…

"Smart," I whispered as he pressed a palm to his chest. "To mutilate yourself in your own defense."

"Foolish to come back aboard this ship and expect not to die."

He came at me again with his blade and that time I rushed toward him. We slammed into each other, but in the darkness, he lost his footing first. He careened to the ground with me on top of him, my dagger at his throat. I jammed my knee against his wrist, pinning his cutlass to the floor.

"You took everything from me!" I screamed, my voice carrying so fully across the ship that I could hear the wood moan and the bell on the figurehead shudder with a low hum.

"Couldn't help yourself, could you?" Vidar chuckled, unafraid of the blade against his neck. "You just alerted my men. Did you plan on killing me even if it meant you'd die, too? *Tsk*. I'm flattered at how you've obsessed over me all these years."

My anger was gnawing at me. I wanted to spill his insides across the wood, but the irrational part of me didn't want to end it like that. No, he deserved so much worse. For my mother. For all the sisters he'd taken. I pressed my blade to his neck hard enough to draw blood and soaked it into my lungs. I could hear another bell being rung. An alarm bell. His crew was coming for me. Vidar could have yelled out to tell them where I was, but he didn't. I could see his eyes staring up at me in the dark, wild and curious.

I leaned in toward him, dragging my nose up the side of his face to take another deep breath before I licked my tongue over his lips. He remained perfectly still as I pressed my mouth to his and bit down on his bottom lip just enough to get another taste of that sweet blood of his.

"I'm not dying here tonight," I whispered. "But you. I have plans for you, my red prince. And it will be sunrise before I let you take your last breath. You've never known pain like the pain I can show you."

Before he could reply to that, I drew back my head and slammed it down against his, knocking him semi-unconscious. I sheathed my blade in my armband and quickly jumped to my feet, heaving his body across the floor. Men were shouting outside, gathering to look for the source of the scream they heard moments ago. But they were looking in the wrong direction.

I kicked the doors to the cabin open and hauled Vidar up until I could hook my arms under his. I made it to the railing before one of his men saw me in the dark night. His white beard practically glowed in the dark. He paused, a pistol in hand.

I knew him. He knew me. We were both there the day Vidar and I signed a silent contract to hate each other. He knew very well what I was going to do to his captain and it pleased me to see the realization dawn on his face. A wicked grin stretched across my lips at the sense of victory I was feeling and he could see it under a flash of distant lightening as it lit up the ship.

"Lovely to see you again, Gus," I said.

He raised his pistol and I raised Vidar's body in front of mine, stilling his hand just long enough for me to roll over the railing and into the sea with his precious captain.

The past is a ghost we shall never be rid of
~Titus

18 Years Ago

"You hear that, my son?" my father said, standing at the bow of the Mother's Fang with his finger pointing toward a small inlet. "Those desperate cries?"

The fog had settled on the placid waters of the bay, making the eerie songs that echoed against the rocky cliffs that much more haunting. But the sounds I was hearing were not the ones sailors talked about. The suffering noises singing from deep within the inlet were the very noises hunters enjoyed the most. Agony. Despair. The tune of monsters defeated.

I looked down at the figurehead, a wooden wolf holding a bell between its teeth, but it was as still and quiet as ever.

"The bell isn't humming," I whispered.

"No, those sounds won't make the bronze hum."

A smile spread across my father's lips, shrouded by his untrimmed mustache. Greasy hair was pulled into a thin ponytail, but I'd learned long ago that there was no one to impress on a hunter's ship. My father would clean up when we returned home lest he face the wrath of my mother who hated the smell of the sea on him. Not a hair had grown on my face yet, but soon I'd be like him, rough and resilient like the two generations of hunters before me.

And this was my chance to finally be a part of a chase. I clutched my cutlass tight and stared into the hazy bay where the broken sails of ruined ships breached the surface of the water like drowning men with their hands stretched toward the sky.

Seeing the ship graveyard just fueled my resolve. It was one of many that tainted the borders of ship lanes across the south sea, but it was the first I was witnessing with my own eyes. It was a violent sight to see wooden maidens of the sea broken, ruined, and forgotten.

The Mother's Fang had seen many hunts and had succeeded in killing more sirens than any other ship in the region. Now I was on it and learning the trade. I squinted into the fog, anxious to find one of the fiends. I'd never seen one alive.

My father gestured to his men. As the wailing grew louder, the crew grew more silent. I watched the movements of his hands, reading his words. He was ordering the men to drop anchor. I could see the land close by. The rocks were sharp and black, perfect for tearing into ships that had sailed off course, but my father knew better than to skim the shore. We stopped in the deepest water of the bay and slowly, the men lowered the jolly boat into the water, being careful not to make much noise. Amongst the loud, pained cries coming from the foggy shore, I doubted we could be heard, though.

"Come, now," my father muttered, turning me to face him. "Look at me, boy."

At fourteen, I was a head shorter than him, scrawny, and my hair was a tawny shade like my mother's. Where he was covered in scars, I was smooth as a baby's bottom. He'd seen everything and I'd seen nothing. This was my moment. I stared up into his dark brown eyes and saw my boyish face looking back.

That was about to change. Boys ran the farm and took care of their mothers. Men braved the sea.

"We row to shore, slow and quiet," my father explained. "You keep your wits about you and you stay close, you hear me? And no matter what, you keep that necklace on."

I nodded once and lifted my fingers to prod at the little pendant under my shirt. Every hunter had one. Without them, the songs were just as deadly to us as they were to any man. It fascinated me that a tiny pendant, forged to be hollow and light, could provide so much protection.

Excitement made my fingers twitch against the hilt of my blade, but I wasn't an idiot. Foolishness got people killed. Recklessness lost them limbs. The crew of the Mother's Fang was smart and it was why they were the best.

I was going to be one of the best.

"If you don't paint your blade today, another day you will, but a move made too soon could get you killed." He paused, his eyes wandering a bit. "Your mother would never forgive me for that."

The corner of my mouth twitched at the humor of his words. My mother always smacked him across the head for leaving first before hugging him like he'd been gone for years every time he returned from a long hunt. I couldn't imagine what she'd do if he got her only child killed.

A hand slapped my back, hardened by the heavy silver rings on the thumb and middle finger.

"Ah," said a rough whisper. "He's smart. He'll do just fine, Woelf."

I glanced over my shoulder at Gustov. He'd had white hair since I could remember and a full beard that he braided into three ropes. And he was the biggest man I knew, built like a bear.

"I know he'll do fine," my father winked.

My heart started to tremble at the thought of going ashore where those awful sounds were coming from. If agony had a voice, that would be it. Shrill, long-winded, and hopeless. They'd sunk their teeth into something horrid, thanks to my father's brilliance, and now they were stuck on land, in pain and disoriented.

The perfect predators were now the perfect prey.

Myself, my father, and eight other crewmen climbed down into the jolly boat, all armed with blades and pistols while the remaining crew took on the important duty of protecting the ship, our only way out. If it went down, we were all trapped like every other poor soul that had seen the bottom of the ocean before their time. Jack, my father's best friend, hummed a quiet tune as he rowed, not a care in the world. He was an uncle to me just as much as Gus. The whole crew was family and I was eager to join them. Eager to prove myself to them all.

Once we started moving inland, I felt my mouth go dry. I'd never taken a life, human or otherwise. But taking the life of a singing menace was the greatest thing a man could do. A blade bloodied by the cunning creatures was a blade worth more than gold could pay.

A blade that had taken a daughter of the sea was a blade worthy of a name.

Mine was yet unnamed, but perhaps soon it would earn its place.

The bottom of the boat scraped against the stone in the shallows. It was then that my father gave the signal. Two men stayed back to defend the boat while the rest of us lowered ourselves into the knee-deep water and ventured to the beach. The water swallowed my legs, eerily warm like freshly spilled blood.

A siren's song could turn a man's free will to clay, moldable by the one whose voice softened his resolve in the first place. It was said to make a man crazy with lust. With desire. With a need to do and be anything commanded of them. Others said it was like knives in the brain, scrambling all rational thought and turning it into obsession. But the songs of that island were nothing of the sort.

On the black sand beach, the violence already peeked its gory head out of the fog. The first piece of the massacre that I saw was hard to make out. Once attached to a body, the torn-up meat of an arm sat on the sand, its blood weeping down the beach with every pass of the gently creeping waves. The bone was stripped on one side showing the thick insides of torn muscle, tainted with a poison so vicious, it turned the blood to something dark.

My father let out a low chuckle, taking a whiff of the salty air.

"Smell that?" he said.

I pulled in a deep breath and found the faint scent of cinnamon on the breeze, but it was tainted. It smelled old and soggy and corrupted by the metallic hint of blood.

My father pulled his cutlass from his belt. Softscale was an old blade with a handle wrapped in crocodile leather. It had been washed in the blood of fallen men and sirens feared it like rabbits feared wolves, for when the blood of victims was folded into the bronze, it was poison to the bitches. So the legends said, at least, though bronze by itself seemed to do the trick if it cut right. I glimpsed the edge of his weapon as he strode up the beach to the black rocks ahead. Behind me, Jack had pulled out both of his pistols.

The reality of our venture hit me like a handful of sand to the face.

I'd never seen a siren with her body attached to her head.

I was about to find out exactly how vicious they were.

More body parts left a trail of gory crumbs leading up the beach, every one of them stripped to the bone and oozing black blood. Rotten cinnamon invaded my senses with more force and I winced.

The wailing echoed from within the cover of the jagged boulders ahead. The breeze whirled around us. We reached the threshold where sand turned to twigs and pebbles… and it all stopped. The breeze. The sounds. Even my heart.

My father held up his fist and we stopped walking, listening to the sudden stillness. I wasn't experienced in the hunt, but I knew something wasn't right. The hair on the back of my neck stood and chills coursed through my whole body. My father sniffed like a dog on a trail and Jack let out a low groan behind me. They knew something was off, too.

"Whole crew," Jack muttered. "They ate the whole goddamn crew."

"No," my father said. "They shouldn't have been able to."

I glimpsed his narrowed eyes and my uneasiness multiplied.

From the sounds, the sirens should have been just behind the rocks, but none appeared. I gulped, the sound of my heart pounding against my ears like fists.

Jack pulled back the hammers on his pistols and I slid my cutlass from my belt, trying to remember my training.

My father turned to another crewman. "Light a torch."

Fire. The only way to communicate when the fog was thick. I watched as the crewman pulled one of three sticks from his cloth satchel and a fire steal from his pocket. The other men encircled him, weapons out. If someone were to attack, they'd go for the torch bearer first before he could light a flame that could be seen from the ship.

But then the silence was broken by a deep woman's laugh that seemed to bleed from the wind itself. My father stepped in front of me and pulled out a pistol to fill his other hand.

"Come out, witch!" he challenged.

From the black rocks appeared the vague shape of a woman. She emerged from the dark stone itself like she was made of volcanic slate, but as she stepped down, her skin shifted and changed like an octopus shedding its camouflage. She became the color of the fog with deep shadows encircling her eyes and darkening the tips of her clawed fingers. She was nude with a dusting of silver across her skin that gave most sirens away. Long, hip-length tendrils of inky hair hung down her back and over her breasts. I watched her stalk down over the jagged rocks with bare feet as if she was floating.

She was as beautiful as a nightmare disguised as a dream. Tall, feminine, and shrouded in an icy chill that pierced right through my guts.

The woman *tsked* her tongue, her black eyes unblinking as she slowly shook her head.

"What a cruel trick, Woelf," she said, her voice seeming to dance all around me. "Hemsbane in the blood." She glimpsed the body parts scattered on the beach. "Sacrifice a few worthless worms just to hunt us down." Her lip curled into a wicked smirk when she looked at my father again. "But as you are willing to sacrifice your people, so am I willing to sacrifice mine."

My father let out a chuckle just as the torch lit fire behind us. The bearer stood, clutching it in his hand and glaring at the fiendish woman before us. Her black eyes flitted toward the orange flame and her jaw hardened with irritation.

"What a filthy thing," she hissed. Then her vision caught the glint of firelight on my father's cutlass and her eyes narrowed. "Softscale. How I've missed you. Still with your poor sister's blood in the metal, I assume?"

My father was past succumbing to the taunts of a siren's words.

"And soon with yours as well, Reyna."

"Please, Woelf," she feigned fear. "Do not hurt us. We are just so starving. I beg you."

Her words faded into laughter like she couldn't keep it together. And then her gaze fell to me.

"A child. I've never liked the taste of them, but yours? I might be able to stomach it. Or perhaps I'll let him watch while I gnaw your skin off your bones… and then I'll be merciful and do him quickly."

My father squeezed his sword but remained calm, standing his ground. I was determined to do the same, but I could not dismiss the fear wrenching my heart. Confidence was terrifying and Reyna had enough to make any man quiver in his boots.

"So? What were they?" Reyna continued, gesturing to the remains of the slaughtered men across the beach. "Volunteers? Murderers? Rapists? No worse than you, I suspect."

"Spare me," my father finally responded, raising his pistol toward Reyna's head. She didn't even flinch. "It doesn't matter who they were."

"I suppose it doesn't. They died slowly either way. And the hemsbane did the trick…" Her smile flattened and her dark gaze seemed to get even darker. "But not to all of us. What a clever plan, shrewd Woelf."

Suddenly, the alarm bell from the Mother's Fang echoed through the night. The men looked back with alarm, but my father kept his eyes firmly on Reyna. Movement caught my eyes in the rocks as more bodies emerged from the black stone. Sirens, every one of them as frightening as the next. Their flesh changed in texture and color to match Reyna's silvery-white hues. Hideous beasts. Black widows in slick, cold skin. And they were all there to devour us.

On the frigid tide, their screams will flood
Their blade is a song and our blade is blood.
~A Pirate Shanty

I awoke to screams. Terrible, blood-curdling screams too high pitched to be coming from grown men who'd spent their lives becoming hard, unbroken killers.

The fight had been short. There were far too many wicked women for our small group of men to overcome. They'd outsmarted my father. Where most people thought they were nothing but bloodthirsty animals, hunters knew better. They'd caught on to my father's tricks.

A crew of criminals had been promised freedom if they could get across the Aisle of the Black Water to the Broken Promises. They were given a ship and as much alcohol as they desired. I was sure they sailed with smiles on their faces and bellies full of rum, but their passage was cut off and they were lured into the bay as most merchants and smugglers were. Their body parts littered the inlet, their blood darkened by the hemsbane that had been added to every bottle of rum they'd been gifted.

Hemsbane. An herb parents put in babies' milk. Harmless to humans in small doses, scentless to sirens, and yet lethal to their wretched insides. The first time a crew was sent to sea filled with hemsbane, the sirens were easy to track and easier to pick off. My father returned with six heads that day and other hunters with none.

But his tricks had failed him this time.

The men of the Mother's Fang weren't dead. We'd been taken across the island to a small cove with those same jagged black rocks. Only I'd been stuffed in a cage. I was cramped, my knees to my chest, and my father was folded into one the same size. He was further up the beach where the water barely licked the bottom of his confines. The bars of both cages were rough with rust and barnacles, which scraped at my clothes and skin. The icy water just barely touched me every time it crept up the sand.

The men were not so lucky. Gus and Matty were pinned by the palms to a couple of old, wooden stumps. Reyna had teased my father by plucking Gus's eye out with her nail and popping it between her teeth right in front of him.

Never had I heard Gus scream like that.

Four of the men had been tied to stakes lodged in the rocks, their legs severed below the knees. They lay against the tide far enough for swarms of bloodthirsty fish and crabs to gnaw at their torn flesh. Two of them were fortunate enough to have died quickly, but not Jack.

Reyna and two of her sirens stood and watched from the rocks, unmoved by the horrendous display. I studied each of their devilish faces. If I did not get a chance to kill them in life, I'd search for them in death, but I would never forget.

I glanced at my father again who stared at his wailing crewmen as if he'd been frozen in time. I could see his jaw clenching and his fists squeezing the bars of his tiny cage, but otherwise, he did nothing. His men were dying slow and agonizing deaths, which the sirens likely wouldn't ease, and they wanted him to watch.

I could only imagine the plan they had for me if making him suffer was their goal.

But I would endure, soundlessly if it was in my power.

My father's tortured eyes turned to me and there was a moment when all of his emotions transferred to me. What he couldn't show. What he wanted to tell me. I felt it all in my soul and it nearly made me retch. My first hunt with him and the legendary crew of the Mother's Fang had been overrun.

Touching my chest, I noticed my necklace was gone. Of course, it was.

I skimmed the faces of the sirens once more, a voice deep inside telling me I was not going to die on that beach. Not easily, anyway. I glared daggers at Reyna, taking in every tiny detail of her venomous features until she caught me staring. Her head cocked to one side, the corner of her thin lips rising into a smile.

I would kill her. Today. Tomorrow. In hell if I had to.

Reyna stood from her stony seat and stepped down the sharp rocks until she reached the sand, her eyes remaining on me. I dared not look away like some pathetic dog. I stared, my nostrils flaring to take in the stink of that bloodied beach.

"What a brave, stupid child you have, Woelf," she said, her voice little more than a whisper. "It is a shame you brought him on this day of all days."

She held a hand out to her side as if to summon something and from the black rocks emerged another figure I hadn't noticed before. She unveiled herself from the stone and appeared almost like a specter in the mist. A girl, barely older than me, with long, raven tresses covering near nonexistent breasts. Her eyes seemed too big for her small face and her limbs were long and thin, disproportionate to the rest of her.

I'd never seen a child siren before. I had never even heard hunters talk about them. They were illusive and coveted by their ferocious mothers. Her black eyes lightened until they were a bright and unnatural gray and she used them to stare at me like she thought I was as unusual as she was.

In the girl's hand was a white dagger carved to a sharp point and etched with designs. She placed it in Reyna's hand and then slowly backed away. The ferocity and hatred that made the other sirens ugly had not yet tainted her soft features, but one day it would. I imagined my face looked much the same until that very moment when I knew I was going to die along with my father and his men.

Reyna *tsked* in my direction and the girl walked obediently toward my cage, picking up my cutlass from the sand nearby to break the latch holding me inside. It was as if the women had found the cages on the sea floor. They didn't even have keys for them.

As soon as I moved, the girl backed away, her expression going rigid like all the others. I crawled out of my confines onto the wet sand, finding my limbs were stiff and in pain. The girl kept my cutlass in her hand like the weapon had always been hers and reclaimed a place on the rocks. As I stood, Reyna walked casually to my father and used the bone dagger to pry open his cage as well. I was no threat to her in my condition and she knew it. She looked almost bored as she stepped away, tossing the bone dagger on the sand before she sat herself on a perfect ledge against the rocks.

For a while, my father didn't move, but when he finally did, he was groaning and grunting with pain as he pried himself out of the cage. He stood, his coat soggy and heavy with wet sand, and rolled his broad shoulders back. The child in me wanted to rush toward him and hug him and beg him to tell me it was going to be ok. The man in me knew it wouldn't be and there was no time to weep.

I glimpsed the dagger on the sand and then Reyna. Were I faster, I could use it and take her out, but the other sirens weren't just there for looks. I was certain they were her guard. They were quicker than men. Stronger. She left the dagger there for a reason and I didn't want to accept it.

"Quite a first hunt, isn't it, my boy?" my father said.

I glanced up at him, fists balled tightly by my sides. He feigned bravery in front of me, but the redness in his puffy eyes was yet another sign that inside, he was a storm of regret and fear. The great Ethelwoelf was defeated and yet there he stood. I didn't know a man could be defeated before he died, but he was. I saw it and it stabbed me right through my chest.

We took a long moment to stare at each other. Words escaped us, but we didn't need them. Everything we needed to say was in our eyes, silent and yet somehow understood.

One of us was going to die. The other had a chance. A slim one, but a chance nonetheless.

In my head, I could hear what my father would say to me if he could speak.

Don't be scared. Every man here chose to hunt. They're dead men and you're not. Be brave and be ruthless.

I'd grown up on his speeches enough to know what was going through his head. I nodded at him once and he returned a slow blink as if accepting what was to come. He was a mountain before a storm, unyielding and unbothered.

"Kill him," Reyna said.

Only her voice was not the voice of a woman. It was the voice of a siren, slow, whispery, and melodic. Beautiful. Mind-warming and yet the thrill of danger coiled its bony fingers around it. It sang toward me, flooding my thoughts. My limbs. It repeated over and over, burning the world around me until the bone dagger and my father were all my eyes could focus on.

And without my necklace, those tones vibrated through me like the threads of a spider's web.

Kill him.

My foot slid forward through the thick sand. My father watched me but made no motion to intervene. I bent to pick up the weapon and rose again to see my father drop to his knees on the ground.

Now I knew a broken man. Now I knew what it was like to die before your heart stopped beating.

"Don't, boy!" Gus's distant voice called out.

I *wanted* to kill him. The more the voice came to me, the more my hands itched to see it done. It was a suggestion first… and then a need. A desire. It tightened its grip until it was my will itself. I clutched the hilt of the dagger tight and moved forward, every bit of my vision focused solely on my father.

Kill him.

I drew closer to him. He was unmoving and kneeling in surrender. My hand twitched to cut a hole in his throat. No… his heart. My eyes trailed across his body in search of a place to cut.

"This will anger you beyond reason," my father whispered, his voice only loud enough for me to hear. "This will turn your soul dark and your heart to bone. It will harden you, son."

"He's your father!" Gus said, his voice growing ever softer behind the nagging whispers saying to end it.

I inched closer, raising the tip of the bone knife to the divot beneath my father's throat where the laces of his shirt were loose and revealed his sun-tanned skin.

"Use it," he said through his teeth, staring up into my eyes. "Bronze and blood, my boy."

Kill. Him.

The dagger slid forward, cutting through skin. Red pooled at its tip and I watched, my hands mine and yet someone else's at the same time. I felt the blade scrape against bone as I dragged it upward, splitting my father's throat up the middle. He rolled his head back and stared up at the clouded sky, eyes wide. His mouth filled instantly with blood and one gurgling breath splashed a warm stream of it across my chest.

My hand released the knife and in turn, the whispering tendrils tied to my will loosened their grip and silence overtook the beach. Not even the backdrop of wailing crewmen could be heard. The sky had darkened as if I'd been standing there for hours over my father's corpse. The bone knife still stood upright in his neck, but his skin had turned pallid.

The greatest hunter on the tides had been reduced to a cold pile of flesh and bone by the hand of his only son. I glanced down at my red-stained fingers and recalled all that had transpired. A heavy knot made my stomach turn and I nearly threw up. I was so outside myself that when two of the women took me by my arms and dragged me back to my little cage, I didn't resist. I was almost a corpse myself, limp and spent and utterly in shock.

Vidar Woelfson had killed his father. That's what they would say. I was a murderer. A stain on my family name. If I was not to be killed next, that is.

Their eyes inspire a thirst
But your ears will betray you first
~A Warning from a Madman

Reyna was not done with me yet. I believed her only regret was not making my father watch.

Her song continued.

For three days, it festered in my head. In my soul. It twisted me into something not myself. Something empty and rotten. My boots had been taken. I wasn't sure why. Maybe she didn't want me hiding anything in them. A sharp stick. A stone I could use to beat someone over the head. I could think of a hundred things I could use against my enemies. I strolled barefoot, back and forth, carving and slicing and serving up pieces of flesh to the bitch and her sirens. It didn't hurt as bad to do it while under the influence of her sickening lullaby, but at night, she forced me back into my tiny cage where she released me from her hold so I could recall everything my hands had done while my mind was being whipped into submission.

A submission my body was all too happy to accept.

They had not fed me over those few days. Perhaps they planned to starve me, force my labor, and leave me to the tide when they were finished getting fat on men I once knew.

Nightmares had never been so vivid. This was not just a bad dream. It was hell itself and Reyna was the devil. No, she was worse than the devil. She was something more primal. More inhuman.

My hands were crusted with salt and blood, my fingernails stuffed with the flesh of the dead. She didn't force me to carve up my dad. Maybe she was saving that part for last just to make sure I was well and truly shattered.

But I would not shatter. I would not break. Not the way she wanted me to.

Wordless and obedient, I served up the men to the demon women, forced to call Reyna "mother" every time I placed a well-cut piece of human meat in her hands. The girl always sat somewhere nearby, watching me as I did my morbid duties, but she had yet to take what I offered up as the others did. In fact, I had not seen her eat in front of me at all.

No matter. Any spark of empathy was likely a trick. None of them could be trusted, least of all the most innocent-looking of the bunch.

On the fourth night of my torment, I curled into my cage, my limbs starting to fail me. Every time I woke from my stupor, half a coconut shell sat near my cage, and from it, I drank fresh water. Their minimal effort to keep me alive a while longer, I supposed.

My senses slowly returned to me. Night had draped its black cloak over the island as I sipped from my nightly ration of water. The women didn't enjoy fire, so all the light I had was from the moon beaming between the parted clouds. On one of the old stumps, Gus barely clung to life. All had died but us, but I knew I would be carving up his body soon enough like I had the rest.

I didn't need to see to know the sirens were still finishing their nightly feast. The sounds alone created an image so detailed that I would dream of it until the end of my days. Gnawing. The ripping of flesh. The slurping of fresh blood and pleasured moans of hungry mouths. Teeth scraping on bone. Tendons snapping.

Soon, it would be my limbs being ripped apart by their savage teeth.

I would endure. No hunter hunted without knowing the risks. Even me. My first hunt was a catastrophe. My last would be a slaughter.

I gazed out toward my father's corpse lying on the beach. It had been left to rot before me for days now. Regret and rage mingled and made a rancid taste in my mouth and an even more foul feeling in my gut.

This will anger you beyond reason… use it. Bronze and blood.

Though I wasn't in control of my actions or my mind then, Reyna could not deafen me to my father's last words.

I balled my hands into fists, my nose twitching at the smell of salt and rot. If Reyna wanted me to suffer the sight of my murdered father, I would. I would stare at him every night if that was what it took to harden me. To make me rigid. To make me a killer.

A stone chiseled enough became sharp. I was going to be the sharpest stone in the black waters. Nothing would bend me because I was already broken.

I stared and I stared, rubbing layers of blood against my palms. It was my blood to bear and I would remember the feel of it. The smell of it.

For hours I watched as the crabs crept up the beach to climb over my father's unmoving form. Their carapaces glistened under the moon.

Better he's in the stomach of sea creatures than those monsters.

It was the slight movement to my right that finally made me turn my head. Looking at the sand, I saw nothing. Well… almost nothing. Two silvery orbs glinted in just a way to let me know someone was there. On the rocks, Reyna and the others had calmed their incessant feasting and seemed to be engaged in quiet conversation in tones my human ears could hardly detect. But someone was watching me. And once she realized I could see her, she moved.

The girl. The skinny young siren that had given Reyna the bone dagger that was still lodged in my father's neck. Curious thing.

Or hungry thing…

I could trust a siren to be nothing but vile.

The girl slowly walked toward my cage, soundless on the wet sand. Her eyes glimpsed the others as if to make sure no one noticed what she was doing, and then she continued, creeping closer and closer to me. The clouds ate up the moon and left the beach so dark it was as if my eyes were closed.

But I could smell her.

I could feel her.

The girl smelled of salt and rain, a testament to her wickedness and deception. No pleasant smell could ever come from a beast like her. It was all part of their ploy.

I could hear her feet in the sand, her steps so soft they were nearly undetectable against the soft rolling sound of the water sliding against the shore. Reyna had no taste for children, she said, but perhaps this young fiend did. I ran my tongue along my teeth, envisioning myself biting through someone's neck and escaping. If my teeth were my only weapon, I'd use them like a wolf.

"Boy," came a small whisper.

She was to my left and if I had a blade, I'd have shoved it right through the bars of my cage and into her eye.

But she was speaking so softly. She did not want to be heard by the others. That sparked my interest. I turned my head toward the eerily pleasant tone of her young voice.

"What do you want?" I said through my teeth, matching her volume.

"Are you hurt?"

The obscurity of her question caught me off guard. There was kindness in her tone, but I knew the creatures were incapable of empathy. My brows furrowed just as the clouds allowed the moonlight to pass once more. The girl's fingers were curled over the bars near my shoulder where her face was so close to mine that I could see a light peppering of silver in her cheeks.

They really were captivating up close… another sign of their malevolent nature. They were meant to draw men in, twist them, and break them. I stared into her eyes and saw temptation. I saw a young girl growing into her wicked nature, but she wasn't quite there.

I could use that.

I shed the ferocity from my hardened features and let the heartbreak claw its way to the surface for her to see.

"I am not hurt," I said in a broken voice.

She bit her bottom lip, an unexpected look of regret glinting in her eyes. She glimpsed the rocks where the others were slowly growing more silent. With full bellies, they would sleep for hours. It was why hunters used feedings to draw sirens out. Killing them after they'd gorged and were too heavy to flee was an effective method. They ate days, sometimes weeks worth of food after every successful hunt.

And they'd just eaten half a ship crew.

"What is your name?" I muttered, trying to draw the girl's attention back toward me.

She was uncertain about something. I needed to exploit that.

Always find the weakness and never let it go to waste, my father used to say.

The girl blinked, dipping her head slightly as if she was hesitant to answer. Perhaps that wasn't the right question.

"I… I'm not hurt," I repeated. "This cage is small, though. My body aches."

She met my eyes again, that time seeming to look deeper. I couldn't look away, as much as I knew I should have. Siren's eyes could make a man melt. It could strip them of their instinct and leave them unprotected.

Her eyes were doing that to me. They were… beautiful. Silver, starlit orbs that glistened like mirrors, showing the world around us in perfect, miniature detail. And the moonlight smiled in her gaze like the moon itself had birthed her.

And maybe it had. No one truly knew how sirens reproduced. Some said they were devil spawn. Others said they were the children of captive men later eaten after their use had been spent.

A gentle metallic clink brought my eyes to the girl's hands. Long, thin fingers curled around the bars, her nails like black talons, but not quite as long as Reyna's. Between her fingers was coiled a thin chain. A necklace. *My* necklace. She caught me eyeing it and pulled it further into her hand.

"My necklace," I whispered calmly.

"It keeps you from hearing our voice," she said, cocking her head like a curious cat. "How?"

"Magic," I shrugged.

Her rapid blinks seemed uncomfortable. She took a glance at my father's corpse, undisturbed by the feasting crabs. In the morning, the birds would join in. Eventually, my father, the greatest hunter on the waves, would be nothing but bones, bested by his own son.

I let the sadness infect me. It seemed to affect the girl.

"My mother hated him," she finally said. "Called him the skinner. He's killed so many of us."

I didn't know what to say to that. It was true he'd killed many of her kind, but sirens had killed many sailors in return.

"This was my first hunt," I said gently. "I don't think I knew what I was getting myself into."

"Your first hunt? Do you…" She dropped her head. "Do you want to hunt us?"

"I suppose it's always been expected of me."

"And now that your father is dead?"

"Now that he's dead… I doubt I'll be far behind."

Her eyes roamed my cramped body. "You're just a boy."

"You're just a girl."

We caught each other's stares and I was unwillingly captured by the strange, almost ethereal glow.

"I've never killed a man," she said.

"But you've fed on them."

"It is our nature."

"But you don't feed on these men."

She paused. "Not in front of you."

It didn't seem right. The witch was feigning kindness and it made my head hurt. Or maybe that was my hunger doing that.

"I've never killed a siren," I returned.

"But your father has killed many."

We lingered there in silence for a while longer until I saw her uncurl her fingers, letting the necklace hang at length within my reach. I swallowed and slowly maneuvered my hand, palm facing up. She dropped the necklace into it and the ice-cold feel of the metal made my pulse shudder. I glanced up at her, waiting for the deception to make itself known. There had to be a catch. A trick. Some sinister meaning behind her returning the only thing that would prevent me from falling under a siren's spell again.

"What are you doing?" I said, lowering my voice even more.

"Promise to leave?" she said, leaning closer to the bars until she was only a breath away. "Leave and never come upon the sea again."

It was a promise I couldn't make. One I didn't want to make. Her mother had given me far too much reason to take to the sea again. I was not just a hunter. I was vengeful. Enraged. Hate and fury were the only two wolves fighting over the scraps of my soul now.

But saying that would not get me out of that tiny cage. So I looked at her, tears of wrath in my eyes disguised as fear. I trembled, doing everything I could not to shout my hatred to the heavens before her.

Closing my fingers over the pendant in my hand, I nodded.

"There is nothing for me on the sea anymore." I turned to look at my father's form in the dark. "All the reason I had to sail is there, murdered by his only son."

For a while, I couldn't look away. The entire moment replayed in my head a thousand times in a blink. It was the cold, damp touch of fingers on my wrist that brought me out of it. It was jarring and not at all pleasant, but it pulled me from that torturous memory, which I was certain would stay fresh for many years to come.

I turned slowly to look at the girl as she withdrew her hand.

"Wait until the moon has hit the peak of the volcano there," she gestured toward the dark, mountainous silhouettes in the distance. "They will all be fast asleep. Your father's crew was quite robust. Your small boat is far down the beach, but you can make it."

My teeth ground at the coldness of that statement.

The girl was about to stand but she paused, biting her lip again.

"What is your name?" she asked.

"Why should you need a name if we are never to meet again?"

The corner of her lips curled ever so slightly. Not in a malicious way. It was almost… serene.

"I like names," she said.

I wasn't sure I wanted to give her my name. Not that sirens held any sway over names, but I wasn't sure a siren deserved to hear it.

Then again, my lies were thick. I was not going to stay off the sea. I was going to bend it to my will one day. I was going to be a menace to her monstrous kind. I was going to take vengeance on every cunning, beautiful, awful creature under the waves and for that, they would need a name to fear.

"Vidar," I said.

Are they beautiful because they are beautiful
Or because they make us believe it so?
~Captain William Foardragun

Present Day

Things were getting interesting. Very interesting.

Why I didn't fight as hard as I was capable, I didn't fully know. Maybe my mind was too scrambled from seeing *her* that I couldn't use my limbs right. Maybe I thought it was a dream a bit too long. Whatever the reason, I let her get the upper hand.

That scarred face had haunted me for eighteen years. Of course, my mind saw a child. A scrawny girl barely younger than I had been when I was stuffed in that tiny, barnacle-covered cage. The face I saw when I opened my eyes was entirely foreign in so many ways. The scar was there, but her eyes...

Her eyes were pure onyx and filled with malice. Pain. Rage and despair.

It was like looking in a fucking mirror for a split second.

But we were nothing alike…

The demon of my past had gotten the upper hand. Whether I'd given it to her or not, I wasn't entirely sure, but she had it nonetheless. I remembered the cold water washing over me. The ocean was rough and she moved through it like a needle through cotton, swift and true. Not that I could see much. I could only feel. She could have drowned me. Could have plunged to the depths where my human bones would curl in and shatter. Where my lungs would flatten. She didn't. Instead, she'd kept me alive and the weight of my limbs on stone beckoned me out of unconsciousness. That and the overly tight binds wrapped around my wrists.

Fuck.

I pried open salt-crusted eyes to see moon-washed land ahead of me. A smooth rock formation created a monstrous arch before me. Around me, the waves crushed the edges of shallow cliffs. Whatever island I was on, it was small. I could see the ocean in every direction. Against my back was a thick rod of some kind. Metal. Clearly not from the island originally. It chafed my forearms where I was tethered tightly against it, hands behind my back.

But none of that mattered when my gaze came upon *her*. She slowly revealed herself against the rocky background, camouflaged almost perfectly. Once she was in view, all of my doubts about her existence washed away. She was there, tall and slender and pale under the moonlight. Any traces of that girl I knew that night had been ripped away, violently it would seem. She wore a thin dress made of strange material laced loosely at the front. It didn't cover much more than her breasts and upper thighs. Every bit of her that was visible to me was marked in some way. Scars. Black tattoos of some kind coiled around one forearm. Her cheek bore the scar I'd given her all those years ago. It was a perfectly straight line from her ear almost to the corner of her mouth.

And the look on her face made her seem like she hadn't slept since the day we parted ways. She held a bone knife in her hand with an intricate handle and a slightly curved and very sharp edge to it that reminded me too much of the one I used on my father.

The corner of my mouth lifted and it made her head tilt a bit. The blackness faded from her eyes until they gleamed silver-gray under the light like two glass marbles.

"You planning on using that to skin me alive?" I rasped, my throat burning like I'd swallowed too much salt water.

She cocked her head again like she heard me but didn't understand. I glimpsed the knife and tested my binds, but she'd given me no leeway to pull free. I didn't expect her to.

She stalked forward, each of her steps silent on the slick stone and reminding me too much of her horrid mother. The material of her garments moved strangely, clinging to her form, until I doubted it was fabric at all.

Fuck me…

It was skin. I wouldn't have been surprised if it was human skin.

"Don't try to struggle," she finally said, her voice unnervingly melodic and calm despite the hate burning in her gaze. "There are three islands in these parts, any one of which I could have brought you to if your crew doesn't think I just dragged you to the bottom of the sea."

She was close now. So close that if I wanted to, I could have kicked a foot out and broken her knee. She didn't seem to care, even when my eyes glimpsed her legs. She just adjusted the knife in her hand to remind me she had it.

"This place is only visible during low tide," she continued, taking another step until she had one foot on either side of my legs. "It's not on any human maps. I've checked."

She dropped to her knees astride my lap. The weight of her on my groin further proved she was real. She lifted the edge of her knife to my chest and let the tip skim my scar where I'd buried my silentium under my skin years ago. She knew it was there. There was no doubt about it.

"By the time the tide rises, you'll be buried beneath it," she whispered, her face close enough to mine that I could feel the caress of her breath on my lips. "In pieces."

I kept my eyes on hers, studying everything about her. It was no use thinking of her as the girl from that cursed island. She was a different creature entirely. So was I.

"So? How do you plan to get me into pieces?" I said.

She slowly cut the blade across my chest, leaving my silentium in place and instead slicing just above it in a diagonal line. Hot blood immediately wept down my skin. I clenched my teeth but gave her no other indication that it stung. She watched me for a sign, though. Oh, she watched me eagerly. She wanted my screams, but I didn't have much else to give in that department. I'd spent my screams through eighteen years of nightmares, hate, and rage.

"Slowly," she whispered, lifting her blade to her mouth. She licked across the bone until my blood seasoned her tongue and then wrinkled her nose in disgust. "Hemsbane. Your blood is bitter with it."

"Did you expect anything less?"

"It makes no difference. I have waited a long time to get my hands on you, Vidar. Do you think I haven't been suffering hemsbane all these years? Your body could be filled with it and I could still devour you before it took effect. I told you I would not forget your name."

I scoffed. "I never expected you to. But after eighteen years, cutting me up in pieces is the best you came up with?"

She shrugged. "I never desired to be creative with my vengeance." Her blade made a quick pass over my chest again, making a parallel cut. That one was a bit deeper and the suddenness of it made me hiss. "I only wish to be rid of you."

Under the moon's muted light, I could hardly tell, but I thought I could see a slight glisten beneath her inhuman eyes.

But sirens couldn't weep. Weeping was for people with hearts and sirens were hollow. I knew that all too well.

"Well," I sighed, lifting my hips to remind her where she sat. "Better get on with it. If I'm to be buried under high tide, you'll want to start."

My lack of distress seemed to make her tense. I couldn't help myself. I smirked at knowing what she wanted. She wanted my fear. She wanted me to plead for my life. Killing me wasn't enough. She wanted me to feel it and the fact was, I hardly felt anything anymore. And the other fact was that my truest fear was that she would take out her vengeance on my crew instead of me. But she'd taken me and I was oddly relieved about it. Another thought that made me smile.

She hated it. She snarled and stood from my lap, looking over my body as if searching for a place to start. She was going to draw it out… if her anger didn't get the best of her. Maybe if I made her lose control, I could get things over with and be done with the whole damn game.

The wet slap of something solid hitting the rocks drew her attention.

Another siren slid from the waves, her body moon-white and almost glowing in the darkness. Silver hair hung over her shoulders and freckles of glowing marks littered her face and the contours of her body. I'd only seen a few like her and never had I left them alive long enough to truly see how their skin glowed like that. Sirens could have been considered beautiful to the untrained eye.

She spoke in a tongue I couldn't understand. Not fully, anyway. Over the years, I'd picked up things here and there. I noticed "ship" and that was the only clue I needed to know they were talking about the Rose.

The pale one's eyes caught mine, but it was hard to tell what she was thinking when there was no color in them. They were just luminescent, white globes that were almost too big for her slender face.

"Your ship's heading west," my little demon said. "Away from here."

Good, I thought.

"Well," I said, adjusting myself as if to get comfortable, but in truth, my ass was going numb and I couldn't really feel my hands anymore. "Torture me how you like. You know how to do it, don't you? Seeing as you're Reyna's daughter."

The pale one furrowed her brows, but my demon? Oh, she looked livid. Her nostrils flared and her fingers curled ever tighter around the hilt of her blade. She was not going to be difficult to anger.

"Come, now," I continued. "You should be ashamed." My tone dropped an octave. "With a lineage like that, I expected more."

For days. For days I listened to the morbid symphony of my father's crew dying. Being eaten. Dismembered. Skinned.

But she didn't care. It was in her nature. She had said it herself all those years ago.

"I wish I was so skilled," I finished.

She lunged forward, grabbing a handful of my hair in her fist and yanking my head back so my throat was exposed to her. The cool edge of her knife kissed my skin and I almost rejoiced at how easy it was to hasten my end.

"Your blood will fill my belly," she snarled. "Your skin will clothe my body."

"Dahlia," the other one said.

I finally had a name.

Dahlia.

My demon had a name.

She pressed the blade under my chin until I felt my skin give and warm blood pool, but she didn't cut. Not yet.

"I will spill your insides at my feet for the ocean to sweep away. The world will forget your name, *Vidar.*"

"Do it already," I strained. "Or are you too weak to murder your mother's killer? I know I wasn't too weak to kill my father's."

Her brows twitched at that. What the hell was her hesitation? I truly wanted to know. And evidently, I had time to figure it out.

"You're shaking, Dahlia," I whispered. "Oh, I must have planted something dark inside you that day. Now that you've got me, you don't know what to do with me. Have I been a part of you too long? Now you don't know how to live without me. What will you hate then? What will drive you, I wonder."

"Kill him," the other one said in words I could understand. Dahlia whipped her head around to look at her. "Swallow your pride and kill him fast or start whatever it is you're going to do. I don't like this place."

Dahlia hesitated for another long breath, tension making the tendons in her neck strain.

Do it, I thought. *End this fucking game.*

A spray of liquid splashed across my face and Dahlia's. Not ocean spray. Something dark. Our eyes were locked for a split second before she turned her attention away from me and to her companion. It wasn't until her fingers loosened in my hair that I was able to look and notice her naked form slumping backward. Innards uncoiled from her stomach and slid to her feet before she hit the stone with a splash, completely limp. Dead.

Dahlia leaped away from me just as a spear shot past her. It landed in the rock not far from my head, thrown with so much force that it remained stuck.

My eyes caught the waves as they lunged upward against the rocky ledges. Appearing from them was a line of figures shrouded in the shadows of night. More sirens, I suspected… until they began to lurch forward. Their limbs were long and slim and their bodies slightly hunched with a significant finned ridge following the length of their spine. The sparse amount of hair they had hung like strands of slimy seaweed over broad yet bony shoulders.

Each figure held a spear or ruggedly shaped blade of some kind and walked with a gait that was eerily in unison with each other. Their faces were long and skinny with eyes that looked too big and empty.

Dahlia quickly absorbed the sight of her very dead companion nearby and then clutched her knife with renewed force, standing with her back to me as the four figures slowly encircled us both.

That crazed fisherman from the Treson docks came to mind and internally, I was laughing at the irony. Although, "weird fish" was an understatement. These creatures were monstrous, towering a hand or two taller than a big man like myself even when they were hunched the way they were.

They began emitting an odd clicking noise to each other that was barely audible over the crashing of the waves hitting the rocks. Once the moonlight hit the nearest one just right, I could see the rows of sharp teeth in its oversized mouth. Gills flared out on the sides of its thick neck making faint wheezing sounds like an old man struggling for air. The nearest one scanned Dahlia and then me with its unnatural eyes before an unnerving sound came from his throat. Something akin to laughter, but absent the vocal tones any human had.

Then it spoke.

The voice was low. Clipped. I couldn't understand a word, but judging by the way Dahlia's weight shifted as if she was further preparing to defend herself, I was betting she did.

And then everything went to the next circle of hell. Dahlia spun around to move away when two of those horrid creatures grabbed her by the arms, lifting her off the ground as if she weighed nothing. She began fighting and thrashing like a wild animal. She had skill in her movements, not that her skill helped at all. Two creatures hauled her to the other side of the island near a cluster of raised rocks, one holding her wrists and the other her ankles like she was a hog carcass fresh from a hunt. Her screams were feral and wild.

The nearest creature took a step toward me, letting me get a good look at its sickening form. It peered down at me with unblinking eyes and cocked its head to one side, planting the butt of its spear on the stone near a large, webbed foot. Its too-long arm twitched, its skinny fingers uncurling to show the claws at the tips.

"Human," it said. "Tasty." Two of the creatures behind it let out the same sort of clicking laughter. All the while, Dahlia's struggles and screams coated the air, muffled only by a shallow wall of stone. "Will eat you after the mudfin." It took a deep breath through those fish-like slits. "Bleeding already."

And that was when Dahlia's screams changed. They became strained. Battered. And slowly, they started to lessen and fade into the night.

Seemed getting myself killed quickly was no longer an option…

They say kindness is laughter
and madness is a scream.
But evil... evil is but a whisper.
~Bishop Doyle II

I did not think I would die on a rock in the middle of the ocean, but there I was… about to die on a rock in the middle of the ocean. It was a pity Dahlia hadn't killed me before the nightmare creatures appeared. I wasn't sure what they were, but they seemed to strike fear in the sirens and that didn't bode well for humans.

I glimpsed the one lying nearby, her innards strewn about like coils of wet rope. Her white face had lost all of its luster and glow. She'd been killed so quickly. Without bronze or a beheading, it baffled me.

Behind the cluster of rocks, there was no telling what they'd done to Dahlia. By her silence, I assumed they killed her which meant I was next once the monsters had eaten their fill.

So… a species that ate sirens. The irony had me smiling inside. It appeared they were not at the top of the food chain. I tested my bonds again, but they only seemed to get tighter. My wrists must have been swelling. Great. I rested my head back on my post to stare up at the thin clouds moving across the dark sky. Waiting to be eaten seemed to be a repeating pattern in my life. Looking down at my legs, I was glad I didn't wake to see them severed. I'd been lucky once again. And if I wasn't mistaken, Dahlia had some odd reservations. I would have loved to get to the bottom of them. But alas, I was about to die.

The faint slosh of water behind me made me pause those thoughts. While sloshing water wasn't unusual when the ocean around us was undulating nonstop, this particular sound caught my attention. I heard something slide on the rocks and as one of those fowl creatures made a half-assed patrol of the island, I watched him, wondering if he'd noticed the disturbance as well. When he turned and started venturing back toward the cluster of rocks where his companions were, the movement continued, creeping up behind me. Then the hushed sound of metal on stone drew my eyes. I glimpsed at the ground beside me to see a bronze blade near my hip. It looked old as if it had been fished from the bottom of the sea.

"How well do you fight, hunter?" came a whisper, so soft I barely thought it was real.

I stared toward the rocks, trying not to be obvious as I said, "Well enough that you know who I am."

She hesitated. "Your ship is far out at sea. You cannot get to it without us. You cannot get to your ship without your boat."

"What boat?" I said, almost laughing.

"You do not think we could bring your fragile human body here without one, did you? You'd have drowned before Dahlia had her fun."

I sighed, leaning my head back against the post. "What do you want?"

"I cut you free, you help kill the xhoth."

I wasn't going to ask her to clarify that. There was only one thing on that island that could possibly be "the xhoth."

"I'm prepared to die here," I said. "Why would I help you?"

She inched closer to my ear, still not coming out of the shadows behind me.

"Because your crew doesn't know what's coming. You could change that. If you care for them, that is."

I tried to bite back the worry that sparked. I was going to try and negotiate with the woman, but my options were limited. I knew she was implying that I help her free Dahlia, which meant she was still alive. I also knew she couldn't do it alone. To be desperate enough to enlist my help meant she had no other choice. It also meant she and Dahlia were close. It was a weakness I could exploit if it ever came down to it.

I weighed my options quickly and ultimately, if I had a chance of getting off that rock alive and back to my crew, I had to take it.

"How many?" I asked.

"Four. My sister waits on the other side of the island to aid us."

"I help kill them and then what? How do I know you'll help me in return?"

"You don't. But I promise that right now, a whole skryll of us is under the belly of your ship just waiting to eat your entire crew alive. You get Dahlia out of this, she calls them off."

She slid the blade closer to me, tempting me to take the offer. I deduced a couple of very significant things in those brief moments. One, the creatures that had interrupted Dahlia's playtime were no friends of hers. Two, she was very important to her companions. It wasn't surprising considering she was Reyna's daughter. It was enough to pique my interest.

With another sigh and a glimpse at the moon, which I thought only moments ago would be my last, I nodded.

"Better get on with it, then."

She sliced my binds instantly, freeing my wrists. My shoulders were cramped. My hands were numb. I was stiff as a goddamn cripple.

But I'd been worse.

I picked up the blade and took a quick survey of the area to know the terrain I had to work with. Rolling my shoulders, I rocked forward into a crouch and glanced over my shoulder to see the woman hiding in the shadows. Like the dead one, she had silvery hair, pale skin and faintly glowing freckles on her admittedly beautiful face. Her white eyes caught mine and she moved back an inch, untrusting.

I wanted to refuse her offer, jump into the sea, and take my chances, but I knew it would have ended quickly, either to drowning, sharks, or one of the many fiends beneath the waves. I shook my head and hissed with aggravation, knowing I had no other choice.

Fuck.

Standing at full height, I tested my mobility as I marched toward the gilled beasts across the little rock island. The water was getting higher and soon that whole place would be under the waves just like Dahlia had said. I was the only one there at a true disadvantage because I didn't have fins.

The first "xhoth" I spotted had his back turned and was staring into the dark sea. I lifted the old sword and kissed the cool metal of its blade before rushing him. He spun as soon as I put my leather boot down hard enough to be heard. I thrust the blade up through his chin until it hit his skull, but it went no further.

Tough creatures. His bones were dense, but all things had a weakness.

He gurgled on black blood before clawing at his wound. I slid my blade free and then jammed it between his ribs, searching for soft tissue. At that point, the little island of horrors was up in arms. The creatures made a terrible wheezing screech as they moved in to fight. I spun just as my first kill crumpled into a twitching mess of unnatural limbs at the edge of the rocks. I kicked him into the water, but just before I took my eyes off the waves below, I spotted something I could use.

A goddamn boat.

I growled to myself, watching for a moment as its wooden edge knocked against the rocks.

So, all sirens were liars. No matter. I needed to kill everything I could lest they follow me on my trip back to the Burning Rose, so I renewed my grip on my weapon and turned as one of the slimy beasts charged my way.

I really would have liked my night to go differently, but death and murder it was.

Suddenly, a figure leaped up from behind the creature and latched onto his back. It was the woman who freed me. She was small in comparison to the xhoth, but she wrapped her skinny limbs around him and her sharp teeth came down on the fleshy bend of his shoulder, ripping a thick chunk right off of him. Dark blood fountained out of his neck and I took that chance to drive him through with my blade.

Chaos ensued. If it was moving, I killed it and I did it furiously. I would have liked to slaughter every last thing on that island, but something in the back of my mind was stopping me. Instead, I held up my end of the bargain, reluctantly avoiding the sirens with every swing of my blade until the island eventually fell silent.

Of course, I'd only agreed to help kill the creatures. What I did next was entirely improvised.

I saw Dahlia's body tied up within the cluster of stones. Her blood painted the wet slate and trailed in red streams deep in the stony grooves beneath her. Black hair fanned out around her head. She was unconscious. Perfect.

Before the excitement of the fight had left me, I bent and scooped Dahlia's body over my shoulder. She was heavier than she looked or I was weaker than I thought after the whole ordeal. Either way, I groaned as I straightened, holding my sword in one hand as I turned to face what was now two silver-haired sirens standing in front of me. The second one must have joined in the fight, but I was too consumed with the slaughter to notice. And clearly, she was wounded by the way her hands were pressed firmly over her side and blood was trickling down her right leg.

The one who'd given me the blade glared daggers at me and I let my lips slant into a smirk, pointing the tip of my blood-drenched bronze at her.

"I held up my end," I said. She stepped forward as if to try and take Dahlia from me and I quickly lifted the blade until the point of it was pressed up against Dahlia's abdomen. So many organs there to slice through. "Ah, ah," I warned. "Now, I can tell she means a lot. She can call off her sisters whether she's with you or with me, but I don't trust her to do it if I hand her over."

"You can't—"

"Get to the boat that's washed up on the other side of this island?" I chuckled. "Not as good at hiding things as you are at lying, are you?"

"If you're going to kill her," the other one grimaced. "Just do it."

"Oh, I'd rather have a nice little chat now that we've all gotten our fill of killing for a few hours. I'm going to take your precious sister with me and if you try anything, I'll cut her open so fast she won't even be able to scream."

"You don't know where your ship is," she retorted.

My smirk turned to a grin. "You know the tides," I said. "I know the wind. I'll find them well enough."

• • •

Damn Gus and his incessant songs. I found myself humming one of his tunes as I rowed off in the boat toward the sunrise. Without the cover of night and the sea mist, I could see the faint peaks of Grissom Island in the distance and I knew my crew was smart enough to use it as a landmark if they were making a sweep of the area. I wasn't worried about finding them. I did, however, find myself looking over the edge of the boat from time to time wondering if I'd see something stalking beneath. No doubt something was down there, too deep for my eyes to find.

I kept humming and shaking my head at the insanity of it all. I was in the middle of the ocean on a dinghy with my greatest enemy tied up and unconscious only a couple strides away from me. I'd discovered another menace in the waters and somehow, I was still alive. I laughed out loud at the whole thing. How many times could I survive impossible situations before death decided he was bored with our game?

When a wave caught the boat just right to make a loud knock against the side and jostle us a bit, I glanced at Dahlia's body secured on the other end of the boat. In the daylight, I could see much more of her than I had previously. Her ashen white skin was so smooth save for the marks that littered it. Scars and new injuries mingled on the planes of her body. I'd adjusted her binds so her wrists were tightly bound with crude rope to the furthest seat in the boat. That scar on her cheek stood out among all the other blemishes, even the thin mark that spanned the front of her throat. It was clean, but prominent, marring an otherwise striking face. She was thin, but not soft by any means. Lean muscle tone made her into something lethal.

On her exposed legs, I saw multiple cuts, but one was quite deep and spanned the length of her outer thigh as if the xhoth had meant to maim her. They hadn't cut any chunks away, so either they hadn't started eating or they had other plans.

When another wave rocked the boat hard enough for Dahlia to roll a little, she sucked in a ragged breath and coughed wetly. Her whole face tensed as she began choking up blood. Turning over, she let what looked like a whole lungful of watery blood out onto the floor. I stopped rowing and fixed the oars on the sides of the boat, watching her.

She was about to realize what was going on and whatever she did was going to determine what I did next.

Dahlia turned her head toward the brightening sky and squinted, groaning through her discomfort before she slowly realized her bound wrists. She tugged on the restraints, testing them, and then her eyes wandered toward me. They shot wide, but not out of fear. It was fury and hatred burning in those eyes like she'd rather get to me than escape.

"Stop your struggling," I said calmly.

She let out a low, animalistic growl, showing her fangs, and struggled to her feet. I furrowed my brows, watching her ignore the deep gash in her thigh as she braced her foot on the seat. The boat rocked violently and with a grumble, I gripped the sides trying to steady it. She was like a wolf caught in a bear trap. I half expected her to start gnawing off her arms to get away.

"Stop," I demanded.

She yanked on her binds, using her foot to add to the strength of her effort. Once. Twice. On the third, the seat splintered a bit.

"Stop!" I roared.

She yanked again. She was fucking strong. I leaped to my feet and marched forward, pulling out that old blade from my belt. Dahlia whipped her head toward me with another snarl, her wrists bleeding from the friction. And, as I would with any wild beast that was out of control, I sought to restrain her. She glimpsed my bronze blade and tugged again, making the seat's middle bend and crack. Then she started trying to capsize us.

"Christ!" I exclaimed, grabbing her by her slender neck and knocking her to the floor.

She writhed beneath me as I straddled her, trying to renew her binds. She attempted to slam her head against mine, but that time I dodged it. I pressed my blade under her chin and still, she struggled and bucked.

It was really hard to threaten someone with death when they didn't fear it.

I should know…

So, since she didn't care whether my blade slipped and severed her artery, I stopped using it to persuade her. Instead, I tossed it out of reach and started to reinforce the ropes holding her in the boat. I tied her arms. Her legs. It was like wrestling a wild stallion, but eventually, I got her wrapped up enough for the boat's rocking to ease. She ended up against the front of the boat tangled in ropes and knots. I sat back on my bench out of breath, sweeping my hair back from my face as I stared at her.

"Are you done?" I asked, perching my elbows on my knees. She parted her lips as if about to answer, but didn't. "So, you don't really talk when you're the one bound, huh?"

Her lips snapped shut in defiance before she scanned the waters around us.

"They down there?" I asked. "Can you all sense each other like that?"

No answer. I groaned and took the oars, rowing leisurely toward Grissom Island. Again, I skimmed the long gash on her thigh. It was no longer bleeding, but it was significant. She saw me looking and her eyes flicked toward it briefly before locking with mine again.

"It'll be a while before I find my men," I said. "Might as well have a chat, Dahlia."

She raised her chin defiantly. So, I did what any sleep-deprived ship captain with a killer siren in his boat would do. I started humming again. When my arms got tired, I stopped rowing and leaned back, hands behind my head, to enjoy the warmth of the morning sun. I switched songs at some point and eventually started rowing again, but Dhalia never moved. I could feel the hate radiating off of her like heat off a piece of red coal. When I took a rest again from rowing, I decided to rekindle the one-sided conversation.

"So, you found the Cornwallis first. No one else slaughters men quite like your kind." Her eyes flitted toward me. "So? Why spare the kids?"

The corner of her lips lifted. "Was saving them for later," she said.

I raised my brows at the sound of her voice. "Right. You mentioned something about dessert. And what were you going to do with them? Pick them off one by one for a few days?"

"Where are my sisters?"

"You know better than me, I'm sure."

"We can't sense each other. Where are they?"

I shrugged. "Wherever they decided to go after I took you."

"Why didn't you kill me?"

"Because your sister said something about a 'skryll' of you stalking my ship and you are going to call them off."

She laughed breathily. "There's no one to call off. There were only four of us and Voel is dead. If anything is stalking your ship, I can't call them off, nor would I want to."

I groaned as I adjusted my sore body. "I figured as much, but I'm still a bit curious."

"So, why'd you take me alive?"

"Because you're going to tell me everything you know about those things that attacked you."

113

~ WICKED TIDES ~

16

Dahlia

If you eat of his flesh,
you eat of his soul.
~The Seer

Vidar found his ship as if he had a sixth sense as to where it would be and his crewmen spotted him so fast, it was like they had a sixth sense about him as well. We drifted up to the side of the giant vessel where his men unrolled a rope ladder. I hadn't stopped glaring at Vidar since I'd woken, hoping by some miracle I would suddenly develop abilities that would snap his neck with a glance.

There was urgent shouting and joyful voices coming from above. To climb onto the ship, Vidar would need both of his hands, which led me to believe I was about to get a chance to escape.

No chance arose.

A rope net dropped down beside the ladder and before I knew it, Vidar was taking it toward me. I knew what he meant to do and I wouldn't make it easy. As he untangled me from the boat and started spreading the net around me, I began to kick and writhe. But the man was strong. Few men could overpower me, but he was and he was doing it with ease. But I was exhausted and my limbs had been tied for some time. I blamed it on my handicaps when he shoved me into the net and it was pull taut around me.

Then the men above started pulling. The twine bit into my skin as I was lifted from the boat like a catch of fish and Vidar ascended the ladder beside me. He boarded before I did and helped his men haul me over the railing and put me on my feet. I stood there, eyes cutting into each and every man's face as I scanned across them. They looked at me like I wasn't real. Like they were having trouble processing my presence.

I supposed they were used to killing us. A prolonged look at me seemed to stupefy the lot of them.

When my eyes reached the back of the group crowding around us, I noticed the burly man with the white beard and aged features. Gus. He was looking at me differently than the others. Instead of wide eyes, his remaining one was narrowed with burning suspicion. I zeroed in on him and cocked my head to the side, holding his gaze until he diverted his.

"What happened to you?" someone asked Vidar.

"We was searching everywhere," another said.

Every voice was laced with concern for the captain. A crew that cared. How sweet.

That meant it would hurt more when I slaughtered them all.

I balled my fists in front of me, which only made the binds around my wrists tighten and throb. I looked for the one I would kill first.

"Was on a rock," Vidar answered chipperly. "And fought my way back. Did you expect anything less?"

The men erupted in relieved hoots as they reached out to pat their captain and welcome him back. It was nauseating. Each one of those men was responsible for the deaths of multiple sisters. I flared my nostrils, sick over the scent of their human skin and filth, and felt my muscles tense to pounce. Even without full use of my arms, I could bite a throat out just fine. I focused on a man with a particularly gnarly grin and a red bandana on his head when the sound of pattering footsteps tapped across the deck. Heads turned as a young girl wrapped in a brown blanket jogged through the cluster of men.

It was Ahnah.

The rage and ferocity slid off my face when I saw those round cheeks. She rushed toward me, misunderstanding the situation completely, and wrapped her little arms around my waist.

I didn't know what to do...

I was meant to be feared. I was meant to fill men with dread and haunt their nightmares and this little girl had ruined that. I didn't hug her back. Instead, my eyes stayed glued to the floor in front of me, stunned and at a loss.

"Da'ya," she said.

Then she continued speaking in that language of hers until Gus shoved through the crowd to pick the girl up and pull her away from me. I didn't want him touching her. I didn't want any of them touching her. Ahnah's little fingers grasped mine, forcing them from their tight fists, and then she was taken away. I wasn't blind to the glare on the old man's face as he carried her as if he thought he'd saved the girl from instant death.

My jaw clenched with unreleased anger as she disappeared through the crowd. And, without thinking, my foot moved forward half a step as if my body was desperate to follow. Vidar's hand shot forward to grab my arm and I stopped, teeth gnashing together in my mouth.

"Back to work," Vidar ordered his men. "Mullins and Boil, come with me."

The crew dispersed, tossing me disgusted and questioning glances as they tore themselves away. Ahnah had made me look soft. I welcomed her affections and cursed them at the same time as Vidar started forcing me to walk across the deck. He led me to the steps going below and it wasn't hard to know where he was going to put me. Most ships were the same.

When we reached the holding cells, I immediately noticed that, unlike the cells on the other ship where I'd found the girls, his cell gates were metal. It was perfect for locking up someone like me. Someone who could splinter a wooden gate and escape.

Vidar swung the gate open and pushed me inside, forcefully spinning me around to face him before I stumbled on my injured leg. The two men behind him had pistols trained on me as he started to loosen my binds. When I felt the blood rush to my fingers, it almost hurt. I watched the twine unravel from my wrists to uncover the raw and chafed skin beneath.

But that was hardly from Vidar's binding. Most of it was the xhoth. I winced at the memory of their slimy fingers on my body and the way they cut deep into my thigh just to test my meat. A few more moments and half of me would have been melting in their stomach acid.

Vidar's thumb brushed over the reddened rings on my wrists, which made me look up at him. His brown eyes met mine, heavy with fatigue but still alert as ever.

"Don't get excited," he muttered, pulling a set of irons off the adjoining gate and locking them around my wrists.

So he wasn't offering kindness. He was just replacing my binds with something I couldn't chew through. But at least the iron cuffs did not squeeze me as tight. They were cold and heavy, but the chain connecting them allowed a little more movement. I sighed and lowered my hands down in front of me. Smirking smugly, Vidar closed the metal gate. The hinges whined with age as it swung shut and latched. There was a heavy lock on the outside that he snapped closed, imprisoning me inside.

Only then did the two men behind him lower their pistols and tuck them back into their leather belts. Vidar tossed the men a brief glance over his shoulder, resting his hands on his hips. Exhaustion was trying to claim him, I could tell. But he was fighting it, trying to put on a strong face for his crew.

"Fix me something to eat, will you?" he said to one of them.

The lanky man with a horribly scarred face gave him a nod.

The other man with the dark skin seemed hesitant but eventually followed his disfigured companion out. Once they were gone, Vidar let out a long breath and leaned an arm through the bars, resting it there while he pinched the bridge of his nose in quiet frustration. I watched him, admittedly intrigued by his behavior. Then I glimpsed his fingers. I could so easily bite the rest of them off and he knew it. His other hand certainly bore the evidence of what my teeth could do and yet he let it rest freely inside my cell like he knew I wouldn't. Surprisingly… I was too curious about everything that had happened to make that move. That would likely earn me a gag or even the loss of my tongue.

"I'm tired," he said, shaking his head. "Don't know about you."

I narrowed my eyes at that casual sentence. After another bout of silence, I was backing up into the cell, distancing myself from the bars until my back hit the wooden wall. Vidar watched me as I slid down and sat on the floor where a thin pad of bedding was rolled out.

"Dessert, huh?" he said. When I didn't respond to that, he just shook his head again. "Does dessert usually react like that or did you sing her into liking you so she and the others wouldn't try to escape?"

I shrugged. "Maybe I did." I looked at Vidar's chest where his shirt was unlaced enough for me to see my handiwork as well as the scar on his sternum. "You going to gag me or cut out my tongue? Don't you think it's a bit dangerous for a thing like me to have a voice?"

"All my men wear a silentium. I'm not worried about that. What I'm worried about is what the hell happened on that island."

His eyes flicked toward the gash on my thigh. Blood had dried and crusted to my skin, but the wound itself was healing.

"Does that hurt? You haven't acted like it does."

"Would you care?"

In truth, it hurt when it happened. It hurt after. Then it all turned off. I could do that. I had to learn how to do that a long time ago. Pain was part of life. Debilitating pain was just a distraction. One I'd taught myself to grow immune to when I was alone in the dark and monstrous ocean for all those years.

But I didn't want to tell Vidar any of that. I didn't want him to know my secrets, my flaws, or my strengths. A man like him was only looking to exploit them.

My thoughts wandered back to Ahnah. He'd used my mercy against me before. What was stopping him now? Would he stoop so low as to hurt those girls? The ship I found them on certainly didn't care for their well-being.

Humans were all alike.

"Do I need to knock you silly so you let someone mend that leg?"

That was more like it.

If my hate could burn flesh, he'd be a charred pile of bone.

"It will heal," I said.

"You hurt anywhere else?"

I shook my head, pursing my lips with defiance. When he realized I was done speaking, he let his fatigue show and lowered his head, running a hand over his coarse dreadlocks.

"Sleep tight, then," he exhaled. "Or do whatever it is you do."

I watched him drag his feet toward the steps and disappear before I finally let myself breathe normally. I slouched, burying my face in my hands and biting back a scream.

I had been so stupid. Why couldn't I kill him? It would have been quick and done, perhaps before the xhoth showed up. Those bastards ruined everything. My revenge. My focus. I could still see Voel lying on the ground, her insides on the outside. She died so fast that I could hardly process what happened. Now, in a cell by myself, the pain of that loss hit me like a punch to the lungs.

Don't show weakness.

I chanted it over and over again in my head. Weakness could be exploited and I knew Vidar did that very well. I was a heartless beast willing to kill any man on that ship. I didn't care if they had families. I didn't care if they begged. I would rip them apart the first moment I got the chance. I wouldn't make the mistake of trying to draw it out again like I did with Vidar. Now he had the upper hand and my sisters were gone.

I stood and started pacing, trying to bury my ire so it wouldn't show if anyone ventured into the hold. I needed to be calm. Calculating. Ruthless.

But no matter the mantras I repeated in my head, my breath still quivered and my eyes still burned with the sadness I refused to let out. I sucked in a deep breath only to catch a whiff of Vidar's lingering scent. Leather, salty sea air, rum, and oak.

Fucking scum.

I memorized that scent, swearing to myself that no matter what happened, I'd always find a way to follow it to his death.

My leg was sore once I let myself feel it. I slumped down again to look at the damage and winced at the ugly laceration with disdain. The bastards had knives made of rock and serrated with shark teeth. The gash wasn't clean and it wasn't shallow. It would have killed a human in minutes. I prodded the inflamed flesh and was pleased to see it already fusing together. It would just be another faint scar in a few days.

I rested my head back on the wall and stared up at the swinging lantern outside my cell. The candle inside was short and almost spent. Perhaps I'd get lucky and the thing would burn out and give me a little darkness to rest my eyes. I stared at it, willing it to dim, and the swinging rhythm of it eventually lulled me to sleep anyway.

● ● ●

The embrace of the cold sea rocked me awake beneath her powerful currents. I could smell blood in the water. The iron tang of it was so strong and rotten. Opening my eyes, clouds of red swirled around me, dying the waves crimson, and within that red cloud floated body parts. Feet. Hands. Legs. Fingers. Items of shredded clothing and a few faces with their last moments of terror frozen upon them. I moved to the surface where the weather was raging. Lune's tears pounded against the surface of the sea, cold and sharp. Frightful thunder rolled through the clouds and shook my bones.

There was a shore nearby. A black shore that smelled of smoke and salt and sulfur.

And on that shore was a man.

The gray colors of the storm shrouded him in darkness, but I could tell by his silhouette that it was Vidar.

Questions whirled through my head. Had I been freed? Dumped? Had the ship been destroyed and I'd blacked out during the whole ordeal? None of it made sense. I swam toward the black sand, nudging body parts aside as I moved. When my tail hit the bank, I forced my body to change, but there was no jarring pain or discomfort like I was used to.

Something was amiss. I glanced up at the thick, black clouds in search of the moon. If I could see Lune, perhaps she'd present some answers, but the clouds completely covered the sky.

I walked along the beach toward Vidar, my steps slow and quiet. He stood still as a statue, his body stripped of his heavy coat and boots, and wore only a pair of leather pants and a thin, tan shirt that was so wet it stuck to him like his own skin. His bare feet were buried partly in the sand as the waves washed putrid water around his ankles over and over again.

The closer I got to him, the more the rain and thunder and the rolling waves melted together into what sounded like voices. Many voices. I couldn't make out the words, but I could hear them. Women. Men. Children. Some were screaming. Others were crying. There were whispers and shouts and angry tones mixed with sad tones and the flood of their inaudible words threatened to crack my skull.

Naked and yet not cold, I trudged closer to Vidar, slowly circling around to the front of him. The bloody water splashed against my calves as I turned to look at him, but he couldn't see me. His eyes were far away and not a hint of emotion touched his features. He looked... dead.

I let my attention wander to the violent scar on his chest where he'd buried his silentium and I fantasized about ripping it out with my nails just to see him writhe as I told him to slaughter his crew. But... by the looks of it, his crew was already gone. Crabs scoured the beach for scraps as pieces of rotting human remains continued to wash ashore.

I recognized the smells. The violence. I even recognized the black sand beach and the volcanic stench in the air. Behind Vidar, stuck between rough rocks, was a rusted, barnacle-covered cage with the skeleton of a boy crushed into the tiny space and suddenly everything made sense.

I looked up once more at Vidar's face. Water cascaded down his cut features and through the blond scruff of his short beard. And yet he still did not notice me. He continued staring blankly into the red ocean.

Something heavy and solid hit the back of my legs with the rush of another wave. I looked down to see the late captain himself, Ethelwoelf, the dreaded captain of the Mother's Fang. To my people, he was the greatest menace and he'd been reduced to a bloated body floating on bloody waters with a dagger in his neck. A dagger that had been embedded there by his son. His skin was pasty and rotten with holes gnawed out by crabs. His eyes had been plucked out by birds and his lips had receded from his blunt teeth, making him an absolute horror to look at.

My eyes crept up Vidar's body again and came to his face. If he wasn't breathing, I'd have believed it was just his corpse stuck upright on a pole. He was so still and unmoving as the voices devoured the space around him.

"I will get you, Vidar!" a girl's voice screamed, shrill and hateful. "I will not forget your name!"

I whipped my head around to search for the source of the voice, startled for a moment by the familiar tone. That scream. That anger. I knew it because it was me.

"You're not scared of her coming for you," another voice said. It was gruff and aged. "You're scared she'll be coming for us. And you'll see another crew taken by the wicked tides."

Still, Vidar did not even flinch. But it was at that point I knew where I was. I narrowed my eyes at his unmoving face and suddenly tasted his blood on my lips.

"If you eat of his flesh, you eat of his soul," I whispered.

I skimmed his hand with my fingertips, remembering the crunch of bone when I bit off two of his fingers. I'd practically swallowed them whole. I remembered because my intent was not to eat him so I did not even chew. It was to maim him. But he got away anyway. Still, I'd eaten of his flesh. His blood found its way to my stomach and somehow into my being. I had tasted him again on that rocky island.

"You're sleeping," I muttered, kicking my foot out behind me to nudge Ethelwoelf's body away from my legs. I stepped closer to Vidar and raised my chin, studying his rugged features. "Not very peacefully, it would seem." Lifting my hand, I let the sharp nail of my finger trace the line of his jaw. "I am so tempted to make this nightmare worse for you. Would skinning you in this dream be as bad as skinning you on that island?" I nicked his chin with my nail and still, he did not flinch, even when the rain washed a stream of blood down his neck. "Or perhaps you're too numb to feel it."

The voices around us persisted until I could catch words here and there. Together with others, perhaps they were significant, but to me, they were only words. Haunting words. Words that clearly meant something to Vidar. I wished I could find a way to use them against him, but they were so damn vague.

"What are you saying?" I hissed, annoyed at the constant babble.

Vidar's body suddenly jolted forward hard enough to push me off balance. I backed away from him as he toppled to the sand, a bone dagger just like the one he'd used to kill his own father lodged in his back. And standing in his place… was Vidar. He stepped over his own body, which quickly began to rot at my feet and attract crabs to the feast.

The new Vidar wore his captain's coat and a leather tricorn hat, but his eyes were no less haunted. He stood at the water's edge, staring out into the reddened sea, and set his jaw like he was preparing for a fight.

And then the voices grew more persistent. The weeping. The screaming. Only at that point, I could feel it. The cold chill of the rain finally found my spine and I shivered. My own voice echoed back to me once more, young and furious.

"I will get you, Vidar! I will not forget your name!"

Another voice joined the fray, one I recognized but never thought I'd hear again.

"Use it," it spoke in a garbled tone. "Bronze and blood, my boy."

I looked down at Ethelwoelf's body to see his mangled jaw moving, stretching salt-swollen sinew as he spoke.

A wave of water washed over him and covered his face in red sea foam before reclaiming him and taking him away from the beach. I watched his body drift away before returning my attention to Vidar only to see his eyes piercing right into me. The dead look on his face was gone and he was very much alive with a look of dull shock in his eyes as if he recognized me. As if he no longer saw through me.

Dahlia

The depths make mad minds
Mad minds seek out the dark
~Unknown

It was easy to know how long I'd been in the holding cell. The tide spoke to me through the wood of the ship, swaying and whispering to my thoughts. It had been little more than two days and the visions of that dream trembled through my mind. I hadn't slept since I woke from it. I didn't dare until I could figure out what to do about it.

What happened was not unheard of, but it was rare. Most men bitten by a siren didn't live to have dreams let alone get close enough to the offender to allow us to walk in them. Most sirens saw to it that they finished their meals. When I swallowed Vidar's fingers, I hadn't intended to eat him. I intended to kill him. It didn't occur to me at the time that we'd ever meet again long enough for me to see the tangled thorns of his mind.

I didn't like it.

It meant we were close. Connected. It disgusted me.

Then again, if I wasn't going to get another opportunity any time soon to finish what I tried to do as a child, perhaps I could use my new unwanted gift to my advantage. Vidar's dreams were haunted. I was about to take the twisted vines and tie them in knots, strangle them, and set them ablaze.

The ship was consumed by a familiar chill that carried a particular scent. It was morning. The sun had just risen which made the salty smell of the ocean breeze more potent. And rain was coming. I could smell that too. I could hear it in a distant rumble from the sky. I sat up on my flattened bedding and leaned against the wall, flexing and stretching my wrists to relieve some stiffness from the cuffs. It was then that Vidar finally returned to my cell gate. He had a wooden bowl in his hand containing a slice of stale bread and some kind of brown stew.

He stopped to regard me for a while, eyeing my thigh where my wound was no more than a light pink line. It would barely scar by the end of it. Not that I cared. Every scar was a symbol of how the world had tried to murder me and failed.

When Vidar's eyes lingered too long on my leg, I cocked my head a little, watching him. My dress was made of thin, pliable leather and laced down the front. There was a space between my breasts where it was bound loosely and it extended to my navel. The uneven, raw hem was slanted, leaving my wounded thigh completely exposed. Human women were always covered in layers and layers of stifling fabric.

I was in no way the typical sight for a human man. Vidar, however, had killed so many of my kind I doubted my exposed skin was what he was staring at. Still, I wanted to gauge his thoughts and slowly extended my long leg out further, giving him a better look. That made his eyes snap up toward mine and he let out a breathy laugh.

"I assure you, I'm not looking for *that*," he rasped.

"All men are looking for that," I replied. "They just don't always say it out loud." I parted my knees, sucking my bottom lip between my teeth and catching it on one of my fangs. Vidar didn't look away from my eyes, though. "It's a cruel, cruel world. I could give you the most wonderful bliss. The greatest pleasure. You wouldn't even know you were dying until it was over. You'd get what you want. I'd get what I want."

"You think I want to die," he said flatly.

It wasn't a question.

"I think you didn't fight very hard when I was going to kill you."

He swallowed. It was the first tiny reaction I noticed from him. But he recovered quickly and sighed, leaning forward on the bars. He hung his arm through and relaxed against the gate, pushing the meal toward me.

"We don't have human meat on board. Only beans and bread," he said.

I let out a deep breath and slowly closed my legs, glaring up at him. Gradually, I stood and walked over to the bars, expecting him to recoil once I was close, but he didn't. He just kept looking me right in the eyes, unafraid and betraying nothing about what he was truly thinking. But I knew from that brief glimpse into his mind that deep within the thick bones of his skull were echoes of guilt and destruction.

I needed to weave some kind of net that could capture all of it and turn it against him. It wouldn't take long if I was focused.

I moved closer to him than I needed to to take the bowl. I cupped my hands around it, intentionally touching him when I did. His skin was rough and well-worn. He was accustomed to physical labor. His blood ran hot, scalding my naturally cold flesh. And when I pulled the bowl from him, I saw the slightest dilation in his eyes. The lantern above swung as the ship swayed and made shadows dance back and forth across his face. He'd be terrifying if I hadn't been eaten, chewed, and regurgitated by a thousand horrors over and over since I was born.

"We don't have to eat men," I spoke softly, the corner of my mouth quirking. "We just enjoy it."

It was the truth… mostly. Sirens could eat anything. We could enjoy it, so long as it had a pulse. But man… man had a particular effect. One that made us stronger. Faster. It made us live longer. Feel deeper. See further. It was exhilarating and potent and nothing compared to the taste.

I hadn't eaten many men since that bloody island. I'd been saving myself for Vidar and the thrill of his capture. I'd fantasized about devouring him since the bones of his fingers cracked between my teeth. Since his blood dripped down my throat. *He* would be my prize for finally setting it all right.

But years of hatred had led me down a dark path. One where my teeth had ripped into the flesh of many foul men.

The thought made my eyes roam slowly down the length of his strong and able body. His pants hugged his muscular thighs tightly. His loose cotton shirt hung thinly on his broad shoulders. Ropes of dark blond hair were half pulled back into a leather tie exposing those perfect, high cheekbones. He looked fucking delicious. If it wasn't for the gate between us and the cuffs on my wrists, I'd have tackled him to the ground. His strength and skill would only prolong the game.

"Those things on that island," Vidar finally said as I sipped from the rim of the bowl. "What were they?"

I shrugged, despite knowing exactly what they were. I continued to sip on the soup and then suffered through the dry bread, knowing I needed to eat something and keep up my strength.

"What did you do to my sisters?" I shot back.

Vidar mimicked my shrug. This was a game I didn't truly feel like playing.

"Tell me about those creatures."

"What's wrong? Did they scare you?"

He glimpsed my scarred leg as if to remind me that they'd almost killed me. But I hadn't forgotten. Vidar, however, was in an impatient mood. He reached out abruptly, grasping the chains on my manacles, and pulled me toward the bars. The bowl went clattering to the ground, spilling the remaining contents onto the floor of my cell. I slammed against the gate, jaw clenched, and saw the anger spread in his darkened eyes.

"I'm only keeping you alive because I want to understand, but if you don't want to help me understand, then I'd rather not keep a siren alive on my ship."

"Then kill me. I know you want to," I hissed. "You've wanted to since that night, haven't you? It's been the only thing on your mind. You made a mistake leaving me alive, so fix your mistake, Vidar."

Part of me wanted him to do it. At least then the torment would stop. But there was the bigger part of me that thirsted for revenge. It forced me to survive against all odds for this particular moment. The moment we finally saw each other again.

"What were they, Dahlia?" he whispered.

"Why do you want to know? It's just something else for you to kill. More monsters in the ocean are good for business, right?"

His other hand moved up to clutch my neck. It was so big it nearly collared my throat completely. He pulled me closer until I could feel his breath on my face.

"Your sister freed me so I would help kill them. So she could save you. That's a lot of faith to put in a man like me. She knew the cost and she thought it was worth it. She was afraid of those things more than she was afraid of me."

"And then what?"

"And then I threatened to kill you if she didn't let me go."

He was already exploiting my weaknesses and I had yet to exploit his. I clenched my jaw, angry that he had the upper hand.

I swallowed against the pressure of his grip and balled my hands into fists. If I was being logical, it would help us both if he knew about the xhoth. They were my enemy as much as they were his. But it was excruciating to think of cooperating with Vidar.

We stared at each other for another grueling moment before I slowly blinked in defeat.

"The xhoth," I said. "It means 'sons'."

His eyes narrowed before he released me. "Why have I never seen them before?"

"Because they're from the deep."

"Like your pale sisters?"

"No. Deeper."

"Why are they here?"

"Why?" I mocked. "Because your hunting us has called them up."

"They were killing you and they killed your sister. Don't tell me they're here to defend you."

"Me? No, they aren't here to defend me," I laughed. "They're here because they're hungry. You've been depleting our numbers for generations. But there's always something bigger."

"They eat your kind?"

I shrugged. "In a sense."

"Speak plainly."

"I can't speak plainly about something I barely understand myself. Those who have been to the depths return mad and soiled by the darkness, and they do not share their secrets with others."

"That cannot be all you know. Tell me more."

"Why? You'll execute me after I give you what you want. My only value is in the knowledge you don't yet have. And you don't have my sisters, so what exactly do you think you can bargain with? My own life means much less to me than you might think."

He blinked at that. I wasn't intending to say it out loud, but perhaps it was a good thing. Perhaps if he knew I didn't care about dying, he wouldn't use the threat of death against me.

For a long while, he just studied me. His eyes narrowed and wandered and then focused on me countless times before he finally stepped forward and pulled a ring of keys from his belt. He jammed one into the gate's lock and turned it. When the gate swung open, I was stupefied, eyes round with surprise.

And then he had the guts to turn his back on me and pick up a bundle of clothing off a stool behind him. He tucked it under his arm and walked right into my cell, confusing me further.

Vidar grabbed my cuffs and unlocked the irons on my wrists, letting the heavy things fall to the floor. My heart was pumping at the discarded weight and the feeling of freedom. I could grab him. Fight him. Break him. He didn't even have his men with their guns aimed at my face. I didn't know what was going through his head. Stupidity. Carelessness.

Whatever it was, it meant I had my chance. My teeth were sharp and his neck was exposed.

But I refrained. I wasn't entirely sure why, but if he was clothing me and uncuffing me, perhaps he had more to tell.

Vidar tossed the clothes at me and stepped back, crossing his arms expectantly. Brows furrowed, I stared at him and unfolded a white cotton underdress and a thin, linen coat with wide cuffs.

"Take off the skin," he demanded.

I pursed my lips and lazily removed my clothes, tossing the old thing at him. He raised a brow when it hit his chest and fell to the floor. Then I replaced my garments with what he'd given me. If he wanted me changed, perhaps it meant he wasn't going to kill me any time soon.

I slid on the cotton dress, not bothering to tighten the ties between my breasts, and then slipped the coat on. It felt awfully heavy, but not overly uncomfortable.

When my eyes darted briefly to the bronze cutlass on Vidar's belt, he moved his hands to hang on his waistband.

"It'd be stupid of you to try," he said.

"Why are you dressing me?" I asked, rubbing the raw flesh around my wrists. "And why is the gate open?"

He turned his back on me for a second time and started walking toward the steps. I was so puzzled, my feet didn't even move.

"I could kill you and your entire crew in the night," I called after him. "I *will*."

He stopped midway up the stairs and ducked down to look at me from behind the roof beam.

"Then you'd be stuck in the same predicament you were before."

"What predicament is that?"

"Not knowing how to sail a ship."

"I don't need to sail a ship," I said bitterly. "The water is my home."

He groaned, rolling his eyes. "If you try to kill any of us, we'll have to kill you." He continued up the steps. "And I think you want to stay alive long enough to see those girls go home."

132

18
Dahlia

You know so little of the sea…
And all the horrors deep beneath
~Matron Ethra

The cotton fabric of my new garments itched. I squirmed in the oversized coat as I followed Vidar up the steps, angered that he had read me so well. I wasn't even sure where the girls were. For all I knew, while I was in that cell, he'd tossed them overboard. Hurt them. Stuffed them in another holding cell of their own.

Only that wasn't the case. When I came up the steps onto the deck, I saw far too many confusing things to process in the few moments I had to soak it in. I saw a good portion of Vidar's crew. Some were wrapping ropes. Others were cleaning. Gus was tying a knot against a post with one of the older girls next to him. She was closely observing every loop he made just as Ahnah had observed me carving the tuna. All of them were eager to learn and… trusting. A couple girls sat to the side, warry of the men, but most of them were fully committed to helping with chores it seemed.

A hole in the clouds let some sunlight through that everyone seemed to eagerly be soaking up, but when I appeared behind Vidar, conversation slowed and eyes started drifting coldly toward me. Gus had the angriest stare of them all. His one eye was filled with more suspicion than ten of the crew combined. I lifted my chin and sighed. I was no stranger to scrutiny. But I was a stranger to letting a stare linger. If I had my way, they'd all be dead already, but slaughtering another crew in front of the girls seemed counterproductive now, especially after Vidar hinted at bringing them home.

I stopped and scanned the faces around me when one caught my eye. One that should not be on Vidar's murderous ship.

Tied to the mast was Meridan, her arms bound tightly with twine. She was dressed in a pair of loose slacks and a large shirt that covered her just like me in filthy human clothes. Our gazes met and my jaw tightened. They'd caught her. Fury boiled beneath my cold skin and I curled my fingers into my palms, letting the pain of my nails piercing my skin calm me.

The metallic scrape of metal caught my attention. I glimpsed Vidar a few steps away with his cutlass drawn.

"Before you do anything stupid, she came to us," he informed me.

My brow twitched with confusion. There was no way Meridan would willingly come aboard a hunter's ship, especially the Burning Rose. The red sails fluttering above us moved like a demon's wings painted with the blood of my people. So either she was there out of loyalty to me, which I never imagined would stretch as far as putting her life in the hands of humans, or she was more afraid of the water than she was of Vidar and his men.

The latter turned out to be the scarier thought but the more believable one. She was the one who freed Vidar in the first place if he was to be believed.

"Why?" I muttered, looking into Meridan's pale eyes.

"We were hoping you would tell us," Vidar said with a smirk. "She's too mad at me to talk."

I started toward her when Vidar stretched his blade out in front of me, stopping me in my tracks. I shot him a glare that could cut flesh and hissed, showing my teeth. Then I slapped the blade away with the palm of my hand. He quickly replaced it, that time with the sharpened edge against my throat. I felt the sting of the metal slice into my skin, making a shallow cut.

"Like I said," Vidar reiterated. "Try anything, and these girls get sold at the next port."

"Still don't know why you think I care about a bunch of human girls."

He cocked his head and stepped in close, keeping the blade in place.

"Ahnah is very talkative and turns out she adores you," he said with disgust, his eyes roaming over my body like I was a rotten stain on his deck. "She must be daft, but it's true."

I pressed my neck against the blade, lifting my chin in challenge.

"You should know by now that content prey is more enticing. Otherwise, what use would our song be?"

"Ah. I must have forgotten," he shrugged, pulling the blade away and abruptly heading toward a few of the girls huddled near some crates. Eyes watched him from everywhere. Even his own crew seemed surprised when he grabbed one of the older girls by the back of her shirt and tugged her up to her feet. "This one is sick and unable to pull her weight."

Vidar swung the blade up to the girl's throat and her friends screamed in horror. A few of the men protested as well with words like "whoa" and "Captain?" But I had no words. My body lunged forward faster than I could control. I intended to pull the blade away and sink my teeth into Vidar's neck when he suddenly tossed the girl aside and countered me instead. I screamed, my voice full of all the frustration and anger I felt toward him. He moved his blade to the side as I lunged. If he hadn't, I'd have skewered myself on it and been content dying as I used my last moments to bite a gaping hole in his neck.

As it was, there was no blade through my stomach, but I was still going for the kill. Vidar spun me around, grabbed my throat with his free hand, and slammed my body down on the floor. Guns were drawn. I could hear each one of them as the men crowded us. Vidar pressed his blade to my neck again and met my eyes, entirely unsurprised by everything that just happened. I was seething, my breath sawing in and out of me.

"Liar," he muttered.

I knew exactly what he meant and I felt ashamed that my secret had been so easily uncovered. Now my worst enemy knew of two things I cared about and he had both of them in his clutches. Meridan was tied to the mast. The girls had nowhere to go. He was winning already and we'd only just found each other again.

"I'll never be a liar quite as good as you," I snarled.

Something flashed in his eyes as if those words affected him but he snuffed it out so fast, I hardly saw it. He looked over me, studying my face meticulously before his gaze settled too long on the scar across my cheek. His scar.

But then he was standing and letting me get off the floor as he slid his cutlass back into his belt.

"The girls are going home," he said flatly.

My eyes flicked toward Meridan. "And my sister?"

"She'll be sharing your cell."

19
Dahlia

We are children of a cruel mother.
Daughters of an absent father.
~ Unknown

Meridan was freed from the mast only to be taken down to the holding cell with me afterward. The hate bleeding off the crew's faces was thick. I could see it in their eyes. None of them had kept a siren alive long enough to interact with one and their desire to kill us made them unpredictable. They were accustomed to capturing and beheading, but now their captain was allowing two to remain on his ship. It boggled my mind. But if there was one thing I could tell, it was that Vidar's men trusted him. Maybe more than they trusted themselves.

If I could bend him, it would bend his crew.

Neither of us struggled when we were taken to the holding cell. I was too focused on being alone to ask Meridan what happened than anything. After we were shoved back into the hold, I watched the two men leave us there in the near darkness, listening to their footsteps fade toward the upper deck. Then I swung around to face Meridan, who had already settled on the floor against the wall.

"I hate it here," she said, her eyes wandering.

"Then why did you come?"

"I didn't mean to. I was nearby, using the ship to deter pursuers."

Our eyes met and I immediately saw a shift in her demeanor. Without prying eyes to peel her apart, she dropped the hard mask and deflated her lungs in defeat.

"Kea is dead," she muttered.

I stilled, unsure for a moment that I heard her right. "What?"

"When he took you, we followed. We stayed deeper so he would not see us. He didn't... but they did. The xhoth. We fled, but Kea was killed." Her voice turned stony and flat. "They speared her right beside me. Dragged her back. I saw them rip into her with claws and teeth. They are a menace. One that rivals hunters like Vidar because they swim our waters. I never thought I'd see the day when they came up from the depths like this. This is the third time we've seen them in as many months."

My heart ached to know that two of my sisters had been killed in a matter of days by an enemy we barely believed existed until they appeared to us.

I had been so close to exacting revenge on Vidar.

I shook my head, enraged that I was being so selfish when Kea and Voel were both gone, brutally murdered by something that wasn't even supposed to be there.

With a deep sigh, I walked over and slid down the wall to sit beside her.

"This is wrong," I said, listening to the vast expanse of rolling water around us. It seemed darker. Deeper. Angrier now that new monsters occupied it. "We both know the xhoth shouldn't be here. Have things really become so off balance?"

"I've never worshipped Akareth. Perhaps this is my punishment. Perhaps he has sent his sons just to eat us all."

"Don't be foolish. Akareth, if he exists, is of flesh and bone like anything else. And so are his sons."

"Either way, now we are trapped between two enemies."

I let out a breath, coming to terms with it all.

Above us, I knew the girls were freely roaming and I recalled the exact look on Vidar's face when he held his blade to the older girl's throat. He was crueler and more ruthless than even his father was. He was part of the reason the sons had crawled to the surface from their dark caverns and trenches. Ahnah still had the will to smile and it was problematic for me to want to preserve that when she was the spawn of the very thing that I hated. Humans. Men like Vidar.

But her smile was too precious to destroy. I knew what it was like to lose it. I might as well have died when my childhood was ripped from me.

I winced at my compassion. It made me weak, but I couldn't help it.

I inched closer to Meridan.

"I don't know how much safer we are on board this ship," I whispered.

"Nowhere is safe. At least if these men choose to kill us, beheading is known to be their most popular method." She swallowed, taking a deep breath of the stagnant air in the hold. "Kea was awake long enough to see her limbs floating away when the sons got her."

I squeezed my eyes shut, saying a silent prayer for her before I let the overwhelming frustration burn through my heart. I didn't have space to hate someone or something more than I hated Vidar, but the sons were making a rotten cavity for themselves in my terrible heart whether I liked it or not.

"What do we do, Dahlia?"

Her voice was smaller than I'd ever known it to be. We weren't used to fearing the ocean like that. We were outsiders. There was a certain unease about being rejected everywhere and having no place of refuge. The sons planted a different kind of dread. One that made me feel helpless.

I balled my hands into fists against my knees.

"There is something awful happening in the water," I said.

"Worse than the xhoth?"

"The men on that merchant ship did not have silentiums."

"Not all men do."

"No, but more than one had had a sigil carved into his skin. Our sisters had visited them."

"You think they were under someone's influence?"

I nodded. "I think those men were doing someone's bidding. Not just anyone's bidding, actually. The symbol was Kroan."

"Then the girls…" She paused "What were the girls for?"

"I don't know. Perhaps the men were meant to bring them bodies. Ligeia's clan hunts these waters. She always had a greater taste for humans than even my mother. And with so many hunters on the surface, she would not be above making men do the work she did not want to."

"I don't want to believe our own kind is swaying men to bring them innocent children, but I do. I also don't want to believe Akareth's sons are now hunting us. What has become of us?"

"Our people are desperate. Hunters are killing us and there are rumors that some of us are being taken alive, silenced, and sold to men far from the sea. Far from our home."

Meridan's face twisted with disgust.

"That they eat our tongues is barbaric enough. Now they must defile our bodies?"

"We devour them completely when it suits us."

"And selling us? Imprisoning us? I'd rather die than be shipped away in chains for sick men to use."

"It is a hateful and endless cycle, Meridan. One we will never escape."

"I wish I could hide in the depths and never come back. Without knowing the xhoth are down there, of course." She paused a moment, picking at her nails. "And the girls? Do you think these men will truly help them or will they all meet the same fate as us? For all we know, Vidar is the foulest man alive. He almost killed that girl in front of you. He doesn't even care for other humans let alone us. How could he be trusted in any way?"

I raised a brow. "You trusted him enough to free him on that island."

She cocked her head. "Desperation is something I'm familiar with, too."

"You shouldn't risk yourself for me. Nor should you have let him go. You should have run."

"You would risk yourself for me. You would deny it, but I know you would. It's in your soul to care about others."

"It's in my soul to kill," I groaned.

"Is it really? You and I have not been to the true depths like others have. Like your mother had. Our minds have not yet been stripped and shattered by whatever is down there. To say it is in your soul to kill is somewhat of a lie, I think. I think we kill for reasons, even if they're our own."

"Does it matter?"

"I suppose not. What are we going to do?"

I rolled my eyes and sighed. "I don't know what we are going to do, but Vidar has already uncovered more than one of my weaknesses and he's already using them against me."

"Then we find one of his."

"I think I have." I inched closer to her, lowering my voice. "You know there are scattered whispers that we can see into the dreams of our enemies if we eat of their flesh."

"Mystics like to ramble about it, yes."

"I've eaten of Vidar," I reminded her. "And I believe I walked in his dreams. I think I am connected to him, whether I want to be or not. Now that we're near, something has changed."

Her white eyes widened a bit when she processed my words. I could see the thoughts churning in her mind just like they'd been churning in mine.

"You can plant seeds," she whispered. "Poison him against himself. Against his crew. Bend him to your will."

"That would take time."

"We may not have time before he chooses to kill us. We will have to take our chances with the monsters below."

"He wants to know about them. It's the only reason we're here. So, we will give him what he wants. It will give us time and I can outsmart him if I have that time." I turned my darkened gaze toward the swinging lamp and ground my teeth. "I can take Vidar's mind apart."

"You could use him. *Make* him protect us. Turn his crew into our own just like that other crew was being used."

It was a lot. Especially for someone like me who was completely unlearned in using a man's dreams against him. It was in our nature to manipulate. To reform a man's resolve. To replace his desires and amplify his needs. So few of my kind stretched that ability further than their voice, but I knew I could do it. I was Reyna's daughter.

And from that point onward, I was going to peel Vidar apart and expose his core. I was going to break him.

Only when we wake do dreams become fantasy.
~Unknown

Having Dahlia in the holding cell was bad enough without her sister there, too. Merilyn, I believed her name to be. I slept like shit the first night she was on my ship. Her presence alone had inspired the demons inside me to wake.

But none of that mattered in the grand scheme of things. The bigger picture had expanded. It wasn't just about killing sirens. Overnight, it had become about this new threat. The "xhoth." They didn't discriminate and my lack of knowledge about them, their tactics, their needs, and their motivation had me on edge. Fuck Whitton's request for tongues and warm bodies to sell. Fuck his love for money and lack of understanding. Something in the ocean was shifting and it wasn't going to obediently remain contained. Evil didn't work that way.

Everything was a mess and it only got messier when the second siren showed up alongside my ship. The same woman who'd freed me on the island. I knew she wouldn't give up Dahlia so easily, so I wasn't surprised. Disappointed, but not surprised. I hadn't spoken to many sirens long enough to judge, but I wanted to say she was pretty level-headed for her kind. She read the situation and understood we needed each other to kill those beasts. What she didn't read was my inability to trust her and how determined I was to get to Dahlia.

For eighteen years, I went over a thousand scenarios in which we would see each other again. I imagined coming across her face in a pile of heads dumped by hunters. I imagined fighting her to the death. I thought of dying at her hands. Of being dragged to the depths in her claws. I imagined her slaughtering my entire crew before I could stop her. I knew she wanted to. She longed to take her revenge on me. I wasn't foolish enough to think that seeing another crew of good men sliced to pieces and skinned alive in front of me was out of the realm of possibilities.

Dahlia had been my worst nightmare and my loudest demon since the day she called my name in anger on that black sand beach. After the day I killed her people in front of her as her mother had done to mine. And now that nightmare was on my ship and in the flesh, longing to rip me apart.

Could I blame her for hating me? No. Just like she had no right to blame me for what I did. I wanted to think she knew how illogical it was just like I did, but neither of us could control the endless circle we were stuck in. Momentum had locked us in motion, constantly chasing the other in hopes of ending the torment only to add more debris to our path.

Gus escorted one of the older girls into my chamber and I could tell by the way she hugged herself with her arms and lowered her head that she was thinking it was for much different reasons than it was. It was not the girl whose life I'd threatened, but this one had seen the whole scenario play out. They all feared me now. Was it worth it to get a reaction out of Dahlia? Maybe. There was no point in regretting it after the fact.

Gus could speak the girls' language. Not well, but even a few words helped us communicate with them. From what we could tell, they were from far up north. It was a place very few ships sailed to. The ice in the water made it near impossible to move through the narrow channels and the cold was unforgiving.

So why the hell did the Cornwallis have the girls on their ship? It was a question I couldn't begin to answer and one that left a cold and uneasy chill in my blood.

On the table in front of me was a map. It was well-used and many of the words were too faded for anyone to read, but I knew it too well to care about smudged islands and stained corners. To my left, Uther was looking over the same maps. When it came to navigating, he was one of the best.

Gus said something to the girl and she nodded timidly, glancing at the map. I saw her eyes searching and trying to understand it, but it was clear after some time that she wasn't accustomed to reading any sort of charts. Her brows worked with concentration before she glanced between Gus and me and shook her head.

"She can't read no map," Gus grunted. "Doubt she's ever sailed this far from home to have a reason to."

I scrubbed my face with my hands and grumbled with frustration.

"Can't get them home if we don't know where that is."

"Sailin' them home seems risky," Uther said. "Even in the warm months."

"I'd still like to know where they're from."

"Could look at the maps from the Cornwallis," Gus suggested.

I cocked my head at him. "We don't have those maps."

He huffed a laugh. "Mullins swiped a few. You know he's teaching himself to navigate. He's got a whole stack stuffed in his personal chest."

I knew Mullins collected any parchment with words and charts on them. To hear that he'd swiped some from the Cornwallis was a relief because I did not want to circle back to that ghost ship.

"Get him for me," I said.

Gus walked to the door, cracked it open, and called for Mullins. He must have been on deck because he was in my cabin in a blink, eager to help.

"Whatever you took from the Cornwallis," I said. "Bring it here."

He nodded and left to retrieve what I wanted. He was back shortly after with an armful of rolled maps and leather-bound papers. He dumped them onto the table and all three of us started to sift through it all, looking for something useful when the girl stepped forward from the corner. I had almost forgotten she was still there. I watched her eyes zero in on a drawing that had fallen out of one of the leather folders. Then she pointed at it, saying words I didn't understand.

On the parchment was a sketch of a mountain with an odd flat top and a large cave opening in the front that looked like a massive beast with a crooked yawn. I picked up the paper to read the sloppy writing on the bottom.

"God's Throat," I read.

The girl kept talking and nodding like I was on to something, but I couldn't understand a damn thing she said.

"Says she's seen that before," Gus said, rubbing his brow. "At least that's what I think she said."

I took one of the maps from the Cornwallis and unrolled it over the one I already had out, searching for that landmark. Or the name. Or even an "X" of some kind that would mark where we needed to go. The girl was the first to pinpoint a place to look. In the upper corner of the map was a scribble of words and symbols that didn't fit the rest of the continents and islands. Among the hand-drawn map additions was a shape vaguely resembling the sketch on the paper.

"Think that's where they're from?" Mullins asked.

"Toluuk," the girl said, pointing excitedly.

"Toluuk?" I asked.

She spewed more words and then nodded, victorious.

"That's about as far north as you can get before the water is just pure ice," Gus pointed out. "I've heard of tribes living up there, but that place don't treat ships too nice. In the warm months, they come south to trade. At least, that's what Yutu told me."

"Yutu? That strange kid you knew as a boy?"

"That's the one. Taught me his language, he did. His dad and mine used to fish together. Maybe that's how the Cornwallis got to them. Maybe they were at one of the ports."

I sighed loudly, staring at the maps again. "The Rose can sail that," I said, hanging my thumbs on my belt.

"Think it's worth the trouble? Getting these girls home, I mean. Could just bring 'em inland, make sure they find work. See to it they don't end up on the streets or in a whore house. We'd be doing them a favor."

I shook my head, reflecting on what a shithole the coastal towns were becoming.

"With the supplies we took off the Cornwallis, we can make that trip if we make a good trade. Port Devlin, perhaps."

"What if their home is gone?" Mullins brought up. "What if they raided it and killed everyone?"

I glanced at the girl, watching her lean over the map with renewed excitement.

"That's not the face of a girl who saw her home burn. And I wouldn't bet on the Cornwallis doing anything so risky. That ship was manned by cunts and beggars."

"Don't matter how they got them. Is there a reason you want to risk taking them that far north?"

"The reason is that we're out here looking for sirens to sell. I'm not showing up in *our* town with a ship full of young girls instead. No one's getting their oily hands on them."

"We've got two of the bitches on board," Uther added. "That's more than enough to see to it we get our pockets filled. And like Gus said, we can make sure the girls get honest work. The young ones can go to the convent until—"

"I said no."

The world was ugly enough. Dragging people from a faraway tribe into the twisted bullshit that was our violent reality was a sin I wasn't keen to add to my long list of offenses. I wasn't a kind man by any means. Maybe I wasn't even a good one, but traveling north would benefit me in two ways. It would give me time to think and it would clear my conscience a bit. I deserved that. We all did. One good act wouldn't grant me passage to heaven, but maybe I'd feel better for a day.

And the days of travel could give me insight into what else was plaguing the ocean as of late. It would give me time with *her*.

With what we took off the Cornwallis, Boil was able to cook up something with a bit of actual taste that night. Merchant ships were always better stocked with luxuries. Naturally, the girls ate huddled together in a corner of the deck. Once in a while, one of the younger ones would laugh, which renewed my hope that they'd forget about their whole ordeal if we managed to return them home.

After the men's bellies were full and their moods lightened, I met with them all and announced the plans to head north. There were a few skeptical looks among them, but I eased their minds by reminding them that we had two sirens on board and a bunch of supplies from the Cornwallis to either use or sell.

Eventually, I won the crowd and everyone went about their business as usual.

After that, there were only two other people on board that hadn't heard the plan. I wasn't sure if they deserved to, but they hadn't eaten since the night prior, so I took a single platter of bean soup and some bread down to the holding cell. I found Dahlia and Meridan leaning against the far wall atop the thin bedding, bored and still. Meridan's head was rested against Dahlia's shoulder, her eyes closed. Dahlia, however, was completely aware and followed me with her gaze as I walked to the front of the cell.

"Comfortable?" I asked.

"Not at all."

I shrugged and crouched down to slide the food across the floor and into the cell. She didn't move.

"Are you planning to sell us?" she asked.

"I'm thinking about it. Your kind is fetching a higher price alive than dead these days."

"Why?"

I shrugged again. "Some men have a fondness for fucking things they shouldn't. I imagine it might be satisfying to defile a thing like you. A thing that man has feared for a long time."

"So, it is a twisted sense of revenge to take our power away." She straightened her head and sighed. "Do *you* want to take my power away? Would you like to put those irons back on me?" Her voice lowered, her eyes becoming shrouded in shadows. "Wet your cock in a body you've longed to destroy for so long? Is that how men get their pleasure? By feigning control?"

There was no fear behind her words. Just taunting calmness. My gaze raked slowly down her body, now clothed in a thin shift and oversized coat. She was a predator. A killer. A monster. Not one bit of her was human, despite how much she emulated one outside of the water. Even with all her hard edges and that long scar on her cheek, she had a rigid and dark beauty to her. One that made my eyes want to keep looking, even if something in the back of my mind told me to run. All sirens had that eerie allure, but Dahlia... Dahlia was different. Dahlia and I had a history that made looking at her even more agonizingly addictive.

"Are you thinking about it?" she whispered. "About spearing me with your cock instead of your sword?" A wicked grin teased the corner of her lips. "You must be wondering which one I would hate more."

Taking a deep breath, I leaned forward on the gate, pressing my forehead to the cold bars.

"All these years, I knew we'd meet again," I said. "My plan was to run you through the moment we did."

"My plan was to devour you."

"Seems we've both been fools thinking it could end that quickly."

"I didn't kill your father's crew, you know," she said, her tone softening and catching me off guard.

"You stood by and watched."

"Killing is what we do."

"Killing is what we all do and yet here you sit, alive. I could have killed you both. I still could."

"Why haven't you? Were I not in this cell, I don't know if I'd have the self-control to spare your men."

"You mean if those girls weren't on board. Why do you want them to live if it's in your nature to kill?"

"They're—"

"Innocent? Like you believed me to be when we were children?"

She swallowed, her teeth grinding as if she were chewing on her words. I waited, but she only responded with silent defiance.

I shifted my weight from one foot to the other. "Tell me something. Do you truly believe that I was wrong to have done what I did? Do you believe your mother to have been good?"

"Do you believe your father was good?"

"Do you believe *you* are good?"

"No," she snapped.

It was at that point when Merilyn awoke to our bickering. She noticed me at the door to the cell and flicked her gaze between us in alarmed confusion.

Dahlia kept her eyes on me. "That we are good is the greatest lie we've ever told ourselves. We are simply caught in the same whirlpool, going in circles, completely unaware we are drowning." She paused to take a breath, her brows twitching. "I believe I tried to be good when I unlocked your cage." Another pause. I watched the duskiness in her eyes become even darker, defying the definition of the word. "And then you turned me into a hateful monster. You turned me into my mother."

She spoke as if that was the worst thing that could have ever happened to her. Her words were rigid and stained. Pained and broken. I recalled for a second what her body looked like when she'd removed her previous clothing to change. She was covered in scars. More scars than I had seen on any siren's body, dead or alive. I had to wonder why. Had she lost that many fights? Had she *been* in that many fights? Or perhaps the scars were a symbol of her victory. I didn't know and I didn't think I cared enough to find out.

The most certain thing, however, was that she was not like others. She did not even harbor the same kind of empty disdain. Hers was her own, built up over the years with me being the pillars on which it was erected. Beside her, Merilyn looked at me like most sirens did, with a sense of abhorrence and fear. That look was what I knew. But Dahlia looked at me with so many years of contempt, confusion, and fire. It mimicked the way I looked at her. I didn't know if I wanted to march into her cell and behead her, ridding myself of her presence for good, or… well, I didn't know what else I wanted to do. I truly didn't and it twisted me up inside.

"We know where the girls are from," I divulged, eager to see her reaction to the fact. "It will take a week or two to get there, but that's the direction we're headed."

She seemed unaffected by the news. It was irritating. I started to walk away, feeling frustrated that I didn't get further than a small argument with her.

"Why do *you* care about the girls?" she called after me. "Rugged killer like you."

I stopped and slowly turned back around to look at her through the iron bars. The cold space between us and the obvious disdain that tainted both our souls made my resolve clear as glass.

"They're young enough," I sighed. "If they go home now before they see the rest of the world, maybe they won't end up like us."

There is serenity in darkness
And peace in oblivion.
~ Eli Williamson

"They're young enough," Vidar said. "If they go home now before they see the rest of the world, maybe they won't end up like us."

I hated that those words hit me like they did. As Vidar disappeared upstairs, I wondered if that was truly the reason I didn't want to see them killed or hurt, too. It was rare to find eyes that hadn't been darkened by violence and loathing. Something in me wanted to preserve it.

What disgusted me more was the realization that maybe Vidar and I had something in common.

"He is a sly bastard," Meridan said, pulling me from my thoughts. "Do you believe anything he is saying?"

"I don't know. All I know is we're behind bars. No matter what happens, he currently has the upper hand."

"In here, perhaps." She reached over and tapped my temple lightly with one finger. "Not in here. Can you control the dreams?"

"I don't know. I don't even know if I'll find him in my sleep tonight. I'm not sure how it works."

"I believe you will find a way. You have to."

I had to…

Meridan's words stayed with me until it came time for the crew to sleep. Thankfully, my own fatigue cradled me at the same time and I found myself dozing on the thin bedding. I didn't know how to find Vidar in my sleep again. The first time was entirely accidental. All I could do was think of him as I drifted… as uncomfortable as that was.

Black sand covered a flat as far as the eye could see. It was dark, but the world was visible around me. Bland. Dreary. I spun in a slow circle to gauge my surroundings only to find the same view in every direction. Dark sand littered with half-submerged whale bones and the skeletons of decrepit ships. It was a graveyard. A place where all dead things eventually ended up.

Above me, a world of gray, blue, and black swirled in slow and eerie motions. Sound was muffled, but I could tell by the muted flashes that a storm was raging above. But the depths never felt the turmoil from the skies.

It was all so familiar.

Looking down, I was in my seal skin dress, the pieces stitched together in asymmetrical patterns like they'd always been.

"Fuck," I muttered.

It was my dream. One I had many times. One I knew very well. Looking around again, I found myself let down by my own mind. I didn't want to be there in that barren wasteland, alone where no light or sound could penetrate. I had gone to the deep ocean before in a feeble attempt to erase myself only to find that it was exactly what I wanted. I enjoyed the silent loneliness. I enjoyed it too much and I almost didn't find the will to return, but now I had something to do. I had Vidar to deal with and I couldn't let that cold, dank world summon me too soon.

I started walking, determined to find a way further from the temptation. The cold sand was gritty between my toes and smelled like salt and rot. A deep moan rippled through the space and as I panned my eyes upward. The monstrous shadow of a whale slowly moved overhead, silhouetted by the dancing light of the storm behind it.

I sighed contently at how beautiful I found it all. I used to enjoy the sun. The breeze. The sound of rain beating on the waves. But my mind changed throughout the years when I realized just how ugly the surface was.

My eyes dropped to the sand ahead of me to see a giant ship rotting in my path. The wood was misshapen and half eaten by the sea and barnacles. The sails were shredded, hanging like wet moss. The figurehead, however, was untouched by time and deterioration. A wolf carved from oak stood at an angle, a bronze bell hanging from between its teeth.

"Mother's Fang," I whispered, slowly making my way closer.

As I neared, I could smell him. His scent had never left me since that day and it had not changed much in the eighteen years we'd been apart. Adulthood had only added the metallic smell of metal and the sweet scent of rum.

Circling around the skeleton of the ship, I found that small, rusted cage in the hollow bowels of the lower deck. Inside it was the boy before I knew him as Vidar. I had seen his face that day, full of fear and sadness. Seeing it in that dreamscape, it was filled with revulsion and fury.

How was I so stupid to not see it then?

Vidar's eyes flicked toward me, but his anger did not wane. He stared into me, tears of blood making lines down his face.

I stepped closer and cautiously crouched down by the too small cage in which he was stuffed, eyeing the lock on the front.

"You seem uncomfortable," I said.

"Come to devour me?" he spoke, his voice hoarse and dry.

"What's your name?" I said, dodging his question.

"They're all dead, you know. Piece by piece. I saw it. Heard it all."

"Cover your ears."

"And my eyes?"

From his lap, he uncovered a rusted nail and quickly jammed it into his eye. I tensed at the sight of the boy gouging out his sight without a sound. He ground it around, making sure it was well and truly mutilated before moving to the other. More blood washed down his young face and down his neck.

Hand shaking, he dropped the bloody nail and gnashed his teeth.

"Doesn't matter, does it? I don't need eyes to see what I saw."

I swallowed hard and looked down at the dark sand around me to find his silentium necklace at my feet. I pulled the chain from the sand and raised it up only to find that the cage was now empty, the gate open with a broken lock.

I coiled the old necklace in my hand and slowly stood, searching the strange wasteland for him. When I heard a man's deep humming nearby, I stopped breathing.

I knew it was him. Somehow, I knew. And as I circled around the decaying ship and found the hull barely intact, there he was. Vidar, grown into adulthood and sitting with one ankle crossed over his knee in a red velvet chair that looked just as aged and rotten as the ship. He wore captain's attire, but his leather hat sat on his knee as he hummed an eerie tune.

Dreams were strange. I wasn't entirely sure whose dream I was wandering at that point. Mine. His. Both of ours stitched together into a venomous realm of horrors. It could have been any or all of those things. None would make more sense than the other.

"…They stripped them to the bone, the sailors come ashore. They broke their backs and ate their hearts, the crew became no more…"

Vidar hummed portions of the song and added words to others, but never finished it. Walking further into his view, I saw him staring out into the vast graveyard around us with unfeeling eyes. Empty eyes. The necklace hung in my hand, but this Vidar didn't need it. His silentium was buried in his chest.

"The son did drive a blade into the chest of the father. And when he slew the bitch he had hate and vengeance to harbor…"

I blinked, realizing quickly what the tune was about. Growing impatient, I tossed the silentium necklace into Vidar's lap and immediately his gaze darted in my direction.

"There's no singing at the bottom of the sea," I said.

Vidar's lips curled into a smirk as he rested his head on his fist.

"Well, well. If it isn't the devil herself."

"The devil doesn't exist."

"I beg to differ. We all see the devil from time to time." His eyes roamed over me once. "Mine happens to dress in skin."

"Seal skin."

I didn't know why I wanted to correct his assumptions. It wasn't as if I cared what he thought of me and I wouldn't have been opposed to wearing the skin of men, but if I was going to appeal to him in any way, I needed him to see me differently.

"Is that right?" he said, narrowing his eyes.

I took a deep breath and peered around at the endless sands once more.

"So? Why are you dreaming of the devil?"

"In this place? You can't tell where we are? This is Hell, isn't it?"

"You seem awfully comfortable in Hell."

He snorted and looked down at the silentium in his lap before picking it up to examine the small, hollow pendant.

"I've been here before, devil."

I inched my way closer to him. "So have I. But it's not Hell. It's just the bottom of the sea. The place all things come when they die."

"Is that not another name for Hell?"

I huffed a laugh and shook my head. "In Hell, you suffer. Here, you simply lay in silence, rotting away, free of pain. Alone. Surrounded only by darkness and bones."

Vidar narrowed his eyes again and slowly unfolded from his seat, coming to his full height. He held his hat in one hand as he stepped to the edge of the hull and then down to the sand in front of me.

"You talk as if you desire this place."

"This place is nothingness. Up there is where the horrors are," I gestured toward the whirling waters above us.

Vidar followed my gaze upward as another wave of lightning lit up dark shadows swimming in the void.

"Hard to believe horrors lay beyond that," he said softly.

"It is beautiful, isn't it?" I muttered back, staring at the barrier.

"Like a lace veil placed over a diseased body."

I kept staring, losing myself in the haunting beauty of it and knowing his words were painfully true. When that realization came, so did the water. It descended in a faint mist at first before turning into a light sprinkle. Slowly, I lowered my eyes back down to look at Vidar. His head was still lifted toward the watery sky above, his eyes closed as the sprinkle turned into rain. Cold, salty rain as if the ocean was falling on our heads. And still, he wasn't alarmed. Instead, he looked... at peace.

Finally, when his head lowered, I found myself entranced by the tears of water cascading down the contours of his tortured face. His lids rose to reveal those deep brown eyes like he was re-realizing where he was. There was a moment between us that stretched on too long. A moment where I felt tethered to him in a way I didn't like. I'd always felt trapped in a feud with him, but this was different.

"All walls must come down," I whispered.

He shrugged a shoulder. "All walls must come down."

"Are you afraid of drowning?"

"Always."

I swallowed, my insides churning at the tone of his words. I wanted to kill him, but I didn't seek him out in our dreams to fulfill that fantasy. I had come there to find a way in. To find a soft spot that I could expose and sink my claws into.

I couldn't tell him I hated him. I couldn't tell him that the dream wasn't quite a dream or that I was me.

So, I spoke in the gentlest way I could.

"Me, too," I whispered.

The ire faded in that gaze of his and as it did, something deep and overwhelming seemed to loom over the watery expanse like a storm cloud. No, a tidal wave. I turned my eyes to the great darkness that seemed to stretch on forever and heard rumbling thunder far within the void. I'd heard the sound before. It was deep and melodic and made of nightmares. My blood went cold. I stared at the overbearing darkness and felt that there was something beyond it. Something behind the shroud. Something not of our world or the next.

Father.

22

Vidar

Beware the silence.
Beware the words not spoken.
Beware the stares not seen.
~ Clea Roberts

Dahlia had been on my ship for two days and the tension was only building. My crew had remained loyal through the worst of times, but there were a few among them who were questioning my decisions. The whispers were faint but present. Why I cared to return a bunch of girls to their home while two sirens were locked up on board with their tongues in their mouths was somewhat of a mystery, even to me. So of course men were talking. Some wanted to return to the harbor and sell them for as much as we could get, girls be damned. Others wanted them dead. Their arguments whispered across the Rose.

Ships and their crews were delicate things. A good captain never forgot that. And with social temperatures changing, we all needed to adapt as well.

Dahlia's presence, though I'd been avoiding it the past couple of days, was becoming a distraction. My plan to use her would go into effect soon, but I needed to get things in order. Feel out my men's stance on it all.

As tempting as it had been to destroy her once and for all and be done with the torment, something told me I needed her alive.

My father may have miscalculated in the end, but he always told me knowledge won every war and with new monsters haunting the tides, Dahlia's knowledge would be crucial.

Or so I kept telling myself.

Up ahead of the ship, a giant fog bank sat over the water like a sleeping monster. I stared at it, elbows perched on the railing, and narrowed my eyes.

Beside me, Gus leaned forward, blowing out a cloud of smoke before sticking his pipe back in his mouth.

"That's a thick fog bank," he grunted.

"We're near the Aisle of the Black Water," I said flatly.

Gus took a deep breath and let it out on a long sigh. "I know. I can smell it in the air. Like blood rotting in a salty tidepool."

"I smell it, too."

"Been a while since we've been through these waters."

"There's no way around that doesn't add a week to the journey. Stick to the course. Make sure shifts in the crow's nest are short. I want everyone sharp."

"Aye. We'll need our senses in there."

It didn't take long for the Rose to become fully immersed in the fog. Clouds above shielded the sun enough without it. It was like sailing through a storm with no wind. The silence was so heavy that I could hear every creak and moan within my ship as she skimmed the water. A siren's song would be easy to sense in that kind of deafening silence, but I prayed we would not hear one in a place where we'd been stripped of our sight.

I stood at the wheel, my wits sharp and my guard up. Four men stood at the railing on either side of the ship, watching what little they could see of the waters below for signs of unwanted guests.

It was a dangerous choice to cut through the fog, but anchoring the Rose in that place would have been twice as foolish. The Black Water was a place of death and had birthed countless horror stories. Some of which were my own. Somewhere in that misty void was the island that made me. The island that took my father. It was a battleground filled with terrors.

Gus joined me at the wheel, arms crossed. His aged face was hardened with suspicion.

"Some say even the bitches themselves think this place too cursed to hunt around," he muttered. "Especially since that night."

"Hunters have died here," I said. "But so did many of their kind."

"What do you make of this endless fog?"

I took a breath and caught faint hints of smoke.

"I don't think it's all fog. Steam and smoke, maybe. There is a volcano in this chain."

"I haven't forgotten that. That added week of travel time is looking mighty good about now."

I almost laughed, but I was far too focused to allow it.

Just beneath us sitting on the deck were two of the girls wrapped in furs. The others had chosen to stay below and I couldn't blame them. Not seeing the surroundings could create an illusion of safety that all humans longed for. Even me, at times.

"Captain!" Jesse called from the crow's nest. I peered up, barely able to see his silhouette pointing starboard.

I followed his gesture toward a faint shadow looming in the white expanse.

"What the hell is that?" Gus said.

I watched the strange shadow grow nearer until I felt certain I knew what I was looking at.

"Drop anchor!" I ordered.

Quickly, two of my men abandoned their posts at the railings to do as I commanded while others filtered out from below deck to see what was going on. The girls, on edge now, scurried downstairs.

"Blade out, Gus," I said as I abandoned the wheel to approach the railing.

The loud unraveling of chains filled my ears as the anchor splashed into the water. Mullins and James were by my side in a blink, watching as the Rose inched ever closer to what was now very clearly another ship. One that had not been there for very long. One that was not sailable and perhaps not even occupied. The wood was blackened, kissed by fire, and the sails were bent and splintered, burned to nothing but bare poles.

"Can still smell the smoke," Mullins mentioned softly as if speaking louder would wake some hidden monster from the fog.

"Uh, should we be anchored here, cap'n?" James asked from my left.

No

"We're not runners or merchants, James," I said with a smirk. "When we smell danger, we follow it."

A small gust of wind passed by the ship and I watched as the fog swirled, giving us a brief glimpse of another large shape further out.

"Fuck me," Mullins muttered.

"Another ship," Gus added, tapping the spent tobacco from his pipe onto the railing. "This hellhole hasn't changed."

"So, why we stopped, cap'n?"

"Because something about all this isn't right and I don't think anyone is going to get to the bottom of it but us," I said, sliding my coat off my shoulders and draping it over a crate. "Mullins, James, Uther, and Tor, lower a boat."

I turned and headed below deck. Gus, always looking after me, followed.

"What about me?" he asked.

"You're to stay on the ship with the others." We came to the cell where Dahlia and her companion were standing alert, sensing everything that was happening. I looked Dahlia right in the eyes as I told Gus, "The pale one stays here. Dahlia comes with me." I pulled the keys from my belt and unlocked the gate. "If Dahlia returns without me, you're to kill her."

Neither woman reacted, but I knew they understood. Dahlia gave Merilyn a slow glance before walking toward the open gate. Mere inches from me, she took a deep breath, smelling the air.

"Interesting place to anchor," she said.

"You're taking the bitch?" Gus said.

"I'm taking the bitch," I said.

I reached out and pulled Dahlia out of the cell by her arm before I shut the gate behind her, locked it, and tossed Gus the keys.

Gus groaned a sigh. "Don't know why they call you 'Bone Heart.' Should be calling you the 'Mad Cap'n' or something."

Pulling up a little stool, Gus sat himself down in front of the cell gate and propped his feet on a barrel. Before he leaned back against the wall, he pulled his pistol from his belt and laid it in his lap, keeping his eyes on the siren still caged.

"Vidar," Gus said before I was out of earshot. "You see any ghosts, you shoot them in the heart."

Dahlia said nothing as we climbed the steps onto the deck. Mullins and the others had the ladder uncurled and two of my men were already in the jolly boat waiting. Uther and Tor were two of my best fighters and sometimes I wondered if they were wishing for death every time we set sail. They certainly risked themselves as if they were asking for it.

"Taking her?" Mullins asked, pointing a finger. "Cap'n—"

"Get in the boat, Mullins, or say you're too chicken shit to go so someone else can volunteer."

He grumbled and shook his head, climbing over the edge of the railing to descend. Uther followed, eyeing Dahlia like she was a leper. I released her arm and she looked up at me, her expression stony and dark. Her eyes narrowed and she canted her head as if trying to read me.

"You enjoy hell, Vidar," she said. "There is no other reason we're visiting this island together after eighteen years. Do you plan to bury me here with the rest of them?"

"I plan to use you."

"For what?"

"Whatever I can. It's in your best interest to be useful to me."

"Perhaps it's in *your* best interest to be useful to *me*." She stepped forward, leaving barely a breath between us. "I have not begun to show you who I am," she whispered.

I reached slowly toward my hip where Lady Mary hung, thirsting to spill some blood. She didn't look at it, but I knew she was aware of it and my intentions. I stepped forward until my chest met her breasts and looked down my nose at her.

"Today, we cooperate with each other and prolongue these lives we so lazily cling to. Perhaps you'll get the chance to kill me yet."

She reasoned with my statement for a moment before stepping away and pulling up the skirts of the clothes she very obviously hated wearing. Then she slung one leg over the railing and descended the ladder. I half expected her to strip and dive into the water, but she was afraid of something below. We all were now. Or perhaps she was playing another game.

Before I followed, I turned to Smalls. He was one of the most level-headed on my crew and with Gus below looking after the other prisoner, he was a good acting captain.

"Any sign of danger," I emphasized. "Ring the bell."

He nodded, resting a hand on his belt where a pistol and a bronze blade hung, ready for anything. He was anything but small, but he'd gotten the name after losing half his cock in a drunken brawl and now he wore the title with a twisted sense of pride.

I climbed down toward the boat and stepped to the front as Mullins and James began to row. My men already knew what to do. We'd done similar things so many times, it was almost routine. There were three harpoons, one on each side of the ship, and nets. They were ready for sirens. I hoped they'd be ready for anything else, too.

The fog was thick and the smells even thicker. It was like a soggy graveyard. I knew the volcano on that black, cursed island smelled of sulfur, but there was more to it. I knew the smell of dead bodies well and the island was surrounded by the stench.

My men pulled scarves over their mouths and noses, but the odor of rotting flesh only familiarized me with what I'd be one day. I never shied from the scent. Glancing back at Dahlia sitting on the other end of the boat, I saw her expression unchanged.

When something bumped the boat, I glanced over the edge to see a bloated corpse full of holes where crabs and seagulls had gnawed at the rotting flesh. The men maneuvered the oars around it just as another drifted by, the stomach hollowed out. I wrinkled my nose at the sour stink as I reached for the man's coat to pull him closer. He was a captain. Foreign by the looks of the beading and embroidery on his collar, but his face was too rotted and peeled to get an accurate idea of what he once looked like.

"Guess we found the crews from those ships," Mullins said.

We finally hit the sand and let the waves push us up the shore before everyone hopped into the knee-deep water. We hauled the boat up onto the black sand beach and then went silent, listening to the too-quiet island. Sounds came back to me from deep within my memories. Wailing voices. Cries of agony. The ripping of skin. The damn pleasured moans of feeding sirens as they ate their fill of a crew that was once like family.

My eyes found Dahlia again as she walked up onto the beach. The way she was staring into the haze made me think she was going through those same memories. But she and I saw that day from different sides of the same coin.

She turned her eyes toward me, straightened her shoulders, and began exploring the beach. My men spread out, blades drawn, and began searching for answers.

The island was the last place I saw my father. The last place the crew of the Mother's Fang put their mark on the world and instead of dying in battle, they died in cruel, helpless agony. That island also saw me take revenge on the bitches who did it.

We had not landed on the same side of the island, but the whole place felt the same. It felt like a great beast mocking us for our tribulations. Jagged rocks made cliffs and passages and there were arches up ahead where red grass and leafless bushes persisted in that wretched place.

I searched the sand. The rocks. Pieces of long-wrecked ships littered the beach. Bones. Jewelry. Remnants of horrors no one was around to hear made its final resting place on that island.

"Cap'n," Mullins said, coming up to me with a wet flag that was tattered to shreds. I looked at it as he spread it out between his hands. "Le Saint. This ship went missing only months ago. Was filled with some of the most notorious hunters, wasn't it?"

"Captain Jean Brigaut," I nodded, recalling the man I saw in the water. "What the hell was his ship doing here?"

"What the hell was the Cornwallis doing so far off course with a bunch of young girls? Nothing's right anymore."

He looked nervous. I didn't blame him. When I'd told my men about the creatures that attacked us on that tiny island, I could see in their eyes that they didn't want to believe there was something worse than sirens stalking the waters. Now it was becoming blatantly obvious that there was more going on.

I turned to see Dahlia far off in the fog, hip deep in the water and tugging on the shirt of a bloated corpse. She was dragging it onto the shore and I wanted to know why. I made my way toward her as Mullins continued to scour the beach. When I reached her, she was just dropping the corpse on the sand. She crouched down over it, tossing his torn shirt off his chest.

No silentium. Jean Brigaut was a hunter. All of his men should have had them. Then again… all of my father's men had them when they were slaughtered. Didn't seem to do much good in the end.

But there was something else on his chest and it seemed to capture Dahlia's interest, though her face barely showed it.

It was a symbol and it was carved into the man's skin like a brand. The way Dahlia regarded it, I was certain she knew what it was.

"What is that?" I asked.

She stood, glancing at me, but she didn't answer. Instead, she turned and continued down the beach. I followed, unwilling to let her out of my sight. When we reached a large structure of rocks, I noticed a shallow cave eaten into the stones. Dahlia walked right in, careless of her bare feet treading on the sharp rocks. The cave smelled like smoke and putrid meat. It was clear why when I saw the fire pit in the center filled with piles of ash and charred bones. I narrowed my eyes at the scene while Dahlia circled the pit and began sifting through the ash.

"Your people don't cook meat last I checked," I said.

From the ash, Dahlia pulled out a necklace. I crouched opposite her near the cold fire pit and watched as her thumb brushed the ash off a silentium pendant. Our eyes met and finally, I saw a hint of confusion on her face.

"Men do," she muttered, dropping the necklace into my hand. She slowly stood as I examined the pendant. "My people didn't do this."

I stood to face her, tossing the useless necklace aside. "Do you understand what happened here?"

"Perhaps. What would you do if I told you? Would you accept it or would you twist my truths into lies?"

"What do you mean?"

"Could you trust me?"

"No," I huffed.

"Then there's nothing to say."

She walked past me, heading out of the cave. I reached out and caught her arm.

"Whatever is happening, you're afraid of it."

"You should be, too."

"I cannot fear something I don't know."

"The only reason I would ever help you understand what's going on is if I intended to work alongside you and that is something I cannot even fathom doing."

"That makes two of us, but that also makes us stupid."

"I made myself the fool the day we first met. We—"

A gunshot rang out from down the beach. Quickly, we both turned and then began sprinting toward the noise. Through the fog, I could see four silhouettes standing together.

"Captain!" James called.

When we got closer, I noticed he was the one that pulled the trigger. There was a body on the sand. A man, half-starved and barely breathing for all of thirty seconds before the wound claimed him. I crouched over him, realizing immediately that he was without a silentium and that his body was littered with infected, swelling wounds. In place of his silentium, was a symbol carved into his flesh, same as the floater. The man would have been dead soon had James not ended him already.

"He came at us," Mullins explained. "Had a rock in his hand and a crazed look on his face."

"Did you talk to him?"

"Asked him who he was. Told him we could help. He was mad."

Dahlia looked over the body, examining it with the same precision she did the other one.

The sound of feet slapping sand drew everyone's attention. Another skinny man with a bald head darted over the hill, shouting madly. I lifted my pistol as he came at me, a big rock in his hand just like the last one. Blackened, rotten teeth sat unevenly in his mouth as he screamed. I pulled back the hammer on my pistol when hands suddenly shoved my arm upward, forcing me to fire my shot into the sky.

Dahlia.

I lowered my firearm and pulled out my blade with my other hand, pressing it swiftly beneath her chin in warning as two of my men tackled the stranger to the ground. Our eyes bore challengingly into each other before she boldly stepped away from my sword and turned to the struggling madman.

"Be calm for me," she spoke in an alluring, gentle tone.

The silentium buried in my chest hummed against my sternum as her voice carried through the air. My men stepped back, alarmed to hear her inhuman tones fill their ears. Those tones were disrupted by our pendants, but to the man without, they were hypnotic. Whimpering, the man rose up on his hands and looked at Dahlia as she moved slowly toward him. I watched as she crouched, reaching out a hand to gently stroke his salt-crusted forehead.

"Be calm," she whispered, her voice like many trapped together in an eerie prison.

The man muttered something in French, his voice trembling and dehydrated. It was not fear I saw in his eyes, but desperation. His yellowed gaze was on Dahlia, unblinking and wanting as if he'd sooner serve her than drink water in his dying moments.

Dahlia spoke back to him in French, her voice no less tantalizing and poetic in another language. All the while, she continued to stroke his face until the man slowly began to lean into her like a babe would his mother. She sat back, coaxing more out of him until his head was in her lap. She ran her fingers gently over the bridge of his prominent nose, his scalp, his ears, relaxing him. Tempting him. Assuring him. My French was shit, but I was able to pick up a few words. Not enough to understand what they were talking about.

"… Pour le fils d'Akareth," he mumbled before his eyes closed and he went quiet.

"Shhh," Dahlia hushed, leaning over the man and pressing her lips to his dirty skin. "Tu dois aller dormir maintenant," she whispered, her song-like tones soaking through the man's muscles until he was completely limp, curled in on himself like a child.

Dahlia's eyes slowly climbed up and found mine. Gently, she set the man's head on the sand and stood to face me.

"You may kill him now while he sleeps," she said. "He wishes for it. I'd do it myself, but I wager you wouldn't like the sight of it."

I glanced at Tor, giving him a subtle nod, and he stepped in to finish the poor man. Dahlia was already halfway to the boat when I caught her, forcing her to look at me.

"You used the voice among my men," I snarled.

"This place is cursed," she said through her teeth. "These sands are haunted by things even sirens fear."

"Was it worth it? Taking his free will?"

"I did not take his free will. Someone else did. The one carving her sigil into men's chests."

I was growing frustrated with her vague answers.

"You know so much more than you're saying."

She scoffed. "Of course I do. And I'll tell you." She stepped in close, lifting her chin. "If you make it worth it."

The briefest sense of desire flashed through my thoughts, followed immediately by disgust and I shoved her away from me. Amusement curled one side of her lips before her eyes shifted away from me toward the sandy hills. I glanced back to see a dozen silhouettes manifest on the null. When they emerged from the fog, they looked similar to the two men on the beach in tattered clothes. They were all starved. Crazed. Some had swords. Others had stones. Sticks. Whatever they could find.

I knew Dahlia couldn't control them all. Nor did I want her to. Seeing her do it to one man chilled me. If I could avoid seeing her do it to another, I would.

The men began to charge, all consumed with madness like it was a disease they longed to spread. My men started firing, but with only one shot in every pistol, we were outnumbered.

I rushed forward, drawing my cutlass to help in slaying the crazed mob. One by one, they fell, each of their faces finding peace in their last breaths as if we'd done them a great favor. They barely tried to fight us. They swung at us but with no skill. No real effort. When they were all dead or dying at our feet, I felt a familiar rage bubbling up inside me. I knelt to wipe the blood off my cutlass with one of the men's torn shirts.

"Get back on the boat," I ordered.

I stood and looked back at Dahlia standing next to the boat. I was about to prod her again with questions when I noticed something in the water behind her. A floating head, perhaps. A body. No… a face. Half-submerged, the face remained perfectly still, inky hair floating like oil around it. Dark eyes pierced through the back of Dahlia's head, watching her.

Dahlia cocked her head at the look on my face when the stranger in the water emerged, leaping from the waves with arms extended. A thin body with sleek muscle and gray skin shot forth. A long, snake-like tail coiled beneath it and propelled her onto Dahlia's back. She fell to the sand, clawing at the wet grit as the other siren dragged her toward the water.

Dahlia turned over, kicking at her attacker when she raised her clawed fingers up and slashed downward. She didn't scream, but I could see she'd been cut. The two wrestled like animals. The woman shrieked words I could not understand before Dahlia kicked her off into the waves. She sat up in the water, speaking in that icy tongue of theirs before lunging at her again.

I sprang toward them with Lady Mary in my tight grip. As Dahlia scurried backward, I surged forward, swinging at the woman's neck. She dodged, but my blade still managed to snag her collarbone. She made a sound so shrill it felt like an ice pick had pierced my skull. Then she dove back into the waves.

"We must go," Dahlia said, lurching to her feet and holding a hand to her bleeding chest. "She is calling others."

My men dragged the boat into the water, heads frantically turning from one way to the other.

"Wait!" a voice said.

My head snapped back to see Uther running from down the beach. I wasn't aware he'd gone so far, but he was desperately sprinting toward us and if he looked that afraid, I did not want to know what might be behind him.

Mullins helped Dahlia into the boat but realized what he was doing quickly and snapped his hands back like she was made of hot metal. Tor and James paddled hard, bringing us back toward the Rose as quickly as they were able. From below, something large bumped the side of the boat. Then another. Bump. Bump. The boat rocked, waves undulating as if to force us back to the island.

23

Dahlia

Blind are we to the evils of our kin.
~Alister Smith

I didn't recognize her, but she knew me. I could see it in her eyes when she tried to kill me. She went for my heart, but she missed it. She spoke something in the old tongue, but her words were slurred. Tired. She had called me "unchosen." It was an insult among the most religious of my people. One I'd heard more than once. When Vidar intervened and she backed into the water again, I knew we were not safe. That island had been claimed for nefarious things. Worse things, I feared, than what Vidar and I had witnessed all those years ago.

On the boat, I watched the water intently, waiting for an attack. Whoever the woman was, she was not alone. I pressed my palm to my bleeding chest, waiting for the assault I knew was coming. She bumped us again and again, trying to capsize the boat from below. When she grew frustrated with her failure, she emerged from the water, leaping toward us.

I had no choice. It felt wrong before I even did it, but she was beyond reason. She'd seen me with humans and word would spread.

I lunged forward, reaching for the bronze blade off the belt of the man rowing in front of me. As the woman soared over the boat, she reached out to take someone with her. I pulled the cutlass free and swung it across her exposed abdomen. She screeched as innards spilled into the boat and her body flipped into the water on the other side. Her long, eel-like lower half flopped against the rowing men and then slid in a twitching mass over the edge of the boat.

Alarmed that I had a blade, the man I'd taken it from spun to face me, pulling a dagger from his boot to point at my head. Just when he pulled back to swing, another scream rang through the air. A second figure bolted from the water, winding like a sea snake around the man. He slashed his dagger into the air wildly as he was drawn overboard and into the water. A third dove forth, going for Vidar. I watched as he spun to grab her, flipping her beneath him. Her tail flailed, nearly knocking another man off the boat, but Vidar had cut her throat so deep that he nearly severed her head.

He kicked the twitching body off the boat and took the place of the man who'd been dragged under, grabbing the oar. There was no hope for him. I knew it and Vidar knew it. He was in pieces already somewhere below and plumes of blood had bubbled up under the boat because of it.

When we came to the ship, Vidar was shouting orders to his men above. The sails were dropped. The anchor was raised. Men were at the railings on each side of the ship, armed and ready. The bells were humming as the sirens spoke and whispered and screamed at the men in a desperate attempt to overwhelm the crew.

Vidar forced me up the ladder first, stealing the cutlass from my grip. Perhaps he thought I'd attempt to escape, but these women weren't my friends. I was as much the enemy as Vidar and his crew were and they made certain I knew it.

I climbed quickly, my fingers slippery with blood, and stood on deck, watching the men organize themselves into their positions. I'd never seen hunters work. I'd never seen how they communicated in the midst of an attack. Not from the inside, at least. I absorbed it. Learned it. I watched them each do their part until Vidar appeared by my side, seizing my arm. Before I knew it, there were irons locked around my wrists. I growled and pulled away from him only to be dragged to the captain's quarters, tossed inside, and then locked behind heavy wooden doors. I slammed myself against them once. Twice. The wood splintered but did not break. And then I stepped back, listening to every detail of what was going on outside.

There was still a mighty ruckus as the ship lurched forward. My sisters' screams filled the air, hungry and incensed.

It wasn't long before the ship was moving with more speed. The sounds of guns firing and sirens leaping and crashing against the side of the ship filled the foggy passage until finally, hours later, everything went quiet. I'd given up trying to get out of that room. It would not matter if I had anyway. I did not care about the crew's safety and I certainly did not want to fight alongside them, even if I had for a brief second. Escaping only to battle what seemed to be a whole skryll of sirens alone while Meridan was still captured below did not seem wise either, so I stayed put.

Necessity made people do questionable things. I convinced myself I did not cut down that woman to save anyone, but only to save myself. She'd have killed me otherwise.

The silence was thick. I could see out a small window and noticed the fog had cleared. We were leaving the most violent of channels in the island cluster. I could also tell that it was late and the sun was low. Seeing any light at all was a relief, though, no matter the time of day. It meant that damned island was behind us.

I was standing against the side of Vidar's table, looking over his maps, but whatever words he'd scribbled on them meant little to me. Hunters' maps were not the same as merchants. Merchants marked safe routes. Hunters and pirates marked the most dangerous ones. The ones more likely to be populated by sirens.

Next to the maps, however, was a leather folder. A corner of charcoal-stained paper stuck out enough to pique my interest and I reached for it, flipping it open in search of things I could learn about the captain. Stacks of drawings spilled out before me. The first to catch my eye was that of a woman. No, a siren. She was beautiful and drawn with expert skill, but she was bound in chains, a fierce look upon her face. Next to the drawing was written a description to compensate for the lack of color.

Bluish skin. Small frame. Golden eyes and red hair. Strong voice.

A Gorgos. I knew of them, but I'd never met one. They were just as formidable as the Kroan, but they lived far to the east. Realizing Vidar had seen one, and in chains, confused me.

I flipped to another page and found more drawings and more descriptions. I even found a rough sketch of a xhoth with sloppy, urgent writing filling the rest of the paper. I saw weapon sketches and designs with detailed instructions on how to create them. Instructions on how to fold hemsbane into a bronze blade. There were sketches of skulls with fangs. Lists of weaknesses he could use against my people.

Then, near the bottom of the stack, one drawing stood out among the rest. It was old. The paper was delicate and worn with creases as if it had been folded a thousand times over. It was a sketch of a girl. A girl with big eyes, long, dark hair, and a bleeding laceration across her cheek. And on that picture was written, *The Daughter*.

Finally, I heard the lock on the door turn and looked up to see Vidar stepping into the cabin. He had an edge to his expression like anything might set him off. I slapped the leather folder closed and clenched my fists, preparing for whatever he might inflict on me to make himself feel better for all that had transpired. I was a siren, after all. I was the perfect doll to meet every blow he wanted to deliver on the sisters he could not reach. If he were like any other cowardly man, he would do just that.

But then his eyes focused on the deep gashes across my chest. They had stopped bleeding, but the wound still throbbed. Blood stained the front of my shift a dark red and the fabric had torn, leaving a significant portion of my breast exposed.

Taking a deep breath, Vidar circled around me to the side of his bed. There were bottles arranged in a small crate near the foot of it and I watched him pull out a clear one full of transparent liquid. From the same crate, he pulled out a roll of white cotton.

"Your men said it wasn't a good idea to go to that island," I said, seeking to measure his level of tolerance. "You did. Now one of them is dead. You lead your men into the mouth of death with no remorse. You are your father's son."

His nostrils flared and I knew I'd struck a nerve.

"Tor was dead long before he became a member of my crew." He lifted his sharp eyes to meet mine. "Losing two sons to bitches like you took his soul years ago. Without a soul, men do not care what happens to them. It made him a good hunter."

He slammed the bottle down on the table and unraveled the cloth as if he were about to mend my wound. I backed up a step.

"I will heal."

"Why'd she try to kill you?"

"You know why."

"Do I?"

"I am the girl who got her mother and her clan murdered by a human boy. And then she saw me with you, no chains and no binds. What would you think?"

"She thought you were working with us."

"Aren't I?" I raised my cuffed wrists up in front of me. "Or is it back in the cell with me?"

He eyed the irons. Then me. Then my chest as if he could not decide whether to kill me, mend me, or fuck me.

Yes… deep in those brown pools, I could see it. He had a flicker of that desire, no matter how much his hatred outshined his lust. He probably despised himself for it if he was not in complete denial.

Then, without a word, he uncorked the bottle and splashed whatever was inside across the open wounds of my chest. It burned like fire. I snarled and pressed my hands to the stinging incisions, but too quickly, Vidar stepped forward and grabbed my wrists. I heard a dagger unsheathe and in a blink, he'd slid the fine point of a concealed blade through a rung in my chain. He pushed me back onto the table, slamming the dagger into the wood above my head so my wrists were pinned. The sting of the alcohol on my fresh abrasions made me feral as Vidar's hand collared my throat. I looked up at him, my fangs piercing my gums and protruding, sharp and aching for violence.

"I am not fond of games, Dahlia," he hissed, squeezing my throat. "I have many questions. Questions you need to answer."

"I owe you nothing," I said, his scent flooding my lungs. His delicious, tantalizing scent. I wanted to taste his blood on my tongue again and feel my teeth pierce his flesh. "You are but a boy dancing on waves where monsters play."

"What did the Frenchman say to you?"

I laughed at his questions and he squeezed my throat harder until I was silenced. Shivers shot through me. My blood pumped furiously through my veins and my head swam as all of my senses clashed together in an instant of breathless bliss. Blackness swallowed my vision. Silence overwhelmed my ears. Pain racked my bones and excited my nerves and for a brief moment, I was being teased with wonderful death.

I came back to myself with a deep breath that sent my blood shooting south. My back arched off the table, one knee rubbing up the side of Vidar's leg.

My eyes focused on Vidar. He was bent over me, hand still on my throat, but no longer so tight I could not breathe. He was looking at me like I had just slapped him in the face.

What cruel god was toying with me at that moment? Vidar nearly choked the life out of me and when I came back, my body craved… something. Touch. Pleasure. Release. A cleansing, perhaps, of the life I was living. My nipples pebbled under my bloody shift, the threat of dying at the hands of Vidar Bone Heart sending me into a daze.

I should have hated the thought, but my body betrayed me.

"Do it," I challenged with a raspy whisper. "I am your greatest enemy. I am the ghost that haunts you in the night. I know I am." My knee rubbed against his hip, my heel pressing against the back of his thigh to draw him closer. "Do it. Finally, watch the life bleed from my eyes as you steal my last breath. Save your crew. Save your sanity. We both know I deserve worse and you want nothing more."

He stared into my eyes, listening to my every word. I lifted my chin, tempting him. It would be easy. I had a slender neck and he had a grip that could break it.

But he didn't.

The moment I felt the slightest hint of hardness brush up between my legs, Vidar stood up straight, that edge returning to his eyes. I could see every muscle in his jaw pulse as he walked around the table and yanked the knife from my chain. I slowly sat up, watching him circle back around with the knife in his hand like he was thinking of just cutting my throat and being done with it.

That would suffice, I supposed, though it was terribly unexciting.

"I am not on your side," I continued, realizing the moment was over.

"Then you are on theirs."

"Did it look like I was?"

"Then whose side are you on, Dahlia?"

I could not answer that. I did not truly know myself. I blinked, unable to form an answer. When Vidar knew he would get nothing out of me, he gestured toward my new wound with the tip of his knife, keeping his distance.

"More scars to add to your canvas," he said.

I remained silent, my thoughts a mess of broken puzzle pieces. Finally, Vidar sheathed his blade and stepped forward, grasping my arm. He led me out of his cabin, across the deck, and down into the hold where Meridan was standing alert at the bars of the cell, waiting. When she saw me, she let out a relieved sigh. Gus was there, pistol drawn as Vidar unlocked the gate and pushed me inside. When he locked the gate again, I turned to look at him, irritated he hadn't uncuffed me.

"I need sleep. Perhaps you'll be more talkative in the morning."

And with that, he and Gus left the hold, surrendering Meridan and me to the darkness of our prison. We hugged only when we knew we were alone and I could feel her trembling. She had heard the battle and the cries of our sisters as well as I had.

What mess had we gotten ourselves into? We had no place among our own kind and we had no place among men. We were trapped in limbo, fighting for something we could not even understand anymore.

Vidar

I am the hate and rage of a hundred men.
I am the last dawn you will ever see.
~The God, Ferros

18 Years Ago

I remembered little. I waited as the girl had said and when it was time, I crawled out of my cage and went quickly to pick up Softscale from the ground where all the men's weapons had been piled. Then I crept to Gus, prying the spike out of his hands to free him. He was barely conscious, but he was alive, even if he had one less eye.

And then, the rest happened as if I was possessed. I was outside myself, watching it all unfold. I slaughtered them all. I slaughtered every last one of them as they slept. Their hot blood drenched my body and I reveled in it. I made my way to each one of them, one by one, until the last one woke to see her sister's dead around her. Reyna. She yelled out as I drove a blade into her gut, drawing out her pain as she writhed. I savored it, hoping I would never forget the look in her eyes as she died.

It was for my father. For the crew of the Mother's Fang. For Gus's fucking eye. For me. Had the girl not let me out of my cage, I would not have been able to catch them off guard. Their bellies were fat and their bodies were slow like wolves after a huge winter meal.

They all deserved to die. They deserved worse.

I was staring at the bloody bodies spread out before me, proud. I deserved my vengeance, but in my rage, I didn't even realize the girl wasn't among them. Then I heard her screams. She came barreling down the hill. She must have wandered off and returned when she heard her sister dying. Part of me didn't want to kill her, but part of me did. She would grow up to be just like her mother one day. I knew it.

Leave none alive. Everyone knew that in revenge, survivors always messed things up. She was a survivor.

When she charged me, I raised my father's cutlass, ready to gut her, but I hesitated. Damn my body. Damn my mind. They were at war with each other and that little hiccup allowed the girl to tackle me to the ground. She was rabid. Madness had overtaken her at the sight of the massacre, but what right did she have to blame me?

"You promised you'd leave!" she cried out.

"I will kill every last one of you!" I roared, trying to wrestle her off of me.

She ripped the cutlass out of my hand and tossed it aside. I lifted my hands to push her away, my fingers grabbing for her throat.

"You are a monster! I freed you!"

"You are all devils! I will hunt you all down if it's the last thing I do!"

She snarled like an animal at that, turning her head just as I was pushing up against her chin to get her off of me. I watched her teeth close over my fingers and felt a horrible pop in my joints. My knuckles splintered and I watched as she tore her head away, taking my fingers with it.

The worst of it was that she didn't spit them out. She crunched once. Twice. Then she swallowed, opening her mouth to let me see her bloodied fangs when she screamed again.

For a moment, her agony was my agony. She was a reflection of me in my anguish and grief and my body stilled, unwilling to accept it. Never could I have anything in common with a monster like her. The only victory in it was that now she knew my pain.

"Vidar!" a voice called.

Gus. The girl looked up, teeth sharp and nails even sharper. Little as she was, she was strong. She'd pinned me with ease and as I struggled, Gus came limping up the beach with a pistol. He fired a shot at the girl and she ducked to the side. I rolled to my feet, using the last of my strength to get off the ground. I ran for my father's cutlass and heard the girl charging after me. She was ready to kill me. I had to be ready, too. I grabbed the blade and spun around just as she was lunging. The sharp metal met her cheek. Blood splattered the already stained sand and she spun, hitting the ground with a shrill cry.

I should have finished it then. I should have run her through. I couldn't. I was a coward. A fool. I ran for Gus as fast as my skinny legs could carry me as the girl struggled to her feet, one hand clutching her face. We ran down the beach to the boat the girl had indicated and jumped in. Inside was a weapon belt and by the luck of the gods, there was another pistol in it. Gus tore it out of the leathers and fired on the girl as she sprinted toward us, hitting her in the shoulder. She hit the ground, shrieking.

We'd made it. We were rowing out to sea. To safety, I hoped, but perhaps to our death. It didn't matter. As we distanced ourselves from that wretched island, her voice filled the air like poison.

"I will remember your name, Vidar!" she screamed. "I will remember your name! I will destroy you and everything you love! I will destroy you, Vidar! I swear to the gods, I will destroy you!"

Present day

I ambled down into the hold, a lantern in hand. The moment the firelight cast its orange hue over Dahlia's colorless skin, my breath caught in my throat. But of all the sirens I'd ever met, there was a human quality to her that hinted she could still be reasoned with.

Or perhaps that was her supernatural charms. Or I was just being a fool…

Her eyes slowly lifted to look at me, dark and endless. Her friend was curled up against the other wall, fast asleep. Or pretending to be at the very least.

"Are you ready to talk?" I said in a near whisper.

She gave it some thought, her face giving nothing away. Finally, I watched her sigh quietly as if in mild defeat. She was tired. I was tired. One of us had to give in.

I held up the key ring and slowly unlocked the gate, watching Dahlia lazily unfold from the floor. She walked over to me, watching me with the same vigilance that I watched her. When she reached the open gate, she held out her still-cuffed wrists as if in a silent bargain.

I grabbed the chain, tugging her out of the cell only to lock the gate behind her. The cuffs would come off when I said they could.

We walked to my quarters where I hung the lantern up on a ceiling hook and then shut the door behind us, latching it. Then I unlocked the irons from Dahlia's wrists, tossing them on the table. The keys I slid onto my belt, buckling them in place so they could not easily be snatched away, and she watched that as if tempted to bisect me just to get them.

The tension between us was like a stressed tendon ready to snap. The way the lantern rocked over Dahlia's head created dancing shadows on her already eerily appealing face. She was a wraith in the dark. A beautiful, venomous thing.

"Tell me what's going on," I began. "I know you understand it better than I do."

She was hesitant to answer. She veiled her fear like it was a sin to show it, but it was there. It was subtle, but it was there. She'd been spooked by that island and sirens weren't often spooked.

"The xhoth," she finally spoke. "They are hungry. And someone is feeding them. Likely to dissuade them from feeding on us."

"I need more than that."

"People like the crew of the Cornwallis. They were marked, just like the men on that island. My theory is the men on that ship were under a sister's influence. The girls were to be sacrificed to appease the sons' abhorrent appetites or to feed a hungry clan. Who can know?"

"And the men on the island?"

"They were simply there to die. They'd been forced to wait there for something and they knew not what it was. It drove them mad. I'm sure hunger drove them to eat one another. In truth, the sons have likely been visiting that place, devouring one or two at a time just to stay satiated and the marks are simply so they know who gifted those men to them. A pathetic attempt to stay in their good graces, I suspect."

"Tell me about the xhoth. I need more if I'm to sail us through these waters."

"They are the sons of Akareth."

I slumped into the leather chair at the far end of the room, regarding Dahlia in her oversized clothes. "Mind telling me what the fuck that means?"

She leaned up against the wall and then slid her back all the way down until she was sitting on the floor.

"They are from the darkest depths where Akareth resides. He is the father of all sirens, if you believe such things."

"Do you not?"

"I've never seen him," she shrugged. "Just as your people worship a god who's never shown himself, my people serve a god who keeps to the shadows. His whispers are all we have."

I swiped a bottle of rum from the table and popped off the cork, letting it bounce to the floor. "How's that work exactly?"

"He calls us to the depths. No one knows how until they've felt the impulse to dive deep into the abyss. If we do not go, we are taken."

"By the xhoth."

She nodded once.

"And what happens in the depths?"

She shrugged again, watching as I brought the bottle to my lips and took a swig.

"I don't know. Nobody knows for certain. Even those that have returned are too broken to say. *If* they come back, they are with child and have seen the wickedness of the dark. Matrons, we call them. If a matron returns, always a cluster of daughters is born and a matron will return to the father every season to bear more. If one of us does not come back... well... they are lost. Some say the lost ones have been chosen to bear sons rather than return. Others say they are forced to bear daughters for the taking. When they can bear no more, they are devoured, ever feeding our great, horrible creator."

I paused a moment, letting her words sink in.

"Is that why you all call each other 'sisters'?"

She stared, remaining silent, but I could see the truth in her eyes.

"Have you ever been called to the depths?" I continued.

The corner of her mouth slanted upward and she huffed like the idea was absurd.

"I have not."

"Why's that?"

"Perhaps I am not worthy. If our father sees all, he surely saw the moment I stupidly freed a boy and betrayed my people. If I am ever taken before him, I will not be returning."

"Do you want to be worthy?"

"I want to kill you," she said flatly, her expression unchanged. "Do not mistake my cooperation as a desire to help you. If the sons came upon this ship, I'd relish the sight of them tearing you apart. I would simply regret being in the middle."

"So why give me this information?"

"Because it doesn't matter. Write as much of it as you please in your leather sketchbook. It won't change anything."

My lips quirked into a half-smile because if nothing else, she was honest.

Like me.

Two mirror images of each other were a dangerous pair.

"No matter. It's clear that the sons and your sisters do not like you," I mocked. "So where do you have to go, Dahlia? You have but one sister left who loves you, if you even value such a thing. Am I wrong?"

Her face remained languid as if my words weren't affecting her, but I knew they were. Things affected her the same as they affected me. If they didn't, she would not have committed her life to avenging her fallen family.

I stood from my chair and slowly made my way toward her, the bottle hanging loosely in my hand. She held my eyes as she stood, her sharp and tainted soul peering back through the chasm of her stare.

"I've come to realize something that I'm sure you already know," I said. "Something you hate to admit. Something that's eating you alive inside." She waited as I took another slow drink from my rum bottle. "This ship—with my men and with me—is the safest place you can be right now and that's why you have not killed anyone yet, as much as it's eating you alive. I think it does matter that you gave me so much information and I think it matters because you want protection. And you know I can give it."

Still, her face betrayed nothing. Not whether or not she was angry over the fact. Afraid. Disgusted. Instead, she let out a long breath as if in silent surrender and her eyes dropped to the bottle in my hand. She reached out, taking it from me and bringing it up so it met her lips. I watched when her eyes snapped back up to mine and she slowly took a drink. Then another. And another. Her lips hugged the mouth of the bottle with delicate grace and when she lowered it, her tongue slid across the corner of her mouth to catch a single drop of the drink before it fell.

The bottle was nearly empty when she handed it back to me and I watched as her black eyes transformed into a rainstorm gray. Her pale, skin gradually took on color right before my eyes until she was a fair ivory with rosy lips and long lashes. She was still thin with slender features that maintained the dangerous aura she possessed, but in a way that was… human.

"So I don't spook your crew," she said.

The way she looked was too familiar and a disturbing thought came to mind. Untrained eyes would never be able to tell the difference. Hell, even my eyes could barely see what she was anymore. She and women like her could so easily walk our streets undetected if they ever chose to.

"Can your sister do that?" I asked, suspicious.

"No. We are different."

"Like a damn octopus," I hissed, walking back to my chair. "Changing like that."

"I change to suit my environment. Among rocks, I can look like stone. Among wood, I can look like wood. Among men…" She paused and then shrugged lightly. "Well, among men, I can hide what displeases them."

I sat down, propping one ankle across my knee as I looked over her. I had plenty of new information to put in my records.

"Do you like this form better? Does it please you?" she asked.

"Stop."

Her lips stretched ever so slightly as if she wanted to smile, but it was not out of joy. It was out of sick amusement. She knew the appeal she had. She could have looked like a fair maiden from the beginning and she chose not to. She liked how uneasy her beauty was otherwise. How it made men shiver. But there was one thing she clearly could not hide and that was the scar across her cheek. It had been made with bronze and could not be disguised. It locked her inside a body that had been terribly wounded in many ways. I glimpsed the slashes on her chest, which had almost completely disappeared, but imagined all of the scars beneath her clothing were still there, whether faint or not.

Near the wall was a wooden chest that I'd pulled from our cargo when Dahlia and her friend first came to the ship. It had other garments in it, all of similar size. Regarding the blood stains and rips in her shift, I decided to give her something else to wear. She watched me stand and open the chest. From it, I pulled a pair of drawstring pants, a belt, and a shirt sized for a large man. I handed the clothes to her without a word and she took them, clearly a little taken aback by the fact that I'd offered them at all. But if we were entering into some kind of truce, I would rather not have her walking in something blood-stained. It defeated the purpose of her putting on a new face.

Setting the clothes on the table, Dahlia dropped her coat from her shoulders. She had no qualms about her nudity. Not like the ladies of land. I stood there as she slid her ruined shift off her body and stepped out of the bloodied fabric. As I suspected, each and every scar was still visible on her skin. Slashes, punctures, and even a large, crescent tear across her ribs that matched the jaws of a shark. I'd never seen a siren's body so heavily marked.

And yet she was still fucking stunning. A sense of shame whispered through my thoughts as I ogled her feminine form.

When she reached for the new clothing, the way she turned her body gave me a glimpse of her back. My eyes narrowed on layers of crisscrossed markings. They were something I recognized all too well.

As she pulled up the pants, she caught me staring and slowed her movements, realizing where my eyes had gone.

"Those are lashings," I said.

"Yes. You humans are fond of them."

She lifted the shirt over her head, covering her body. She was swimming in it but belted it at the waist, making it seem more like a tunic.

"You've been captured before?"

She let out a breathy laugh like the question was ridiculous. "Captured. Whipped. Chained. Raped. Mocked."

"By who?"

She shrugged again in a manner too casual to suggest she even cared. "A Russian man and his crew four years after the island. I was with them for a week, but they were so fond of their drink. I took a man's cock with my teeth when he foolishly put it in my mouth. From there, it was carnage." Her lip curled and as she swept her hair over one shoulder and began braiding it, she stepped toward me. "But don't worry. You're still the only man I've ever enjoyed the taste of."

"I am not the only man to have wronged you, but I seem to be the only man toward which you've directed your ire for all that's been done."

"You're still alive, Vidar. And... you were the *first* man to wrong me. The space you occupy in my nightmares is vast."

"Have I made a mistake, Dahlia?" I muttered. "Should you still be in chains, behind bars?"

Her face hardened as she finished her long braid. "I should be dead," she whispered.

There is one thing that can destroy as easily as it can create
And that is trust.
~Unknown

Vidar took me back down to the cell where Meridan was now awake and sitting against the wall. Our eyes met for a moment as Vidar stepped in with the keys and unlocked the gate. Meridan stood, watching as he opened it and stepped aside. Her gaze flicked toward me with concern and I just gestured with my chin, coaxing her out.

"What is happening?" she asked.

"Merilyn," Vidar greeted with a sigh. "Dahlia will explain."

"Meridan," I corrected.

"That's what I said," he spoke over his shoulder, making his way back up the steps and leaving us both alone.

Meridan's lips were parted with shock. She stood just inside the open cell, waiting for an explanation.

"We can't go back in the water," I said simply. "I believe Vidar and I have agreed not to kill each other until we understand what is truly going on."

"You believe?"

"It was unclear," I rolled my eyes. "But this, as ridiculous as it sounds, is the safest place we can be."

"Is it because you were attacked on that beach?"

I nodded. "And because of what happened to our sisters."

I stepped back into the cell. Vidar hadn't told us we could sleep anywhere else, so I slumped down against the wall with a quiet groan. Meridan sat down beside me, waiting for me to keep talking.

"What really happened?"

"She tried to kill me," I explained. "A Kroan."

"They've tried to kill you before."

"This time it felt different. Men try to kill us. The sons. Our sisters. I don't know what side I've been fighting for all these years."

"Our side."

"Voel and Kea are dead, Meri. Linya died just last year to hunters. The tides are changing. I feel it. We've been killing each other for so long, but the sons coming from the depths twist everything up. And we cannot fight a war with just the two of us."

"Then we run. We go far out to sea. To the other side of the world. I don't care."

"I can't. I don't deserve peace. I deserve to see the end of this wretched road. I deserve to stay on these wicked tides, being tossed this way and that."

"But Vidar is on the same tide and you've been harboring your hatred for him all these years. Take your vengeance. You've done it." She gestured toward the open gate. "You've made him trust you. This is the time you've been waiting for. Take their silentiums and bend them to your will."

I thought about him and the things he said. I had nowhere to go. The safest place truly was on his gods forsaken ship.

I never thought it could come to such a thing.

"I can't," I whispered.

"Why?" Meridan hissed. She scooted closer to me, speaking in hushed tones. "You showed mercy to him once before. In that cage.

He's manipulating you again. You're weak to him and he will use that to destroy you all over again."

Her words stung. I'd considered that idea numerous times just walking from his cabin to the cell. I was still considering it. It angered me to think it could be possible that he was using me all over again, but what he'd said was just as true. We were stuck. We were enemies to our own kind. Enemies to man. Enemies to ourselves if we could not be smart. But Vidar had fought the sons once and survived. He'd fought others like me. He was strong and if we stayed on his good side (or as close to it as possible) we might just survive long enough to be the victors in the end.

"I have no reason to love our sisters anymore," I admitted. "They've declared me as worthy of death as they consider humans to be. And now the sons wreak havoc on our home. The waves will see more blood very soon. I stayed loyal to them for years, Meri." I ran my fingers over the newly healed claw marks on my chest. "But I believe I'm realizing just how alone we've been. There is nothing to cling to. It is you and me and that is it in the end."

I stood up off the floor, walking toward the stairs. I needed fresh air and to hear the waves and the wind.

"Kea and Voel died helping you get revenge on that man up there," she said. "For you to side with him—"

I spun, grabbing hold of Meridan's neck and driving her back against the wall. I was bigger than she was. I was Kroan. Stronger. I was a killer, born to wrestle men to their graves and tear out throats and hearts with my bare fingers. She was small. Her kind were shy and she was out of place on the surface. The moment I overpowered her, her eyes went wide and her body stiffened.

"Who was it that cut him loose in the first place?" I said. "Let's not forget that you trusted him first. And I am not siding with him. The thought alone makes me sick, but the waters are not safe, Meridan. For either of us. Killing his crew and him leaves us with another empty ship and all those girls we both swore not to kill. It leaves us stranded with an ocean full of killers and monsters around us. Do you understand? I cannot lose you. If I lose you, I truly will have nothing to fight for. So silence yourself and accept our fate for what it is today. Tomorrow may be different, but today, we are here."

She nodded timidly and took a deep breath as soon as I released her. I had not touched her in that way in a while, but fits of anger were something I'd been unable to control for some time. Frustration ate at me. Madness caressed my thoughts at all hours of the day. Perhaps I'd never made a right decision in my life, but I was too tangled in the web to be anyone else. I was too far across the line to take anything back.

"Forgive me," I whispered, stepping back. "You know I would never blame you if you left."

She slowly shook her head, her shoulders slumping with defeat.

"Like you, I have nowhere else to go. No one else to cling to."

"Then we remain lost together." I stepped away from her again, putting more distance between us. "Stay here. I will find food for us both."

I ventured up the steps, feeling strange being unhindered, and found a group of Vidar's men on the deck, gathered around in conversation. The conversation seemed a bit heated. When I saw Vidar leaning up against the mast, arms crossed, I could sense the exasperation on his face by the way he was pinching the bridge of his nose.

"Never have I questioned you, cap'n," one man said. "But to let those bitches walk freely on this ship? It's madness. I have half a mind to say you're under their spell."

"We are near Port Devlin," Vidar said. "Like always, you're free to leave. Find work on another ship."

A couple of the men shook their heads at that.

"This is the damn Burning Rose," Gus spoke up, puffing on his pipe. "And this is Captain Bone Heart. The lot of you won't find a better ship and any other captain would have taken a finger just for questioning him."

"Maybe hunting isn't as lucrative as it used to be," someone said.

"This isn't hunting. If we were hunting, those women would be dead," another man chimed in.

"Governor wants 'em alive. That don't mean we should let them walk around like part of the crew."

"Maybe voting in a new cap'n is in order," another spoke up.

Vidar looked the culprit in the eyes and straightened off the mast, stepping into the man's space. The man immediately dropped his shoulders like a dog coming face to face with a wolf.

"Go ahead and vote, then," Vidar said, staring unblinkingly at his crewman. "But I'm willing to bet I'm the only one on this ship ready to die for it."

I believed him wholeheartedly and so did his men. Their talk of dethroning Vidar seemed to end as quickly as it began and slowly, men began to disperse. Gus leaned up against the mast beside Vidar, speaking softly so other ears could not hear. I walked onto the deck and caught both of their eyes.

Vidar had been the one to free us from the hold, but he still seemed almost offended that I'd ventured out of it. I raised my chin at him and slid my hands into the pockets of my coat.

"Need something already?" he asked.

"We're hungry," I said.

Gus and Vidar exchanged a look before Gus strolled off, blowing smoke into the air with a long exhale. Vidar groaned, rubbing the back of his neck as if to relieve tension, and pushed off the mast.

"Come, then," he sighed.

I followed him below deck into a small kitchen area. The man with a terribly scarred face was playing a card game on a table with a teenage boy I'd never seen. Both of them stopped what they were doing and stood when we entered, whatever joy there was in their faces extinguished with my presence.

"Boil," Vidar said. "Our guest is hungry."

I didn't expect him to leave me with his beloved cook and the boy and he didn't. He grabbed an apple from a wooden bin and sat on a stack of crates with one foot on a rickety stool as he carved into it with his dagger. The apple was overripe and before he even took a bite he was cutting away bruising and brown spots.

Boil groaned as he stood, telling the boy to grab something from a drying rack. When the boy returned, he had half a slab of dried meat, which he placed on a thick cutting board for Boil to begin slicing into. I stood at a distance, watching the precise cuts the cook made in the salted chunk. He put a few on a plate before the boy returned again with a round loaf of bread that had a heavily browned exterior. When the cook cut into it, the inside was still soft and preserved. None of it was fresh and none of it looked particularly appetizing, but I hadn't eaten food with taste in a long time.

With a full plate in hand, Boil walked around the table and set it on the corner for me, wiping his hands on his stained apron. The boy kept himself near Vidar as if for protection, watching me vigilantly. I turned my gaze from the boy to Vidar, then to the food, and lastly, to Boil and his haggard face. I scrutinized at him the longest, curious as to how he'd been marred so badly. Most of his hair was missing, replaced with rough skin and discolored slashes. Even one of his eyes was foggy.

"You stare long enough, you might see the devil, lass," he said, his voice just as rough as I would have expected with an accent different from the other men.

I cocked my head to the side. "You think you see the devil looking into eyes like yours?" I took a step forward, lowering my voice. "That's not where the devil is." We stood there, staring at each other for a long while until I finally glanced down at the plate. "Thank you for the food."

He shrugged. "It isn't anything fancy, but it keeps our bellies full."

"Will you be replenishing your food stores at the next port?"

"That and other things," Vidar spoke up, his mouth full of apple. "Port Devlin isn't big. It's just the last port before the sea opens up and there's nowhere else to stop."

"I know it," I said, taking a tiny piece of meat between my teeth. "Never been inland, but I know it. The fishermen there leave us alone."

"That's never stopped your kind in the past."

I didn't argue out loud, but I knew a few of my kind who had not killed before they were provoked to do so.

As I chewed on my salted meat, I glanced up at Boil again, my gaze tracing every gnarly detail of his face.

"What happened to you?" I asked.

"A bad fire. An angry wife. Ugly as I am, my mistakes match," he chuckled.

"You're not ugly. I've known a great deal of ugly things in my life." My eyes flitted briefly toward Vidar. "I find your face far easier to look at than most on this ship."

That drew another chuckle from Boil. When he smiled, the scarred skin around his mouth grew taut and smooth. It was oddly satisfying.

"Never has anyone said I'm easier to look at than the captain."

"Billy," Vidar said to the boy. "Why don't you take some of the best apples down to the girls."

The boy nodded and began sifting through the remaining fruit for the least bruised ones.

I wanted so badly to ask to follow. I hadn't seen Ahnah and the others since Vidar had imprisoned Meridan and me and I longed to make sure they were alright, but my attachment to them had been exploited already. I didn't need to let that happen again. I acted cold to the mention of them and took another piece of meat in my teeth, chewing slowly as the boy skirted past me with an armful of apples and a loaf of bread.

"They're fine, by the way," Vidar said. "They're growing a bit too comfortable with some of my crewmen. Especially Gus, but I think that's because he knows how to talk to them. They keep calling him grandfather."

I wanted to smile, but I withheld it. Vidar, of all people, deserved to see me smile the least. So few ever had and I didn't want to make him one of those few.

"When we get to port, I've told Gus to bring the girls to an inn with Mullins. They'll look after them. Being off the water for a day or two will do them good."

"Then I want to go, too."

"No."

"I wasn't asking."

Vidar rubbed his brow with his fingers as if annoyed. "Fine. The little one might like that, I suppose. She can't stop asking about you."

Ahnah. The girl was too attached for her own good.

"They're just strangers to you," I said. "I still find it difficult to believe you care what's good for them."

"And I find it difficult to think you care at all."

Our eyes locked for a moment as if our silence was an accusatory jab.

"We both already know our motives when it comes to them," he said. "Thank God we have that in common lest we use them against each other."

"I suppose it is good. Though it is harder to use your crew against you." I looked up at Boil. "They are all so much more difficult to hurt than a young girl would be."

Both men scoffed, but I doubted it was because they didn't believe me. I imagined they were used to hearing threats and my words were only more of the same in a way.

"Yes, and we're running out of sisters to use against you," Vidar countered, reminding me that I'd lost Voel and Kea.

"Oh, but it's in your best interest to keep Meridan safe while I'm here," I said, reaching over to the slab of meat on the cutting board. In it was a rib bone, which had been partially exposed after Boil had carved it. "Without her, I have nothing, and when I think I have nothing," I paused, bringing the boned meat to my lips. "I am so willing to destroy *everything.*"

I opened my mouth. My teeth sharpened as I bit down over the bone and broke it beneath the pressure of my jaw. It filled the room with a loud crunch when it snapped. The meat and shards splintered between my molars as I picked up the plate of food. I took the slab of meat with me, still chewing as I left the kitchen and the two men behind.

I had a sister to feed.

Blind is not the man who cannot see.
But the man who sees and realizes nothing.
~Hector Stone

There was an incessant voice in my ears like the high-pitched ringing after getting hit in the head. It stabbed at my thoughts, causing everything around me to disappear into a blur.

Everything around me… which was nothing.

I was in a deep void. One where the echoes of that screaming noise was all-consuming. I could hardly breathe. I could not move. I only knew that I was slipping deeper into the cold, dark depths toward something awful.

I reached up toward the faintest bit of light above me. I could hardly see my own hand. Try as I might, the light was only getting further away from me and as it did, another voice rang in my thoughts. My own. It kept saying what I somehow already knew.

I was being dragged to the depths. I was being dragged to a hell I did not want to go to. A place where I knew only suffering was waiting for me. Endless suffering. Stagnancy. The slow destruction of all that I was.

I reached further, wishing for a way out. A lifeline. Anything to hold onto so I would not sink to a place I could not return from.

And then I felt it. Fingers wrapped around my wrist. Everything went dark once more, even the light above me. And then the cool kiss of wind on my wet skin shocked my eyes open. A stomach full of water was regurgitated from my mouth as if I could not breathe underwater and I nearly drowned.

Beneath me was black sand. As I pushed up on all fours, I dug my fingers through the wet grit, relieved beyond reason to be on land and not in the water.

I never imagined I'd feel that way.

"Your screaming could be heard from the heavens I imagine," a voice said.

I rolled with a start to find a man sitting on a pile of black rocks nearby. The ocean still massaged the shore, reaching up the beach as if trying to beckon me back. But the ocean was no longer what occupied my thoughts. It was the man on the rock. Vidar fucking Bone Heart. He had one foot propped up so he could perch an elbow upon his knee. He was in his captain's coat, his dreadlocks tied back with a red sash. In front of him, his bronze cutlass was standing, point in the sand, and he was twirling it slowly, but his eyes were on me.

"I did not think I would ever be pulling *you* out of the water like a drowning damsel."

"You know me, then," I blurted out.

Dreams were strange. Unpredictable. He could know my face one night and not know me the next. I was clearly unprepared to fall into his head that night. The shock had rendered me stupid.

"Of course I know you. I've been hunting you since we were children. I never thought this is how I'd find you."

"And how exactly have you found me?"

I stood, black sand weighing down my wet, cotton shift.

"Calling for help."

"And why would you help me?"

"Curiosity, I suppose." He stood from the rock and began pacing along the beach, running his fingers over his blade like he was caressing a lover. "I have killed you so many times in this place, you see. I've slit your throat on this very beach over and over and yet I find you alive over and over."

"Perhaps you cannot kill me. Have you thought of that?"

"Many times." He stopped and looked up at me, his expression flattening. "We make our own hells, do we not?"

"Then your hell is not being able to finish me. Is that it?"

"My hell is not knowing why it does not please me to kill you over and over again."

We stood, staring at each other for a while as if words could no longer communicate our thoughts. And then it occurred to me how I'd been ripped from my own nightmares and fallen into his as if I barely had control of myself anymore. As if sleep was no longer safe now that I'd meddled with our connection.

The waves crept further up the beach, reaching for me. I inched backward, staring at the sea foam like it was poison. That stabbing tone needled through my head again, making my vision waver. Whispers of the deep language tore through a deafening noise only I could hear and I recoiled, pressing my palms to my ears.

"Have you gone mad?" Vidar said.

"I believe I have. You may get your wish soon."

I turned and began marching away from the beach to wherever the hell I was able in that strange dreamscape. If it was distance I needed from the water, so be it. But as soon as I gained any space at all from the beach, Vidar was beside me, the sound of his cutlass sliding into its sheath startling my senses. I whipped my head toward him, the sudden motion amplifying the ruckus in my head. The chorus of noise around me was a venomous thing that sunk right into my bones. The incessant sounds pulled me off balance and I teetered, finding the ground uneven. As I stumbled, Vidar's arms were around me, keeping me on my feet.

My fingers gripped his coat in an effort to stay upright. Bodies pressed together, we found each other's eyes and remained that way, unsure exactly how we'd ended up in that position.

Despite that, neither of us chose to move. Dream or not, I felt everything. His warmth. The beat of his pulse. The roughness of his salt-stiffened coat.

"Do not tell me some unseen force will best you before I have a chance to figure out how to bring about your demise."

"Is it really so important that you are the one to deliver the killing blow?" I said with a sneer.

"If only to make sure it sticks."

"You've failed at that in the past. Maybe you are not suited for the task as much as you wish you were. There are—"

I was cut off by another wave of dizzying beckons from the sea. I winced, trying my best to block them so I might figure a way out of the nightmare I'd gotten lost in.

"If it's so important to you that you be the one to destroy me, then come up with a way to distract me," I said.

"Should I know what it is I'm distracting you from or—"

"Just distract me. Take my mind elsewhere."

He chuckled as if I was joking and it only angered me. I pressed my lips together just to keep from biting off his ear or some other appendage he might need. If I was dreaming, the best course of action to avoid whatever force was luring me out was to wake up.

But I couldn't. Lune help me, something was keeping me there.

Perhaps if I hurt myself. A jolt like that would force me awake. And since Vidar was anything but helpful, I decided to abandon his company.

"You are useless," I hissed, turning to make my way down the beach in hopes of finding a cliff to leap off of.

Suddenly, a strong hand was around my wrist. I was wrenched back and before I knew it, his fingers were around my throat. Vidar's face was a mix of frustration and anger as he drove me up against the rough stones. Our eyes locked and like two stones striking to make sparks, something flashed between us. Heat. Electricity. I wasn't sure what it was, but it made my pulse jump.

"Useless?" he murmured. "I am all you have."

Like a blow to my chest, those words knocked the air out of me. When Vidar's mouth crashed into mine, my heart ceased entirely. His hand squeezed me tighter and his lips were desperate as if he was truly trying to suffocate me. Hate and yearning were bitter on his tongue, but I did not fight him. Despite every fiber of my being wanting to escape, I didn't. I let it happen.

I wanted it to happen.

Because when he kissed me, the noises stopped.

• • •

Six days on that ship free of iron bars or chains was the strangest feeling. Seeing men go about their business while Meridan and I stood on the foredeck of the ship, feeling the misty ocean air on our cheeks, felt unreal. In the six days we'd been allowed to roam, the men became marginally less tense around us. A few of them never took their eyes off of us and many of them had added excessive amounts of hemsbane to their diets. I could smell it.

Meridan and I were of different descent. Where I could change to look more "human," she could not. Her skin remained almost translucent white. Her hair was a pale silver and her eyes never gained color. She could not pass for a human even if she dressed like one.

I was determined not to leave her side. Unlike me, she'd never been a captive of humans or hunters before. She'd never known how cruel the touch of a wanting man could be and she was just as unable to get comfortable as half the crew was.

Since we'd been let out, I saw Ahnah and the girls a couple of times in passing. Ahnah seemed to understand that our affection for each other could not be shown so openly, but when she and I caught each other below deck with only dusty cargo around us, we snuck long hugs. She would speak a few words I couldn't understand and I would give her the smile I was unwilling to give anyone else.

And then we would part ways.

Why I adored the young girl was not as much of a mystery as I once thought it was. She was the innocence that was denied me. Perhaps in protecting her, I could prove that not every human was like Vidar. Not everyone was stripped of goodness.

Maybe it was a twisted sense of redemption I was after. A need to be validated.

As Vidar said, there was hope yet that she and the other girls would not end up like us. The fact that it was important for both of us to keep that darkness from them spoke volumes about our tainted souls. I couldn't say there was any light left in me, but at least I could recognize it in others.

On deck that day, Mullins was sitting on a barrel strumming his fingers over a small, hollow string instrument and singing an upbeat tune to which a few of the girls were dancing. Or jumping. I wasn't sure it could be called dancing. Billy joined them, his footwork equally uncoordinated. Gus was behind them, leaning against the railing with the same old pipe in his mouth, but his eyes were on me like he expected me to dive in and tear everyone to bits.

If I was going to do that, I would have done it already…

Vidar stepped down from the helm looking exhausted. He'd been at the wheel since before most of the crew had woken up. I watched as Ahnah danced in a circle, stumbling into Vidar as he passed. I stiffened. The girls had warmed to him over the days, but they were still wary, and rightfully so. He'd held a knife to one of them and they weren't soon to forget. But Ahnah, the naïve little thing, turned and grabbed his hand as if asking him to join.

Vidar rolled his head back with a groan, trying to get around her. When she did not allow it, he feigned irritation and stooped, tucking her little body under one arm like she was a sack of flour. She giggled so loudly as he carried her around, pretending she wasn't there. Her laughter was almost infectious. Almost.

And then he set her on a pile of linens like she was a piece of cargo. Smiling, he said something to Gus and patted him on the shoulder before retreating to his cabin.

I pursed my lips, staring as Ahnah continued to dance, despite that she was out of breath. And Gus was back to watching me, catching the suspicious glint in my eyes.

"They're getting so comfortable with them," Meridan muttered. "Even after what that other crew did to them."

"So are we," I confessed. "We must stay sharp, no matter how well they play their roles."

It was late in the day when the lantern lights of Port Devlin came into view. Meridan was growing increasingly nervous as we approached and as if on cue, Vidar came up behind us.

"Merilyn will have to stay on the ship unless she wants less forgiving eyes to see her."

"Meridan," she replied.

"*Meridan* will have to stay on the ship."

I nodded and gave Meridan a glimpse. She didn't look keen on going ashore anyways.

In Vidar's hands was a leather hat with a floppy brim. "Hide your hair in this," he said, tossing it to me. "There's another ship on its way and men can get rowdy here."

"I can take care of myself."

"Even so, I don't want to make a scene that will make everything harder than it needs to be. This place is the only port around and it attracts all manner of people. Pirates, mostly. But other hunters, too."

I rolled my eyes and started twisting my hair into a knot on top of my head. Then I pushed the hat over it to hold it in place, hating how constricting it all felt. In the oversized shirt and coat, I looked as much the young sailor as the rest of them at first glance.

The men rolled up the sails and anchored while one of the boats was lowered for part of the crew to row ashore. Going with them felt odd, but behind us, another boat filled with the girls, Gus, and Mullins was rowing in our wake. It would be the first bit of land the girls had seen since they'd been taken, I assumed.

The men of the Rose still looked at me with sideways glances, cautious of my existence. One in particular, Uther, stared as if there was no one else in the boat. I was certain that would not change anytime soon, but I didn't care. Our cooperation was a truce, not an alliance. If I didn't have anything to lose, I'd be putting their own blades through their hearts, but I had Meridan and the girls.

When we arrived on shore, I stepped off the boat onto a rickety wooden dock. The port was small with a sparse amount of buildings that looked to have been built in a previous century. The air smelled heavily of firewood and bread and fish. As we walked inward, I saw drying racks with small silver fish carcasses hanging in the sun. Those who roamed the muddy streets looked as if they'd been following the same routine for generations. Old farmers, shopkeepers, and fishermen ambled about with their wagons, baskets, and sacks, hauling goods from one place to another.

I'd been to Port Devlin before, but never in the form of a woman. I'd circled it from time to time looking for hunter's ships, but its people were too disconnected to be of interest to me. I'd known other sisters who fed on those who ventured too far out to fish, but I never cared to do the same.

I had a more aggressive palate.

"Brom and Nikolas," Vidar said, speaking to his men. "Gather what food we need. I believe Boil gave you a list."

"He did," one man nodded.

"Get on it. If another ship is about to dock, they'll be looking for supplies, too, and I want the best before they get their hands on it. I'll get us rooms for the night."

The two men set off to do what they were ordered to while the girls, Gus, and four other men from the Rose remained with us.

"What of your other men?" I asked. "They do not want time ashore?"

"They'll get it tomorrow. Part of the crew must always be on the ship."

I raised a brow. "Did that work for your father's men?"

Vidar smiled and leaned in close to me as we walked. "Say something like that again and I'll pour hot bronze down your throat."

I rolled my eyes and followed him and the others to an inn. It was small, but inns had taverns, so most of the noise was coming from that one building. It was made of brick that had eroded over time and the wooden doors leading in were thick and warped. They whined as they swung open.

Before going inside, Vidar turned to his men and me and held up a hand. "Stay here with the girls until I get the rooms. I don't know the crowds yet."

I remained with the girls, glancing back to see Ahnah clinging to one of the older ones. The one Vidar nearly killed to gain my cooperation. She seemed to favor her and the older one seemed quite protective. Of course, all of them seemed protective of each other. It made me miss Voel and Kea, but I knew missing them would do me no good and I hadn't known them as long as Meridan. I was fortunate for that.

I schooled my features just as I met Ahnah's eyes. Even after everything, she found a way to smile up at me and I couldn't help myself. I gave her a weak smile in return and even that seemed to overjoy her.

I longed to know what that kind of joy felt like. Even when I was her age, I wondered.

"Lord only knows why the brat likes you so much," Gus said.

I glanced over at him leaning against the outside wall of the inn scratching his head.

"Children are fickle. She'll bore of me soon enough."

"Don't think so. I don't speak every word of their language, but I know she says the word 'Da'ya' almost every day."

"Can you blame her? These girls were taken by men. Men hurt them. You are a man and I am the woman who killed her captors. No matter what you think of me, that fact remains true."

"You're no woman," he sighed. "But kids don't know better. I suppose I see your point."

I slid my hands into my coat pockets, inching closer to Ahnah just to let her know I was still there to protect her. That even if I was keeping my distance, I was still her friend. I knew abandonment and betrayal and I knew what it could do to someone. If the only thing I could do was keep her from feeling betrayed, I would.

"You think those fish men Vidar talked about would come here?" Mullins asked me.

I shrugged. "They don't discriminate. They'd devour me as easily as they'd devour you."

"And sirens like you do discriminate?"

I smirked at him, letting a fang peak out from behind my lips. "You're still alive, aren't you?"

When Vidar came back out and waved us all inside, I took up the rear, making sure none of the girls were left alone on those dank streets. We walked through the whole establishment, up a wide set of wooden steps, and down a hall lined with doors. A short, plump woman with breasts spilling over a cinched bodice pointed out four different rooms before waddling back down the stairs to the tavern.

"All the girls in one room," Vidar said, his eyes meeting mine. "Including you."

I was surprised to hear him say it. I knew he didn't trust me, but it seemed he finally understood I wasn't going to hurt the girls.

And I could protect them better than anyone.

The other men divided into the rest of the rooms as I walked into the largest of the four with two bunk beds against the walls. A couple of the girls would need to double up, but I doubted they'd mind. I knew I was destined for the floor, but I didn't care. I'd been sleeping on harder surfaces for days.

With the door closed and all of us in one space together, I gave Ahnah another smile and she rushed over to hug me. The little thing was a warm glimmer of light in an otherwise cold and desolate wasteland. She started spewing words I couldn't understand until her older companion stepped up beside her.

"She miss you," she said in a heavily accented voice.

I raised my brows at her. "You've learned how to speak their language."

"Little," she nodded, gesturing with her hands. "Maps. I help."

"You learn fast. What is your name?"

"I, Sakari. Ahnah," she said, pressing her hand to her chest. "Mother… my sister…" She gestured to her belly, unable to find the words.

"Your niece. Her mother is your sister."

"Yes," she said, somewhat uncertain.

"And the others?"

She started to explain in her own language, peppering words I could understand in the mix like "home" and "taken."

I got the picture. Then she proceeded to tell me the other girls' names. Kimi. Aponi. Halona. Knowing their names made a difference. Since much of my purpose had been stripped in recent days, I made them my new purpose, and knowing their names solidified my decision. I would need something to drive me until the day came that I could get my revenge the way I intended to get it.

After what seemed like ages, there was a knock at the door. I walked over and opened it to find Vidar leaning on the doorframe. Downstairs, the tavern sounded livelier and someone was even playing music, though the singing left something to be desired.

"Thought everyone should eat," Vidar said, looking past me at the girls.

Half of them were already sleeping, but the other half were alert and attentive. I glanced back at Sakari.

"Hungry?" I said, gesturing to my mouth.

She nodded and without hesitation, I stepped out of the room, skirting past Vidar and heading to the stairs.

"You should stay close," he said, catching up to me.

"Why? Do I not look human enough to blend in?"

"You look plenty human to the untrained eye, but that other ship just docked and men from the sea like pretty women. Keep your hat on."

I looked over my shoulder at him and narrowed my eyes.

"Feeling protective?"

"Of the others, perhaps, because I know what you'd do to them if they even put a finger on you." To drive the point home, he lifted his hand where two wooden fingers were strapped on in place of the ones I'd taken. "I don't want a scene."

I rolled my eyes and continued into the tavern where the men from the Rose were eating stew and drinking warm ale.

"I'll try to contain myself," I mumbled.

I walked up to the bar where the plump woman was lining wooden mugs out to be filled. She caught sight of me as soon as I arrived and instantly her expression warmed.

"Ah! A lady in my tavern. Color me pleased. It's not often we get feminine faces in this port."

I smiled at her, leaning forward. "I've got a whole room of young ladies upstairs and they're famished."

"Saw those girls when you all came in." Her eyes moved to Vidar, who took up the space beside me, and her face soured. "Thought Cap'n Bone Heart here was doing a different sort of business."

"Thelasa, you wound me," he said, pressing a hand to his chest. "You don't think they're a bit young for me?"

"You'd be surprised what kind of nasty business I see passing through here."

"I'm never surprised," Vidar said under his breath, placing a few coins on the counter. "Fresh loaves of bread, cheese, and stew for six mouths."

Thelasa swiped the coins and stuck them in the pocket of her apron, pushing a brown curl of hair behind her ear.

"And for you two?"

"Nothing," I said.

"Two mugs of ale," Vidar answered, his voice overlapping with mine.

I shot him a look and he just shrugged

When Thelasa returned with two mugs, I glanced down at the foggy liquid and winced at the smell.

"What? Don't like ale?"

"It has a rotten taste. I will never understand why men drink it."

"And I'll never understand your taste for human flesh."

I sighed and picked up the mug, bringing it to my mouth. I forced down a big gulp, displeased at the bitter tang. Vidar huffed a laugh as he took two big swigs and leaned back on his elbows, watching his men engage in careless conversation. There was tension in his brow as if something was bothering him and he had far too much reason to be bothered for me to question him. He cared for his crew and I hated to relate to that.

Realizing how many vulnerabilities I had made me stiffen. I was too exposed. I'd attempted to make myself stronger by evading attachments in the past, but I failed time and time again. My soul longed to have companionship and it was my undoing. It would be forever because I could not stop.

It didn't take long for Thelasa to bring out a few loaves of bread and some cloth-wrapped cheese. The stew, however, seemed to be brewing in the back and would take a little time. It smelled mildly seasoned and meaty, unlike the stale porridge that the girls had been served on the ship.

In the corner of the tavern, a pair of old men played string instruments while one of them sang in a raspy voice about beautiful women in big cities made of gold.

Soon, I caught Mullins walking down the steps with Sakari by his side. She was looking shy but eager, her eyes darting curiously around as she came into the tavern. Mullins brought her to the counter, his hands stuffed into the pockets of his worn trousers.

"Found her standing at the top of the steps," he said. "She looked curious. Thought it couldn't hurt."

Vidar didn't look happy at first, but within moments, he warmed to the idea of her being there. He handed her his half-full mug of ale with a smile and she took it, hesitantly looking at the contents and giving it a sniff. She didn't recoil like I would have expected. Instead, she took a good-sized sip, cringed, and gave it back. Mullins and Vidar chuckled and she laughed with them, bashfully covering her mouth.

"These girls haven't been out much I think," Mullins said.

Sakari noticed the music before noticing the food and gravitated toward the men playing. Her face lit up at the sound and she stood near one of the tables closest to them to listen, gently swaying to the melodies.

She and the other girls had been on the Rose for days and no man had touched them or given them a reason to be afraid, save for the first night when Vidar had used her against me. She seemed to have gotten over that and looked like she was feeling nothing but safe among the men. It boggled me. I kept a close eye on her, holding my mug but not drinking the bitter contents.

Finally, I saw Thelasa filling bowls in the back with stew. I was eager to go back upstairs and get away from the increasingly rowdy men in the tavern. They were growing louder with every passing moment and I could do without their boisterous laughter and excessive drinking.

Just as Thelasa was walking bowls over to us, the front doors to the tavern rushed open. No one cared except for me and Vidar and a few of his less intoxicated crewmen. From outside came a whole new group of strangers I didn't know and by the look on Vidar's face, he recognized them. I dipped my head to keep my face hidden in the shadows of my hat and watched as a dozen men strolled in, clearly in need of sleep and drinks.

I didn't have time to study them fully before Vidar straightened, his eyes landing on a tall young man with a slender build and orange curly hair.

"Fuckin' hell," he hissed, slamming his mug down on the counter and splashing warm ale across the wood.

Amongst the newcomers, one of the other men caught sight of Vidar and paused, squinting. The corner of his mouth lifted into a grin, but there was no kindness behind it. A few days' worth of stubble traced his jaw and a head of thin hair was tied into a ponytail.

"Ah!" he said, announcing himself to the tavern, but mostly to Vidar. "So those were the Rose's sails I saw out in the water."

Vidar's jaw pulsed with tension as he stepped away from the bar, hanging his thumbs on his belt.

"Collin," he greeted coldly. His eyes shifted to the boy again and his anger began to give off a dangerous scent that only I could smell. "David," he said. "What the fuck are you doing with Collin Jones, boy?"

The boy's face went rigid with disappointment. He didn't speak. He simply dropped his gaze elsewhere, a sense of shame on his cowering expression.

"I see you know my newest recruit," Collin said. "He said as much. Called you a bastard if I remember correctly."

Vidar did not take his eyes off the boy as Collin spoke.

"Well, we're not here long," he continued. "The hunt never ends, but my men deserve a drink."

The new crew began to make themselves comfortable around the tavern as Thelasa and her sparse amount of employees began to deliver drinks. Vidar turned to Gus, saying something to him that I could not hear over the noise, and then marched clear across the tavern toward the young man. Collin let out a guffaw of amusement as Vidar took the boy by the arm and led him out like a disobedient child.

Gus moved gradually to my side, watching the newcomers as vigilantly as I was. Mullins moved inward, taking a place near Sakari as if unwilling to leave her to the wolves that had crowded the space. I watched them with as much caution as I did the sailors.

"Boy's like a son to the captain," Gus said, slouching onto a stool beside me. "Fucking Collin has no business bringing him into his crew."

"Vidar was younger than he was when he slaughtered my mother," I said, my eyes on Collin as he propped his feet up on a table and drank from a wooden mug.

"We all know how that turned out. Which is why he doesn't want David on a ship."

I turned to look at him, finding it strange that he felt it necessary to even speak to me let alone tell me who David was.

"Why do you think I care to know this?"

"I don't," he shrugged. "I personally don't think you're even capable of caring about anything at all. I think that's what makes us so different."

I wanted to argue that, but what did it matter? The more anyone knew how much I actually cared, the more I was stripped of the armor that had been keeping me alive.

"Perhaps I don't care," I said.

"See, that's where we're different. You know, after we left that damn island, first thing the captain did was report the loss of his father's men. The next thing he did was make sure the families of the men were taken care of. A fourteen-year-old boy did that. Then, he learned to fight with his left hand since you damn well bit off his fingers on the right. Now?" He laughed. "Now, you best fear the man. We call him Bone Heart cuz the bastard just don't die. Death favors him. Won't take him, no matter what he does. And you? What did you do after that day? You kept killing. You kept eating."

I would have turned and sunk my thumbnail into his other eye were I not distracted by the tavern's activities. Gus, nor any of the men from the Rose, knew a damn thing about me.

"You can think what you like, Gus," I said. "Doesn't make a difference to me."

Glancing at Sakari, I noticed one of the other men approaching her with eyes that could only portray one thing. Hunger. I narrowed my gaze, watching and waiting for a reason to hurt him when Mullins stepped in and nudged himself between them. Sakari inched behind him, side-eyeing the stranger.

I knew sailors and I knew hunters and I knew men. It would not take long for drink to loosen their control. I glanced at the counter and the two bowls of stew sitting beside the bread and cheese. The rest had been forgotten with the new arrivals.

But I needed to get Sakari upstairs, food or no food.

"You have a look," Gus pointed out.

"I have no look," I countered, watching Mullins and Sakari again as another man joined the pursuit of the young woman.

"Oh, yes you do. It's the same look a snake has when it's coiled in the grass about to sink its fangs into something."

I took in a deep breath, catching the scent of the room. So many filthy men. So many filthy souls and dirty hands. The crew of the Rose was well into their leisure time, their bellies full of drink and their ears full of conversation. No one but Mullins and Gus was paying attention to Sakari or anything else for that matter.

I was growing increasingly uneasy as time passed. I was itching to slaughter the lot of them for no other reason than to lessen the number of threats in the room. Suddenly, one of the men snuck a hand past Mullins and slid it between Sakari's thighs, gripping her firmly. Mullins shoved the man away and immediately, men were standing from the tables, ready to brawl.

It was sickening. All over one young woman. They were no more civilized than a pack of wild dogs. I stood, about to intervene before Gus gripped my wrist. He stood instead and walked over to the altercation.

"She's with us," he said.

"Who says?" one of the strangers barked.

"We do, you rat," Mullins spit.

"Practicing a little skin trade, are we?" Collin spoke up, laughing in that obnoxious manner again.

"Not your business," Gus argued.

While everyone was distracted by a battle of dull words, I saw another man sneak around, his fingers twitching to touch Sakari. The moment the doors opened and Vidar walked in with the young man, everyone's attention scattered in two different directions. Mine was the only one on the man going for Sakari. He rushed up and wrapped his arms around her, lifting her with a playful yet sickening laugh. One hand slid over her modest breast and she squealed, kicking her legs.

"Hey!" Vidar roared.

Most men looked his way, including the one who'd just assaulted Sakari, but my eyes saw only him. I zeroed in on the hand that was still around her unwilling waist as she struggled to get away from him. Mullins turned to push him away when the man pulled a pistol from his belt, aiming it at his head.

"Oy!" Thelasa shouted. "We have ladies of the night here for that. Leave the damn girl alone."

But they were deaf to her words.

My teeth throbbed in my mouth. My fingers stung as my nails grew from the sensitive beds. His scent was all I could find in the array of odors filling that tavern and I focused on it. While his back was turned, I rushed him, leaping onto his body. He went careening against the wall as my teeth closed over the side of his neck. With one turn of my head, his jugular and a good chunk of flesh and sinew was ripped away. Blood spurted over me, hot and bitter. The man clawed at his open wound as I got to my feet and spit a mouthful of his flesh from my mouth. My hat fell, letting black hair spill over my shoulder.

All eyes turned to me and in my ears, I could hear muffled screaming. I saw pistols aimed and blades drawn and no part of my mind could convince my body not to cut down the ones wielding them. I lunged, pushing Mullins aside and leaping onto the nearest sailor. Gunfire rang, breaking the pattern of furious shouting. These men were hunters, but I had no truce with them. Not like I did with Vidar. I had no obligation to spare any of them and I certainly had no desire. They were merely a proxy for what I wished I could do to the crew of the Rose.

It was in my nature to kill and no matter what, the men reeked of siren blood. They'd killed many of us. Perhaps they'd done worse. All I wanted to do was kill.

Screaming. Gunshots. Tables were being flipped and swords were clashing. The taste of blood coated my tongue and flesh was lodged in my teeth. Another man charged me, blade raised. I leaped at him, my thumbnails piercing through his eyes. All I could think of was Sakari and even Meridan. Meridan was like me and these men were killers. Fiends. Even if she was on the Rose, she was vulnerable if anything happened.

I had bitten into three of them before I spun to see Sakari wrapped in the arms of one of the strangers, a knife to her throat. I hissed, blood dripping down my chin, when the pop of a gunshot rang in my ears. Something hit my shoulder and sent me stumbling forward. Three men moved in, grabbing at me with their hands. Within seconds, my arms were being painfully twisted behind my back and wrapped in thick twine. I struggled, but the hole in my shoulder had rendered me unable to fight all of them off. Someone managed to stuff a rolled cloth in my mouth and pulled it tightly behind my head.

Everything was a blur. I barely heard the words that were spoken around me. All I felt was hot rage and searing disdain as the tavern sat in ruins.

"Fucking siren!" someone shouted.

Sakari was screaming, but soon, her screams were as muffled as mine. They'd gagged her.

"Take them both!" another voice said. "Could both be sirens."

I was dragged outside onto the muddy street while inside, I could still hear men arguing. No one was fighting anymore. Something had happened to make them stop and I was unwilling to think it had anything to do with me. They would be happy to be rid of me, I suspected, but Sakari? I had hoped they cared more about her. I only prayed they wouldn't allow the other girls to be taken so easily.

Vidar

Vengeance is more blinding than the sun
Yet darker than the night
~Unknown

"What the fuck?" I growled, shoving David outside as the rest of Collin's rotten crew filtered into the tavern. David stumbled onto the street, tossing me a disdainful look. "What in the hell are you doing with Collin Jones?"

"He offered me work and I needed work," he said.

"I told you to take care of your mother. Have you left her all alone, then? You left her for your selfish and foolish pursuit of coin and excitement. Is that it?"

"She is dead!" he barked. "The day after you left, she saw fit to leave *me* alone in this world just like *you* left me alone in this world. Jumped off Roger's Point right in front of me, so fuck Treson and fuck you. Collin needed a deckhand and I needed work."

The news of Agnes's suicide was a knife to my heart. I had always suspected her mind was not right. I'd suspected it never would be right after everything. I didn't know how to fix her and a part of me didn't want to carry the burden of trying. Perhaps it was selfish, but I was not the right man. I was too broken to mend her the way she needed. Still… knowing how badly I'd failed at taking care of David and his mother had never been more blatantly clear than at that moment.

"I'm sorry," I said. "Your mother… she was not right. I couldn't replace your father. I—"

"You didn't have to replace him. You just had to be there."

There was bitterness in David's voice, but the sorrow had long passed. He'd expected her to do something drastic, too, even if he never spoke of it. It pained me to know he had been preparing to be alone for so long and I'd left him to that task like a coward. Guilt stabbed me as I tried to contend with the news, but I was no stranger to the feeling.

"Leave Collin's crew and join me on the Rose," I offered.

His jaw ticked as if he was considering it, but he didn't have time to say anything before I heard Mullins raise his voice inside. Collin's crew had never been the civil type. Knowing they were inside with my men was an uneasy thought. I sighed sharply and shook my head.

"This discussion isn't over," I said, walking back toward the doors. "If you're going to be on the water, you should be on my ship. Not his."

I walked back inside to see a face-off between a few of my men and Collin's crew. The damn shits couldn't be in a space together for two seconds without someone getting hurt. Upon my reentry, eyes flicked in my direction, but near the back, one of Collin's men stepped up behind the young woman Mullins had brought into the tavern and picked her up in a maliciously playful manner that she clearly did not like.

"Hey!" I barked.

And all hell broke loose.

Dahlia was still at the bar, but as soon as the man assaulted the girl, she rushed him, leaping onto his back and sinking her teeth into the side of his neck. I saw it happen, but it didn't really become real until the man was toppling to the floor, blood spurting from his open throat.

"Fuckin' hell!" someone shouted.

Pistols were being aimed. Blades were being drawn. The music stopped and was replaced by madness. Mullins tried to get the girl out of the fight, but he was knocked onto a table and she was left having to fend for himself. Gus threw a mug at a man's head. James was shoving a man into the wall, pushing his pistol hand upward so it fired into the ceiling.

I spun around and drew my pistol from my belt, grabbing David by the back of the neck and throwing him behind an overturned table for cover.

"Collin!" I roared, grabbing his wild gaze from across the room.

I was ready to blow his brains out, laws be damned. I lifted my pistol and watched him duck behind a few of his men. I fired, grazing the man's cheek and hitting a pillar behind his head.

"Fuck!"

Someone rushed me with a blade and I grabbed hold of his wrist, pulling him in and slamming my head into his. For a moment, my sinuses exploded with pain, but the man was knocked to his knees and that was good enough.

"Can't get one night of peace, can we, cap'n!" James shouted over the noise.

"Fuckin' siren!" someone yelped.

I whipped my head toward the other side of the tavern to see Dahlia in binds, practically being carried through the crowd. Behind her was the girl in a similar state of restraint.

I rushed to intervene, shoving men aside. I was ready to gut every one of them. I'd been waiting for an excuse to end Collin since the day he became the captain of his own vessel.

"Take them both!" Collin shouted over the ruckus. "Could both be sirens!"

I turned toward his voice to see a man beside him with his pistol trained on me. I stooped just as he fired it. The wall behind me splintered when the bullet hit it. When I recovered, Collin had David beside him, the barrel of his gun pressed to the side of his head. David's eyes were wide with shock and I was rendered useless at the sight.

"Stop!" he ordered, malice in his conniving eyes. "Now, we came here for a nice, quiet night of drink, but looks like I've found a rather unexpected bounty. Sirens mingling with your crew. Either you didn't notice, which is highly unlikely, or something very sinister is going on here. Either way, I'm taking them."

"She's not a siren," Mullins spoke up, pointing at the girl just as she and Dahlia were dragged kicking and thrashing out of the tavern, a knife at her tender throat.

"Oh, I wouldn't say that. These creatures come in so many shades and in so many innocent masks. In't that right, wolf cub?"

I cringed at the name.

"He's telling the truth. She is not," Gus intervened. "She is simply a worker here at the inn."

"I very much doubt that with the way the other one protected her. But either way, I'm taking them. And when Whitton finds out what strange dealings you've been engaging in… well… perhaps it will not be worth it for you to return to Treson Harbor at all."

I had no words. I looked Collin in his putrid, yellowing eyes and ground my teeth to keep from rushing at him. Honor was a foreign concept to him and I knew he was more than willing to pull the trigger on David. The boy meant nothing to him. I was inclined to believe he only absorbed him into his crew as a way to use him against me in the first place.

Looking at me, Collin smiled. He was always smiling, but I suspected it was because he had no idea the thoughts he'd stirred in my head. Before me, I did not see a man. I saw a corpse, gutted and lifeless. That was all he was to me and I was going to make it so. The hell he suffered in my head was limitless the moment he put that pistol to David's temple. My hand squeezed the hilt of my cutlass, eager to drive it through his gut.

"Nothing to say?" Collin said, shrugging as he shoved David toward the door. "Perhaps you've come to your senses. Perhaps this game on the seas does not suit you anymore, Bone Heart. It appears you've gone a bit soft." The rest of his men filtered out of the tavern, backing through the door so their eyes could remain on my crew. Those who'd been slaughtered were left on the floors, already forgotten.

When Collin's crew had gone and the tavern was left in disarray, my eyes remained on the doors. I could feel my heart hammering in my chest and heat rising in my gut. Hate had a distinct feeling. It was overwhelming and somehow sickening. It was a psychosis that I knew all too well and seeing Collin take from me in the manner he did, all cocky and derisive, teased a monster in me.

"Cap'n!" someone shouted.

I spun on my heels to see Uther knelt over Brom's bleeding body. I rushed to their side, grabbing Brom's hand as he reached up. Blood pooled in his gasping mouth.

"Brom," I said.

"Got shot, cap'n," he coughed.

"Looks that way, you crazy bastard."

Scanning his body, I found his hand cupped over his stomach. Slowly, I pulled it away to see streams of blood pouring from his abdomen.

"Ahh, you'll be fine," I said.

"Aye," he shuddered. "Been shot worse."

When our eyes met, the truth of it bounced between us. We both knew he was dying. I squeezed his hand and by the mercy of the gods, I watched the life fade from his green eyes, taking his suffering with it. Uther was still kneeling on the other side of his friend's corpse, his eyes reddened with sadness. The two were like brothers and they'd both joined my crew at the same time.

I ground my teeth together and gently placed Brom's hand on his chest.

"Those weren't sirens," Uther said. "Those were men. Are we fighting men, now?"

I glanced up at him from the crest of my low brows. "I'll fight whoever I have to fucking fight," I snarled, standing.

The silence in the tavern grew as the men came to terms with Brom's sudden death until finally, Mullins stepped up beside me.

"We really going to let him do this, Cap'n?"

"Not a chance," Gus said.

My jaw clenched and slowly, I slid Lady Mary back into my belt.

"Gus," I said calmly, staring at the door where Collin had disappeared with my things. "Gather the girls. Stay with them. Thelasa will help you."

"I know where to take them," the woman said from behind the bar, shaking as she stood.

"Everyone else," I continued. "Return to the ship."

"What will happen when he tells Whitton about all this?" someone asked.

I cracked my neck to one side, relieving some tension as I marched toward the door.

"Whitton won't hear a damn thing about this."

28

Dahlia

Withered are we when we dream of water
With our roots trapped in sand.
~ The Flower Bed

"Move, you dirty dogs!" Collin shouted, his two men dragging me through the mud toward the docks.

I tugged and writhed to get free of their grip and once it angered them enough, they lifted me. One carried my kicking legs and the other had hooked his arms under mine. Every kick and thrash was met with more force. Ahead of me, Sakari was wide-eyed, constantly looking back at me for reassurance.

It was the same way Meridan looked at me sometimes. The same way Kea used to. And though Voel never needed my reassurance, she always knew I was with her.

And I'd failed them all. I didn't ask to lead them, but they expected it from me nonetheless and my selfish vengeance had skewed my judgment.

What the fuck was I doing?

Sakari had no weight to her. A lean diet on ships had weakened her, but even if it hadn't, she was small. She was dragged down the dock into a boat and gagged as if the men truly believed she was like me. A siren. They could not be more wrong. I doubted Sakari had ever hurt anything in her life.

I gnawed at the gag between my teeth. Not that my voice would do me any good when all of the men wore silentiums, but my teeth were sharp and could break bones.

It was no use, though. As soon as they flung me in the boat, they were coiling ropes around my legs and adding more to my wrists like I was a carcass fresh from a hunt ready to be carried on a pole to the fire. Immediately, the men started rowing with vigor, despite how tired and hungry they looked. They must have come to the island for supplies and rest just as Vidar and his crew had, but with Sakari and me in tow, they were making a run for it.

And Collin could not hide the unease behind his pretend confidence. The way he was retreating revealed something to me that I doubted he wanted people to know. That he was afraid of Vidar. His eyes kept glimpsing the shore as the boat gained distance as if he was nervous he'd see him coming out of the tavern.

But he didn't. Part of me wondered if Vidar cared that Sakari had been taken. I wondered if he cared that I'd been taken. Perhaps we were just two less burdens on his ship. Either way, I wasn't going to be a quiet prisoner on another man's vessel.

I began to struggle again, knocking one man into the water when I thrust my legs out. The men began to scurry about trying to control me. I twisted, opening my mouth enough to feel my jaw snap. It was painful. My cheeks stretched and an irritating discomfort shot up my temples. Many sirens could open their mouths wide during feeding, but it didn't mean it was enjoyable. But, doing it meant I was able to push the gag out with my tongue. I twisted around, biting into the nearest limb. My teeth sunk through salty flesh and I ripped the large chunk away, realizing I'd bitten into someone's forearm.

Horrified screams rang in my ears. The man stood and stumbled over his crewmates, falling into the water in a bloody mess as I spit the mouthful of skin onto another man's lap.

The boat was in chaos after that, but my efforts were doused when the butt of a man's pistol collided with my head. My skull cracked under the pressure and instantly, everything was black.

When I woke, the soft spray of sea air was kissing my cheeks. The sun was coming and going behind clouds, its bright light pulling me from my unconsciousness. That, and Sakari's terrified cries.

When I realized what I was hearing, I instantly woke, my eyes bursting open with alarm. I was on a ship, but it was not Vidar's ship. My memories returned and I realized it was Collin's. I felt a terrible pressure on my wrists. I was so tightly bound that I could hardly feel my fingers. The ship was moving fast, rocking against the waves like it was off balance, making me realize how well-designed the Rose was in comparison.

I could tell the men of Collin's crew were low on energy and unenthused… until it came to Sakari. A few of them were eyeing her hungrily while two of them were poking and prodding at her chest, trying to undo the ties that kept her breasts concealed.

I started to growl like a damn animal, flashes from my past overlapping with what was happening to the innocent girl.

"Finally awake!" Collin called out, strolling down the steps from the helm. "And just in time."

"Don't touch her!" I shouted. "She's not like me. She's human."

"Then why are you so protective of her, witch?"

I didn't know how to answer that in a way he would believe and I knew it wouldn't do any good anyway. I glared as he came to crouch in front of me, just out of reach of my legs.

"You say we are monsters and yet you do not care whether it is one of my kind or a young human girl you are hurting."

Collin only laughed at my comment. Shifting my eyes toward the doorway leading down to the lower deck, I saw the orange-haired boy emerging into the daylight. He had a conflicted arch to his brows when he saw Sakari in the men's clutches and me tied to the base of the mast.

"Vidar loves you," I shouted toward him. "I saw it in the way he looked at you."

"Shut up," Collin ordered.

"Do you think this man took you with him because he cares about you? No, it's because he knows Vidar cares about you and he needed leverage. He reeks of malicious intent."

"The gag!" Collin ordered one of his men. "Shut her up."

"That girl," I continued. "Her name is Sakari and she is human. Vidar was protecting her. He would not want you to be a part of this. A part of hurting an innocent girl."

"And what about you?" David said, his eyes still glassy with indecision.

The back of Collin's hand slammed against my cheek before I could answer, snapping my head to the side so hard, I tasted blood between my teeth. I felt it flooding my mouth and looked back at him with a half-smile, knowing that I was going to kill him, no matter what else transpired on his ship.

"Oh, I'm a monster," I said, loud enough for only Collin to hear.

One of his other crewmen showed up with a black contraption. I barely got a look at it before it was being fitted over my head. The leather harness covered my mouth and buckled under my chin and behind my ears, preventing me from being able to open my mouth at all. I struggled until the men began harassing Sakari again, playing with her like she was a toy. When one of them managed to tear her top open down the front, I screamed profanities against my gag, watching her small breasts spring free. She curled in on herself, but the men began to grab at her arms, laughing as they ripped at her clothes.

David was watching nearby, mouth agape like he wanted to say something.

He wasn't as vile as the other men. I could see it in his posture. If I could appeal to any of the damn humans, it was him. When his eyes caught mine, I shook my head, silently pleading for him not to let those men violate Sakari. He gulped, his jaw pulsing before he rushed in and grabbed one of the men by the shoulder. His intervention was as indecisive as his expression, but it got everyone's attention.

The ropes around my wrists were tight. I tugged, testing them. The twine was rough and old. As the men got into a tussle over Sakari, I started to writhe against my binds. I pulled with all my might, tucking my thumb into my palm. When I felt the sharp pain of my joint giving, I pushed through it, watching David get overpowered by his larger, more violent companions. All the while, men started moving to fight over Sakari while she wept in the middle of the mob.

Hungry sharks, all of them.

With another tug, one hand slipped free, my thump popped clean out of the socket. Once one hand was free, the other slid out with ease. I rose to my feet and rushed into the mob, nails extended. I drove them into the side of one man's neck just to get him out of the way as I shoved at the one with his slimy hands around Sakari's arm. She screamed as I wrestled him off of her. Men shouted and the ringing of blades being drawn pierced my ears. But I didn't care much about getting skewered, as long as I ripped some men apart as it happened.

Sakari shrieked again, tugging hard as she desperately tried to keep her shirt closed in the process. Three men rushed me and as I reached for Sakari's captor, he threw her hard to the side. I heaved the man against the railing and thrust his head back so hard his spine cracked. His body went flaccid as a beached squid as I rolled him overboard and turned to see Sakari on the floor. Limp.

One of the other men had David by the arms, restraining him. His eyes were on the unmoving mass between us, too. As the ship rocked, Sakari's body rolled, and beneath her head was a solid metal spindle with layers of thick rope wrapped around it. Blood started to pool beneath her so fast it was creeping toward my feet already, sinking into the grooves of the wood. I listened for her heartbeat. Her breath. Anything to indicate she was alive, but her death had been as instant as the stranger's who'd thrown her.

Fire ignited in me. It made me nauseous. My vision turned red, but my hesitation was too lengthy. Three men rushed me and restrained my arms as David was hauled down to the lower level by the back of his coat.

"On the mast!" Collin barked.

The men hauled me to the mast once more where everything happened too quickly. My hands were raised above my head and despite my struggling, I was immobilized by too many men. My palms were stacked, one on top of the other, and before I knew it, Collin had emerged with a long dagger. He reached up and slammed it forward. The burn of the blade sliding through my hands was nothing compared to the ache I was feeling over my failure.

Hands immobilized, the men began wrapping the rope around my standing body, securing me to the mast like a fucking sacrifice.

"You bitches are hard to contain," Collin said, yanking another dagger from the belt of one of his men. The ship rocked, pulling at my body and the blade pinning me to the wood. "But I have ways. Which is why I'm so good at bringing live specimens back to shore." He waved the dagger in front of me teasingly and then swiftly jammed it up between my ribs. I stifled a scream behind my teeth, unwilling to give him the satisfaction.

And then he twisted.

I was completely restrained and unable to thrash against the tight ropes. I just felt the cold steel moving inside me, poking at my innards.

"Took me a while to figure out which places I could cut your kind without you dying. You have quite a lot."

I looked up into Collin's dull eyes and watched him as he twisted the blade the other way. I wanted to cry out, but I knew better. I knew what he wanted, what he liked, and I wouldn't give it to him. I'd been used and tortured by men before. If only he knew what happened to them.

"See, I've found that if I don't use bronze, I can poke you lot full of holes before you start to fade."

Finally, Collin pulled the knife free and stepped back as blood began to trickle down my side. It would heal soon, but not before I lost a good amount of it. The point was to weaken me, I was sure.

"See, we were cutting your tongues out long before bringing you to shore," he continued, wiping the bloody blade on the sleeve of his crewman's shirt. "But our governor likes his tongues fresh."

I didn't think I could hate someone more than Vidar, but Collin was taking up so much space in my head, Vidar had all but been forgotten. I was going to kill Collin. I was going to tear into him while he watched and that smug look on his salt-burned face would be molded into a perpetual mask of terror and regret.

As I bled, he walked to Sakari's body and waved a hand over her like he was bored.

"Get her off my deck," he said.

Two men ambled over to her, picking her up by the feet and arms, and tossed her limp form over the railing and into the sea. I watched, unblinking as the girl disappeared. And in her last moments, she'd been broken and tainted. She died that way. After everything she'd endured, she died afraid and violated.

Another wave undulated beneath the ship, rocking it just enough to tug on my hands and send a shock of pain through me. It was enough to pull me back from my vengeful stupor so I could properly think. Or at least properly process things.

As the crew began to disperse, overtaken by the fatigue they likely went to the island to relieve, I stood tied to the mast trying to slow my heart. The less blood I lost, the more likely I was to keep up my strength. I needed to heal. I knew the wound in my ribs would close soon. Likely by morning. The dagger through my hands would not allow that hole to close, though.

One step at a time.

Night crept up over the ocean, turning the sun's yellow hues on the surface of the waves into the blue tones of the moon. Silence fell over the ship. Some men were sleeping. Others were trudging around doing aimless tasks. Every time they passed by me, their eyes looked over me like I was a rotten slab of meat.

But they were starving and would eat anything. They'd violate me eventually, whether I was conscious or not. Despite humans claiming we were the demons, they enjoyed indulging like it was their right. Like they enjoyed us.

Slowly, more men began to fall asleep, but not me. My eyes saw everything and as the darkness thickened, my gaze sharpened. I'd stopped bleeding and I saw all I wanted to do play out in my head over and over.

The more I thought about my vengeance, the more the blood loss got to me. It would pass. I only prayed it would pass in time. The night was quiet. The sails barely fluttered in the wind. I could hear the soft hush of the breeze skimming the water and focused, trying to will strength back into my muscles. But focusing on the sounds of the ocean only brought an unwanted tone with it. Voices. They whispered in the wind. Dozens of them. Slowly, the whispering became a deep, bass noise that resonated from the cavernous ocean, making the water ripple around the ship. Like a pod of whales was circling beneath, the air hummed with the eerie sound. The sound from my dreams.

I peered out toward the sea, my spine stiffening. I skimmed the water for any sign of something more dangerous than my captors. Something from the deep. But as I scanned the horizon, something else caught my eye. There was something under the shadow of a cloud and veiled from the moon. It was getting closer. When the moon's light finally touched it, I saw sails.

Another ship. It was coming straight toward us. I looked around to find that no one else had spotted the coming vessel. Vidar's crew was alert. They were constantly searching the waters for danger. Collin's men were fatigued and starved stupid. No one was even in the crow's nest.

I looked up, balling my hands into fists as best I could around the dagger pinning them together.

Pain is your strength. Pain is in your soul. Pain makes you stronger.

I chanted those words in my head as I started to slide my hands up the blade. The stinging agony coursed through me, but with blood loss and elevated arms combined, it didn't hurt nearly as much as it could have. When I reached the hilt, I held my breath and curled my fingers over it, hooking them on the small hand guard.

And then I tugged.

My arms fell limply in front of me, what blood I had left rushing to my fingers with painful speed. I stifled any noise I might make behind my gag, glancing at the blade still pinned through my palms. I needed to get it out, but I was limited. The rest of my body was still tightly secured to the mast with thick ropes.

Looking up, the other ship was visibly closer. I stared as the moonlight kissed its sails. Even from that distance, the tinge of crimson was unmistakable.

So, Vidar had come for David. Or perhaps Sakari. He certainly would never come for me, but it did not matter. I did not need saving.

I watched the Rose suddenly come about, turning so the length of it was visible to me rather than the front. Suddenly it occurred to me what he was doing.

Just as two men were coming up from below deck, a flash of orange revealed exactly where the Rose was to them. Their heads whipped to the side just when the low pop reached their ears, but by then it was too late.

The canon ball hit the side of the ship just at the water line. They were a bit out of range, but they were moving fast. The ship quaked at the impact and suddenly the crew was once more awake and discombobulated. Their alarm bell was being rung, the brass sound of it sharp against my ears. Men were shouting, but before long, another canon fired. That time it hit high enough to send splinters of wood flying into the air around me.

Quickly, I started to maneuver my hands, prying the blade out of my palms and biting through the pain. I was regaining feeling, but not much. I had to accept that my vengeance would not be nearly as sweet in my weakened state.

Finally, the knife pulled free. I gripped its blood-slickened hilt and began sawing through the ropes. As soon I broke the coils, my restraints were gone. They fell at my feet and I stepped out of them as another canon ball hit the mast above my head. I ducked out of the way as the giant pillar cracked and bent, rocking the ship violently. Men were scurrying about, but Collin's ship was full of harpoons and ropes. He was a hunter and his ship was built for hunting, not fighting other ships.

The Rose was a killer.

Broken are the seekers of light
For light can never be captured
~ The Sun King

"Fire!" I hollered, standing at the railing.

Smalls expertly positioned the Rose, coming parallel to the Widow's Smile. When the first canon fired, it nearly missed. I knew the range of my ship. Perhaps I was a bit overeager, but Collin and his men were not equipped for a battle at sea. That much I knew. We were privateers, but his ship had been designed to hunt sirens. To trap them. It was small and outfitted with nets and harpoons. The Rose had once belonged to pirates before I liberated her. She was designed to maim other vessels and for the first time since I acquired her, I was using her to do just that.

Collin had been an idiot to challenge me. On the sea, where no one was watching, I would tear him apart and leave the whispers of his demise to the fish as they ate his remains.

"Fire!" I shouted again.

Each hit dealt more damage than the last and the closer we came, the better I could see the deck where Collin's men were scurrying about like chickens without heads.

The plan was simple. Dangerous, as usual, but simple. All Smalls had to do was get the ship close and I knew he understood how to do that. I'd taught him, after all. And before me, his father captained a similar ship in the Navy.

As we sailed closer, I could see someone on the deck. Someone out of place. Under the moonlight, it wasn't hard to see that it was Dahlia. She was shimmying out of loosened ropes on the mast just as a canon ball tore it down above her head. She darted to the side, a small dagger in hand, and began cutting through men, appearing behind them like a shadow only to slice them open.

A dozen of my men stood behind me, ducked low as Collin's crew began firing blindly at us with muskets. The idiots.

"Hooks ready!" I ordered.

Four men stood and rushed to join me at the railing, tossing grappling hooks across the water and onto the rigging as Smalls drifted parallel to the Widow's Smile. With Dahlia distracting them from behind, my men began to swing across. Once the hulls of the ships were nearly brushing, I leapt onto the railing and bounded across to the Widow. I landed on top of a man as he scampered in confusion. Drawing my cutlass, I ran him through. As soon as another charged me, my pistol was drawn. One squeeze and the metal slug was between his eyes.

My vision skimmed the chaos for David and instead found Dahlia, blood dripping down her chin and soiling the front of her chemise. Her eyes were black as obsidian and feral. She met my gaze for a split second before she turned and sprinted down toward the lower level. I intended to follow, but the battle distracted me. Eighty men converged on that deck, painting the Widow's Smile red.

I damned the laws and rules the moment Collin threatened me. The moment he took David with him. The moment he stole the girl.

When he took Dahlia…

I cut through men with a fury I had been keeping tethered inside me. One after another, Collin's crew fell. They were tired. Poorly fed. They were unmotivated and uncivilized. Collin had created a crew from street rats and criminals and in battle, it showed.

The Widow's Smile was beginning to drift off tilt. She was taking on water. Soon, she'd be another sacrifice to the hungry ocean. A relic on the bottom of the sea. Forgotten.

Seeing a gap in the masses, I took the chance to head toward the hold only to see David emerge on deck. Herding him up from behind was Dahlia, the dagger still in her hand. I half expected her to use it on him. To cut his throat in front of me would have been the perfect vengeance, but she didn't. Instead, she shoved him toward Mullins with force just as he was rushing past them. Mullins quickly took him and started dragging him toward the Rose.

I marched toward them before I heard my name roared over the ruckus.

"Bone Heart!" Collin yelped.

I spun to see him with a pistol poised toward my head from across the deck. Just when the crowd shifted, he pulled the trigger. Fire lanced through my ear and I staggered, pressing a hand to the side of my bleeding head.

He'd missed.

I looked back up at him, my fingers tightening around my cutlass. As I was moving toward him, he began frantically loading another slug into his pistol. I wiped my bloodied hand on my shirt and shoved past stumbling combatants as the ship tilted further to one side. The floor was uneven and soon, we would not even be able to balance on it. But I only needed to kill one man. The rest could drown for all I cared. As they leaped and fell into the water, I knew very well that they'd all perish there before long.

I was near Collin when Dahlia came out of the clusters like a wraith, jamming her knife into his stomach. Her blow was met by the sound of his pistol firing again. Dahlia twitched just before she wrapped her other arm around him and dragged herself and him over the side of the ship.

I rushed to the railing just as they hit the water and disappeared beneath the surface.

"Cap'n!" someone shouted.

I looked up at James waving his arm at me from the Rose. The Widow was sinking and David was safe on the other ship. But not the young girl.

Dahlia would have brought her out of the hold if she had been down there. If she didn't, it could only mean one thing.

I growled at the thought and quickly dove down into the water. Men were frantically trying to find purchase and were being shot down as they clamored for the nets hanging over the side of the Rose. I grabbed hold of one and climbed up out of the water but stopped to look back, waiting for Dahlia to surface. I wondered how deep she would take Collin. I wondered if she'd drown him, eat him, or slice him to pieces down there.

All around, men were thrashing in the water, realizing quickly that they were all about to die there. If any managed to survive my wrath, perhaps I would take them into my crew, but it didn't look promising for them. I watched them fight each other to grab hold of anything they could until a dark shape burst from the waves, taking one of the men under quicker than I could process.

The air shifted. The water seemed to get colder. A thin fog suddenly rolled in like a beast coming to toy with its prey.

"Sons!" Meridan screamed from above.

I held fast to the netting as men were plucked from the surface and dragged beneath by shadowy hands. The chilling sound of clicking and shrieking filled the air, mingling with the blood-curdling screams of dying men.

"Cap'n!" Mullins yelled. "Climb!"

I stayed silent, watching when suddenly I saw her. She burst from the waves, her movements terribly off. She seemed desperate, using only one arm to push through the water. I absently reached for her.

"Here!" I called to her.

She moved toward me as fast as she was able, stretching out to take my hand. We were mere inches away when she was abruptly sucked down again

"Vidar!" James chided.

But I was not in my right mind. I sheathed my cutlass and I leaped off the netting into the water like all my years of honing my skills had vanished. I dove beneath the surface to see near darkness around me.

But it was far from silent. That deep, rhythmic clicking persisted loudly down there. The muffled cries of men in agony filled the water. The moonlight barely breached the surface, but one thing was visible. Dahlia's black fins were iridescent amongst the blackness. The slight sheen of her lower body caught my eye and I swam toward her. I found her struggling against the long, wiry limbs of her captor, the dagger still in her hand. She was pushing desperately for the surface of the water. It was the only reason she hadn't been dragged deeper like the unlucky men around us.

I was a good swimmer, but no match for her kind in the water. I knew that. I did the only thing I could and I reached for her. She reached up, her hand finding mine in the madness. I kicked toward the surface as she thrashed to break free.

And as if we'd been sent a blessing from the heavens, another figure darted into the frenzy. White in color and glowing like moonlit snow, Meridan swam by me and pulled my cutlass from my belt. In a blink, she'd thrust it into the neck of the attacking son. His clicking turned to high-pitched whining that nearly broke my eardrums

Quickly, Meridan hauled Dahlia and me to the surface and we pushed for the nets. Meridan's legs emerged before she even got out of the water and she began scurrying up the netting.

"Climb!" my men were calling.

Dahlia, half-conscious, clung weakly to me as I lifted her from the water. I should have dropped her. It would have saved me. It would have saved my men.

But I didn't.

I pulled Dahlia up and secured her in my arms as James and Mullins climbed partway down to aid us. Smalls was steering us away, pulling us from the sinking Widow and its debris.

I pushed Dahlia upward and as quickly as we were able, we passed her from man to man until she was onboard. And by then, she was not moving at all. Meridan jumped over the railing beside me and rushed to her sister's side. She was lying on her back, her shirt clinging wetly to her form. Billy came running up with a lantern, shedding some much-needed light on Dahlia only to reveal the blood gushing from her side.

She had been shot. I'd suspected it, but now I knew. She was clutching the wound, but it wasn't her only one. She had holes in her hands. Tears in her clothes. Her long, black tail, at least twice as long as her body, sat limp and littered with deep abrasions.

Meridan hissed at anyone who tried to touch her, including me. She pulled Dahlia into her lap, pushing her wet hair off her face.

"I can help her," I said.

"She doesn't need your help! She needs the water."

I gestured toward the infested ocean around us as my men continued to fire on attacking beasts, pulling up the nets with haste as the ship gained distance from the massacre.

"Be my guest."

She gave me a glare that could cut skin and cradled Dahlia tighter.

"The island. There are caves," Dahlia muttered.

"We're going back to the island," I confirmed. "Can you make it?"

Meridan took a breath and calmed herself enough to give me a tense nod.

"Will *we* be safe on the island?" I asked.

"The sons cannot stay long from water. Not like us. But no," she said, looking up at me. "We will not be safe. Safety is a fantasy you humans cooked up in search of bliss."

I shrugged. "I'll take that over being on the sea right now. To port!"

It is when we cease seeing with our eyes
that ugly things transform into diamonds
~Mother Anne Stillington

It was midday before we returned to Port Devlin, but it was overcast. The season of storms was earning its name and I could smell rain in the air. Once we anchored, no one stayed aboard the Rose. Not after the sons had devoured Collin's entire crew. They were voracious beasts and they wanted Dahlia as much as they wanted humans.

As soon as we were in the shallows, Meridan took Dahlia's partially conscious body into the water without even a warning and disappeared beneath the dark waves. We came to the docks and headed inland, eager to gain some distance from the shore. All the while, David kept his head down like a beaten dog. I hadn't said a word to him during the entire journey back. He knew he'd made mistakes. I knew I had, too. I was at fault as much as he was and neither of us wanted to admit it aloud.

Coming to the inn, I immediately walked in searching for Gus and the girls. They were down in the tavern sipping on warm broth and nibbling some bread when we arrived. Gus got a look at my torn ear and the dried blood on the side of my face and shook his head with a sigh.

"What happened then?" he asked.

I skimmed the girls, catching the little one's distressed gaze as she scanned for the young lady that had been taken. Knowing she wouldn't find her among us made my heart sink a little.

"Gone," I muttered to Gus. "The lot of them."

"Don't look like it was an easy fight."

I touched my stinging ear and shrugged. "It was easy enough." I glanced over my shoulder at David and gestured toward the girls with my head. "Can I trust you to look after them while you get a bite to eat?"

He nodded silently and dragged his tired feet to one of the tables as Thelasa brought out a fresh bowl of broth.

"Got the boy back looks like. What about the girl?"

I shook my head. "Haven't asked what happened yet, but I didn't see her when we boarded. And Dahlia looked mad enough."

Gus lowered his head with a grumble and scratched his scruffy chin.

"Sakari, her name was. Was the little one's aunt. And where's Dahlia?"

I shrugged again, stepping over to the bar and pouring myself a mug of water from a wooden pitcher. I took a few sips to wet my dry throat before I spoke again.

"She was hurt. Meridan said she needed the water, but she had to wait till we got to the shallows."

"Why'd you have to wait."

I took another sip. "Because those slimy creatures showed up. Whole crew saw 'em this time. Devoured whatever was left of Collin's men. Tried to take Dahlia, too. We had to sail inland before Meridan would risk going in the water again."

He scrubbed his face with another groan and leaned an elbow on the bar beside me.

"Why did I ever think our days of sailing would become simple?"

"When have they ever been simple?" I snorted.

"Go out, hunt, bring back heads. Simple. Now we're making alliances with sirens, fighting other crews, and being attacked by creatures from the deep."

"First, what we have with Meridan and Dahlia is hardly an alliance. Second, Collin was a prick. I was bound to kill him out here or in a tavern back home sooner or later. And…" I paused to shake my head with defeat. "The sons are just in the middle of it all. As far as I'm concerned, they're just something else to kill."

I glanced at David as he carefully sipped warm broth from a bowl. Across from him, a few of the girls were quietly huddled together, heads down and eyes closed as if in silent prayer.

"How's he doing?" Gus asked.

"Don't know. Haven't spoken to him yet." I took a couple breaths before continuing. "Agnes took a leap off of Roger's Point, according to him. Just after I left the harbor. That's why he joined Collin's crew. Boy's as lost as I was at his age. I just didn't want him to find the path I did. It doesn't lead anywhere good."

"Ahh," Gus huffed. "Woman was having a hard go at it since Jack. Don't blame yourself."

"It's hard not to, Gus. I was trying to make good on promises to myself and I failed at that."

"What promises?"

"I promised I would protect them."

"Too much weight on one man's shoulders will break even the strongest back." He slapped me on the arm and then turned back to the table. "I'll talk to him if you like."

I nodded. "Might be best. Don't think he likes me much right now."

"Thelasa says Oscar Keith has a few hunting cabins inland he'd be willing to rent out for us since the inn's getting a little full. I, uh, I promised the stock of furs to them as payment."

"Good. They'll make use of it better than we would. Might be best for me to sleep elsewhere tonight anyways."

"Hmm. Sensing some restless nights ahead?"

"They're always restless, Gus," I smiled tiredly.

"That they are."

I stood off the bar and set my mug down, rolling my sore shoulders.

"Take care of the girls."

"Aye. And David. You have my word."

"Aye, and David. Thank you." I turned to Thelasa as she walked behind the bar with a few empty cups. "Doors locked tonight, Ma'am."

She snorted. "We lock our doors every night here, sir. And bolt them. We've had our fair share of conflict on our island, believe you me."

"I'm sure you have," I smirked.

"Get some rest," Gus interceded, shoving at my shoulder.

I shrugged off my coat and headed for the doors, swiping an almost full bottle of rum from behind the bar on my way. I was in great need of time alone. Before I reached the exit, I turned to David, placing my fists on the table and leaning forward. His eyes met mine like he was a little boy about to get a spanking.

"I don't care if you hate me," I said to him. "I hate me. But these girls here just lost someone because Collin wanted to have some wicked fun. You want a job? You look after them because they need us."

His eyes scanned over the girls once and then returned to me.

"Who are they?"

"Scared, unlucky girls is all. They just want to go home."

It was a vague answer, but it was all I had for him. Subtly, he nodded and something in my gut said he was being honest. I saw the guilt radiating off of him, and if he truly was like I had been at his age, he was eager to redeem himself.

I slapped my hand against David's back and then continued to the doors, coat in hand.

"I tried to fight them," he blurted out, stopping me. "That… woman. She tried to help her. And then they put me in the hold for speaking up. When the ship was taking on water, she got me out. I… why did she do that?"

My eyes lifted to see Gus listening in on every word. He looked just as conflicted as I felt hearing about what Dahlia did.

But I was too damn drained to think about it all just yet. I nodded and continued toward the door, brows furrowed.

"Up the hill and then down again into the valley where the trail narrows," Thelasa called to me. "The cabin with all the overgrown ferns is where you'll be staying. Oscar already done it up with sheets. You want a bath, you'll have to take it in the lake."

I waved at her over my shoulder, lazily exiting the tavern and making my way along the damp street toward the hills. Port Devlin was a small part of the island. Once I got to the top of the null, I could see the rest of it. Most of the island was groves and fields with a few cabins and houses peppered throughout. They were mostly self-sufficient but traded for warm clothing and food from time to time when winters grew harsh. Descending the hill, I watched a green landscape pass me by. There were tall trees, small streams, and pens full of sheep, and in the distance, I could hear crows cawing as if to mock all of my recent losses.

Farther from the small town, the silence engulfed me. The breeze was there, but it was bearable, even with the biting chill riding it. I reveled in the lonely walk, fighting an onslaught of invading thoughts.

I'd lived with guilt my whole life. I'd always dealt with it by putting a bottle in one hand and my cutlass in the other. If excessive drink and a blade didn't finish me and I saw morning, then it wasn't my time because it was beginning to look like nothing else was capable of killing me.

Death had a sick sense of humor. He took the ones who cherished life too soon and spared those who desired to see the end of it.

Rubbing my tired eyes, I noticed the path narrowing just as Thelasa said it would. And as if it appeared out of nowhere, I saw the cabin in an overgrown patch of weeds and ferns. I trudged along, feeling sticky with salt and grime, and came to the door. Not far from the cabin I saw the muted sunlight glinting off the surface of a placid lake. I supposed that was my bath if I found the energy.

But I didn't have it. Not yet. My mind was too burdened and my body too tired. I lifted the latch on the door and headed inside, finding a pile of wood already stacked by an iron stove.

Oscar's cabin was full of luxuries I didn't expect. I would have taken a pile of wool blankets under the stars if it came to it, but instead, I got a bed and a fire.

Immediately, I stacked a few logs with some kindling into the fireplace and ground the fire steel I found sitting on top of it until a spark caught. As the flames grew, I sat back on a thick wooden chair against the wall and released a breath, letting the tension in my muscles trickle away. Across from me was a bed with a wooden headboard made of curved beams. There were two small windows and a small, round table, but otherwise, the cabin was vacant like no one had used it in ages.

I nearly fell to sleep in the chair, letting my thoughts wander to places I'd tried to keep them from for years. Just before I surrendered to rest, I lurched out of the chair, tossed off my boots and my belts, and fell onto the thin mattress on the bed. I didn't even pull the covers over myself. I just let sleep take me and hoped it wouldn't be plagued with incessant dreams.

● ● ●

Gus was very aware of how much my time alone meant. I hadn't returned to the village and even as the next day passed, I was still in need of solitude to plot our next moves. And to reflect on all that happened and all that had gone wrong the last few days. My decisions had been unlike me since Dahlia reentered my life. The mere fact that she and her sister were still alive was proof of that. My men were taking notice and some were proving less tolerant than others. But the tides were changing and the sons had twisted the normalcy of things into something unpredictable.

It was late in the day when I finally decided to take a dip in the lake. It was going to be cold, but when was I not cold? I took my bottle of rum with me, planning to use it to warm my blood.

I walked over barefoot until I reached the gravely edge of the water. Even just on my toes, it was ice, but the shock would invigorate me. Runoff from the mountains was usually chilly no matter the season. I knew that much. I set my bottle down and sucked in a breath before diving right in. The water was ice on my skin. It took the air out of my lungs, but after a few forced moments of immersion, I relaxed, rinsing my hair and scrubbing at my body with my hands, making sure the salt was being cleaned out of the fibers of my clothes as well. Lastly, I cleaned my throbbing ear, wondering what the damn thing would look like once it healed over.

Once thoroughly cleaned, I grabbed my bottle and waded further down the bank, sipping on the rum to keep that warm feeling in my stomach fresh. I found an outcropping of rocks that made a shallow, crescent-shaped landing. I lifted myself from the water and onto the rocks, finding a place to sit and lean up against some smooth stones. And from there… I simply stared at the calm, quiet waters and the trees swaying on the opposite bank. I watched, I drank, and quieted my thoughts.

Night cloaked the sky and still I sat, my clothes nearly dry and my skin icy, but I barely felt it anymore. It was either I froze or I found something I could destroy and destroying things had caused greater problems in the past.

The moon seemed to grow larger the longer I looked at it, framed by a ring of clouds. The gentle sounds of wind whispering over grass and through trees could have lulled me to sleep if I wasn't beginning to get stiff against the rocks.

On the ripples danced the blue half-moon like a reflection in a mirror and I watched it. It sat mostly unmoving aside from the flutter of wind that disturbed the water's surface from time to time.

And then a shape moved beneath and disrupted the perfect image.

A long, slender shadow lurked just under the water, hair flowing like silk as she moved. Slowly, she surfaced. I watched as her head gradually crowned and she opened her near-black eyes at me. She was entirely silent as she drifted slowly toward the edge of the rocks, quiet as a predator stalking a lamb. She watched me closely, waiting for a reaction to her siren form up close as if she thought I'd suddenly raise my blade to erase her from existence now that she was with a tail in front of me.

But she wasn't the same creature she'd been only days prior. The image of her shoving David up from the hold as Collin's ship took on water flashed before me. I was conflicted, seeing both a monster and an ally looking back at me.

While I did not gasp in astonishment at her form, I could not deny its horrifying beauty. She drifted to the rocks, lifting her torso from the water. Her breasts were humble and bare, though mostly covered when her long, dark hair clung to them. Her skin was pallid but with a silvery undertone beneath the moon's light. Every striation in her slim muscles was visible in that form as if she was built to make a man uneasy. Sharp nails clung to the stone and three slits under her ribs pulsed subtly with each breath as she took in the cool night air. Behind her was a long tail that swayed slowly back and forth. It had a slick, blackish-silver sheen to it. Down her spine was a sharp fin that stretched down to where her knees should have been and at the very end was a flare that cut through the water like a blade.

And her scars. They set her apart from any soft beauty she might have had.

I peered into Dahlia's black eyes, seeing the slightest glisten of light behind them like a star in the night sky. It was terrifying, like the lure of a deep-sea fish enticing a meal.

She found a flat corner of stone and folded her arms atop it, resting while she watched me. I took another swig of my drink and then relaxed my wrist on my raised knee, swallowing down the satisfying burn of the rum.

"How did you get here?" I asked.

"Most bodies of water lead to the ocean somehow. But I walked, in fact. I can do that."

A soft breeze whistled through the stones around us, but Dahlia seemed entirely unaffected by the chill.

"And your wounds?"

"They healed, as they always do."

I nodded, tapping one of my rings on the side of the rum bottle. I watched as Dahlia's gaze slowly traced over me and paused on my torn ear. I did not expect her to care, so when she reached toward it with her hand, I turned from her touch, furrowing my brows. She drew her hand back with a sigh.

"Humans are so fragile," she whispered, regarding me like I was a riddle.

"Yes, we are," I muttered, my thoughts wandering back to Agnes.

"What did she mean to you?" Her voice barely cut the silence and it took me a few moments to realize what she was asking about.

It was as if she could read my mind.

I didn't know how she even got that information. Perhaps Meridan had relayed something she overheard as we sailed for the Widow's Smile. Or perhaps Dahlia listened more thoroughly than humans ever could. Both were likely.

"The boy's mother," she continued. "She must have meant something for you to be losing yourself in drink." She paused, resting her chin on her arms. "Did you love her?"

"I suppose in a way I did. Not the way she wanted me to." My eyes wandered for a moment before meeting hers again. "Not the way *he* wanted me to love her."

"The boy? In what way did he want you to love her?"

"Like his father should love her. But I am not his father."

"Where is his father?"

I took a deep breath. "Your mother and her sisters killed him on that island. He'd just been born. Never knew him." I saw nothing in Dahlia's face that said she felt anything for that statement. I didn't expect her to. We'd felt more pain than most and knew how to swallow it. It was a pattern that no longer surprised us. "Jack was like an uncle to me. So when I returned, I promised myself I'd take care of his family. His wife and his young son. Most of the other crewmen didn't have families."

"Did you not have family?"

"I had a mother." I took another small drink. "She left the coast behind and headed inland." I glanced at Dahlia again, watching her gaze drift off into a memory. "David is my family like my crew is my family." I swallowed, finding the will to say what I wanted to.

"Then you drink for them, too. They will all die on the sea if you do not give up your ship and this life you have."

"Is that a threat?"

"It is a warning. I will die in the sea, too. It is only a matter of time."

There was no malice in her voice. Her words seemed suspiciously genuine.

"This is the second time you've told me to stay off the water," I said. "You said the same thing to me as a boy."

"I was a fool. I still am," she scoffed. "A fool for trusting you after what had been done to you. Naivety is not just a human trait, I'm afraid."

"What made you unlock my cage, Dahlia?" I said.

Her eyes crawled up to mine, gray and pleading as if she did not want to answer.

"If I tell you, you will use it against me," she whispered.

Perhaps I would. I couldn't lie and tell her there was no chance of that. When she did not answer, I decided to offer something in trade. Something that might reveal one of my weaknesses.

"Thank you. For getting him out."

She blinked, taken aback by my gratitude.

Straight faced, she said, "I don't know why I did it. I suppose the way he looked when Sakari died said he was not like them. Not like us. Not yet."

"I'm doing my best to keep it that way. He makes it hard."

"It is good you have him. All sirens are family. Until they're not." Her fingers lightly feathered over her throat. "When my blood sister found out it was my fault my mother and her sisters were killed, I was cast out."

I ran a finger across my neck, indicating her scar.

"And that?"

"Her way of banishing me. They all hoped I would die and I nearly did. But hate can keep you alive and it did that for me. Whether I wanted it to or not."

I took a deep breath and let it out, lifting my other knee to perch my other elbow. There was a cloud of regret hovering over both of us. It was thick and heavy and stirred emotions that we'd been stifling for years. I could feel it on my skin like an oil slick and something told me Dahlia could feel it, too. We were a pair of broken things being held together by thin, cotton sutures that were soon to break.

"I long for it to stop," she whispered.

I glanced slowly her way to see her gaze drifting far off again.

"I long for relief," she continued. "I believe I'm at the end of my rope, you might say. I long to answer for my failures and my mistakes and yet Lune has not seen fit to let me die yet. She dangles chances before me that I cannot reach and then steals them away, filling my heart with more pain than I ever thought I could bear. But I am a dam waiting to burst and all in my path may perish." She took a couple long breaths before continuing. "I let that girl die. I tried to save her and they killed her. And now Ahnah's been stripped of something she will never get back. I let my sisters get swept away by the sons. I let my family get slaughtered by a young boy." Her eyes met mine again. "I freed you because neither of us wanted to be there and only one of us was in a cage. I watched you for days as my mother killed all those men and I felt… wrong. I thought I could let you go and they would all think you'd escaped. But you came back."

She took a few more deep breaths, her brows knitting with uncertainty. "We created something that day. Something awful, in each other. It grows more venomous every day. I am the storm," she whispered. "And I fear the destruction I will bring if someone does not stop me."

"How does one stop a storm?" I muttered softly.

"We both know you cannot."

I watched her turn and duck back into the water. Her long shadow curled around and then swam back out into the lake just as rain began to gently pelt the surface of the water. She left me there in that empty silence with her words echoing in my mind. So much pain laced her tone. So much longing and desperation was hidden under her words and as I sat there mulling it all over, something deep inside me desired to be that relief she spoke of. Not just for her, but for me.

31

Vidar

I am the storm
And I pray for those who do not hear me coming
~ Coranthus

Slightly tipsy, I traipsed back to my cottage, my half-empty rum bottle in my hand. The cool air soothed the burn in my chest at the thought of all the things that had happened over the past few days. I itched to relieve myself of all of it just like Dahlia did. In Treson Harbor, I'd have visited the brothels with too much drink in my belly to truly enjoy myself and take out all of my tension on a willing body. One that could take a hard fuck without complaint or judgement. But on that island, near such a small port, there was no such relief.

At least, not the kind I was used to.

I entered my cottage to find candles lit around the room and standing in the center, dripping wet and clothed only in an oversized shirt, was Dahlia.

Her chemise was thin and had soaked up the water from her body and hair, making it easy to see her breasts and pert nipples through the light cotton. It was doing nothing to clothe her really. She was a Grecian statue, every contour of her body on display. I stepped forward, my eyes skimming down her long, bare legs and back up. She watched me with a sense of hope in her gray eyes and somehow, I knew exactly what it was she was searching for.

Shame and longing and a whole hurricane of emotions were buried within the armor of her being. The words to admit it were imprisoned deep in her throat.

But I didn't need to hear them. I knew. Somehow, I knew what she wanted—what she needed—like she'd told me already outright. Like a part of her had confided in me without a voice. And what she was asking for was something I needed to give.

"This is not the place I expected you to come," I said. "Not if it is comfort you seek."

"I am in search of a certain torment and there is no other place I could think of."

Those words teased a part of me I had not even wanted to admit existed.

I took a deep breath, catching the subtle trace of ocean and rain as her scent filled the room. Then I lifted my rum bottle to my lips, locking eyes with her as I took one last swig. My head wasn't swimming, but perhaps my nerves were loosened up just enough. Then I strode further into the room until I was barely a step away from Dahlia. She didn't move. She was not prey. She would not cower from me and I knew it. She watched as I slowly lifted the bottle to her lips. Our eyes were still locked as her lips sensually parted. Then she reached up and took the bottle, tipping it until she got a good mouthful. She swallowed it without a wince and handed the bottle back to me, her tongue swiping over her bottom lip and sending a flurry of awareness straight to my cock.

I took the bottle from her and slowly set it down on the table, taking another deep breath.

I was everything she hated and more and she was everything I feared. Together, we were a flood. A tempest. A destructive force capable of tearing things down to the very core, especially each other.

But we were trapped in the same prison no matter how much we hated it. We were debris in the same flood. Dust in the same zephyr. We were out of control, but always blowing in the same chaotic direction.

Silence swelled within the space between us. Heat coiled within me thinking of all the years she'd been on my mind. Dahlia had haunted me, whether in sleep or not. She desired something and I could absolutely give it.

"How are your injuries?" I asked. "Truly."

"I heal very quickly. But it would not matter either way. We both know it."

I turned to her, meeting her eyes for less than a breath before I had her throat in my hand. I pulled her close at first, jaw clenched, and then drove her back until she hit the wall. I pinned her there, squeezing her neck and watching her eyes widen at my assault.

But then realization set in and I felt her body melt beneath my punishing touch. Her breath came and went with a shudder as she lifted her hands to grasp my wrist. She didn't fight me, though. She just watched me, waiting. I squeezed a little harder until I could feel her pulse beating against my fingers. My lips hovered over hers, feeling her last breath leave her before I cut off her air.

"You are not leaving this cottage until you've made your throat raw with screams," I rasped, my lips barely brushing hers. "So do not stifle them. I want to hear them, loud and clear."

Her body melted again, her hands loosening on my wrist. I watched her eyes start to roll back and then I released her, allowing a rush of air into her lungs. She was breathing like she'd almost drowned, but I did not plan on letting her get comfortable. I gripped her neck again, pinning her but no longer choking her. Already, tears were forming in her eyes. She fought for an adequate breath and as she did, my free hand slid down between her legs to find her folds hot and slick with arousal. I parted her with my fingers, stroking up her seam and over the sensitive bud. Her body quivered and as she sucked in a startled gasp, I pressed my thumb into her throat, denying her another breath.

I stroked her again, pushing my knee between her legs. Her hips rolled toward me, seeking, and I circled her entrance. Immediately, my cock hardened behind my leggings, hungering for the body I was about to defile.

I drove two of my fingers into her wet sheath, enjoying how her body went taut at the invasion. I allowed her more air, soaking up the sweet whimpers she made as I pumped myself inside her. I moved hard and fast, taking her breath away not with my grip but with the fingers in her cunt. Her knees began to shake and I pulled out of her, sliding my other hand to the back of her neck and gripping a good handful of her hair. Tugging her head back, I forced her to look at me and lifted my fingers to her lips, sliding them deep into her mouth.

Any other woman would have gagged, but not Dahlia. I imagined the day she bit off my fingers and shoved deeper until I could feel the back of her throat.

"Bite any more fingers off and I'll gut you," I snarled, pinning her tongue to the bottom of her mouth. "Taste that? That's you hungering for me. Did you ever think you'd want me like this?"

I withdrew and watched her eyes flutter closed. Tears welled with every assault, but she did not fight me. She so easily could have. I knew how strong she was, but every attempt to struggle was weak and restrained. Her protests were a lie.

Releasing her, I unbuckled my belt and slid it out of my pants loops in one, swift tug. The leather slapped against my hips as I grabbed the back of Dahlia's neck once more and drove her toward the bed. Once her knees hit the mattress, I turned her, pulling her damp shirt off her body until she was nude. Her skin was cold, chilled by the sea and wind, and her appearance had not gained that false, human color she'd been parading lately. She was a siren, through and through. Her complexion was like ash and her scars were all the more prominent when she was that shade.

I pushed her onto the bed, sliding my belt between my teeth so I could pull my shirt off. If she was going to be exposed to me in all ways, so was I. I didn't have as many scars, but my skin was no blank canvas either. Bullet holes, knife wounds, and two missing fingers made it easy to see that I hadn't grown up inside some luxurious mansion. But where her skin was pale, mine was tanned from the sun. We were opposite in every way except our pain. That much we shared.

I took my belt from my teeth and put a knee on the bed between her legs, driving her further up the mattress. Then, grabbing both of her hands, I lifted them above her head. Her fingers curled around the wooden headboard.

"Hold onto it and scream if you've had enough. Though it may not do you any good."

She watched as I lifted the folded belt over her and brought it down against her thigh. A loud slap reverberated through the room and on her skin was left a red welt.

But she didn't make a sound.

Her jaw clenched and I watched her body bow off the bed a bit, but she remained with her hands gripping the headboard. I brought the belt down across her hip. Then her ribs. Her breast. Her other breast. I avoided her face, but even so, no blow drew even a peep from her. She tightened her jaw and squirmed every time I made contact with her skin, but she never screamed.

I feared she'd be able to hold out all night. I thought I might enjoy that, too. Welts were forming all over her front, but she barely even gasped with every lash. I saw her teeth bite down on her lip hard enough to draw a tiny drop of blood and finally, I decided I was the weaker between the two of us.

I eyed a particularly dark welt across her ribs and hit her hard, seeking to make her scream and end the torment. It worked. Hitting the already stinging flesh made her yelp and once the barrier had broken, she was a mess. She drew her legs up as if to shield herself and I forced them back down, her knees on either side of my hips. She'd released the headboard with her hands, but I only captured them, using my belt to bind them above her head once more.

She was whimpering. Tears wet her cheeks and rolled into her hair. Her lips were trembling and her chest heaved with strained breaths.

Were she human, I'd have known I went too far, but she wasn't human and I needed to keep reminding myself of that. She wouldn't break. Not even if I kept going for hours.

Hooking my hands around her knees, I pulled her down until her arms were stretched taut against the binds. My groin rubbed up against her slick heat and I felt the painful strain of my eager cock fighting my trousers. The scent of her arousal was intoxicating and those stressed cries coming from her mouth made every inch of me yearn to be inside her.

Growling, I rolled Dahlia onto her stomach and pressed a hand to the small of her back, pinning her flat before I stood to undo my pants. I slid them off my legs and kicked them to the side, watching as my cock sprung free. The damn thing was far too eager to fuck a siren and the thought sent chills down my spine. But it didn't stop me from wanting to continue.

Kneeling behind Dahlia again, I lifted her hips off the mattress, my fingers biting into her backside. She was pliable and willing, every inch of her surrendering to my touch. Leaning over her, I let my cock press against her back and licked my tongue up the divot of her spine. I threw her hair out of the way so I could kiss her shoulder and then I slid my teeth over that same skin, biting down. Dahlia gasped loudly and let out a little scream as I sunk my teeth deeper. Copper tinged my tongue before I drew back and glimpsed the crescent marking on her skin.

Why I loved the look of that bite mark so much was lost to me, but it made my cock pulse with need. I reached down and stroked myself a few times, trembling under my own touch. I needed to be inside her. Even then, her scent was hypnotizing me and I was losing my mind. The way her pained breaths filled the room made me feral. I reached forward, grabbing her hair and wrapping it around my hand. I tugged until her head was craned back and I notched my cock at her sopping entrance.

In one, fluid thrust, I was sheathed inside her. I let out a shuddering moan when I felt her squeeze me, so tight and hot. Her muscles went rigid as I stretched her, but once I was buried deep, she let out a raspy sob. I pulled out and sunk back in again, driving her forward with the force. She moaned loudly, her fists clenched against the headboard.

I took her hips with both hands and pulled out of her all the way before dragging her back onto my length again. Dahlia began a rhythm of gasping moans that turned into desperate cries as I rocked in and out of her. The room was flooded with sounds of agony and pleasure and the crude cadence of our bodies slamming together.

But it wasn't enough. Dahlia was disconnecting. She was giving in to the wrong thing. She was giving in to a pattern and that was where I needed to interrupt her. I wasn't a pattern. I wasn't something to go numb to. I wanted her to feel every bit of what was happening.

I pressed her down onto the bed flat, my cock still deep inside her. I pinned her with my full weight, coiling my hand around to the front of her neck. As I took on a new tempo, I pulled her chin up, forcing her back to arch. I thrust hard and deep, plunging into her without mercy as I squeezed her throat.

"I'll fuck you raw unless you come," I rasped into her ear, picking up speed. "Come for me, Dahlia. Come with me inside you. Come with my hand around your throat. I know you need it. The pain. The release."

"I let them die," she whined, her words like the head of an arrow hitting my chest.

"Yes, you did. Now, answer for it."

I fucked her hard. Brutally. I crushed her beneath me until I felt a sharp intake of air sweep through her lungs. I squeezed her throat even tighter, my teeth grazing the shell of her ear before biting the lobe. Suddenly, I felt her whole body seize. I gripped her jaw and forced her head to turn, locking my lips against hers just as her release rippled through her body. She let out a choked cry against my mouth and when I released her, that cry turned to a shuddering moan.

It was fucking music to my ears and the way her walls quivered around me had me on the edge of coming myself.

God, why was everything about her in that instant making my chest swell? It shouldn't have. I should have been disgusted, but instead, I was starved for her. Being inside her and feeling her unravel beneath me was some kind of twisted relief that filled me with satisfaction.

I rolled Dahlia onto her back. She was still in the throes of tortured ecstasy, her body still trembling, but I gave her no reprieve from the torment as I forced myself back into her heat. Tears still streaked her face and when I drove into her again, she tossed back her head with a throaty moan. I watched her fingers wrap around my belt and longed to feel those nails on my bare back. But as soon as I reached for the belt around her wrists, she looked up at me, her brows furrowed.

"No," she protested.

The look of pain on her face threw me off. Her tears ceased being from getting choked or slapped and seemed to mean something entirely different. She was in anguish from the inside and her soul was screaming for a different sort of release. One I feared I could not give her.

I pulled back my hand and braced myself above her, driving myself deep. She gasped, closing her eyes, and instinct drove my fingers around her throat again. She tipped her chin up, welcoming the assault, so I pressed my thumbs into her windpipe and watched her eyes roll back. I thrust into her. Harder. Faster. Every stroke drove me closer to my own pinnacle and as I witnessed consciousness begin to slip from her, I felt the tension in my core snap.

Dahlia suddenly seized again, pushing up on her heels as if about to struggle for air. I released her and she sucked in a ragged breath, her back arching off the bed with another climax. The sight of it undid me and I came. I came hard, pleasure exploding through me like wildfire, catching every nerve from my stomach to my toes in an uncontrollable squall of euphoria.

Slowly, my release ebbed, the pleasure trickling away until I was spent and breathless. Beneath me, Dahlia was panting, but her body had relaxed, her wrists hanging limply in the loops of my belt. She pressed her lips together as if to suppress something. There was still great pain in her face. I could see it in the way her eyes were screwed shut and her brows were knitted together.

The monster I believed her to be was unprotected now. She was naked in more ways than one, her heart and soul displayed to me like she'd been split down the middle. I didn't know if it was trust or desperation that made her that way, but considering our past, I was inclined to believe the latter. She'd been desperate for relief and it was clear she could not simply reel it all back once she got it.

I finally pulled from her heat and rose to my knees, reaching for her binds. Once I unwound my belt, she lowered her hands to her chest and took a couple deep breaths. Then she opened her tear-filled eyes and sat up, forcing me out of the way. I stood as she did and watched her hurry to the door, toss it open, and head toward the lake. I stayed in the cottage, watching through the open door as she retreated and disappeared.

Whether she was ashamed or overwhelmed or regretful, I didn't know, but I knew what I saw and what I felt. She wanted—needed—whatever we'd done. She needed the pain. The torture. She needed the release and I needed it, too. Perhaps not in the same way, but I did.

That did not mean I was not confused. I was beyond confused. I'd fucked plenty of women, but never anyone like that. Never in a way so dramatic. What we'd done was more than a simple roll in the sheets. What we'd done unlocked something in both of us and I wondered if either of us would ever be able to admit it to the other or if it was just going to be yet another emotion we fought the rest of our lives trying not to feel.

Like stars falling from the sky
Joy is bright yet fleeting in the dark
~ Unknown

The next morning, the clouds had thinned, but the ground was newly wet from a downpour that had moved across the island in the night. I was wearing my coat and hat that day as I trudged along toward the inn. A couple of days by myself had not mended me completely, but I had known from a young age that the only cure for my insanity and anger would be death. In life, I only needed to endure.

Outside the inn, a few of my men were lounging against the wall on rickety wooden. By the way they greeted me, they were well rested, too, and in better spirits.

I moved past them and entered the tavern where more of my men were sitting around quietly eating smoked sausage and toasted bread. I paused at the door until I saw Gus and Mullins at a table in the far corner. I made my way toward them, pouring myself a mug of water as soon as I arrived.

"Morning," I said lazily.

"You look refreshed, cap'n," Mullins commented.

"Where are the girls?"

"Upstairs with our boy, Billy, and Thelasa."

"And how are they doing?"

"They're not as talkative, that's for sure."

I sipped on my water and slowly pivoted to face the room, catching a figure on the opposite side dressed in a deep blue dress and a tightly cinched corset. I paused, my cup midway to my mouth as I watched her speak with one of the tavern hands. When she turned, my breath caught.

Seeing Dahlia dressed like a lady, her long, black tresses braided over her shoulder, was not something I imagined ever seeing. Especially after the previous night when I'd seen her at her most vulnerable. At her most broken. She looked proper and held herself like she was not a demon of the sea but a well-mannered woman of the land.

"Ahh, right," Gus said. "She and Thelasa got to talking early this morning. Thelasa thought it was inappropriate for her to be in tattered men's clothes and put her in one of her old dresses. The men rightly don't know what to think."

"She looks so human that way," Mullins said with a shiver. "I don't like it much. But Thelasa insisted."

"And she knows what she is?"

Gus nodded once. "Said something about seeing her throw herself at the men when they threatened Sakari and now she's wearing one of her dresses. I swear, the people on these little islands aren't always right in the head."

"Thelasa's seen a lot more than she puts on. If she wanted to give Dahlia a dress, then what are we to say about it?"

Dahlia's eyes made their way toward me and our gazes locked. My heart skipped a beat. It truly was unnerving how she could make herself look like a woman when all of us had seen how she could rip into a man. We knew the teeth behind those lips and the malice behind those storm-gray eyes. To one who did not know the beast beneath the skin, she was beautiful. Even with the scar on her cheek, she was a head-turner.

"Captain," Gus said. "We should probably talk."

"About?"

"Well, about Brom. There've been whispers about. Some of the men don't much like the way things are going."

"Who?"

He shrugged. "Just whispers. But maybe we should have a chat with Uther. He and Brom were good mates."

I nodded solemnly. "I'll talk to him."

But then my eyes fixed on Dahlia again and I felt a need to speak with her first.

"Cap'n?" Mullins said.

I set my mug down and started toward her. "We're leaving today. Make sure everyone is ready."

Dahlia kept her gaze on me as we both converged at the bar. Images from the previous night crept back into my head. The sounds of her pained ecstasy. The memory of her bare skin and heavy breaths. Of my cock surging inside her.

Fuck.

"It's unsettling how easily you slip into the role of innocent beauty," I said to her.

"Only simple men cannot see through me. Are you simple, Vidar?"

"Am I?"

"There was a time I thought you were."

"And now?"

She shrugged and looked away for a moment, her long nails tapping on the countertop.

"What did Thelasa say to you?" I asked.

"Kind words laced with suspicion."

"Did you compel her?"

With a smirk, she pointed toward the ceiling. There was one bronze bell hanging in the middle of the room. There was another at the door and another on the corner before the stairs. She would not be able to use her voice even if she wanted to.

"Your boy stares at me when he thinks I do not see him," she continued.

I saw her eyes flit to another corner of the room for a brief moment. Looking over my shoulder, I saw David just coming downstairs to sit with a couple of my men. He slouched into a chair, looking defeated.

"He's conflicted. His father was killed by sirens and he was saved by one," I said.

"Are you conflicted?"

It took me a few seconds to speak. Not because I didn't know what to say. I knew exactly what to say. I only wondered if I should.

"More than I have been in a very long time."

She looked up at me, her gaze searching. I felt split open under her scrutiny. I felt naked and skinned and somehow, it did not bother me. Her eyes bore into me like knives, but I felt as if there was very little there that she had not already seen. Just like I was beginning to think I'd seen most of her. Of all the people in our lives, we hated each other the most, but we knew each other the best.

It was a disturbing revelation to know you related to your enemy more than your loved ones.

"I do not want to leave Meridan in the water for long," she said, breaking our silence. "She refuses to come ashore."

"We are leaving soon. I think my men are fed and rested by now."

She nodded and turned from the bar. Even her mannerisms had become human. That predatory sheen in her face was gone. That squared posture was relaxed. She was so good at pretending.

Before she walked away, she turned one last time, leaning a bit closer to me as she spoke.

"Thank you. For offering me what I needed last night and not thinking me too disgusting to give it to me."

You're not disgusting.

I was unsure where that thought had come from, but it was immediate. I turned my head to look at her, realizing just how close she was to me. I could feel her breath on my chin. Smell rain and salt in her hair. I clenched my jaw, trying to stop more images from the previous night from breaching my thoughts. We both needed something and we gave each other the opportunity to take it. It was nothing more than that...

The sound of many footsteps coming down the stairs drew both our gazes. Turning, I saw Thelasa and the girls emerging from the inn upstairs to have a bite to eat. The little one saw Dahlia and her solemn face turned downward. Hesitantly, Dahlia veered in another direction, avoiding her.

My eyes lifted to see Gus staring at me, his one eye narrowed. The old man didn't miss much and I was sure he'd caught on to the way I was looking at Dahlia. I couldn't blame him for being cautious because I knew how I was looking at her, too.

And I sure as hell wasn't looking at her like the enemy that morning.

33

Dahlia

*A sorrow never felt
is a disease never cured
~The Wanderer*

I stood at the edge of a rickety dock where it was clear boats no longer came. While Vidar and his men loaded up fresh supplies onto the Rose, I stood looking out into the gently rolling waves. Thelasa had given me an old dress of hers and being so tightly cinched into the heavy fabric was making me a little irritable, but she insisted. She gave me a strange speech about not proving her wrong and not breaking her trust, but I didn't hear all of it. I was mostly focused on the way she touched me without fear.

People didn't do that.

If they lived long enough to know what I was, they usually looked at me with hate, disgust, or dread. Perhaps Thelasa had been a little shaky when she handed the dress to me, but she covered her fear well. I half expected the dress to have been soaked in hemsbane, but the fibers were clean.

When I finally spotted Meridan's ghostly silhouette beneath the water, I straightened. Her head breached the surface and her white eyes fixed on me. There was a sense of bitterness in the way she ogled my dress like I was wearing the skin of our own people. As she drifted toward the dock, she lifted her head fully from the water and pursed her full lips with disappointment.

"Are you one of them now?" she muttered.

I knelt on the dock's edge and hung my feet over. I had removed my shoes as soon as Thelasa walked away and hid them in a corner. I hated the feel of shoes. And it made shifting that much more tedious. Feeling the cold water around my ankles soothed my dry skin.

"The tavern woman simply gave me the dress to make her feel less uneasy in my presence," I sighed. "I suppose it does make me look eerily human."

"Human. And ugly."

I snorted at her comment as she rested her elbows on the dock beside me.

"What's going on?"

"We're leaving. Vidar swears we're not long for the shores where the girls were taken."

"Well, the waters are quiet at the very least. I've been keeping to the grottos, but even so, I've not heard the xhoth since we arrived."

"They're busy gorging on that other crew, I'm sure."

The horrifying thought that I was nearly devoured alongside the men came to me and I shivered. It must have been more visible than I thought because Meridan raised her head, alert.

"What is it?" she asked.

There were many things I wanted to say. She didn't know what happened between Vidar and me and I feared what she would think if I told her. What we did the previous night was beyond the game of manipulation I was playing. I went to him selfishly, in need of relief. Of pain. Of feeling. I hadn't tried to manipulate him. I simply offered myself in hopes that he'd accept, and he did.

No, I was not going to tell her about that yet.

But I had much more to say and it was eating at me.

"I hear them," I said.

Her brows furrowed. "Now?"

"No. I mean, I hear their words. Their voice." I looked at her, catching her gaze. "In my dreams. They're calling to me, Meridan, and I don't know why."

"Our people… they go to the depths and they come back with child or—"

"I know. I know what going to them will do to me. If they choose not to tear me apart, I'll return with no shred of myself left. So my choices are death or madness. I can only…" I choked on my words, trying not to sound as broken as I was. "I will never see the light again, whether I return or not. I will never know freedom and they will never grant me the relief of death. It is the only hell I will not stand for. I will die before then."

She reached out and grabbed my hand, squeezing it in her long, bony fingers.

"I will not let them have you."

"You cannot stop them. And I don't expect you to."

"Then what will you do? Being in the water is more dangerous than ever if the father has set his eyes on you."

"Then I must not go in the water."

She tore her hand away as if she'd burned herself. "You cannot stay forever on land."

"Then I have nowhere."

When I arrived at the dock where the men were loading themselves into a boat, I saw Meridan's pale silhouette heading for the Rose. I picked up my thick skirts and stepped toward the edge of the dock when a hand appeared in front of me. I looked up to see Gus offering to help me step down. I swallowed, wondering if he might just pull me onto a blade the moment I accepted his help.

But then… would that be the worst thing?

I slowly placed my hand in his, feeling all of his rough callouses rub against my fingers, and stepped down into the boat. I was getting strange looks from all the men, but not hateful ones. Not anymore. I wasn't sure how to take it.

I sat down and glimpsed Vidar at the head of the boat coiling a long length of rope as the men began to row. It was strange not being in the water with Meridan, but the beckoning from the sons had planted seeds in me that I was not used to feeling. I feared the water now. I'd been afraid of things before, but never like that.

Fearing men and monsters was one thing. Fearing my own madness was another.

When we arrived at the ship, I found that climbing the ladders in a dress was not an easy task. I felt like I was wrapped in kelp. I finally reached the railing to find Vidar there with another helping hand. I hesitated even longer that time, unsure what to do with that kindness. Or whatever he intended it to be. I took his hand nonetheless, swinging a leg over only to get myself even more tangled up in the fabric. I stumbled a bit to get on board and quickly righted myself, pulling my hand out of Vidar's.

"The girls are below deck putting out their new bedding from Thelasa," he said. His eyes skimmed over me and my troublesome dress. "No need to wear that here. You're not trying to impress anyone."

I stepped away from him with a single nod and waited by the railing as the last of the men boarded. Once the jolly boat was secured, the men all began dispersing to their duties. The sails were dropped. The anchor was raised. Words were exchanged. It was almost another language the way Vidar barked orders, helping with things around the ship to get her prepared to sail.

I made myself scarce, walking to the far end of the deck as men moved about, but no matter where I went or what the men were doing, my eyes found Vidar again and again. He removed his coat almost as soon as he came aboard and he'd rolled the sleeves of his loose, cotton shirt up to his elbows, showing off leather cuffs and jewelry and a forearm tattoo that looked like a tentacled sea beast. I glimpsed the leather bracer laced to his right forearm, securing false fingers where real ones used to be, and was reminded of our brutal past.

But it seemed less significant that day.

He was moving large sacks of beans down into the kitchen. The way he slung one sack over his shoulder and held another in his hand made my blood warm.

How he touched me the previous night still burned on my skin. My lips still tingled and my tongue still tasted of him. It should not have been that way. I had intended—I had hoped—to get what I needed from him and be done with it, but he'd left marks on me. Marks I could still feel. Marks that were not just on the surface where they could be seen.

I'd been foolish. There was not one person in the world that I had ever been truly vulnerable with. Not Meridan or Voel or Kea. Not my mother or my other sisters. And yet some broken part of me sought out Vidar when I was at my weakest and I let him see me stripped to the core.

Pain and punishment had been my salvation before. Guilt followed me like a parasite, choking the will to exist right out of my soul. I craved pain. I needed to hurt for all that I'd done or failed to do. I couldn't do it myself. Every time I tried, I found I was a coward. A part of me prayed someone else would end it so I did not have to.

And then I saw Vidar on the edge of that lake, the black cloud of sorrow and regret hovering just as thick over his head as it was above mine. I was drawn to it. Admittedly, I sought it out, thinking perhaps if he was just as wounded as I was then he'd be more inclined to do something so outrageous as touching me.

If I could not punish myself, I trusted he could. And he did. I laid myself open to him, stripped of pride, of armor, begging for relief. He was a cruel man and I needed cruel hands to absolve me.

And when he put his hands on me, the sting of agony and the threat of obliteration was as sweet as I imagined it would be. I felt all my hate and torment pouring out of me and relieving the pressure that had been crushing me for so long. Every time his belt met my skin, my tears brought me closer to peace. Every time he squeezed my throat, I found my mind empty of the torturous voices. And when it ended in dizzying pleasure, it was as if something was finally right with me.

Just thinking of it all again sent a chill through me. I shivered as Vidar reemerged from below deck, picking up another load of heavy materials to bring to its rightful place. The chills tickling my skin became heat. A prominent heat that coursed through me, touching all the places it shouldn't have.

I was falling apart. Glimpsing Vidar's bracer again reminded me who we were. We were not friends. We were not partners. We were two people who had hurt each other in ways no one could come back from.

Slowly, as Vidar disappeared below deck again, I lifted my fingers to my cheek and gently traced the long scar from the corner of my mouth to my ear.

I couldn't forget who we were. What we'd done. One night of tormented desire couldn't change that.

When I saw Meridan's white figure slink over the railing, naked and soaking wet, I started toward her. The men noticed and I saw sneers on the faces of some, but for the most part, they consciously were looking away. When she saw me approaching, she folded her arms over herself and turned to retreat to our quarters, which was still the holding cell, where she could cover herself up. I followed her, eager to get out of my corseted dress.

The Rose was on its way. Meridan helped me out of my dress so we could get comfortable. She pulled on a thin shift with long sleeves and I slipped into a pair of drawstring pants and a shirt and belt again. By midday, the island was out of view and we were once more in the open ocean. The sea was anything but safe, for siren or man, and the crew had their eyes peeled for anything breaching the surface. Bored, I decided to help and stood out on the foredeck, watching the waves for threats as the hours passed. Unable to stand the light for long, Meridan stayed in the hold, making the space as comfortable as possible using whatever new supplies we were allowed.

When shifts changed, I stayed put, pacing slowly from one place to another until I saw Gus walk out and sit on a water barrel with his pipe.

He glanced at me, but his eyes didn't linger as he started to blow smoke rings into the breeze. With the sun out and the clouds thin, he seemed to be enjoying the warmth for a while as he rested his old bones. I glimpsed him from time to time, my mind turning. Every now and then, he caught me looking at him and I wondered what he thought of me. I knew Vidar's father was close to him. I knew the slaughter of his crew had affected him like it did Vidar. I knew he was a hunter like the rest of them, ruthless and fierce despite his frail age.

He probably hated me.

But I was used to being hated.

I turned and started walking in his direction. When he saw me coming, he barely paused smoking his pipe.

"Gus," I greeted.

"Dahlia."

I took a deep breath and kicked an empty wooden crate over to sit on it.

"There a reason you're filling this space with your presence?" he asked, his tone solidifying my suspicion that he hated me.

"Yes. I have a favor to ask."

"Ask away. Don't mean I'll grant it."

It was fair. I didn't expect anything much from him.

"You speak to the girls," I said. "You understand their language."

"I understand enough."

Sakari lying on that ship's deck, her head bleeding and her body limp, flashed across my mind. I swiped it aside, trying to focus on what I wanted.

"How do you say, 'I'm sorry'?" I asked.

Gus paused, resting his pipe hand on his stomach as he blew out a breath. He wrinkled his forehead like he didn't think I was done with my sentence. Then his face softened.

"Oweh," he said softly.

"Oweh," I repeated.

He shifted his weight with a groan. "Oweh tia paloei."

"Oweh tia paloei."

He nodded and cleared his throat as if a little uncomfortable. "I'm sorry. For your aunt. That's what it means. I'm sorry for aunt, actually. Don't know how to say 'your.'"

I blinked at the fact that he knew my intentions. When our eyes met, he looked a little defeated. He slumped back against the wall, pulling in a lungful of smoke.

"You know, either you're the best actress I've ever seen, which isn't too far-fetched for your kind, or you truly care for those girls. What I can't figure out is why."

I hesitated, watching one of his smoke rings float away and dissipate.

"I believe I was caught in the middle of a war I did not want to fight when I was a girl," I said. "And it turned me into a horrible monster."

Gus slowly nodded his head, coming to understand my meaning. Luckily, he didn't push it further. I wasn't sure I could truly explain my motives even if I wanted to.

"Boil made beans and pork," he exhaled. "Should get the meat while we have it. I hear pork tastes like humans."

I raised a brow at his comment and then rolled my eyes. "Humans are greasier."

He paused mid-breath to stare at me and then, the slightest hint of a smile graced his lips and I couldn't believe the sight. The joke was morbid, but amusing in some darkly satisfying way. Still, it was Gus. I shook my head and moved to retake my place near the railing for a few hours more.

"Thank you," I muttered as I walked away.

When my few hours were up and the night was thoroughly upon us, I ventured down into the hold where Meridan was picking at a plate of food.

"Food's bland," she said.

I shrugged. "And what would you call what we usually eat?"

We both half-smiled with amusement as I continued to the other cabins. In the largest of the divisions was a space full of beds and hammocks where half the men were already napping while others took shifts around the ship. Further in was a smaller cargo room where bedding had been laid out for the girls. I slowly headed toward it to find most of the girls already sleeping, but Ahnah was awake, her fingers black with charcoal as she sketched designs on a piece of paper. She had a few other pictures spread out around her on the floor. Someone had given her supplies to draw and she was fully taking advantage.

She looked up at me with a sad, flat look on her young face. She no longer smiled when she saw me and it broke what little was left of my heart in two. I wasn't too sure if I was even welcome around her. I was the last one to see her aunt. We were both taken and only I returned. I couldn't imagine what was going through her head.

"Ahnah," I muttered.

She sat back from her drawing and folded her legs beneath her, wiping her blackened fingers on her skirts. I stepped closer, sitting down on the floor and leaning against the opposite wall.

"I wish we could understand each other," I said. "So I can tell you how truly sorry I am. Oweh." Her eyes fluttered up toward me. "Tia paloei. For Sakari. Oweh."

Little glistening tears formed in her big eyes as the words reached her. She stared at me, her lips slowly parting, and blinked, letting a couple of those tears trickle down her cheeks. And then she stooped forward and crawled on her hands and knees toward me, curling herself up in my lap. I stiffened at first, but when I realized she was crying, I couldn't help myself. I wrapped my arms around her and I squeezed, pulling her close.

I'd failed her. I wasn't sure if she really knew it, but I had and I hated myself for it. But I wouldn't fail her again. I would see her home. I would see her removed from the horror and death that haunted the water like I wished someone would have saved me as a child.

As Ahnah wept quietly against my chest, Meridan found her way to us. I found her staring quietly at the weeping girl in my arms, her head cocked. Maybe she agreed with my need to be with Ahnah. Maybe she didn't. But then she locked eyes with me and gave me the subtlest nod of approval. I didn't want to be at odds with my only remaining sister and the only person I could trust. That acceptance was everything.

Meridan left me there with Ahnah that night. Uncomfortable as I was against that wooden wall with no bedding for my bones, I didn't want to be anywhere else. I couldn't imagine it. I felt my own sadness in Ahnah that night and I'd wished a thousand times before that someone—anyone—would cradle me while I felt it.

I had never been allowed to feel it. To feel was practically a crime. I'd never gotten the chance to let it pass through me. It simply remained, growing and rotting and killing me. Now, I was a husk of the child I was and all I could do was feel that lost sorrow through Ahnah's tears. And it was there in our shared pain that I found sleep.

Until those horrendous, toxic tones found their way into my slumber like the barbs of a sea urchin. Wet fingers gripped me, pulling me somewhere I didn't want to go. All was black and I felt the pressure of the deep sea squeezing my lungs.

Was it real or was it a dream? Was Ahnah still in my arms?

Meridan, I called out, finding I had no voice. *Meridan!*

Father is hungry, Dahlia, said a deep, unnatural voice.

Those fingers touched me everywhere. My arms. My face. They slid into my mouth. Into my throat. They gripped my jaw and pried apart my teeth. They ventured lower, finding places I desperately didn't want them to find. And yet it was still dark. Cold. Stifling. I screamed, but no voice came out. I wanted to move, but nothing happened. I felt their cold presence in my bones. In my stomach. In my lungs. In my womb.

I needed someone to hear me. Terror crashed through me like a wave of burning flames and his name rolled from my tongue in a panic.

Vidar!

34

Vidar

What we love most goes unrealized
Until we've lost it and know not what to do
~ Lady Madeline

It was late in the night when I finally settled in my cabin. Sleep did not come easy with the images of those vile creatures devouring Collin's crew like a swarm of ravenous sharks. The seas had become twice as dangerous with their presence.

But they were not the only things haunting my thoughts. I found myself lying on my bed and staring at lines of moonlight from my window. The clear skies were unusual and welcome that night. Seeing the blue light on my walls made me think of Dahlia's pale skin, though, and the brilliant, dangerous grey color of her eyes.

I found myself trying to sleep with visions of her behind my lids and the sound of her voice in my ears. Dahlia, who'd haunted me since I was a boy only possessed me as an adult. I hadn't escaped her. I wondered if I ever would.

The deeper I fell into sleep, the more she took up space my thoughts. I could hear her breathing as if she were lying beside me and somehow, it lulled me into a deeper slumber. Each time I took a breath, she let one out. And as I exhaled, she breathed in. My heart slowed and I felt my body melting into my bedding as the ship rocked upon mild-mannered waves.

Please, whispered a voice. Her voice. *I'm afraid.*

I was partially conscious, my mind floating between dreams and reality and the voice felt the same. It felt like a ghost.

Vidar, she said, her voice a soft whimper. *Please. Help me.*

I opened my eyes to the sound of crashing waves and rolling thunder. I was on that black sand beach, soaked to the bone by pounding rain. I rose to my feet, a stabbing chill coursing through my blood. I could barely see. The chaos came so abruptly. Waves pummeled the sharp stones further down the beach, sending icy sea spray into the air.

"What the fuck," I hissed.

It was a dream. I knew it was a dream.

How did I know it was a dream?

I needed to wake up.

A large wave hit the beach, pushing a flood of water onto the sand until it reached my knees. I fought the current and moved further up, trying to see through the raging downpour.

"Vidar!"

Dahlia's scream was shrill and full of distress. I spun around to see darkness so black it was like a curtain. From it emerged Dahlia in a pure white dress, her face twisted with panic. She rushed forward as if in retreat and crashed into me, clinging to my body like I was her only anchor. But as quickly as she reached me, she was torn away. Her body was yanked to the ground at my feet and suddenly dragged back toward the darkness. She cried out, clawing at the sand.

I sprinted after her. She reached out to me and I dove, barely brushing my fingers against hers before the darkness swallowed her like a hungry beast.

I woke with a jolt, nearly choking on my own breath. My room was around me again. The ship was rocking more noticeably as if the water had become angrier.

Something was wrong. Something I could feel in my chest like the pain of a thousand losses had suddenly bubbled to the surface again. And one loss was yet to come. I jumped up and rushed clumsily for my door, emerging on deck and into the night. Nothing seemed amiss. Nothing but the figure walking to the edge of the ship as if she meant to jump into the cold water.

"Dahlia," I said.

She did not hear me. Or she did not care.

"Dahlia!" I called out.

The few men keeping a lookout turned at the sound of my voice as I headed toward her.

"Cap'n?" someone said.

The urgency was mine. No one else felt it.

Dahlia reached the railing and swung a leg over, absently moving her body toward the water.

"Stop her!"

My men were confused. Too confused to act. I rushed toward her as her feet left the ledge and wrapped an arm around her waist, pulling her against me. Her body went rigid as I hoisted her back over the railing. I fell backward, grunting when her weight slammed into me. Suddenly she was flailing.

"Dahlia," I said.

She was panting as she rolled over to get away. Only then did I see the knife in her hand. She spun toward me, straddling me as she raised it over my chest. I could hear my men pulling their blades and pistols.

"No!" Meridan screamed nearby.

"Don't!" I ordered my men, reaching up to grab at both of Dahlia's wrists.

She snarled as I tossed her to the side and restrained her beneath me. Meridan rushed in to pry the knife out of Dahlia's hand and was quick to step away again, a look of shock on her pale face.

"Dahlia, wake up!" she screamed.

She craned her head to look up at her friend, tears shining in her eyes. "Meridan, please," she begged.

"What's happening?" I said.

"She cannot go in the water," is all she managed to say before I'd had enough.

I stood, pulling Dahlia off the floor with one heave and tossing her over my shoulder.

"It is not her fault," Meridan said after me as I hauled her down toward the hold. "Please, do not hurt her!"

"I will not hurt her."

I arrived at the hold and took Dahlia inside, laying her down on the bedding she and Meridan had made up for themselves. When I looked back, Meridan was standing outside the gate, hesitant.

"You may stay with her or not, but I'm locking this gate tonight."

She nodded and took a step back, confirming she didn't want to stay inside the cell. I wasn't sure if that was because she didn't want to be locked up or if she was afraid, but the look on her face suggested Dahlia's behavior had unsettled her.

Dahlia, like a tired child, curled up against the wall and pressed her hands to her ears as I stepped out. Though, in truth, part of me wanted to stay. She looked in pain and not the kind of pain we both were used to. Locking the gate behind me, I turned to Meridan, who was staring at her friend like she was dying.

"Explain," I said.

"You won't understand."

"Do your best."

She took a deep breath and sighed, hugging herself with her arms. I hated the timid way they were both acting. If sirens were so afraid, it couldn't mean anything good for us men.

"She explained how the sons work to you."

"Yes. They call you down to breed is what I gathered."

"To breed. To break us. Like men without silentiums, we sirens cannot resist when they summon us into the depths."

"So they're calling her? Why now?"

"Why ever? No one knows. We are at the sons' mercy. At the father's mercy. Piling pirates and sailors on an island in hopes of satiating their appetites could never work forever. They feed on *us*. She is Reyna's daughter. Reyna bore many children with three journeys to the deep. The father favored her. It was only a matter of time before the sons took notice of Dahlia."

"Dahlia has sisters."

Meridan nodded. "Ligeia remains. Poel went to the depths and never returned. The others disappeared years ago like many others. And unlike some of those zealots, she doesn't want to go to go down there."

"Why would anyone want to go?"

"The Kroan especially dedicate themselves to the father. They're more religious than most. Some prepare their whole lives to give themselves to him in whatever way he pleases, but many fear him and his sons as we do."

"You call serving these creatures a religion?"

"There are some that don't believe in Akareth. So, yes."

"Do you believe in him?"

"I've seen enough to know *something* is down there that changes us. Once returned, something is forever missing. The returned feel nothing. It is said that looking upon the face of Akareth will tear the mind and soul apart and while some see it as a great cleansing, others fear it. And perhaps it is because Dahlia has never been down there that she is still as kind-hearted as she is, even when her sympathies got her people killed. When a child of Akareth grows in a woman's womb, it creates a hole that cannot be refilled and we are tricked into thinking we are stronger for it. That the empty space is for the father. In truth, I believe every mother resents her child for what she lost."

"Do all sirens believe this?"

"No. But her people did. Do you ever wonder why it is the Kroan of all sirens that choose to meet you in every battle? They are bloodthirsty and broken creatures. They are the closest to Akareth in spirit, it is said." Her eyes turned to the semi-conscious Dahlia. "She has a sliver of light in her that you should be very glad still exists. None existed in her mother. She had only enough room in her soul to care for Dahlia in the end. And I believe even that is something Dahlia's been lying to herself about her whole life."

Everything she said chilled me. I realized my understanding of her people was not nearly as sound as I had believed it to be.

"Have you been down there?"

"There'd be no mercy in me if I had, Vidar. Though, sometimes I think being stripped of feeling would be easier."

"You truly believe that? Would you go down there if you were called?"

She paused, narrowing her eyes at me. "I don't believe I'll be called. I am different."

"How?"

"My father was human."

I had to repeat those words a few times in my head to truly hear them.

"Your father was human? How is that possible?"

"I don't know, but to my people, I'm nothing. To Dahlia, I am family. I don't want to see her get pulled into the darkness."

A stretch of silence grew between us as our eyes wandered back to Dahlia lying in the cell. She was quiet now, but I knew she was not sleeping by the way her fingers slowly played in her hair.

"How do we help her?"

"I don't know," Meridan said solemnly. "I've never known anyone to even try to resist Akareth, let alone succeed in escaping him."

"Then it may not be impossible."

Meridan glanced up at me, her eyes wide and unblinking as if she couldn't believe her ears.

"You want to help her," she finally asked. "Why?"

"Helping her helps me. These past days have proven that."

Madness is the monster come
to eat the things you love
~Marcus Crow

I felt hollow sitting alone in that cell. The air had grown severely cold in the days passing so I knew we were in a very different place. Not even Meridan had come to see me since first greeting me the moment I opened my eyes and I suspected it was because she was afraid. Neither of us enjoyed the idea of disappearing into an abyss only to return as something not ourselves. Seeing me out of control must have spooked her. All our pain and suffering could not be traded for a farse of a life. A false mind. Going to Akareth meant I would never be the same and even death was better than that fate.

When I heard heavy boots descending down the steps, I turned to see Vidar approaching the cell with a tight bundle of clothing under his arm. He looked surprised to see me awake and paused before coming closer to the bars. I wasn't sure what he'd seen or how exactly things played out. I only knew what Meridan told me. I had attempted to go into the water before Vidar pulled me back and I drew my knife on him.

Faint echoes of my cries for help were the only other thing I remembered.

Vidar leaned against the gate and hung his hand through the bars, regarding me thoroughly. There was an empty plate of food in front of me that I'd forced myself to eat in hopes that it would fill the void I could feel growing inside, but it did nothing.

"We're getting close to shore," Vidar said. "One of the girls spotted a landmark, so we're heading that way."

He pulled a keyring off his belt and raised it toward the lock.

"Should you do that?" I muttered.

His eyes met mine and he paused. "Meridan says it's unlikely the sons will come this far north."

"They're from the deep. I assure you, the waters where they're from are just as frigid. The cold will not dissuade them."

"Have you heard them the past couple days? Or felt them? I'm not quite sure how it all works."

I shook my head and immediately, he slid the key into the lock and twisted. He pulled the gate open and stepped inside the cell with me, motioning for me to stand. On strangely sore legs, I got to my feet as he unrolled what I could now tell was a leather coat with a hood. Our eyes met for a moment and behind both our gazes were words we could not say. I felt them hanging in the air, silent and restless.

"Turn around," he finally said.

Slowly, I turned so my back was to him and he maneuvered the coat over my arms. It was heavy and thick and smelled like oak and rum. Like Vidar. When I faced him again, he casually adjusted the front of the coat, slipping two of the wooden buttons on the front into their respective loops.

"You don't have to do that," I said.

I huffed a sigh. "Do you even need a coat?"

He was avoiding eye contact when he said it.

"It helps," I said.

"I haven't known you to feel warm, Dahlia. Your blood seems to run cold."

"Our warmth is deeper. Less obvious. But it's there."

His eyes met mine, a struggle raging behind his irises. His brow was taut and I could see the tiny muscles in his jaw pulsing. I desperately wanted to know what he wasn't saying, but I had no right to force it from him when I was withholding something, too.

"Captain!" someone called from above.

Both of us turned away and began heading up the steps. Men were jogging to the railing on either side of the ship and peering over into the water. Among them was Meridan. When she saw me, she gave me a subtle smile as if she were ashamed. I shook my head, hoping she knew she was blameless. I knew tossing me in that cell was best and I did not hate her for not wanting to see me through the worst of it. I would have barely noticed her presence anyway. Over the last few days, I was so far from myself with the incessant voices in my head that I could barely recall how much time had passed.

I strode toward her and we both walked to the railing to see what was going on.

Below, the water was littered with thin slats of white ice. The Rose easily navigated through it, but it wasn't the ice the men were staring at. It was the shapes beneath it.

Ghost-like in color, the figures darted in and out of sight alongside the ship. I counted four of them. They stayed submerged, deep enough that nets would not snag them. Swimming with them was a pod of strange whales, all white with gray spots. As they breached the surface, water sprayed upward into the air, misting the ship.

"They're so beautiful," Meridan muttered.

Vidar turned to us. "Have you never seen them before?"

We both shook our heads.

"The Maruhk do not leave the ice," I said. "That's why we call them 'coldfins.'"

"They've likely never seen sirens like us before, either," Meridan added.

Suddenly, a few of the girls ran up to the railing, smiling as they pointed into the water. Every man on the boat turned to ogle at their enjoyment, confused.

"God help us," Gus groaned. "They're calling them 'sea angels.'"

I recalled what Kea said when we first encountered the girls, but I still couldn't quite wrap my head around a culture that saw sirens as anything more than a deadly threat. I'd been fighting humans since I was a child and my mother had been fighting them since she was a child. Generations of sirens and humans did nothing but kill each other. And now I was watching the young girls being giddy over the sight of a small group that didn't even want to come to the surface.

Uther slammed a fist against the railing and pulled out his pistol. Vidar quickly waved him off.

"Put it away, Uther," he commanded.

It took a moment for him to comply and when he did, he was not happy about it. His eyes flicked to me as if he wanted to turn his aggression my way, but then he finally conceded and paced to the other side of the ship. With him were three others that did not seem to be enjoying the journey or the company.

I looked up at Vidar and could tell the exact same thoughts were going through his head. He and his crew were fighting generations of killer instincts as they watched the skryll swim alongside the Rose. The ship was full of harpoons, nets, and canons, and yet they weren't using any.

I was sure it was killing them.

When Vidar met my gaze, there was so much there that I still didn't understand, despite having walked in his dreams for many days. But, for once, his hatred was buried beneath a need to see things through. A need to finish what we'd started.

Hours passed. The sun was slowly descending toward the western horizon and the Rose was taking a beating from ice that was floating in patches on the water. We could see land on either side of the ship, salted with snow and frost. Mountains stood as tall as the clouds on one side and before the day had ended, one of those mountains stood out to us. It was oddly shaped with a flat top and a massive cave entrance at the base. The girls moved to the foredeck, pointing.

Vidar and I exchanged another look Ahnah ran toward me and took my hand. She tugged me toward the front of the ship, speaking with excitement as she gestured toward land. It wasn't hard to tell that we'd made it to their home. The girls were practically crying.

The sun was growing ever closer to the horizon when Vidar called to anchor just off the coast. The sirens in the water had disappeared where the water seemed placid and the wind was soft. Once the sails were up and the boat was lowered, the girls seemed almost willing to jump in the water and swim to land just to get there faster.

Vidar began naming men to accompany him to shore and included Gus seeing as he was the only one to know any amount of the girls' language. He also picked two of the oldest girls, leaving the rest to wait on the ship. Lastly, as everyone was climbing down into the boat, he turned to me with a subtle nod of his head.

"The girls trust you more than any of my men," he said.

I stepped forward, but Ahnah still had a hold of my hand and pulled me toward her. Glimpsing the look on her face, I knew she wasn't going to let me leave without her. I tossed Vidar another look and after a few seconds, he rolled his eyes and waved us both onward.

I helped Ahnah climb over the railing, making sure her short legs were secured on the ladder before I climbed over myself. Beneath her, Vidar descended the rungs slowly, making sure he was positioned well enough to keep her from falling. When we'd all piled into the boat, Ahnah was at the front with Vidar, staring longingly at the beach as it neared. Somehow, after the loss of her aunt and all the horrors she'd seen, she was still just an innocent soul inside a young skin. She was trusting. Vulnerable. Precious. I found myself staring at her with envy, wishing I could have known even a day of what it was like to be so pure. Instead, I was a canvas of violence and quarrel. Of wrong decisions and consequences.

Coming to the shore, the men rowed as close as possible to land. In the icy water, no one was about to get their feet wet prematurely. Before the boat was even on the rocks, the girls hopped out and started running inland.

"Hey!" Vidar said, jogging after them.

They were headed straight for the monstrous cave mouth which, now that we were closer, I could see light through. There was something on the other side.

We ran after them until we were swallowed by the eerie shadows of the tunnel. It felt like being in the belly of a great beast. The humidity and the smell of old water only added to the atmosphere. Our footsteps bounced off the walls of the giant, hollow space, creating a ruckus. The men fell silent. Some of them rested their hands on their weapon belts as if they thought something might leap out and devour us all.

Beneath us, the muddy ground was trampled and firm. Footprints were smashed into the soil along a very particular path and when I looked up at the walls, I forced my eyes to adjust to the near darkness to see carvings etched into the black stone. Drawings of animals. Men. The sun and moon. Water. And, unsurprisingly, sirens, their fins long and slender. They were carved out in groups. As we walked onward, more images filled the walls. Sirens and men meeting at the water's edge. Men fighting giant beasts. Men in boats. Children walking hand-in-hand.

"What is it?" Vidar said. "What can your eyes see?"

I hesitated to answer, unsure whether I wanted to. "Carvings," I said. I swallowed my fascination and turned to keep walking. "We're clearly going the right way."

The cave narrowed toward the end of the long passage until it finally opened into a vast valley framed by tall, pointed trees. The land was white as far as I could see. Mountains made the horizon look like a row of giant's teeth and a thick forest spread out along the base for what seemed like miles.

"Holy hell," Vidar sighed, watching the girls jog tiredly toward rows and rows of snow-topped cabins made of leather and wood. "We fucking made it."

"And it isn't destroyed," I said, glancing his way.

When our eyes met that time, a sense of accomplishment was shared between us. In an instant, my thoughts raced with unlikely ideas. The idea that we were enemies—that we were hateful, cruel creatures capable of little more than mindless violence—but we shared one simple goal. The bizarre feeling of being of the same mind as Vidar cracked and splintered my thoughts.

"We should see to it that their safe," he said, clearing his throat.

I nodded, straightening my shoulders to follow after the girls. As we got closer to the village, figures began to filter out from the buildings. Men. Women. Some wielded spears or daggers. Others seemed too old or too gentle for either. I caught Mullins putting his hand on his belt where his pistol was stuffed behind the leather and eyed him from behind. Vidar walked beside him and shook his head as the villagers closed in on us.

Ahnah's attention locked on an elderly woman with silver hair who walked with a limp. She sprinted toward her, breaking into tears as they met and embraced. Watching the two reunite filled me with a warmth I didn't think I was capable of feeling. I could smell their joy and relief on the chilly wind like a freshly blossomed flower. I stopped, listening as they exchanged words in their beautiful language. The other girls dispersed, finding their loved ones in the small masses of people while a row of armed men created a loose blockade between us and the village.

Gus said a few words, causing a couple of the villagers to perk up. Their eyes flitted amongst each other until a few of them lowered their weapons. Finally, one of the older girls in the group spoke up, pointing at us and speaking to our defense. At least, I assumed that was her intention when the rest of the villagers started lowering their weapons.

The elderly woman hobbled our way with Ahanh clutching her hand. There was a beauty to her serene yet wrinkled features when she wove her way through the armed men and stood before me. She stared up into my eyes, her clouded gaze examining every scar and contour of my face before a warm smile met her lips. She spoke to me in words I couldn't understand and then surprised everyone with words I could.

"Thank you," she said. She lifted her hand and slowly brought it to my face. I pulled back an inch before I let her touch me, caught off guard by the lack of fear in her. "Beautiful angel."

Never did I imagine those words would be associated with me. I stared at the woman, unable to find words to respond.

"You know our language," Vidar said.

The woman pulled back her hand and turned to him. "Yes. Some of us do."

One of the village men stepped forward, his long, deep-brown hair tied into an intricate braid. He stuck the butt of his spear in the ground and nodded.

"We have traded with outsiders before. We get seed and livestock in the cold seasons. Only…" His expression soured as he scanned Vidar's men. "The last ship to come here was unfamiliar and left with far more than we were willing to give."

"The girls," I said. They nodded. "That ship was the Cornwallis and those men are dead. Killed by my sisters and me."

The old woman smiled knowingly. "We knew the sea would protect them."

I wanted to say that wasn't the case and that she was being naïve. That the sea would have swallowed them whole if they hadn't been found by me first. Or, other sisters would have found them and gnawed the meat from their bones before letting the deep have their remains. I said none of it, though. Instead, I stayed silent, watching the village slowly relax in our presence like my existence was somehow a comfort. It was perplexing, to say the least.

"And, pirates?" the old woman said, looking over Vidar and his men.

Mullins cleared his throat. "Privateers, ma'am."

"Independent," Vidar added, hanging his thumbs on his belt.

Gus just huffed a laugh at that. "Don't think we'll be answerin' to anyone after this. Our cap'n is just a man with a damn heart is all. And I think your little ones won over more than one crewman on the Rose." He smiled down at Ahnah and she gleamed back at him.

"Our Ahnah is a gift," the woman said, her eyes glistening with unshed tears. "Which is why we are so glad to see her and these girls safe, even if it is not all we have lost."

Vidar and his men exchanged looks before Vidar said, "There are others on my ship, waiting to come ashore."

The villagers' eyes lit up, but I caught the solemn wilt in Ahnah's smile and the way her gaze slid downward like a dying flower.

"All but one," I added softly. "Sakari was lost to another crew, I'm afraid. One not as decent as…" I eyed Vidar for a second. "As the crew of the Burning Rose."

There was a short but heavy silence among us after I said those words. I hadn't expected them to come out of my mouth and neither did anyone else.

But it was true. When it came to the girls, at least.

"I am Taupek," the woman said as if sensing something needed to be said to cut the tension.

There was a deep and painful crack in her voice, though. One I was certain was tethered to the news about Sakari. I regretted my role in her passing and revisited the incident when I saw the look on Taupek's face.

"I am Ahnah's grandmother," she said.

"Sakari was your daughter?"

She shook her head. "The daughter of my late husband, but I loved her like my own. I… she will be missed."

I heard Ahnah snivel and glanced down at her wiping her eyes.

And like the coward I was, I turned away from her, seeking something else to focus on.

"The others," the man said. "Can they come ashore?"

Vidar nodded. "We can send for them now, but the weather is harsh and the journey was long. We'd be grateful for lodging and food and supplies for our journey back."

"Stay for a while," Taupek said. "We have empty lodging since one of our elders passed and their children married."

"Enough for my whole crew?"

Taupek nodded and then turned to a few of the men, speaking in their native tongue. They inclined their heads and then headed into the village.

"We will prepare food and beds," she said.

Vidar shrugged. "Then we will retrieve your girls."

I turned to accompany the men back to the ship to get the others when Vidar grabbed my arm, pulling me close.

"Stay," he said quietly. "They seem warmer to you than to us." He paused and glanced sideways at Ahnah as she and Taupek walked away. "And the little one wants your company."

"I got the woman's daughter killed," I whispered.

"You did no such thing."

I clenched my teeth, preventing any further arguments. Vidar's eyes bore into me, keeping my gaze. I realized then that his words were meant to comfort me. Comfort from Vidar was not something I ever thought I'd get. Not in that way. Slowly, I let my eyes fall to his hand around my arm and watched him gradually release me.

"Alright," I agreed. "I will stay."

36
Dahlia

Mothers know, and they whisper
"You are safe" even when the monsters
are breathing down her neck.
~ Ophelia Quin

I followed Taupek and Ahnah, watching as she spewed long sentences to her grandmother that I couldn't understand. There was a heaviness to both their tones as if they were talking about Sakari and when I heard her name uttered between them, I was certain. Taupek glanced back at me and slowed her pace even more than her limp already forced her to. I stepped up beside her as we strolled through the village. I could smell salted meat and fish among the thick scent of wood smoke.

Venturing further, I smelled something I was unfamiliar with. Something thick and musky with hints of dirt and grass. A long, square building sat off the path with a large, wooden round pen in front of it where two giant beasts leisured about nibbling dry grass. I slackened my gait at the sight of the four-legged animals.

"Horses," I whispered.

"We have eleven of them," Taupek said. "Have you not seen one before?"

"Wild ones. From a distance. Never have I seen them so close."

"You will have to visit them in the morning when you're rested."

I blinked, trying not to gawk at the creatures like a child as we passed. I had seen them before galloping across the beaches of some of the large islands. They were gorgeous things, but I'd never tried to get close. The sound of their hooves slamming against the ground was reason enough for me to keep my distance. I never imagined they were so large.

Ahnah's little voice stole me from my thoughts as she rambled to her grandmother.

"She tells me you have a companion," Taupek said.

"My sister. Meridan. She waits on the ship."

"She is welcome here."

"Why is that?" I asked, furrowing my brows. "You know what we are, yes?"

"I do. We all do."

"You would welcome a monster into—"

"Monsters are different to everyone. To you, men are monsters, yes? To a mouse, a fox is a monster."

We walked in silence for a moment as I absorbed her words. "On our way through the ice, we saw others in the water."

Taupek smiled as if the thought of the coldfins elated her and I couldn't grasp it.

"It is a great honor to see them."

"It doesn't make sense," I uttered under my breath.

"You come from a place of war controlled by the ones who can be the most ruthless. I can understand how things might seem strange to you here, but we are far from your home, are we not?"

"You seem educated for being so isolated from the world."

She sighed, placing a hand on her hip where her pain seemed to be the worst.

"I was taken a long time ago like these girls. I saw and learned many things before I found my way back here to have my first daughter."

"Ahnah's mother."

She nodded once. "She was a product of horrible acts, but I loved her just the same. Until she died and we surrendered her to the sea with many others during a great fever."

I took a deep breath and let my thoughts wander back to Kea and Voel. The pain of losing people was something every being in the world had in common, whether the loss came early or later in life.

"Here," Taupek said, gesturing toward a small cabin just off the main path. "This hut is empty."

I turned to look at her, a thank you teetering on the tip of my tongue. Instead, I just inclined my head and then glimpsed Ahnah. She gave me a shy, solemn smile and I returned it with as much subtlety.

"Sakari was like a sister to her," Taupek said. "We will have a farewell ceremony for her tomorrow when the village is fed and rested."

Ahnah muttered a few words to her grandmother and Taupek smiled.

"She wishes for you to help us prepare food. She says you're good at it."

"I carved some fish in front of her," I scoffed. "I wouldn't say I'm good at it."

"Then perhaps we will put you in charge of the fish while the rest of your people come ashore."

They turned and began walking away.

"They're not my people," I blurted. "They're… hunters."

Taupek turned back to me, her lips parted with surprise before her expression softened.

"Hunters *kill* sirens," she spoke, continuing on to another part of the village. "Are you coming?"

I was quickly put to work preparing salted fish stew and bean buns as Vidar and the others retrieved the rest of the crew. It was hours before everyone had come to shore and with them, they brought what little supplies they could spare to thank Ahnah's people for the hospitality. I watched tear-filled reunions unfold around me as everyone gathered in a longhouse at the center of the village. A large fire pit burned warmly in the center and above it were rabbit carcasses slowly cooking over the flames.

Aside from the obvious sorrow hanging over the place for those lost, the villagers seemed overjoyed to be reunited with their loved ones. Their delight filled the air with a sweet and spring-like scent that I wasn't used to. I could hardly tell who was family and who wasn't. They all seemed so close.

Glimpsing the crew of the Rose scattered throughout the gathering, I realized how similar they were in that sense. None of them were related by blood and yet they acted as if they were.

Beside me, Meridan helped pluck rosemary and chives from their stems and roots to drop into the stew. She wasn't speaking much. Of everyone, she was the most obviously inhuman. She'd been given a hooded coat with a fur trim and she kept the hood up to shadow her pale features. Despite the village being adamant that they had no ill feelings toward our kind, I could tell Meridan was uncomfortable. I kept her close, hoping my presence would sooth her.

Food was divvied out among all those present and everyone enjoyed it with full appreciation. It was the best food I'd had in a long time. Even Port Devlin's bread and stew could not compare. Quiet conversation filled the house, but the gathering was far from being a celebration. Many were sad. Some of the girls learned their loved ones did not survive the attack that took them from their home and things seemed quite downhearted. But the relief I saw because they were home was worth the struggles we endured to get them there. It had given me a sense of purpose that I didn't think I was missing.

The night moved swiftly. Most ate their fill and surrendered to exhaustion or retreated to corners where the villagers set up fur-covered cots for people to sleep. The longhouse grew quiet save for snoring and the crackling of the fires and torches. The leftover bones and scraps were given to a few wolfish looking dogs that seemed to roam the outdoors like wild pets and a majority of the villagers dispersed to their homes.

A few of the stronger men stayed in the longhouse and by the weapons tucked in their belts, it wasn't to be social. They were subtly keeping watch. As much as the girls vouched for us, we were still strangers and Vidar's crew looked like any other pirate crew.

I was sitting at a table sipping tea from a bone cup with Meridan for a while before she walked off without me. She seemed deep in her thoughts and as someone who knew the feeling, I didn't want to intrude. I stayed at the table watching the room in silence until Ahnah strode up to me and sat by my side. She didn't say anything. She just rubbed her tired eyes, attempted to smile, and fall to sleep with her head on the table. It didn't take long for Taupek to appear with another young lady to take Ahnah to bed.

Rather than follow her granddaughter to their cabin, she stood beside me, her hands tucked into the furry sleeves of her coat.

"She adores you," she said.

I lifted my cup to my lips and took a sip of tea. "I was nothing like the sirens you're used to when she first saw me. I have no idea why she's taken a liking."

Taupek sighed and sat down on the wooden bench, perching an elbow on the table.

"This place has seen more violence than we'd like to admit. We've rebuilt many times."

"Pirates?"

"Sometimes. Other times, neighboring tribes. We are separated from the world, but we know it's a cruel place. Sometimes that cruelty finds its way here. Ahnah is young, but she understands what evil looks like. She must not see evil in you."

"My soul is darker than you know."

"Darkness and evil are different."

"The things I've done—"

"You brought our girls back," she cut me off. "I do not care what you've done, Dahlia. We thought them dead before today."

A splash of warmth touched my heart at those words. I knew what I was. Who I was. I thought I did, at least. I thought I understood my place in the world, among men and sirens, but evidently, I knew nothing.

Or perhaps I was being made a fool for questioning it.

"I am old," Taupek continued. "I must rest. You should, too. Your journey has been long."

"I am not tired."

She stood with a groan, her old joints creaking. "Then perhaps a dip in our spring will help. I find the warmer water soothes the joints and the mind. It's down the path just past the bend."

A comforting bath was the last thing on my mind. Relaxing was a luxury I hardly deserved, but once the longhouse became too noisy with the heavy breathing of passed-out sailors, I decided to leave. I strolled toward the cabin I'd been given where I suspected Meridan was already trying to sleep, but once I reached it, I surpassed its door and continued down the trail. At first, it was just to think and be alone. It was a long walk, but I enjoyed it. Even in the cold, it was peaceful. If I happened upon a spring, I would take it as a sign that I needed the time alone.

I strolled for some time, wondering if there was an end to the road when the air started to smell warm with the scent of salt and stone. I realized I had indeed managed to walk all the way to the spring. I would not have gone in if I didn't also sense something else. *Someone* else. Someone I barely saw at the gathering in the longhouse. I could smell the rum and oak of his clothes and hear the steady patter of his heartbeat. He was alone.

I headed around a tall wall of rocks, following a few torches that were lodged in the ground. Turning the corner, I saw a wonderful pool framed by slick rocks and green, thriving plant life. As soon as I stepped onto the warm stone surrounding the water, I was hit with another whiff of his intoxicating scent.

In the haze of steam coming off the pool, a figure stood hip-deep in the spring. I could see the muscular plain of his back and his broad shoulders and the scars that decorated his tanned skin. His golden dreadlocks were pulled back with a leather string as he leisurely scrubbed days' worth of sweat and salty sea air from his body.

I stood at the corner of the wall and watched him through the thin vapor as he bathed. Cocking my head, I wondered when he would notice me only to hear him chuckle at my presence and turn.

"The way you're looking at me doesn't seem nearly as murderous as I'm used to," he said, his deep voice filling the space.

I took a long breath of the air infused with Vidar's distinct scent. I stepped forward and slid my leather boots off my feet, setting them aside. As Vidar continued to run his hands over his wet skin, he watched me and I began to undress until I was naked before him.

A set of natural stone steps led into the water. Slowly I descended them, letting the spring warm my cool blood. It wasn't hot, but in that frigid place, it was a wonderful feeling. Sinking down to my neck, I pushed off and swam to the other side of the large pool, dunking my head beneath the water to saturate my hair. When I came up, Vidar was still casually watching me as I leaned up against the stone opposite him. A crack in the clouds above let Lune through to illuminate the clearing and the beam cast a pillar of light right in the middle of the water. Vidar stepped forward into the center of it and I was struck with an infuriating sense of lust.

"Does your change call to you in the water?" he asked, sinking down so he too was submerged in the spring.

"It calls to me on land," I admitted.

"Do you want to change now? In my presence?"

"I would not subject you to the pleasure of watching me squirm," I said. "It is not pleasant. We are two creatures in one skin. From one form to the other, it is like being cut down the middle only to be turned inside out. For a split second, it feels as if all my guts and insides are outside, there for the taking."

"And yet your kind take to land as if it is nothing."

"Pain is something all creatures have in common. We are born screaming. We die screaming. Enduring through life only prepares us for the excruciating end."

"Then why do you fear the xhoth?"

I paused, taking a breath to calm the nerves he'd agitated.

"The sons do not just hurt us. They transform us into things that are soulless. I am tortured by my pain and my hatred and fury. By you. But my mind has remained my own. Madness has not gripped me, or so I think, but if I surrender to the deep, I will be lost. I have fought too hard not to become…" I stopped for a beat, tasting the bitterness of my words before I said them. "My mother."

"I thought you loved your mother."

I took a deep breath, watching the light dance on the ripples of the cloudy pool.

"Have you ever heard a whale cry out beneath the water, captain?" I said, my memories moving like waves before my eyes. "When they see their young killed, there is a certain tone in their song. In the water, it is not just a sound. It is a feeling that crashes through you. You can feel it in your bones for miles. In your lungs."

Silence stretched between us as I came back from the horrors.

"I have not," Vidar muttered softly.

I lifted my eyes to him again. "I loved my mother, but to think she ever loved me like Ahnah loves her people. Like you love your crew. To think she would have ever cried out for me. That would be foolish. One who has been to the deep cannot love. We live to serve the father, Akareth. I insulted him by betraying my mother. Since that day, I have prayed to Lune. Blasphemer is only one name they call me because I will not serve a god that turns his daughters mad."

Looking up, I saw Vidar staring at me with such focus that it was almost unnerving. I narrowed my eyes at him.

"What?"

Shrugging, he said, "I am only trying to figure out if you're attempting to manipulate me in some way or… if you have a heart."

The corner of my lips lifted and I slinked through the water, moving slowly toward him. I could have eaten him alive. He was alone. I was stronger. His cutlass was on his belt too far for him to reach. He knew it and like always, he did not shy from me. I slithered close to him, my teeth throbbing at the smell of him. At the sound of his pulse fluttering through the water like a beacon.

"You will never know, no matter what I say," I whispered, bringing my face dangerously close to his. "I can lie as well as I can speak the truth. I know you can, too."

He lingered there, his eyes locked onto mine as I inched closer to him, yearning for his dangerous heat. When his hand jutted out of the water and grasped the nape of my neck, I did not pull from his cruel touch. He tangled his fingers in my hair, pulling my head back.

"I never expected to trust you," he said, his other hand coming out of the water with a dagger in it.

He pressed the blade to my neck, letting my skin taste the sharp edge, and I smiled with excitement.

"And here I am the fool for thinking you'd be unarmed," I said.

He watched me as I surrendered to his grip as if waiting for me to do something. All I wished to do was dissect him and the only way I could do that while under his blade was to toy with his mind. His body. It was something I had been yearning to do for some time.

Slowly, I slid my hand up his thigh, crawling my fingers along his body until I felt the length of his cock thick and hard in my hand. I did not need to say anything. The silence said it for me. Vidar was aroused and by his greatest enemy, no less. I wrapped my long fingers around his shaft and watched his lips part as I slid my fist upward to the very tip. When I slid it down, he shuddered, his hand gripping my hair tighter.

"Take the blade from my neck," I muttered.

Slowly, he moved the dagger and loosened his grip on me. I looked up at him from hooded eyes and slid my hand along his length again before slowly sinking deeper into the water. But once my mouth was submerged, he took my hair again and stopped me from going under.

"Do not think for a moment I am letting your teeth anywhere near *that*," he said.

I smirked at his caution, but too soon, Vidar's lips were almost on mine. My heart skipped at the thought of kissing him. Since that day in Port Devlin, my body desired things it never had before. Things I was certain only Vidar could give me. I *wanted* him to kiss me. I wanted to taste his lips. Feel his arms caging me against him. Feel the sting of his touch and the caress of his skin.

But too soon, someone else entered the space. I pushed away from him, my heart racing with unanswered anticipation. Looking up, I saw Meridan in the haze, watching us.

Vidar cleared his throat and stood from the water, unashamed of his nudity as he ambled over to his clothing and slid them on over his wet skin.

There was a terrible, unfinished feeling in my gut as Vidar walked out of the clearing wrapped in a fur blanket. But he was right to leave. Meridan had a disapproving air about her that I felt was directed at me. I had been feeling it for some time.

Once we were alone, she undressed, sliding into the water beside me. Her pale skin nearly matched the milky color of the spring. She could have gotten lost in that pool for days. I wanted to ask her what was on her mind, but her silence was telling of her mood. I let her stew in her thoughts for a while, waiting for a chiding remark.

"I thought it strange you did not come to bed, so I followed you," she said, combing her fingers through her long, silver hair. "You are getting tremendously comfortable with him,"

"Comfortable is the last thing I feel around him," I said.

"You touch him as if you are."

"I touch him because I know—"

"You are growing to care for him," she interrupted, turning to look at me with those foggy eyes.

I couldn't deny it and I wasn't sure if it was because she was right or if I was simply confused. Either way, I said nothing and Meridan didn't seem thrilled about that.

"Meri, whatever your reservations, you can rid yourself of them. Vidar remains a tool and nothing more."

She remained silent, slowly pulling knots from her hair. I waited patiently, trying to put Vidar out of my mind. At least, for the moment.

"I told you long ago that my father was human," she began. "I told you he raped my mother and I was the product of hatred. That's untrue. My mother loved my father. So much that she left me with her clan to be raised under hateful hands so she could live her life with him. They called her a traitor. They called me a blight. They murdered them both. So, I left."

"Your mother loved a man?"

Her head turned swiftly toward me. "They are manipulative creatures, men. Vidar has his claws in you and you do not even know it."

"He does not have his claws in me. And I would never think to leave you behind in pursuit of a man. A human, no less. You are all the family I have."

Her eyes searched mine for lies, but she found only the truth. It was all I had. I loved Meridan.

"Kea and Voel are gone," she said, lowering her gaze. "I would be alone if I did not have you."

I reached out to her beneath the water and grasped her hand.

"You will never be without me."

"And if the sons manage to tempt you into their dark waters?"

"They won't…" I hesitated to finish that sentence. "Not if I am with Vidar."

"What does that mean?"

"I don't know. He is the only one who heard me when I called for help that night I almost jumped off the Rose."

"Is it your dreams?"

"I fear I've lodged myself too deeply in his thoughts and he in mine. But as long as he can hear me, perhaps the sons will not be able to tempt me away."

Her jaw tightened. I could see she was conflicted about the whole ordeal, but it was all the truth. Then, as if surrendering, she nodded and squeezed my hand.

"We are in a strange place at a strange time," she said. "Promise we will navigate it together."

"I promise."

Not death do we mourn
But the things that were
and now will never be again
~Unknown

Three women stood at the very edge of a low cliff over calm water. The ocean whispered as it moved and the biting breeze wept with the villagers as the three women sang. Their voices were sorrowful and beautiful, a haunting lullaby on a dreary day as Sakari's family and friends bid her farewell. Vidar and a few from the crew stood off to the side, watching but not participating. I kept a little distance as well and stood near some large rocks to observe, soaking in the looks on every person's face as they paid their respects. Ahnah held on tight to her grandmother's hand, tossing me innocent glances now and then.

I tried to smile at her each time, but it was hard. I didn't want to smile at a funeral, but I felt the need to reassure her somehow. Of what, I didn't know. I wasn't planning on replacing Sakari, so what could I give Ahnah besides smiles and hugs?

When the women stopped singing, a dozen or so villagers with a long flower garland stepped toward the cliff and slowly tossed the beautiful creation into the cold sea.

Another song began, that time by the men. By then, I was beginning to catch on that they weren't songs at all but prayers. Each time someone began, the others would bow their heads.

I recalled funeral practices from my childhood, which consisted mostly of feeding a body to sharks or cannibalizing it. The first time I saw my mother sink her teeth into a dead sister, my stomach turned. The second time, I wondered what my own sister would taste like if it ever came to it.

When Vidar killed my mother, the last thing on my mind was eating her. I wanted nothing more than to kill him for shattering my world beneath my feet.

A world I didn't even love.

The only world I knew.

It was all such a mess and nothing made sense.

A sudden feeling like someone was standing right behind me made me turn my head. Meridan was sitting beside me and immediately looked in the same direction as if she felt it, too. Behind us was nothing but a tundra of dirt and snow. I focused my eyes against the too-bright landscape to see a woman standing near a cluster of stones. She was as white as the snow with white hair and dark, inky eyes. Her long, slender form was covered by a thin dress that looked too large on her frame.

I stood and Meridan stood with me, just as curious as I was to finally talk to one of the coldfins. Quietly, we made our way toward her as the funeral kept on. Just when we were close enough to speak to her, she slipped behind the rocks as if to coax us away from prying eyes. Turning around the stones, we found her standing there, her gaze regarding us both like we were not real. I noticed then that she was nothing like us at all. Her features were so delicate. White, short fur covered her shoulders and the tops of her arms and a dreamy sheen made her flesh look like the top of sun-kissed snow. And her eyes were like onyx with no color in them at all. Slowly, she started to pace, her eyes studying.

"What is your name?" she asked, her head canting subtly to one side.

"Dahlia."

"Meridan."

"You are a Kroan, from Theloch," she said to me before turning to Meridan. "And I've seen your kind before. The Naros."

"I am from Underhome," Meridan confirmed.

The woman studied me again "And you live in warmer waters. What are you doing here?"

"We came to return the girls home."

"Men took them. Men like the ones you are here with."

"Different men. My sisters and I killed those men."

"You and your sisters. I see only two of you."

"The others were killed."

"Southern sirens and men have been killing each other for a long time. We may stick to the cold, but we know the ways of the world. Why are you with them?"

"It's complicated."

"Nothing is complicated."

I swallowed, taking a deep breath. "We had common interests and we chose to work together for them."

"The common interest being the girls."

I nodded. Slowly, the woman took a step forward, her eyes roaming across my body like she didn't think I was a siren under all the clothes.

"Why would men and sirens care about those girls enough to work together?"

"Does it matter?"

"It matters if you've brought notice to our home. We do not want conflict here."

"Would you rather we didn't bring them?"

She paused, her black eyes telling me nothing. And like the frozen waters she lived in, her expression was cold.

"We care about the people here. We rely on them." She inclined her head. "I thank you. But we know far too much about Kroan zealots and their violent delights."

"I am not associated with a clan. I was cast out a long time ago."

"For the best."

"What about you? Humans fear us, but these people talk about you as if you are gods."

"And it has kept them content."

"So, you live here? Alongside them?"

"Not exactly."

"They do not fear you so you must not eat them."

"These people believe they came from the sea long ago. They believe when they die, they return to it and are reborn. They age, we visit them, and we take them. And we take the sick. The disturbed."

"You take them… and feed on them."

"We get what we need and they believe their loved ones have passed on to the form from which they came."

"But it's a lie."

"The world is built on lies. Ours keep people satisfied and functional and they keep us fed without war. Happiness, after all, lasts as long as the veil remains over one's eyes."

"And you've been doing this all along?"

Her gaze was unblinking, so dark I could see myself looking back.

"Your people have been at war with men for generations," she said. "Which life would you prefer? If it is war you want, you'd have killed the men you came with before ever arriving on these shores."

The statement made me pause. I knew no other life. Fighting hunters had been the focus of my people—what used to be my people—since I was born. Of all the daughters of the sea, the Kroan were the most spiteful. Since before I was born, it had been the way of things. Trying to imagine a life absent conflict made me wonder if I would even know how to function without the violence.

"What's your name?" Meridan finally asked.

"Teles," she answered.

Though it was hard to know exactly where she was looking, I sensed she was staring past us. Her head cocked and she blinked, her shoulders relaxing.

"They are finished with their goodbyes," she said. "There will be a celebration now."

"A celebration?"

"They will celebrate Sakari's return to the sea and the time they had with her." Teles stepped in close, looking up at me. "I smell blood on you, Kroan. Shed any here and it will not go unnoticed."

Her head snapped toward Meridan for a moment and then she slowly backed away, inching toward the water's edge just past the rocks. I watched her slide her loose-fitting dress off her shoulders, letting it fold to the ground. She stepped delicately out of it, unaffected by the biting cold, and glided into the water off the edge of a slate of ice. As if she never existed, she was gone.

As Teles said, the tribe began celebrations as soon as the sun began to descend its peak. There was a large fire in the courtyard where tables were full of salted fish, milky drinks, and fruits. Boil was eager to help make the food and Billy seemed tied to him at the hip. There was even music. Flutes, drums, and upbeat singing filled the air as people seemed to forget about the sadness of the morning and replace it with joy.

Whatever the milky drink was, it was strong smelling. Something fermented, I gathered. The men enjoyed it and after a while, they were laughing and singing boisterously. Sea shanties being sung off-key replaced the drums. Mullins and James were making fools of themselves, stumbling about with wide smiles on their faces. They were trying to dance in unison, but each time they lifted one foot, their other would fail them and they'd stagger. Some villagers laughed at their clumsiness while others tried to teach them how to dance properly.

It was a wonderful mess.

Even Ahnah had taken on the task of getting scrawny Billy to dance with her. She had a smile that stretched from ear to ear and poor Billy was doing his best to seem unenthused.

I was snacking on a handful of berries that were so sweet, they made my jaw hurt. I wasn't accustomed to sweet foods. Or foods that did not come from something that once had a beating heart, for that matter.

Meridan was enjoying the fruit as well while she watched the festivities. Neither of us had ever been a part of something so… blissful. The Kroan did not have feasts or celebrations. Not like that. I knew the Naros were even more elusive. It was all so different and yet, I didn't hate it.

From the longhouse, I saw Vidar with one of the male village elders and Taupek. He and the elder shook hands and I wondered what it was that they'd been discussing inside while the others were getting rowdy. I watched him from afar as a young woman strode up to him with a cup of the strange drink. He smiled at her and she inclined her head bashfully as if asking a question.

I bristled at the sight. Her mannerisms suggested she was attracted to him. Her shyness. The way she lowered her head with a smile. It all seemed so transparent.

When Vidar took a sip of the drink, the young woman giggled and then set the cup down on a table before boldly dragging him into the courtyard where people were dancing around the firepit.

I couldn't take my eyes off of them. They were joined by Mullins and David, who was smiling for the first time since Vidar had taken him from the other ship. One of the young girls was trying to keep up with his rapid foot movements and laughing at her inability to.

The dance was in good spirits. Everyone was switching partners and enjoying themselves, but time and time again, the woman found her way back to Vidar, her hands touching his body every chance she got. And she was beautiful. There was an innocence to her youthful face that put light in her eyes. A light I knew I didn't have. Long, umber hair was braided to her waist and she had a round face untainted by scars and violence.

I took a deep breath and snatched a piece of salted fish off a platter in front of me, tearing into it with my teeth. Meridan's hand came out to touch my arm and I glanced at her, realizing my emotions were getting the better of me.

I'd never wanted to claim Vidar in any way besides a fatal one. For eighteen years, I imagined what he looked like and I saw myself killing him in so many ways. I prayed to Lune that I would one day get that chance and hoped another wouldn't steal the opportunity away. Now, seeing a young woman practically parading herself in front of him was making me seeth. She was touching him, offering him drinks, and it all made my teeth gnash. It shouldn't have… but it did.

Whether I wanted to destroy him or not, he was mine. A very possessive, overwhelming part of me knew it and it burned in my chest like a pit of flames. I didn't want to look at the young woman for fear of imagining terrible things. One last glimpse in their direction and I saw Vidar pulling her close and teaching her the foot movements of some dance that matched the rhythm of the music. The woman was stumbling and both were amused. The big smiles on their faces fed the flames of my jealousy.

It was so easy for me to see myself sinking my nails into the woman's eyes, plucking them out, and popping the orbs between my molars. How simple it would be to bite into her throat and drown her in her own blood. I wondered what one so innocent would taste like.

No.

It was my nature to wonder.

What wasn't my nature was the desire to cage those urges so that I did not disrupt the happiness unfolding around me. I didn't want to ruin it. I didn't want to be the reason everything fell apart nor did I want to be the reason another blameless child's life was destroyed.

So I watched Vidar and the woman have their fun. I watched until both were out of breath and they finally parted ways. Beside me, even Meridan had a smile on her face and that was something I never thought I would see. Eventually, Mullins swayed his way toward us, gulping down another cup of the fermented drink, and held a hand out to her.

Meridan hesitated and then giggled—*giggled*—at Mullins and took his offer.

I was dumbfounded as I watched her prance away with him and join the fun, but I wasn't pleased by the looks on some of the men's faces as they passed. Uther and a few others sat by themselves at a table, watching, but not participating in the celebrations. I feared they would never warm up to us.

Not that I should care.

I was surprised by Mullins as much as I was surprised by Meridan. Though he'd been civil most of the time, his dislike for sirens had never waned nor did his expression of it. Now he was dancing with one and smiling about it.

Meridan never allowed herself to have fun. I watched her join a circle of skipping girls around the fire and couldn't help myself. Vidar and the woman were forgotten. Seeing Meridan let down her guard and wash herself of her sorrows and fears was perhaps the brightest image at that feast.

Long into the night, things finally began to die down. The younger members of the tribe retreated to their homes to rest. Then the elderly disappeared while the men of the Rose found corners and benches to pass out on. Young ladies from the village gently coaxed a few to their feet to take them somewhere they wouldn't freeze to death in the night while the stronger men dragged others away. A couple crewmen still sat by the firepit singing slow shanties with drunken slurs, still sipping their drinks, but otherwise, everyone had gone.

Including Vidar. I saw him walk away on his own some time ago and had expected him to return, but he never did. My gut turned at the idea that he might have been with the young woman somewhere private. The image of the two sweaty in bed with her moaning beneath him made my nostrils flare.

I balled my fists on the table, recalling the direction he'd gone when he left. I took a big swig of water and then stood from the bench, heading out toward the cave. I thought it strange that he'd gone that way, but perhaps he and his little admirer wanted time alone somewhere remote.

The idea sickened me.

Nearing the cave, I saw the illumination of a torch deep in its cavernous depths and paused. Perhaps it was not smart to pursue him when I was so clearly unhinged about the thought of him fucking a woman. I was liable to kill someone and Teles had warned me against such things.

But I was not a smart woman when it came to my impulses and I trudged on, my soft, leathery boots crunching on the frosty ground. I was prepared to see something I didn't want to, but when I got closer, I realized my suspicions were wrong. I smelled only one presence. A familiar one. One that made me feel stripped all over again. Through the darkness, I could see him, alone, standing in the cave with a torch raised toward the wall of the long passage where I knew the carvings littered the stone. Beside him, he'd also built a small fire to stay warm. He was planning on staying a while.

I could have turned back at that point. He was alone and my jealousy was misplaced. I could have left. I *should* have left.

But I didn't. I went forward.

Dahlia

There is no curse so great
as seeing a future you cannot have
or a past you cannot change
~Alisaen Ducroix

"Where is your sweet admirer?" I said, announcing my presence as I neared Vidar's makeshift camp.

He glanced my way and I was struck by his firelit brown eyes. His mouth curved into a smirk as if my question pleased him in some way.

"I have no idea what you're talking about," he played.

"You do. You only danced with one girl tonight."

"She's sleeping, like all the rest, I suspect."

"Your men are being hauled off like corpses to their cabins. Seems they cannot hold their drink when it is made by foreign hands."

I stood beside him, looking up at the carvings to find he was studying a set of figures hunting a massive whale with tiny boats and spears. Nearby, a carving of the sirens swimming in a skryll beneath a canoe led to other carvings deeper in. I didn't know what to say. I was certain the depictions were as confusing and foreign to Vidar as they were to me. We both just stared at them, likely thinking the same things.

"The world has been making less sense to me since you slithered back into it," Vidar finally said, sighing as he stepped over to a stone and sat himself down.

He jammed the torch down between two rocks, standing it at an angle before he perched his elbows on his knees. That's when I noticed his leather folder full of drawings on top of another stone and the charcoal stains on his fingers. He'd been copying the images from the wall onto his own paper for safekeeping.

I found another stone suitable for sitting across from him and took a seat, watching the firelight make flickering shadows on the walls.

"What are you doing out here?" I asked.

"I knew there was more on these walls than you let on. I needed to see it."

"Always searching for new knowledge."

"Always."

"Why learn about us when you just intend to kill us?"

"I take it you've never heard the saying, 'Know thine enemy,' before." I shrugged in response. "My father thought he knew his enemies. It got a lot of men killed."

My eyes wandered for a moment, thinking back on that day. "I didn't know my enemy, either. I didn't know how cunning he could be until I unlocked his little cage."

"Deep down, we both know we cannot blame each other for what happened that day."

"And yet we've held onto it for eighteen years, letting it kill us and keep us alive at the same time."

Vidar scrubbed his face, taking another long look at the walls of the tunnel.

"Well, it's been exhausting. I'm here to make sense of things," he sighed, picking up a stick and breaking off little pieces to toss in the flames of his campfire.

"What things are you trying to make sense of?"

"You, for starters. You defy everything I've ever known. It was all black and white before I saw you on that cursed island. Sirens were creatures of evil. We were the ones to rid the world of them. Deep down, I knew you weren't like the rest. Not yet. And I used that to my advantage to survive."

"I am like the rest now."

He snorted, running a hand over his hair. "I've never met a daughter of the sea that has to convince herself so often that she is awful."

"Awful creatures can do good things and still be awful."

"Then I am no less awful than you. You, Dahlia, are an enigma. Born from the vilest creatures to ever rule the seas and yet you released a boy from a cage so he would not get eaten. You saved young girls from men and sailed with your greatest enemy to see them to safety. You freed my… David from certain death when you could have let him drown to spite me."

"Are you here to reason that I am a virtuous person under the ugliness, Vidar?" I said, glimpsing the walls. "Do you see these carvings and wonder if I am not the monster you've always thought me to be because the Maruhk somehow avoid war with humans?"

He tossed his stick into the flames with a groan and shook his head. "Perhaps I am."

"The Maruhk are sirens, but they are not the Kroan. Just like your nuns and priests are human, but they are not hunters."

"And what are you?"

Our eyes locked and I opened my mouth to defend myself only to find that words had abandoned me. I was no more Kroan than he was. I was nothing. I was just… me.

I understood myself just about as much as Vidar did. After the time I'd spent with him and his crew and with the girls, I was starting to think it felt nice not to be looked at like an evil menace.

"You should go back. It is cold out here," he said flatly.

"I don't need—"

"I know. Your warmth is deep, as you said."

I pulled my coat tighter around me, leaning in toward the heat of the flames.

"My warmth is deep," I spoke, pausing a moment to wonder if I should go on. "My heart is even deeper." I lifted my eyes to meet Vidar's again, a knot in my chest making it hard to think. "But it's there, I assure you. Buried beneath armor far thicker than your own."

I lost myself in his eyes and he in mine as if some thin shroud had been lifted and our vision was clearing. Vidar was the first to divert his gaze only to toss another stick into the flames. A flurry of red sparks flew up between us.

He cleared his throat and spoke softly. "Would you ever tell me how to get through that armor?"

My stare remained on his face, which had become blurred by smoke. "No."

He smirked faintly. "So, I'll have to figure it out on my own then."

Finally, I let my eyes fall to the fire. "I fear that you will," I said so softly, I wondered if he could hear.

When Vidar stopped poking at the fire, I knew he understood. I couldn't bring myself to meet his gaze again for some time after those words had slipped. Not only did I fear what he would think of them, but I feared the weakness I had just exposed.

When I could finally bring myself to look up, Vidar was leaning forward on a long stick, his hands overlapping the top of it for him to rest his chin. He was just staring at me, no readable expression on his face for me to scrutinize. I cocked my head to the side, admiring the strong angle of his jaw. The quirk on his lips. The strength of his cheekbones and brow.

Then that young woman slipped back into my memory and a wave of uncomfortable heat roiled in me. I narrowed my eyes at him and when he noticed, he raised a brow.

"What are you thinking about, Dahlia?" he whispered.

"That woman you were dancing with. Do you desire her?"

He set his stick aside and slowly unfolded from the stone, coming to his full height. I stood, wanting to be on equal ground as he stepped toward me.

"What if I did?" he said. My jaw tightened at the idea. "She was beautiful, was she not? Young. Human. And she has never wanted to kill me. Or eat me, for that matter."

I took in a deep breath, but that only filled my lungs with Vidar. The heat inside me was both irritated and desperate and it sickened me to think I had no control over it.

"Why would you care about what I think of her if I did go to her tonight?" Vidar added.

"I don't want to hurt her," I confessed, stilling myself as he moved in closer to me.

His head canted to the side. "Why would you hurt her?"

I peered up at him, pleading silently for him to understand. The mere thought of him wanting her made my fists clench. I swallowed down any response I might have given him and watched as the realization dawned on his face.

"I do not even know her name," he finally confessed, his eyes dropping to my mouth in a way that made my body shudder with excitement. "Dahlia," he emphasized, his hand slowly coming up to slide around the back of my neck.

He fisted my hair and tugged, pulling my head back. The burn that radiated across my scalp at the pressure made me gasp as I was yanked against the heat of his body. Could I have fought him and pushed him off of me? Yes. But that nearness was something I'd been wanting for days. Ever since he'd cleansed me of my guilt with harsh and rewarding pain. Ever since it was his hands that pulled me from the edge of the ship and kept me from jumping into the sea where the sons were waiting, I'd wanted them on me again. I wanted to say it, but the confession felt like defeat and stayed lodged like a piece of glass in my throat.

Vidar's other hand slid up to grasp my jaw.

"Do you want me?" he whispered, his lips hovering over mine. I thought he would kiss me before he suddenly twisted us around and slammed me against the cold, hard barrier of the cave wall. "Or do you just hate the idea of another having me?"

"Perhaps I do. But if I am to confess something so outrageous, perhaps you can divulge why you stole me from the railing the other night when I was about to surrender to the sons. You could have been rid of me. So why'd you do it?"

"That is easy. You called to me."

"Did I?"

One hand released my hair, sliding down my body, through the opening of my coat, to the drawstring of my leggings. I pressed my hands to his chest, but I did not shove him away when he slid past the waistband and delved between my legs. My heart was racing at his touch. I parted for him, unsurprised that he found me wanting and wet.

"I imagined it, then," he said, his fingers parting my folds. "What wonderful timing."

"Why did you pull me back?"

"Why would you want to hurt a woman simply for dancing with me?"

Two of his fingers slid into my entrance, stretching me around him. I gasped when his hand closed over my throat and squeezed. Heat enveloped my body, coiling deep inside as his fingers thrust up inside me again.

It was exactly what I wanted. I wanted him to touch me. Hurt me. I wanted his attention, as pathetic as it was. I wanted his eyes on me and his hands against my flesh. I clutched his coat in my fists and dragged him closer, spreading my legs as he played against my clit with his thumb.

"I didn't want you to want her," I panted. "I wanted you to desire me."

He thrust his fingers deep, nearly lifting me off the ground. I whimpered, throwing my head back. He assaulted my neck with his mouth, licking a slow trail along my throat. And by Lune, I was hungry for it. The feeling of his hot breath against my cool skin silenced all other thoughts. The way his fingers stretched and ravaged me demanded my nerves pay attention to only him and nothing else. The way he pinned me to the wall was a demand to give up control and for some reason, I wanted to. I wanted to relinquish everything to him and set aside all thoughts and doubts and fears.

He pumped himself inside me again and again, his thumb pressing against my sensitive bud. I had never felt pleasure from a man until that first night beneath his harsh touch. It was an all-consuming pleasure that left me broken and comforted all at once. I thirsted for more of it. For more of *him*. For that unique liberation.

Opening my eyes, I could see the darkness down the tunnel over his shoulder, facing the coast. The firelight around us created shadows across my vision, so it took a breath or two to realize one of the shadows was solid.

The shadow stepped toward the very edge of the firelight's reach and I saw a tall, pale form with hip-length black hair clinging to her still-wet figure. Her black eyes were sharp with hatred as she lifted her hand. In it was a bone dagger much like my own.

I was instantly ripped from the throes of pleasure when the woman launched the dagger toward Vidar's back. Without thinking, I spun him around so his back hit the wall and I pushed myself away from him. The dagger hit the rocks with a loud clank that echoed through the hollow passage.

"Traitorous cunt," the woman hissed.

She looked half starved and her eyes were red and crazed as if she had not slept in many days.

"Ligeia," I muttered.

"You keep taking and taking," she said. "And leaving us to clean up the mess."

"What?"

"The men you killed. They were meant for the sons. They would have left us alone, but now they hunt and you are here, fucking a human."

I heard the metal of a blade unsheathing and glanced back to see Vidar shrugging off his coat, his cutlass in one hand. He paced like he was about to fight a pack of wolves for a fresh carcass.

"The father wants you," Ligeia continued. Her gaze bore into me like two poisoned picks digging right into my soul. "And I can give no more of my sisters to appease his hunger. You've angered the sea."

"So, he calls me and not you, sister," I said. "It must be torture to know that."

"You will surely not be spared for what you let that man do to mother. Akareth loved her."

"Akareth loves no one."

"You did this!"

"We both know this has little to do with mother and more to do with the fact that you wish it was you who was chosen. Ligeia, the loyal little bitch always striving to be the favorite and yet your name is not the one being whispered on the waves."

"They'll tear you apart, bit by bit, your body and mind, because you're not a believer," she said through her teeth. "And we'll kill your hunter. In front of you, as you both deserve."

"We?" I laughed. I crouched to pick up the bone knife from the ground and snarled. "Have you other sisters, then?"

She cocked her head at me, flashing her fangs when she smiled. Her eyes darted to the space behind us and both Vidar and I spun around only to see the flash of a pistol firing. It was blinding in the darkness. The sound ricocheted through the tunnel, but I did not feel a thing. Instead, I saw Vidar stumbling back into the wall, his hand clutching his shoulder.

When the white spots from the muzzle flash had cleared, I saw Uther standing at the mouth of the tunnel, his pistol smoking. Behind him were four other men looking on while their captain bled.

"Sorry, cap'n," Uther said. "Nothin' personal, but since when are we fucking sirens?"

Vidar growled as he stood, blade still in hand. Shouting rose up from the village as people awoke to the loud gunshot. The other men pulled out their weapons and began to advance and I quickly ran toward Vidar, lifting the knife in front of me as if it would help against men with pistols. Vidar pulled his own, aiming it over my shoulder at Uther with a scowl.

"So this is your pathetic little attempt at a mutiny, is it?" he said, unafraid.

My eyes darted toward Ligeia to see her jeering at the whole ordeal. Why the men were ignoring her was made clear when I glimpsed Uther's chest to see that he wasn't wearing a pendant. None of them were. In a blink, my mind sored back to that black-sand island. I remembered him being the last man on the boat during our retreat. Had he been wearing his silentium then?

"You've been following us all along," I said. I addressed Vidar. "She's been in his head since the island."

"Fucking figures," he spit.

The men from the village drew nearer and I heard Gus shout at Uther. The men turned on each other, whipping their pistols around. Meridan came darting out of the crowd and leaped onto the back of one of the traitorous crewmen, her teeth clamping down on his ear. He screamed, firing into the ceiling of the tunnel. Vidar lifted his pistol, swinging it over my head and turning it on Ligeia. She ducked and the bullet rebounded off the wall with a spark.

Suddenly, one of his men charged at Vidar, swinging his sword as if they'd never been friends. He fought him, but in four moves, despite his injured shoulder, he had slammed the man's head so hard against the wall that he wavered and plummeted to the ground. Uther charged Vidar next and before I could think, I lunged, driving my blade into his gut four times in quick succession.

He didn't even look like he felt it. He slammed the hilt of his cutlass against the side of my head and I saw spots for a second before I recovered and stepped away, dislodging the blade from his stomach.

Another one of the once loyal crewmen rushed forward and Vidar tugged at my arm, spinning me around to the back of him and blocking the man's blade with his own.

I looked up at Ligeia. She absorbed the situation and when she realized her poor, enslaved puppets were going to lose, she bolted toward the coast with a hiss.

"Meridan!" I shouted. Immediately, she was at my side, her lips bloodied. "She cannot get away."

We both took off after her, but my sister was as fast on land as she was in the water. For all we knew, she had others waiting for us, but I didn't care. She could not leave.

When we exited the cave, Ligeia veered off toward a cliffside. We followed, but before we reached her, I stretched out an arm and halted Meridan. Ligeia spun to face us as two other Kroan emerged from the frosted stone ground, their bodies uncurling from the rocks and shedding their gravelly color.

"All of Theloch will descend on this place," Ligeia threatened. "And every place you go will fear us as we rise up in your wake."

Meridan and I wasted no time. We charged toward the intruders without remorse or hesitation. We had not fought our own in years, but we knew how to do it. We combined our efforts, tearing into one before even thinking of the others. Ligeia inched toward the cliffside, staying far from my blade. Just as I was about to finish one of the strangers off, the third tangled her fingers in my hair, dragging me backward. I launched my feet up, flipping over her skinny form and driving my knife into her side. She screamed as I twisted it and then dragged the sharp edge through her stomach. Blood and organs spilled to the ground in a steaming heap.

Ligeia roared with fury and suddenly reached out toward Meridan. I threw my knife. It whispered past her head, cutting deep into her scalp, but it barely slowed her. The third stranger, though wounded, had enough in her to rush at me, a smaller bone dagger in her hand.

A pistol blast rang through the air and her head snapped back before she crumpled to the ground. Glancing sideways, I saw Vidar marching toward us, his eyes set on Ligeia and his cutlass clutched tightly in one hand. My sister wasted no time and grabbed Meridan by the back of the neck, dragging her toward the edge of the cliff. I watched in horror as the two toppled into the water below.

"Meri!" I shrieked.

I stepped toward the ledge to see the water bubbling up where they'd disappeared beneath the waves. Vidar moved up by my side, sheathing his blade.

"She cannot leave," I said, tearing off my clothes as fast as I could. "She will tell others where we are."

"You cannot go alone."

"I have no choice."

When I hit the water, it was like hitting a slab of solid ice. The cold swathed me in a suffocating cage. My vision was skewed by a flurry of bubbles, but I could see them. Ligeia's dark hair mixed with Meridan's silver locks flitted through the water ahead and as soon as my body was through changing from one form to the next, I darted after them.

39

Vidar

We all serve a dark god
Bound by lies and tyranny
~Dema Dumos

One of the women in the village was sewing me up with a bone needle and a thread while I stared across the room at my wounded men. The mutineers had all been killed on the spot while Boil, Jesse, and James all rested on cots, recovering from their wounds. Thankfully, they were minor. A couple of split lips and bruises, but we'd all gotten out of it unscathed, for the most part. Gus came to sit beside me as the woman stitching up my shoulder knotted the string and severed it with a small knife. I had been lucky. The slug went clean through my shoulder and left nothing behind. It hurt like a bitch, but I had been hit worse.

Gus reached out to poke at a bruise on my temple.

"Fuck off," I said with a groan, swatting his hand away.

"Quite a night," he said. "Quite a week, actually. We haven't buried this many men in years."

"Uther, the bastard," I said through my teeth.

"He lost his silentium."

"On the island. He was the last in the boat."

"You think one of them bitches snagged him and planted ideas?"

"I do. But he didn't agree with leaving Dahlia and Meridan alive in the first place. How much of it was under her influence?"

"And the others?"

"Each of them spoke up when I let Dahlia out of the holding cell." I glanced at Gus, searching his one good eye for truth. "You think all of this was a mistake?"

He sighed heavily. "I think I trust your decisions. Like I trusted your father's."

"My father's got a lot of people killed."

"And yours may do the same one day, but I've never stepped foot on a ship thinking there wasn't a chance I'd die on it. We all make choices. I recall one of your choices being to save my old ass on that very island where your father died. We choose to sail those dark seas."

"Full of dark fates," I sighed.

Gus leaned over to look at the healer's handiwork.

"Stitched you up good, she did. You lost a fair amount of blood."

"Been here a couple days and already brought the storm with us."

"These people are resilient."

I nodded and searched the room for my coat and weapons. I found both lying across a stool and put them on.

"What are you doing?"

"We need to bury the men."

"Smalls and the others are already on it. You need to let that shoulder heal."

"Then I'll go to the water."

"I don't think that's smart."

"Dahlia's been gone for hours. If she's dead, we're about to be visited by something far worse."

Even thinking that she might have perished in the water made me feel as if I'd been punched in the stomach.

"What are you going to do? Take a swim to find her? Last I checked, you don't sprout fins and we humans don't take that freezing water well."

"Doesn't matter."

"I'm not going with you. My joints are hating the cold as it is," he threatened as I walked out of the cabin into the chilled, early morning air. "Mullins! Dammit, go with the cap'n."

Mullins was just outside sitting with a few other crewmen around a fire. He stood quickly when I walked outside, rubbing fatigue from his eyes. My men were somber, sitting with the bodies of the mutineers. They'd all been covered up with thin blankets and were ready to be buried. No one liked to see their crewmates dead, especially by their own hands, but the sea tested men. Sometimes they failed and they let the madness and chaos claim them.

"Where we going, cap'n?" Mullins asked.

"He's going down to the water to find his precious siren."

Mullins fumbled to grab his gun belt and jogged to match my pace. As we departed for the coast, I saw my men staring at me from all directions. One of the lingering stares was David's and as we passed, he set down the bowl of food he was eating and quickly caught up to us.

"Stay here, David," I ordered.

"Not likely."

"We're all glad you are alive," Mullins said as we left the village. "But we all see it, you know."

"See what?"

"That you care about that woman."

I tossed him a glare and then grumbled my irritation. "Don't matter if I care about her or not. She saved my life last night."

"I'll say," David added, walking as if he'd regained some of his confidence over the past few days.

"True, that is," Mullins added. "We all saw Uther go at you with his blade. The way she stabbed him." He shivered. "Don't think anyone's going to try to touch you with her around."

The thought made my already spinning head spiral out of control. I had seen Dahlia drive her knife into Uther. It was the second time she'd come between me and someone trying to kill me.

When we exited the cave and came to the water's edge, I noticed the silence first. The water was placid and so blue it seemed tampered with. Up on a cliff, I spotted a villager with a bow and arrows strapped to his back. He was diligently scanning the water, but not likely for the same reason I was. Another lookout stood further down the beach.

"They sent these men out to keep watch as soon as you went in to get stitched up," Mullins said. He buckled his belt around his slender hips and chose a direction. "I'll start patrolling down that way."

I nodded as he headed down the rocky beach. David sighed and tied his coat tightly closed. Looking at him, I was reminded how young he was. I was barely younger than him when my life fell to pieces and though I tried to keep his together, I had failed.

Maybe there was no helping the course of things.

David headed in the opposite direction as Mullins without a word.

"David," I said, catching him before he hiked too far away. He turned and I slid Lady Mary out of my belt, handing it to him. "Take this."

"Lady Mary?" he said, wrapping his fingers around the hilt.

"You see one, you gut her."

"What about you?"

"I've got my pistol."

"I've got a pistol."

"Just take it. Bronze is better for killin' them. We'll get you your own soon."

He looked down at the cutlass. Lady Mary wasn't pretty. She was full of nicks and she hadn't gotten a good cleaning in some time, but she was sturdy. He ogled it as he walked away, but once more, he stopped before he was too far.

"I want her to be alright, you know," he said. "As foolish as it sounds, I do want her to survive. When I was about to drown on the Widow's Smile, in that damn holding cell, I called out to the men and none of them stopped. They was all trying to save themselves. Then she showed up. Dragged me out of there and to the surface. If she can do that, then I can wish for her safety, right?"

The thought of Dahlia going down into the hold to fetch a boy she didn't know was a puzzling one. She was a conundrum. From the day she freed me from that cage, she had been a giant mystery.

And I wanted to see her safe.

"Go," I said, jerking my chin. "Keep an eye out and don't let your guard down."

David nodded and then finally slid my cutlass into his belt as he patrolled the other side of the beach.

The day dragged on with nothing to focus my attention on in the water. In the distance, I caught the spray of a whale breaching the surface once or twice, but no sirens. Not even the locals. It irked me a little that they hadn't intervened when the damn Kroan waltzed onto land to attack, but we didn't know them well enough to place any real blame. Perhaps they were of a weaker, more cowardly sort.

The lookouts had switched shifts many hours into the afternoon and when the sun began to sink toward the horizon, Mullins returned from his trek, tired and hungry.

"Going back for some food," he said. "I'll grab us all a bite."

He hesitated before leaving as if waiting for me to tell him I was finished searching for her, but I didn't. I was willing to camp at the water's edge if I had to. My shoulder was sore and I was tired, but I kept my eyes on the water. I alternated between sitting and standing all day and leaned up against a large rock once Mullins left toward the village.

Down the beach, David strolled into view and gave me a nod, letting me know he was alright before he began another walk along the water.

It was all ridiculous. I wanted to reason that I was just volunteering to help the other lookouts in case another threat burst from the water, but I was there for far more selfish reasons and it was to see Dahlia returned. Some nasty voice inside me told me she wouldn't. After all, other sirens were not her only threat in the water. She still had the sons to contend with. I wanted to know what possessed her to leave like she did when she knew the dangers waiting for her, but I could not ask her if she was lost to us. If she did not come back.

The sound of steady wind was broken by water sloshing nearby. I stood and peered down the icy bank. It could have been anything. An animal. A siren. I wanted it to be Dahlia, though.

When I saw a hand jut out of the water, I narrowed my eyes, hoping. Then a head of black hair emerged and I started jogging in her direction, hand on my pistol in case it was not the siren I wanted to see.

But then that scar gleamed in the late afternoon light just right.

Dahlia clawed at the ground, dragging herself out of the sea with a strained grumble. My body wanted to grab hold of her and hoist her into my arms, but I tamed that impulse. It took every fiber of my self-control, but I did it.

"Did you get her?" I asked, trying to sound casual when really, my heart was racing.

She lifted her other arm out of the water and slung something on the ground at my feet like a heavy sack. When it rolled, I saw a woman's gray face, jaw slack and eyes rolled back. Rigid torn flesh encircled the red crevice of her severed neck. I cocked my head at the trophy.

"You could have just said yes."

Dahlia untangled her fingers from the mangled hair and continued pulling herself onto land with great effort. She was exhausted. More than that, she was in pain. I stood a step away as she rolled onto her back, revealing two deep, crescent-shaped patches of flesh riddled with teeth marks. Scrapes trailed down her arms and bruising covered one side of her ribs like purple paint spills.

Halfway submerged in the water was her long, eel-like tail, glistening under the muted sunlight with faint, silverish hues amid her black lower half.

She let out a strained sound, clenching her teeth as her tail began to curl in on her like a dying snake. But in doing so, the black dissolved behind peeling, disintegrating layers that turned to the skin I knew so well. The sinew and muscle split down the middle like a serrated knife had taken to her flesh and bones cracked and splintered, creating two limbs from one in a manner that was both fascinating and grotesque.

Finally, her tail was no more and in its place were her long, bare legs. I gave myself two breaths to gather my thoughts before I was sliding my coat off my shoulders. I stepped toward her, kicking the head aside like a piece of waste as I draped my coat over her naked body.

Immediately after Dahlia had shifted, Meridan burst out of the water in a hurry. Her shift was just as unnerving, but fast. I noticed there were no wounds on her aside from a deep gash on her arm that had already stopped bleeding.

"She needs help," she said quickly.

Clearly.

Dahlia was shivering. I wasn't sure if it was the cold or something else that had rendered her so helpless, but she was terribly weakened. Her wounds were severe and I still did not know how the icy waters affected her, but she was frail and spent.

Once she was thoroughly wrapped in my coat, I slid an arm under her legs and another around her back, hoisting her off the cold ground. David came running when he realized what was going on.

"You found her," he panted, quickly sliding off his coat and handing it to Meridan as if she were a lady and not a flesh-eating siren.

"She's hurt," I said.

Dahlia was almost limp initially, her eyes opening and closing as I carried her from the shore. Then her limbs went completely lax. Her head rested on my shoulder and she nuzzled into my warmth.

"That's it," I muttered. "Just relax. We'll get you fixed up. David, run ahead and tell them we'll need help."

He nodded and sprinted through the cave toward the village.

Dahlia mumbled something so softly, I could not make it out. I bent my head down toward her as I walked, realizing she was quickly losing consciousness.

"What's that?" I whispered.

"Are you alright?" I heard her say faintly.

I laughed, barely believing my own ears.

"Yes, I'm alright. I'm Captain Bone Heart."

"Your heart is not made of bone. You will realize it eventually."

I hastened my step. As I did, I felt her cold fingers shock the flesh at the center of my chest where my shirt plunged just past the scar over my sternum. My eyes darted toward her touch as she traced the ragged skin.

"It is good you have this."

"I'd have to agree with you. So? How far did you have to chase her to get her head?"

"Not far. But the fight was long. She did not want to die, of course."

I turned toward her forehead, my lips unintentionally grazing the top of her head.

"But you were stronger."

"I had to be," she replied, her words laced with fatigue when she tossed Meridan a weak glance.

As I strode forth toward the village, I felt her already slack body sag further against my arms like she'd finally passed out. I only prayed it was exhaustion and that no internal injuries were rendering her so weak.

My arrival in the village set off a chain reaction until my men and a dozen villagers were meeting me in the courtyard. Two elderly women rushed to my side, their hands going swiftly to Dahlia in search of injuries. One of them began pointing toward a cabin and I could only assume that they had a place for her to heal there, so I headed that way without a fuss. Onlookers seemed concerned, hovering just close enough to see who I was carrying but not close enough to be in the way. Even my men looked bothered to see Dahlia unconscious in my arms.

When I entered the cabin, there was a cot made up with thick furs beside a fire that burned calmly in the center of the round building. I laid Dalia down only for one of the women to shove me to the side. I stepped back without protest, confident they knew how to tend her wounds better than I could. I would have splashed a bit of alcohol on it or stuck Lady Mary's red-hot blade to her bleeding injuries. Dahlia, for once, deserved more graceful ministrations and I let the ladies work as I turned to face Mullins, David, and James standing just outside the door. I pushed my way through them and began a hunt for a new coat.

"She gonna be alright?" Mullins asked, trace amounts of genuine concern in his voice.

I turned to him, the bite of the afternoon chill nipping at my neck, and shrugged. "Don't know. Nothing we can do right now, though."

Saying those words stung. I didn't like feeling helpless. I didn't like not knowing, either. But I knew it was best to find a place to bury my thoughts for a while until the women finished their work.

Better yet, I needed a drink.

I had a new coat. I had a bit of drink in me. I spent another few hours sitting in the courtyard where the large fire never seemed to burn down completely. The warmth of it was soothing and with the village winding down, it was a good time to rest without having to lay down and close my eyes.

"Going to sit out here all night?" a voice said.

I turned to see Gus ambling toward me, hands deep in the pockets of his thick coat.

"Thinking about it," I said.

He came to stand beside me, peering over the crackling flames. I'd never stayed in a place so quiet. In Treson Harbor, the water was rough, the people were rowdy, and the bells were constantly ringing. So far north and so far off the beaten path, things were… serene. Even a few unwelcome sirens had not shaken the village enough to put them in a frenzy.

"This place isn't like home," Gus said.

"No, it's not. But that attack proved it can be just as dangerous."

"Maybe not. If there was no one left to return, there is no one left to tell them where these people are. Or where we are."

"Bad things always find good people, Gus. We both know that."

"Do we? Cuz we have never been good, boy. How are we to tell?"

I huffed, about to laugh, but not quite amused enough to put the effort in.

"Maybe we don't know much about good and bad. Maybe there's nothing to know," I shrugged. "People think there's a line between the two. There's no line. If there is, we just hop from one side to the other when it suits us."

"You're right on that. We're all going to hell," he chuckled. "But may we be in heaven for half an hour before the devil knows we're dead."

"We'll be lucky for that."

We stood for a moment longer before Gus slapped me on the back and started to walk away.

"She's all mended, your siren. She's sleeping."

My instinct was to head to the very place I left her when I heard that news, but I refrained, keeping my urges buried where the world couldn't use them against me. I wanted to go to her, though. I wanted to see the state of her. Make sure she was alright. Sickening as it was to admit, I prayed for her to heal swiftly. I prayed for it because… she did not deserve the turmoil she'd endured the past eighteen years. Of that, I was certain now.

Gus retreated to get some rest and I headed to the last place I saw Dahlia. When I opened the door, the scent of herbs and oils wafted out toward me in a wave of warm, smokey air. There was one woman in the cabin rolling up cloth. When she saw me, she gave me a half-smile and then carried her items out into the chilled air, leaving me alone with Dahlia.

I pulled up a leather stool beside the cot where she slept like the dead under layers of fur and wool. I wasn't sure exactly what I was doing there. It wasn't as if my presence could hasten her recovery, but I remained there anyway, watching her.

It only took three breaths for me to see her as the most gorgeous creature I'd ever laid eyes on. Despite the scars and the strange tone of her skin and the ferocity in her eyes, she was beauty incarnate. She was strength, resilience, and mystery captured in the skin of a mystical creature.

Without realizing it, I lifted my hand and gently dragged my fingers down her cheek where the scar I'd given her marked her cool skin.

It made her mine.

What the fuck was wrong with me? My heart flipped in my chest, making me pause. Warmth flooded my veins and I pulled my hand away, unnerved by the feeling, when the door to the cabin opened. I glanced over to see Meridan standing in the doorway with a fresh bowl of water. She paused at the sight of me.

"What are you doing?" she asked.

"Looking after her."

"*I'm* looking after her."

The corner of my mouth lifted. "Yes, you are."

Realizing Meridan was feeling uncomfortable with me present, I stood from the stool and took a step toward her. Her ice-white eyes looked up at me, unyielding.

"Do you truly think me a threat after I carried her back here?"

"No." Her gaze dropped for a moment to peer at Dahlia. "Not in the way you'd think."

"What does that mean?"

"Nothing," she avoided, skirting past me to put the water bowl down beside the bed.

Sighing, I headed for the door, feeling sleep clinging to the back of my eyelids.

"It might not be real, you know," she blurted out, stopping me in my tracks.

"What might not be real?"

"What you're feeling for her."

"You don't know what I'm feeling for her."

She rolled her eyes toward me as if to call me an ass. "I smell it on you. I hear it in your pulse. You humans are so revealing."

I turned toward her, taking a deep breath in preparation for the things she was about to say. By the looks of her, she was wondering if she should.

"She has been in your dreams," she said. "She has seen your deepest fears. She's been visiting your sleeping mind since you took us prisoner."

"Since when can you do that?" I raised a brow.

"Not us. Her. She ate of your flesh. You've been attached to each other since you were children. It's been a rumor that our kind can do it, but we do not often leave men alive after having a bite. So the things you are feeling, perhaps rethink them."

My chest clenched, a sense of betrayal swelling inside.

But did I ever fully trust them enough to justify feeling betrayed?

I crossed my arms over my chest and glared, jaw clenched.

"Why would you tell me this? You're putting her and you in danger by confessing something like that. If it's true, I could have your heads."

Anger coiled in my gut at the idea. To think I had protection against their words only to fall victim to an equally violating manipulation made me sick. I looked at Dahlia lying there on the cot, unmoving and vulnerable.

"I could kill you both," I said under my breath.

"I am telling you because I've watched her try," Meridan continued.

"Try what?"

"Try not to care for you."

Those words caught me off guard more than the news of her invading my sleeping thoughts.

"You're talking in circles."

"I hate it. I hate to see her head turn from me, but I am speaking the truth. I have no reason not to. I just wanted you to know because somehow she's grown affection for you. Or whatever equivalent emotion we possess. Enough that she's making stupid decisions." She lowered her eyes to the wash bowl where she was rinsing strips of cloth. "And the more she cares about you, the more she will put herself in harm's way."

I watched as she brushed the cloth over Dahlia's arm, cleaning dry blood from her skin. I knew guilt when I saw it and she was rank with it.

"What happened out there?" I asked.

"What always happens. She put herself between me and something awful. And she nearly died for it. And now she's proven she will do that for you." Her gaze once more lifted to mine. "I've come to find it is a curse to watch her suffer in my stead and now you may find what that feels like."

The idea of Dahlia risking her life for me was absurd, but I'd witnessed her kill two men who were a threat to me.

Or perhaps it was just another trick to chisel out a place for herself in my good graces.

"Why does she not wake? Her wounds have surely been worse," I pointed out, ignoring the anger festering inside me at Meridan's confession.

"We heal best when we sleep."

"Would she not heal faster in the water, as she did at Port Devlin?"

"Not this water. It is not hers. It's too cold."

I gave it some thought and then sighed, "What about the spring? It's warm." Her head snapped up as if just remembering the spring existed. "We'll take her on horseback."

"Why? After what I've told you?"

I stepped forward, urging Meridan to move as I scooped Dahlia up in my arms. My shoulder cried out at the movement, but I ignored the inconvenience with a groan.

"Because I would hear it from her mouth when she wakes," I said, walking out.

With Dahlia wrapped in a single blanket, I carried her toward the round pens. A young man was tending to the horses when I arrived, but upon seeing Dahlia in my arms, he understood what I needed and nodded. He was quick to toss a thick blanket saddle and a soft halter onto one of the mares and even helped hoist Dahlia's barely conscious form onto her back.

"Get on," I said to Meridan.

She drew back like I'd insulted her. "We do not ride."

"I'll walk the horse. All you need to do is sit, but Dahlia won't stay upright on her own."

She bit her lip, thinking. When she finally inched toward the mare, she snorted, stomping a hoof on the ground as if sensing Meridan's unease. I stroked the mare's forelock and made a few soft, hushing sounds until she calmed while the young man helped Meridan onto the horse's back. She looked awkward and stiff, but once she was distracted with Dahlia's wellbeing, she seemed to settle in. I shook the hand of the young man and walked the mare out of the pen and onto the path toward the spring.

I set a brisk pace with the mare in tow. Eventually, we reached the pool and Meridan slid off the horse like she'd been hanging on for dear life the entire ride. I pulled Dahlia down into my arms next and carried her toward the water. Meridan took the blanket off of her as I knelt to lay her down in the pool. I watched as her body sunk beneath the surface and though I knew what she was, seeing her fully submerged made me want to immediately pull her back up so she would not drown.

But I was supposed to be angry with her after what Meridan had said. Still… part of me was in denial. Perhaps it was all a lie to regrow tension between us, though I couldn't fathom why Meridan would want to do that at the expense of their safety.

"Thank you," she said softly. "I will look after her here."

"Don't thank me yet," I groused.

"What will you do when she wakes?" she said quickly, a hint of regret in her tone.

"I have not decided," I grimaced. "But pray she stays out of my head tonight."

I moved toward the horse and swung myself on her back. I knew Meridan had no use for her in my absence, so I urged her into a trot back toward the village, eager to get some space. I returned her to the round pen and to her caretaker with a nod of thanks and strolled back to my cabin. On the way, I sent a few of my men to the coast to help patrol the water in case those witches were not the only ones skulking around. If we were going to be staying longer in the village, we might as well pull our weight.

Inside my cabin, the silence should have helped me clear my head, but instead, it fed the haze. Everything Meridan had told me struck a nerve. Maybe two. Or three. Things between Dahlia and I had become such a blur and it left trails of debris in my thoughts that rattled everywhere I went.

I slumped onto the pile of furs and thick blankets that were layered on the floor for me to sleep on and stared up at the ceiling for a moment. Unable to rest my eyes, I reached for my leather folder of what now seemed like just a mess of knowledge and scribbles. I had only a couple of pieces of paper left.

I grabbed a fresh piece of charcoal, ground it to a nice tip, and began to pull threads from my memory to create one image that I was certain would haunt me to my grave. I sketched until my fingers were black and my eyes were heavy, letting my hands do the work.

Dark seas, dark fate, to the ocean we go
With a heart full of vengeance and a tale of woe.
~ The Wolf Cub

Darkness was all around me, thick and stifling like the smoke of a giant fire. At first, it was almost a relief to be surrounded by absolutely nothing. No noise. No chaos. There was a time that I thought I thrived in chaos, but deep down, I knew I eventually would seek peace.

But that darkness wasn't peace. Despite the emptiness it was trying to disguise itself as, it was full of strife. I looked down at myself to find I was dressed in my captain's attire. My heavy boots. My cotton trousers and slouchy shirt full of sweat and blood stains. I was even wearing my coat, which had once been a deep red but was now barely a dark brown.

There was… *something* in that darkness. Something unseen. I didn't know how or why, but I knew in my gut that it was large. Formidable. Something of life and death. Of sanity and madness.

Terrifying.

A great beast made of nightmares and oblivion, hungry for flesh and souls. I could not see it. I could simply feel it and it reminded me what fear was.

A shuddering breath pierced the suffocating silence and I spun, realizing ripples beneath my feet as if I were standing on water. And then I saw her. Dahlia was standing before me dressed in a thin, white dress through which I could see the silhouette of her slim yet strong form. Her heartbeat flooded the strange, hollow expanse of that wretched place. She was afraid. I was standing right in front of her and her eyes were looking somewhere beyond. Somewhere that terrified her. As if invisible arms were wrapped tightly around her, she seemed unable to move.

"Dahlia," I said.

She shivered at the sound of my voice, but still, she could not see me. I moved forward, reaching out to grab her shoulders and give her a little shake.

"Dahlia."

She screwed her eyes shut and suddenly, like she'd been freed of her bonds, she let out a whimpering breath, and her muscles gave out beneath her. I held her aloft until her eyes fluttered open and she finally looked up at me. Her lips parted as if she was about to speak before a slew of shadowy figures appeared around us like a pack of rabid dogs in search of flesh. Suddenly, Dahlia was ripped from my grasp and sucked into the darkness. I reached for her, lunging forward only to feel my foot sink into the ground.

I was in an endless body of cold, dark water with no indication of which direction was up. But there she was below me being pulled deeper into the void. I reached for her but she was too far from me and drifting farther. A flood of slimy hands rose up from the black to wrap her in their bony, webbed fingers. Blood filled the water around us in thick, wafting clouds. I swam as fast as I could, but I was getting nowhere.

And then everything changed again as if I was a rope swinging on a mast in high winds. I was flying from one disaster to the next and that time, I was in a prison cell. One I knew well because I'd been there before.

I was in Treson Harbor.

How I got there, I didn't know, but I had been stripped down to nothing but my trousers. No boots. No coat. My body ached, slouched on the stone floor of a small cell, my wrists bound to chains that coiled at my sides.

A familiar laugh echoed through the hall and it made the sour taste of bile rise in my throat. Whitton walked into my cell, his fat body shrouded in streams of moonlight bleeding through a barred window. His outfit was as meticulous as ever with threads too perfect for his character.

"You were supposed to rid the seas of singing bitches," he snorted. "Not rid it of the Widow's Smile." He clicked his tongue, pacing slowly. The sound of his heeled shoes on the stone floor made me want to cut off his feet. "All for the one woman you've been wanting to kill since you were a boy."

I tested the chains on my wrists to find they only stretched enough for my arms to lift over my head. Even if I wanted to, I would not be able to reach Whitten and wring his thick neck. I slowly stood, glaring daggers at the bastard as I came to my full height over him. He smirked, picking something out of his teeth with his fingernail. The sound of him sucking it loudly off his finger made my eyes narrow to envision all the ways I'd break the bones of his face if only he took one more step toward me.

I'd always hated the man, but now, that hate had grown into a disease and seeing him again made me murderous.

Whitton took a lantern from the wall and chuckled as he crossed the hall outside my cell and ventured into the one across from me. As the lantern light flooded the room, I noticed a body chained to the wall, hands raised above her lax and unconscious form. My lips parted, but I refrained from saying her name in front of *him*. Somehow, I felt as if he would be able to use it to do terrible things.

Just as Whitton lifted his slimy fingers to touch her cheek, more figures lurched from the shadows around him. Tall, hunched, and in a state of perpetual wetness, four xhoth closed in on Dahlia as if Whitton did not exist to them nor they to him.

I stepped forward, my heart beating against my sternum like a wild animal against the bars of a cage. My chains snapped with tension and Whitton whirled to look at me with a wheezing laugh.

"You may be Vidar Bone Heart, but even you cannot break iron chains."

He stepped away from Dahlia and hung the lantern on a wall hook as the sons put their hands all over her body.

He looked me right in the eyes as he said, "I only want the tongue. Her body is yours."

The sons hissed, their oversized eyes glowing in the darkness. One of them wrenched Dahlia's head back so hard, she was awoken by the force. Disoriented and only half-conscious, she gradually took in her surroundings. Her eyes widened with dread when she saw the xhoth hovering over her, their fingers exploring every inch of her. The thin shift she wore did little to shield against their touch.

Dahlia squirmed, testing the metal binds around her wrists. She bore her teeth, kicking and struggling only for one of the monsters to grab hold of her jaw and force her head back even further. The same beast reached deep into her mouth as she writhed in protest.

"No!" I bellowed just as he pulled back his hand and I heard a terrible, wet ripping sound.

Dahlia's noises turned to strained, agonized screams as the xhoth turned with her torn tongue in his grasp, dripping with hot blood. Whitton held out his hand and the xhoth dropped the strip of raw, bleeding meat into his palm.

"Whitton, you bastard! You know not the pain I will inflict on you," I roared.

The xhoth returned their attention to a coughing, whimpering Dahlia as Whitton turned feral and bit into the raw tongue like an animal, covering his mouth with her blood. Dahlia screamed, gurgling as blood filled her hollow mouth. The beasts ripped her from the wall and threw her to the ground before me. A red pool formed beneath her mouth when she rolled to her stomach to spit it up.

"We break body," one xhoth said, his voice just as unnerving and grotesque as I remembered it.

"Then father break mind," another said.

In the corner, Whitton was now crouched over his gory meal, tearing the tongue to shreds between his blunt teeth.

"What the fuck?" I rasped.

Dahlia was crawling forward, blood continuously gushing from her mouth. I tried to get to her, but my irons kept me back and I couldn't help shouting in desperation. Two of the xhoth grabbed hold of her ankles and dragged her back so that another one could rip into her dress. He tore it right down the middle and sunk on top of her, pinning her body to the floor as she screamed.

A coward would have turned away. I was no coward. I pulled on my chains until my wrists were bloody and ground to the bone. Until I'd stripped the skin from my hands, but still I could not get to her. I watched as they violated her. Sadistically. Aggressively. It was only when Whitton appeared in front of me, his face covered in blood and pieces of Dahlia's shorn tongue between his teeth. He had but a tiny piece left and he quickly grasped my hair, shoving the bite down my throat with a stream of boisterous, infuriating laughter spilling from his mouth.

The moment I felt it slide down into my stomach, my mind imploded with fury and madness. I tugged once more on my binds and felt my arms break free. I rushed at Whitton and took hold of his fat throat, digging into him with my fingers until his flesh gave. Blood spurted from his neck as I drove him up against the wall. I slammed his head back. Once. Twice. Again and again, I smashed his skull into the stone until it no longer made a thumping sound, but a noise akin to tossing a slab of meat onto a stone cutting table. His body slumped against me and I stepped away with disgust, my vision red.

Pivoting, I saw Dahlia straddling one of the hissing beasts. The others lay dead around her, their insides on the outside as she continually jammed a sharp piece of metal into the corps's chest. She was covered in blood. In dirt. In soot. She was an animal.

I moved toward her, grabbing her arms before she could bring the shard down on the xhoth again. She jerked around to look at me, her eyes red and swollen, but she did not truly see me. She was panting, her face awash with blood.

And then realization dawned and she quickly got to her feet to embrace me. I would have embraced her back. In that hellish place, I wanted to.

Only she couldn't. The darkness swallowed us and tore us apart like the current of the ocean on a stormy day. Then everything fell quiet and still as if I'd returned to that nothingness from which it all began.

Dahlia's screams faded into a dense silence and the pain on my skinned wrists ebbed, leaving me feeling empty and weightless… until I opened my eyes and saw the wooden thatches of my hut above me. A thin layer of sticky sweat made my shirt cling to my chest as I rose up from my bedding to find I had returned to what now seemed a forgiving reality.

Taking in a few deep breaths, I came to my senses. The horrors in the dream faded and what I felt for Dahlia there transformed. She was in my head, just as Meridan said she had been many times. How many times had she invaded my sleep without me knowing? How much of what I was feeling was by design?

I pressed the heels of my palms into my eyes and groaned.

I had been a fool.

Empty silence may greet you in death
But in life, memories never leave you
~ Hugh Teller

I burst from the warm water with a gasp, my body trembling with memories of the son's slimy hands on me. In me. The dream was a horrid one and I felt it all as if I were there. I'd stumbled once more into a nightmare that wasn't mine and found myself the subject of torture. Torture at the hands of the things I'd been running from my whole life and a fat man in a gaudy blue outfit. The rage I felt at seeing him devour my tongue as if he was better than the sirens he plucked them from ate a hole in my chest.

But the sons. They were my nightmare, not his.

None of it made sense, but it didn't have to. Dreams didn't often build themselves with plain weaves. They were crooked and askew and that particular one was a deformed disaster of tangled webs. A hybrid of two people's twisted minds, I suspected.

I felt sick as I moved my still attached tongue in my mouth. When I had opened my eyes to see the sons standing over me, jeering with their jagged, crooked teeth, I wished for death instead. My greatest fear was being used, tattered, and emptied out by their sadistic hands and there I was, their fingers down my throat, wishing it would all end.

I waded toward the edge of the pool, looking around at my surroundings. I was alone, from what I could see.

My heart was racing, sending blood through me so fast it was almost painful. My mind should not have gone immediately to Vidar, but it did. He'd been screaming my name as the sons ripped into me. He'd been fighting thick chains trying to intervene.

And I vaguely recalled him meeting me at the water's edge and carrying me into the village when I returned with Ligeia's head.

And now I had found myself in his nightmare where he was unable to save me.

On a rock, I found a bundle of thin blankets and a cotton dress. I took it and slid it over my wet body, loosely tying the laces over my breasts. Looking around again, I tried to remember how I got to the spring.

A pair of urgent footsteps drew my attention. I looked over my shoulder just as Meridan slid around the corner, nearly slipping on the slick stone. When she saw me, she blinked as if surprised to see me awake.

"You must run," she said.

"Why?"

"Vidar is coming. I told him about the dreams."

"You what? Why?"

"I have not been myself. I have been foolish. I see the way you look at him and I wanted it to stop. I—"

She ceased talking when the heavy thrum of hooves could be heard drawing closer to the spring. I stepped around the stone wall to see Vidar just up the path on horseback, galloping across the packed mud. The moment I met his eyes, I could see the tension in them. Instantly, I wanted to shout at him. I wanted to explain myself and the way things had changed since I first set foot on the Rose, but seeing that great beast hurtling toward me made me rethink that.

"Dahlia, run," Meridan urged.

"He will hear me out," I said, trying to convince myself more than her.

"You cannot risk it. You've only just healed."

She pushed me away from the spring and I turned to her. "Where will you go?"

"It doesn't matter. Just go!"

She pushed me again and I stumbled out into the open as Vidar careened up to the spring, pulling the horse to a skidding stop. I spun around and took off toward the trees. Not out of fear. Out of a need to survive long enough to explain.

"Vidar, don't!" I heard Meridan shout.

"Stay out of this!" he roared.

I looked back long enough to see that Meridan was safe. I saw Vidar leaping off the horse and sprinting toward me. I couldn't even tell if he had his weapons. I just kept going, hoping whatever position we found ourselves in next would be one that would allow me to speak.

The trees were thick and tall the further I ran. I was barefoot and the stones and frosted ground hit the soles of my feet like glass.

"Dahlia!" Vidar bellowed. "Stop!"

As if I was going to suddenly start doing as he said. I leapt over logs and rocks and ducked under snow-salted branches trying to gain enough distance to gather my thoughts. But Vidar was fast. Outrunning him would not work. Not when he was born with legs and I was born with a fin.

I reached a small clearing covered in yellowed grass and patches of snow. In the middle was a thick, fallen log lying as high as my hip. I jumped over it and turned to face Vidar once something—anything— was between us. I saw him race into the clearing and slide to a halt on the other side of the log, his eyes glaring daggers at me.

"Stop running," he panted.

I shook my head in defiance. "Stop chasing."

He moved to one side and I moved to the other, keeping my distance.

"It's true, then" he muttered, regarding me like I was a stranger.

I shook my head, but did not say anything. I couldn't deny his accusation, as vague as it was. I knew exactly what he was talking about. Pressing my lips together, I straightened my shoulders and fortified my thoughts.

"How long?" Vidar said, stepping toward the log. I backstepped, ready to take off again.

I was not accustomed to running, but I'd made it so far with him. A part of me didn't want to ruin that. If I didn't run, I would have to fight and one of us would perish in that confrontation. I knew it.

"How long?" he barked. "Since we were children or since I brought you onto my ship?"

"It doesn't matter."

"It matters to me."

"I didn't know I could."

"Then how did you?"

"The first night on the Rose, I slipped into your dreams by accident," I shrugged.

"And then?"

"And then…" I raised my eyes to meet his, steeling myself. "And then I decided to use our twisted bond to manipulate you since my song could not."

Vidar's lip twitched. I could see the muscles in his neck and shoulders tighten. He lunged for the log and bounded over it. I nearly tripped over myself backing away, but I managed to slip away from Vidar's outstretched hand. I took off again, searching for an even path to run on, but the woods only looked thicker moving forward. So, I just ran with no destination in mind. I stumbled and Vidar crashed into me, his arms coiling around my body. He slammed me against a tree, his forearm pressing against my back while he twisted my arm behind me with his other hand.

"You've been toying with me the whole time," he breathed harshly against my ear.

"Now you know," I said through my teeth. "I have been in your head, even if you've woken every morning remembering nothing of the dreams we've shared."

"If ever there was a part of me that wanted to trust you—"

"I am a siren! My existence is the result of violence and hatred and I am nothing more than a monster. You knew it the first moment you saw me."

He shoved off of me, allowing me to turn and face him.

"Was it your plan to convince me otherwise then? With the girls? By saving David? Was it all part of this morbid fucking dance of ours?"

"Would you be surprised? I am an outcast. Your ship was the safest place to be. I needed to make sure it stayed that way."

A flash of sorrow burned behind Vidar's rage before he cleansed it with the flames of his disappointment.

"And Uther? Laurence? All those men who betrayed me. The men I *killed*. Did you play a part in that?"

I winced with surprise. "No. That was Ligeia. I thought all of your men were with silentiums."

"I was and you found a way to get in my head."

"Because I've tasted you!" I shoved him angrily, appalled that he suspected it was me behind his men's uprising.

Although, who I was only weeks ago would have enjoyed seeing his men try to kill him.

"We are bonded because of what happened on that island when we were children. And I used it against you. I wanted to destroy you from the inside out since I could not do it any other way. That's all I've ever wanted. I have wanted you dead, Vidar."

"Then prove it and kill me," he said. "You say you invaded my dreams to manipulate me, then be done with it and take your revenge, Dahlia. Prove you are the same kind of monster I have made a living off hunting and we will end each other, here, tonight." He moved in closer and I stiffened. "Or admit what you've been too afraid to tell me since that night in Port Devlin."

My heart hammered in my chest. My lip trembled and I could feel the cold around me fighting to snuff out what little warmth I had left in me. I felt Vidar's gaze searing into me, forcing truths from me that would both wound and liberate my soul.

"I am a devil," I forced out, the words bitter on my tongue. "I am a killer. A beast. Trusting me would be suicide."

"Lies."

"Believing I am more than my mother will leave you wanting."

Every word I spoke was sour bile on my tongue because I knew it was not entirely true. I was a killer, but I knew that wasn't all I was.

He thrust me back against the tree again, raising his chin with disappointment. I could see his nostrils flaring as he breathed like he longed to shout and curse at me, but he didn't. I spun to move away when he suddenly braced his hand against the trunk, blocking my path. I stiffened, pressing myself against the pine and preparing for a fight when he pulled a knife from his leather bracer and handed it to me, handle first. I glimpsed it warily, narrowing my eyes.

"Go on, then," he said. "Cut it out."

My gaze flashed to his in disbelief. A deep "v" plunged down his shirt where loose laces barely kept it together. I could see his jagged scar stretched over his sternum, beautiful and gnarly.

"What?" I spoke.

"You speak as if you're just as vile as the rest. So, slice me open, take the thing that is keeping you from invading my waking mind, and do what you claim you're built for. Cut it out, Dahlia. Take my free will as your mother once did. Kill me, if that's your wish. There is no reason to keep me alive, after all. The sons won't find you here. Perhaps you were pretending all along to care for the girls just so I would bring you here. Is that it?"

When I did not take the blade, Vidar stepped back and turned it toward himself, pressing the tip into this already scarred skin. I watched it sink in and with nothing more than a stifled groan, he sliced upward.

"Vidar, stop," I hissed. "You've gone mad."

"Was that not your intention? To drive me mad?"

He clenched his jaw with a low growl as he dug into the shallow wound with the knife's tip and a small, bronze pendant slid free, bloodied and warm. Crimson wept down the groove of his hard chest and stained his shirt, but he ignored the mess he'd made.

I stared wide-eyed at his chest when Vidar tossed the little pendant at me without a care and then threw the knife to the ground. The blade lodged in the grass, standing upright. I caught the pendant in my hands and stared at the seemingly worthless piece of metal. Such a tiny thing and without it, he was without armor.

"You're a fool," I whispered.

He raised his arms up in presentation and cocked his head. "I'm without a shield. The boy in the cage who killed your mother has no silentium to protect him. No men to pull their guns. No bronze blade to slit your throat. What will you do now?"

The puzzle pieces were trying to align, but they wouldn't snap into place. My mind was in pieces and trying to think of an answer to that question had me feeling crazed and almost panicked. I screwed my eyes shut and shook my head.

"Do not ask me that."

"You can't do it. Why, Dahlia?"

"Stop it."

"Here I stand, alive. I thought you were a killer. I thought it was in your nature."

"And I thought you would have killed me before you let it get this far!" I paced backward, raking my hands through my hair. "The plan was simple. I was to manipulate you into feeling something for me. I needed you to not kill me before I could kill you, but I needed your ship to stay away from the sons and to know the girls were safe. That much has never been a lie. I peeked inside your soul, looking for the softest parts. The parts I could use. All you had to do was care for me in the end so I could win this stupid game." I took a breath to let my words sink in, for me and for Vidar. "And all I had to do was not feel something for you in return. I failed at that, as I've failed at so many other things.

I feel too much for you, Vidar. My heart aches for you, my greatest tormentor, and it is ripping me apart, a fact you enjoy, no doubt."

Tears stung my eyes and blurred the image of his face. I tried to keep them from falling, but they, like so many other things, were beyond my control. They soaked my cheeks, sapping the strength from my limbs. My walls had crumbled. I had surrendered to something I never wanted to surrender to and I felt the weight of it pulling me down.

"I walked in your dreams and found myself weakened by you yet again."

Slowly, his expression went lax as if some burdensome weight had been lifted away. It confused me. I expected to see ire. Disdain.

"That dream—that nightmare—I don't even know whose it was," I admitted. "I've not been able to tell for a while. It pains me to realize how many fears we share. How many weaknesses. We are so similarly broken that I cannot distinguish one nightmare from the next and it's turned everything upside down. In trying to twist and bend you, you've twisted and bent me and you didn't even know you were doing it."

Rather than speak, Vidar just stared at me, his chest bleeding and his heart beating so loudly, it drowned out my own. I didn't know what I expected him to say.

I never thought my heart could ache without being pierced by a man's blade, but Vidar was proving me wrong.

Unable to take the weight of his stare any longer, I pivoted and started to walk away.

"So, you'll run," he said after me. "I think you are many things, but never have I thought you a coward."

I stopped, balling my hands into fists. I could feel my fangs aching and my heart thundering against my ribs. Frustration and need clashed inside me and created something monstrous. Something I didn't know how to tame.

I turned toward him again, my eyes darkening. I could see his warmth. The ripple of his pulse in the air. I could see it because I was a predator, but instead of hungering for his flesh, I hungered for his touch. My insides burned to feel him. To taste him. My instincts screamed at me to tear him apart and resisting the primal voices in my head was driving me insane.

But… it was almost thrilling, too.

I walked toward him, narrowing my eyes as my hands shoved against his shoulders. He stumbled backward, hitting another thick tree. The impact made him grunt. Taking a deep breath, I caught the tantalizing scent of his blood and peered down at the red stream coming from his chest.

"Do not forget what I am, Bone Heart," I hissed. "Not when you are so rash, you tempt my impulses. I will show you how soft your heart truly is."

I threw the silentium pendant at him as I moved forward.

"I have not forgotten what you are, Dahlia. It's who you are that intrigues me. No. It's more than that. Perhaps I am damning myself for saying it, but you've captured me. Whether it was with your hypnotic dreams or not. I am a traitor to myself for admitting it."

His words took me aback. My body just kept yearning to be near him when I should have kept running. My heart missed a beat and I remembered how good it felt to kiss him. I wanted to feel that again. I wanted that bliss over the pain and violence that plagued me. Over the hate and anger. Over all the things that I thought made me who I was.

But a reprieve from it all was the last thing I deserved.

I was being ripped down the middle.

I turned away to make another retreat when he reached out and clutched my arm, spinning me to face him. Before I knew it, he was crushing his mouth to mine.

I wanted it so badly. I needed it, but still, I denied myself and I tried to push him away. He held fast, instead pulling me closer. His fingers bit into my thighs and he hoisted me off the ground. I struggled from his grip and landed on my back beneath him on the cold grass. Relentless, Vidar continued to kiss me, his tongue pressing into my mouth as if he'd forgotten my teeth could bite it off.

I turned my head to the side with a snarl. "Get off! You should want me dead."

He shoved his way between my legs, sliding the thin, damp skirt of my dress up my thighs. I bucked as he pressed his lips once more to mine. His tongue darted into my mouth again and a wave of hot excitement washed through me, making my core pulse with need. I continued to fight him, sinking my teeth into his bottom lip until he bled. Vidar drew back, growling at the pain, but the sight of blood on his mouth sent another delightful flood of anticipation through my veins.

"You discover I've been assaulting your dreams and you hunger for my body instead of my death," I panted. "You truly have gone mad."

I drove my thumb against his shoulder where I knew he'd been shot. Vidar roared and sat up on his haunches, out of my reach. Blood blossomed on the fabric of his shirt where I'd irritated the wound, but he did not relent. He grabbed my knees and drew me against him until he was once more pressed between my legs. Heat fluttered through me at the sight of him covered in his own blood. Yet, he was still overpowering me.

His strength over me was thrilling. So thrilling I lost myself in trying to test it.

I reached for the fallen knife, driving it toward Vidar's ribs. He caught my wrist, slamming it down and pinning it above my head.

"You cannot fool me, Dahlia. I do not even believe you're fooling yourself."

By Lune, the way his cock hardened against me in our struggles made me ravenous. I pressed my heels into the ground and lifted my hips to meet him. His other hand collared my throat and squeezed, trapping me in place.

"I'm done dancing with you," he said against my mouth. He gripped me tighter until I could not breathe. "It is you I crave."

He ground his hips against me, stroking his swelling desire between my legs. Then he released the pressure on my neck and I gasped, letting my breath out on a moan. More tears gathered in my eyes as I lifted my head, licking my tongue across his bleeding lip to get another taste of him.

"Then lay claim to me, Vidar," I said, breathless. "Or something else will."

What that something else was had haunted me since birth and it could not be explained as one thing. The sons and the madness they wrought. The idea that I might one day want to end it all against the tip of my blade and be the coward so many thought I was. The dread of being alone when I had never truly wanted to be. It all clashed together into a dark, empty creature that had been clinging to my back my whole life like a parasite, feeding off my soul.

But Vidar silenced that creature. When we were fighting. When we were kissing or fucking. When we were wondering how to end one another. He stole my thoughts from it all and he blinded me to the things I did not want to carry anymore.

Tears spilled over onto my cheeks and I trembled, savoring the taste of the man—the hunter—who'd twisted me into such a mess. I did not want his mercy. Perhaps I never had. I wanted his ruthlessness and his brutality.

I ground myself against him, lifting my head to take him in another kiss and he reciprocated with vigorous need. He released my wrist and in turn, I released the knife, using my freedom to wrap my arms around him as he forced a hand between my legs.

I was wet with anticipation, a detail that did not escape him as he parted my lower lips and stroked me. I twitched at the shock of pleasure and tore at Vidar's shirt, searching for bare skin. When I found it, I couldn't help myself. I was ravenous, dragging my nails against the flesh of his arms until I felt him hiss at the pain.

He forced two fingers into my heat and I gasped, my head falling back and breaking our kiss.

"Tell me now what it is you want," he rasped. "Do you want to run? Do you want to kill me and be done with it?"

"I want you," I confessed. "Against all reason, I want you."

His mouth moved to my neck as he thrust his fingers into me again. Impatient, I sunk my teeth into his shoulder, nearly breaking the skin. When he drew back, I rolled him off of me and moved quickly over him, straddling his hips. My loose dress slouched off one shoulder as I sat up astride him. Seeing him beneath me woke something I did not know was there and a primal, possessive beast roused from within. I pressed my hands to his chest and curled my fingers, my nails biting into his skin. Vidar groaned through his teeth, his hands grasping my hips.

"You are mine," I muttered. "You know you are."

I shimmied down enough so that I could unlace his pants and reached inside, exposing the thick, hard length of him. I wanted nothing more than to put him in my mouth and suck him to completion, but I recalled what he said to me in the pool. Looking up, I caught him staring at me with a brow raised. Teasingly, keeping my eyes locked on his, I licked a slow, torturous trail along his cock before moving myself over him again and poising my entrance against his tip. Vidar, hands on my hips, watched himself disappear as I sunk down on his length.

I hungered for the stretch. For the sense of fullness. For *him*. We both moaned when he was fully seated inside me and I began to move, trying to savor the sensation. Vidar, now the impatient one, reached up and grabbed the back of my neck, pulling me down to him. Our lips met and he locked me in his arms as he pumped his hips upward. Harder. Faster. When our mouths parted, I was sobbing, my body burning with desire. Vidar clutched at my dress, pulling the whole thing over my head. Once my breasts were free, he was quick to lay claim to one with his mouth. His teeth closed over my nipple and I cried out, jolts of pain and pleasure blossoming inside me.

Vidar, thirsting for control, rolled me onto my back and thrust into me without restraint. Every rock of his hips drove him painfully deeper, but I welcomed the agony. The intensity. It made everything else disappear. I wrapped my legs around him, clutching him tightly as he ravaged and claimed me. When I felt that edge coming, I began to speak in tones I hadn't used in a long time. Tones that I knew Vidar would sense despite that he could not understand the words.

He drew back to look at me, slowing his rhythm as he took my throat again in his grip.

"What are you doing?" he said.

I placed my hand on his wrist but did not fight him. "My pleasure will be yours," I breathed. "And yours will be mine."

"What are you saying?"

"Words you need not fear. Please. Give us this."

He narrowed his eyes, suspicious, but relented, continuing to rock into me with renewed force. And I continued to speak in hushed, strained tenors, words that opened a window through which we could both see the other. *Feel* the other. Our pleasure and pain and desire married in that moment.

"Harder," I breathed.

He seized both of my wrists, lifting them over my head as he thrust, the force of his body driving my back roughly against the ground. I could hardly breathe. My mouth was agape but soundless. And then the wave came rushing forth until I felt myself descending over that sharp ledge into complete bliss. The knots unraveled inside me, letting all the pieces fall into place. I choked on my cries as I came and as if in unison, I felt Vidar's muscles go taut and he too was riding our climax. My vision blurred and every bone and muscle and nerve in my body shivered with release.

Vidar continued to thrust into me, torturing us both as we came. Liquid heat spilled inside me, claiming my body. My soul. It seemed unending. There was nothing outside of us. I'd lost my breath in the chaos of it and when the perfect assault finally ebbed, I was a boneless, spent mass beneath the weight of Vidar's body. He collapsed on top of me, his breathing labored. Our bodies were slick with blood and sweat and the air filled with our combined scents.

"Fuck," Vidar breathed against my ear.

His cock was still inside me. Neither of us wanted to move and were content savoring the serenity that followed. Our hearts slammed against each other, flooding my ears with their frantic cadence. I turned my head toward Vidar's ear where Collin's pistol had torn the cartilage. I breathed against it, my lips whispering across his lobe.

Something was balancing on the tip of my tongue, wanting to be said, but I wondered again if it was true. If it was the right time. If it would ever be the right time. He was without his silentium and I could command so many things from him.

But all I wanted to command was that he be mine.

Because deep down I knew—I'd always known…

Vidar Woelfson *was* mine.

We are both whole and broken
When we find we love something we cannot have
~ Rich are the Broken

Morning was teasing the horizon when Vidar and I trekked back to the spring. Grazing on the plant life around the pool was the giant beast he rode in on. The horse. The animal was large with hooves that could crush a skull, but it was beautiful with a soft, gray coat that matched the season of storms. I paused as we approached, staring at it as Vidar grabbed the ropes that were draped over its thick neck.

"Come," he urged, holding out his hand to me.

I cautiously approached, my heart beginning to race when the animal lifted its large head. It snorted, shaking out the coarse hair that grew down the ridge of its neck and I tensed.

"Have you never seen a horse before?" Vidar asked.

"From afar," I said, watching the horse's black eyes take me in.

He beckoned me forward again and hesitantly, I stepped toward the creature. Vidar reached out and took my hand, pulling me even closer.

The horse bobbed its head again with another snort, stomping one of its solid feet into the ground.

"Shh, girl," Vidar hushed, his voice calm and soothing.

I pulled my hand from him, nervous. It wasn't often that I shied from anything that could kill me, but I'd always wanted to see a horse up close. Ever since I was young. Watching my presence spook her made me wonder what she saw in me. A predator? A fiend?

Vidar stroked the horse's long muzzle a few times, steadying its nervous movements until it stilled again. And then he looked at me, gesturing for me to approach.

"She's afraid of me," I muttered.

"Show her she doesn't have to be," he said, once more holding out his hand to me.

I inched forward and slowly, Vidar raised my hand toward the animal and pressed it flat against her muscular neck. I felt her skin twitch beneath my fingers. Felt the fiery heat of her body. Her strong pulse soared under my touch, powerful and alert.

"I never imagined I would touch one," I admitted. "I've seen wild ones on the islands. I used to watch them run when I was young. It amazed me that they could move so fast."

I could see Vidar staring at me in my peripheral and slowly panned my gaze toward his. Something was on his mind, but I couldn't tell what it was. His hand remained pressed over the top of mine, his thumb stroking my knuckles.

"They used to be my favorite as a boy," he said, releasing me. "So? Are you ready to ride her?"

My eyes widened at the prospect. I knew men rode the giant animals, but it amazed me that he even offered. Smirking, Vidar grabbed a thick tuft of the mare's mane and leapt up onto her back with very little effort. He situated himself astride her, adjusting the thin ropes in his hand that wrapped around her long muzzle.

"I learned to ride on the fiercest of them," he continued, offering me his hand.

My heart was doing somersaults when I gripped him and he hoisted me up onto the horse behind him. It was far off the ground and as she sidestepped, I could feel every muscle move beneath me. Every breath coursing through her giant lungs vibrated across her body. I wrapped my arms around Vidar's waist and held onto him, certain the animal would throw us off of her, but she didn't. Vidar clicked his tongue, tapping her ribs with his heels, and she trudged forward.

"His name was Dawn," he continued. "He hated saddles, so I often rode without."

"That such a strong creature lets men ride it is fascinating."

"They don't all let men ride them. And I regret that defiance is often met with cruelty."

"As it is with all things," I said with regret. "Sometimes giving up is worse than the punishment, though."

I nuzzled against his back and the warmth he provided as we rode back toward the village. My limbs were frozen and my body ached, but none of it mattered. My nerves savored the echoes of how Vidar felt inside me. The way he claimed me and commanded me and pushed away the darkness.

Nothing had ever been able to do that. Not even for fleeting moments.

I rested my cheek against his shoulder and closed my eyes, finding that I didn't want to be without the bastard. Some pathetic, sad, weak part of me wanted him. Needed him. I locked my fingers together against his stomach, listening to the gentle thrum of his heartbeat and the rhythm of the horse's gait like they were a lullaby.

"We are so different, Vidar," I muttered. "How is it that I have waited more than half my life to kill you and now…" I trailed off, turning my lips into his shoulder. "I almost died trying to save you."

I felt his hand slide across my forearm to cup mine. It was affectionate and affection was something I didn't know how to digest. No one but my sisters had ever offered it in any form.

Not even my mother.

"You may yet be a monster succeeding in tearing me apart from the inside, Dahlia," Vidar said. "But the fool in me refuses to end you. So, I suppose we do have something else in common. Neither of us seems capable of destroying the other."

"I don't believe that. I believe you've destroyed me, Vidar Woelfson. Just not the way you intended."

When we returned to the village, the horse was left at the round pen, and Vidar and I continued inward. I was eager to put on a coat and some shoes. Or at least get somewhere to rest my aching feet. When we came to the longhouse, I saw Meridan sitting outside with Taupek and Mullins. She stood as soon as she spotted us, her lips parted with concern when she saw my stained and torn dress. I strode toward her, despite the stabbing pain in my soles from running across frozen branches and rocks, and cupped her face in my hands.

"Are you alright?" she whispered. "I'm sorry. It was stupid of me to tell him—"

"I'm alright," I answered softly, kissing her on the forehead. "I'm going to rest."

"With him?"

I nodded. "You must trust me. Please."

She bit the inside of her lip and then finally inclined her head. Sighing, I turned back around to see Vidar waiting for me on the path.

"Cap'n?" Mullins asked, pointing at the blood that stained his shirt over his shoulder and down the front.

We were both aware what it looked like. It looked like we had just tried to kill each other.

It wasn't too far off from what actually happened…

Vidar shrugged, grinning. "Do I look bothered, Mullins?"

I ambled toward him and his eyes flicked to my feet and the way I was trying not to seem uncomfortable. In two strides, he was next to me, lifting me into his arms so I would not have to walk anymore. I saw his jaw tighten at the pain in his shoulder, but he completely dismissed it.

"You don't have to," I said.

"Aye. Doesn't mean I don't want to."

. . .

One more lick of Vidar's expert tongue over my clit and I was stifling a cry behind my hand and squirming against his mouth. He continued to torment me with his lips until I was finally spent and shaking. Emerging from between my legs, he surged over me, bracing his hands on either side of me so he could claim my mouth in a kiss.

For two days, we shared his hut, though it prevented us from ever getting a good night's sleep. We were addicted to what happened in the woods and spent hours every night finding new ways to experience it again and again.

Vidar fell to his back atop his furs and blankets, joining me in staring up at the ceiling to catch our breath. During those two days, something swelled in my chest that had not been there before. It was heavy and almost painful, filling a hollow space that had been there my whole life. A space I thought was meant to be there, vacant.

"Will you ever let my mouth do the same for you?" I asked, distracting myself from the deeper feelings.

Vidar chuckled. It was a sound I had come to enjoy.

"With your affinity for biting off limbs? No."

I bit my lip to keep from smiling when Vidar rolled over, propping himself on an elbow over me.

"Do that again," he said.

"What?"

"Smile."

I pressed my lips together, unsure how I was supposed to just smile. I could fake it. I was good at that. But I didn't want to fake it anymore. When he lifted his hand and let his fingers whisper over my lips, it was like he was doing it for me. I felt my face warming under his touch and it spread across my mouth into a soft, subtle grin. Vidar mirrored it, his eyes roaming my face like he was seeing it for the first time.

That heavy feeling in my chest grew, making my heart skip. I stilled as Vidar's fingers continued from the corner of my mouth along the scar that stretched across my cheek. He didn't say anything, but I could practically hear his thoughts rattling inside his skull.

Slowly, I sat up beside him, a large fur tucked around me, and reached for his right hand. He hadn't taken off his leather bracer in ages. Not in front of me, at least. Gently, I pulled his hand into my lap and started to loosen the leather strings keeping it tight to his forearm. A strap buckled around his elbow and I pulled that free as well until it was loose enough to slide free. Slowly, I pulled it from his arm and the two false, leather-bound fingers with it.

I set the bracer aside and let my fingertips trail lightly down the top of his hand. Turning it over, I did the same to his palm, studying his imperfections.

That horrendous day was imprinted in my mind like a brand. His screams and mine mingled in my ears and I blinked the images away, lifting my eyes to his.

The word was there, right behind my lips, begging to be set free. One word. One, simple word.

"Sorry," I whispered, my voice quivering.

Vidar stared for a moment, processing what he'd just heard.

And there I was, truly naked in front of him. Vulnerable. The perfect prey. If he wanted to kill me at that very moment, I did not have the will to stop him.

He raised his free hand and cupped the side of my face, his thumb brushing my marred cheek.

"I'm sorry," he whispered back.

I sighed as if a burdensome weight had been expelled from me. Vidar leaned in and our lips met. But that kiss was different. It was slow and gentle. The warmth of it spread through me like sunlight on chilled skin. When we parted, I slowly licked him off my lips, savoring the taste of him.

"When I was injured, I know you stayed by my side," I said. "I could feel you there."

"I tried. Meridan had gotten a little possessive."

The thought of Meridan made my heart ache a bit. I knew her feelings toward Vidar and I knew her reservations. And now it was blatantly obvious that I cared about him.

"She is afraid I will abandon her for you," I said softly.

Vidar huffed a laugh as if the thought was too outrageous to fathom.

"She has her reasons," I clarified.

There was another bout of silence as he mulled over my words.

"Do you believe that I am a monster?" I whispered.

"I believe you are as monstrous as you've needed to be to survive this shit world we're in. And you are no more monstrous than I."

"Two monsters in a shit world sound rather formidable."

"And dangerous." He paused, tucking a strand of hair behind my ear. "There are worse creatures than us, Dahlia. Much worse."

"I know."

"I don't intend to let them live."

I studied his face, trying to find what was behind his eyes when he said those words. It was unclear at first until my mind crawled reluctantly back to our shared nightmare.

"That dream we had. Was it my nightmare or yours?" Vidar asked, as if reading my mind.

"I don't know anymore. Being overtaken by the sons is my worst fear, though."

"Maybe not being able to stop it is mine." He paused a moment and I could practically see him returning to that dream. "I felt something in the darkness. Something awful. Something not of this world."

My brows knitted. "You felt him. Akareth."

"That can't have been my nightmare."

"No. No, that's mine. Then, who was that man who ate my tongue?"

"Governor fucking Whitton," he sighed.

"You want him dead."

"I want plenty of people dead, but he holds a special place on the top of my list."

"Why?"

He perched an elbow on his raised knee. "Because he's the worst of us. He's what people are becoming. Ignorant. Entitled. Cruel."

"No worse than most, I'd wager."

"Worse in different ways. The world was simple. Violent and horrid, but simple. Men like him will complicate it. Before I left, he ordered me to stop killing and start capturing. For your tongues and for your bodies. Under the control of men like him, the brothels will be full of your kind."

"You cannot keep a siren in chains. Though I'm not surprised you are trying."

"Not me. I want no part of it. My men have been on the fence about the whole thing since we set sail."

"You wanted no part of it? Even before us? This?"

"Even before this. Don't get me wrong. It wasn't out of kindness that I disagreed. I wanted every siren dead. Outside of you and Meridan, I think I still do."

"I don't know what I want."

"You want something different. That much I know. Otherwise, all those girls would be dead."

I slid closer to him, my nails lightly caressing his bare back. The wound where Uther had shot him was healing nicely, despite my tearing the stitches in the woods.

"Perhaps we were meant to be good," I said, pressing a kiss to his shoulder. "We just missed a turn somewhere on our paths."

"You mean the turn that would have steered my father's ship away from that island?"

I held his eyes for a while, soaking in the gold flecks that littered them in the firelight.

"I am glad for it," I confessed. The words nearly broke me. "That day stripped a mask from my face that I didn't know I was wearing. Painful as it was, I do not think I could bear having to wear it my whole life."

Vidar reached up, taking my hand from his shoulder and pressing my knuckles to his lips.

"You forced my eyes open, Dahlia. I pray I never close them again."

"And? You know now that even in sleep you cannot be rid of me. The only way to sever this bond is to kill me."

"I'll not be doing that anytime soon," he said, placing his hand on a stool to stand.

The stool tipped his leather folder of papers onto the floor. I glimpsed the many charcoal drawings and canted my head at one in particular as it drifted toward me and landed near my feet. A new sketch. I reached out and picked up the parchment, staring at the face of a woman, her hair blowing in the wind. On her cheek sat a long scar which was all the indication I needed to know it was a drawing of me.

But... I was beautiful. The drawing was delicate and the lack of malice in the eyes made it look like an entirely different creature to the one I'd always envisioned myself being.

Vidar crouched to scoop up the drawings as I ogled the piece.

"Why'd you draw this?" I muttered.

"Because you haunt my dreams. Quite literally. I draw what I want to understand and I've wanted to understand you for some time."

I took another moment to soak in the picture and then slid it back into the folder for him with a sigh.

"You know a lot," I said. "But you don't know everything. The one with the blue skin. The Gorgos. They're from tropical waters. If you saw one, she was displaced. There's been a lot of infighting among my kind. More than I'd like to admit. And if the sons are truly surfacing, they could be migrating."

"There's been a lot of infighting among humans as well. There always has been. We move to avoid it and it follows. We have that in common."

I pulled my knees to my chest and looked up at him as he set the leather folder back on the stool.

"You're a product of that. Do you regret killing your sister? Your blood sister, I mean."

I shook my head with a shrug. "No less than I regret killing the men on the Cornwallis." I dragged my finger across the scar on my throat. "She gave me this. There was a time that I wanted to please her like I wanted to please my mother, but in the end, our shared blood meant so little to me." I paused for a moment, watching Vidar get dressed, and then glanced back at the folder of sketches. "That drawing. It's beautiful."

His eyes met mine and a handsome grin spread crookedly across his lips. Reaching out, he took my hand and lifted me to my feet, pulling me against him.

"Would it surprise you that much to know that you are that beautiful to me?"

"Perhaps." I ran my finger lightly down the healing cut on Vidar's chest. "I do not know how to navigate these waters. You think I'm beautiful. I believe you to be charming. With our past—"

"I don't care about the past anymore," he grumbled. "There are many names there that will be lost with time. But I'm still making my mark on this world and I won't have it be a tragic one like those before me."

"You truly think there is any other mark we can make, you and I? A siren and a pirate."

"A privateer. We're different"

"Right. Privateers kill lawfully. Then what do you call what happened to the Widow's Smile?"

"An accident."

I almost laughed. Almost.

"We accidentally murdered them all, then."

"That's a way to put it, love."

I glanced up at that word, even if he had used it casually, and that slanted grin returned to his lips.

"What? Like the sound of that, do you?"

"I—I don't know." My mouth opened and closed like a fish out of water as I attempted to form words.

"It's just a word," he groaned as he continued to dress himself. "Like lass or sweetheart."

I pulled on a pair of leather leggings and a tunic and coat, shielding myself against the cold now that Vidar wasn't pressed against me.

"I know what it is," I said, stepping past him to leave the cabin.

Vidar attempted to grab my arm and I slipped out of his grip, moving into the chill of the morning air. I folded my arms over myself, breathing in the fresh breeze and soaking in the sun. When Vidar emerged, he was in his captain's coat instead of one of the thick, fur-lined ones everyone else was wearing. I looked him up and down and furrowed my brows.

"Didn't mean to hurt your feelings," he said. "I won't say it again if it—"

"Do I look like someone so easily hurt?" I said flatly.

"Not at all."

"Why are you wearing that?"

"I am going to talk to my crew. About leaving."

"Leaving?"

He shrugged. "We were never going to stay here forever."

Of course, he wasn't. I felt foolish for being so surprised by the notion and shook my head.

"I'll tell Meridan."

Without giving him another chance to cut off my retreat, I left. I walked with the scent of him still in my lungs and the warmth of his touch fluttering across my skin.

Vidar fucking Bone Heart. The captain of the Burning Rose. Hunter of sirens and scourge of the sea. My mother's murderer. The wolf cub from the Mother's Fang. The golden-haired bastard had done it. He'd found a chink in my armor. I had heard so many human stories about it feeling good to care for someone. It was supposed to be exciting. Warm. Instead, I was afraid and it left an absolutely wretched knot deep inside.

The crew of the Rose gathered in the longhouse where Vidar divvied out jobs for everyone to prepare for departure. He tasked many of the men with getting supplies and negotiating good prices with the villagers. Not that the village was asking for much after we'd returned their girls to them.

Meridan and I stood at the back of the building, watching while I strung a thin twine string through Vidar's silentium pendant. Now that it wasn't under his skin, he would need to wear it another way.

Seeing him in his captain's garb, speaking to his men, had never captured my attention quite like that. Every single one of his remaining crewmen was watching him as if he were the only person in the room. They were loyal, even if there had been a hundred reasons for them to leave for a less dangerous life. Even if they had to watch him kill the traitors.

Glancing at Meridan, I imagined Voel and Kea being with us, but like so many others, they'd been claimed by the horrors of our ugly world too soon.

When the meeting was through, Vidar got caught up in talking with Gus and Mullins in the back corner as the rest of the crew dispersed to do their jobs. I narrowed my eyes at them, wondering what they had to talk about without the rest of the men present.

Once they finished, Vidar headed my way, but rather than stop, he passed me by and walked outside. I walked after him, confused.

"You didn't say where we're going," I pointed out. "Should that not be the first thing you decide before setting sail."

"My crew knows where we're going. We knew before we anchored here."

"Can I ask where that is?"

We wove between two cabins and he still wasn't looking at me. Irritated, I hastened my step to walk beside him.

"Vidar, you—"

Quickly, he took a step toward me, herding me toward the wall of a cabin until my back was against it.

"You can ask," he said calmly. "But it won't matter."

"And here I thought perhaps I was a part of your crew after saving your life," I said. "After not killing all of your men, despite the many chances."

"I cannot begin to thank you for everything."

"Is there another way you test your crewmen's loyalty?"

His eyes wandered.

"There is no test."

"Then it's because of what I am that you are not being honest with me."

I saw the tension in his jaw before it happened and yet I still flinched a bit when his hand came up to slam onto the wall beside my head. Anger seeped like salt on a wound into my thoughts, rotten and unwanted.

"You are angry with me? What right do you have to be—"

Both hands suddenly cupped my face and his once tense features became tortured and twisted.

"You're staying here," he said.

I blinked. "What?"

"You're not coming with me, so you don't need to know where we're going."

I reached up and ripped his hands off my face. "You dare to leave me behind after everything?"

"I am a hunter. My place is on the sea. And now new monsters have surfaced. People won't know what to do about them, hunters and fishermen alike. I'd say my job just got more lucrative."

"You think my place isn't on the sea?"

"The sons don't know you're here. These people love you. You'll be safe."

"That's not safety. That's a prison."

He took a deep breath, seeming defeated, and stepped away from me. "I'm sailing tomorrow. And you should stay. I want you to stay, Dahlia."

I stared at him, waiting for him to change his mind, but he would not relent. His mind was made up and I had no say in his decision. Part of me couldn't help but think it was his plan all along to leave me behind, whether in the sea or in an icy village. The sense of betrayal was like a jagged little stone in my gut, churning and sharp. It hurt. It hurt in a way I was not trained to withstand.

"I will do as I please," I hissed, pushing him away so I could rid myself of his presence.

When the stars fall
I will be your candle in the dark
~ Until Nothing

I stood leaning against the outer wall of the longhouse, watching as men, villagers and crewmen alike carried supplies toward the beach to load up the boat. Meridan watched me, but she and I hadn't spoken in depth about my feelings. I feared she would not enjoy the fact that I wanted to be sailing with Vidar over staying in the village.

It was a ridiculous idea. The north was frigid and unforgiving. Everything unresolved was out there at sea and I knew I would not stay long in that place. Vidar was a fool for thinking I would.

Most of the crewmen said nothing to me as they filed toward the coast to leave, but Gus, in passing, inclined his head.

"Can't say we're best mates," he said. "But you're more decent than a lot of humans I've met, I'll say that."

"You're somewhat decent yourself, Gus," I said flatly.

He limped off, groaning through his discomfort when Mullins strode up, a large sack over his shoulder. He shrugged toward us and then bowed exaggeratedly with a flare of his hand.

"Ladies," he said. "It's been a horrible pleasure."

His eyes flicked briefly to Meridan and the slight pause in his breath caught me off guard before he spun and walked away, whistling some upbeat tune. I whipped my head toward her, brow raised, but she just bobbed a shoulder, oblivious.

He favored her over me. He had since the beginning.

Vidar didn't speak to me that morning until everyone was gone and he was the only one who had yet to venture back to the Rose. Only then did he meet my eyes as he walked past, heading for the coast. I did my best to seem indifferent, but I wanted to hurt him. I wanted to make him feel something like I was feeling something, but he appeared unwavering in his choice. He looked at me, his thumbs hanging on his belt, and set his tricorn hat atop his head.

The gods had made him beautiful in their own, tormenting way and I'd never despised it so much. He didn't even speak to me and I had no words for him that were kind, so I refrained as well. Instead, I reached into the pocket of my coat and pulled out his silentium, now strung onto a necklace. I handed it to him and straightened off the wall.

"It was stupid of you to remove it," I said, turning to walk away.

"I have no shortage of stupid decisions," I heard him say under his breath.

I walked to the courtyard where a few others were gathered to say goodbye to the remaining crew. Ahnah was there and beamed when I showed up. She waltzed over to take my hand. She thought I was staying, too, and I did not dare tell her otherwise yet.

I watched from a distance as Vidar shook the hand of one of the village men and the two began walking toward the tunnel to leave. Seeing his back like that did something to me. Rage and bitterness and pain tangled and twisted in my chest where my heart was supposed to be. Once more, Vidar was causing me pain where I should not have felt any and I wanted to sprint after him and tear him to pieces for the offense. To have earned my affection only to abandon me was something I would not forget.

Again…

Once he had disappeared into the cave, my heart struck my sternum like it was trying to follow after him. Pathetic.

Ahnah squeezed my hand and I looked down at her confused little face. Her forehead was scrunched as if she was asking a question, but even when she spoke, I couldn't understand her. When she remembered her words meant nothing to me, she pointed toward the cave where last I saw Vidar's departing silhouette. Then she pointed that same finger toward me before tapping her hand on her chest.

I shook my head at her but she insisted, pulling from my grip and pointing again toward the coast. Frustrated with her implications, I turned my gaze toward Meridan, hoping for some clarity. She shrugged.

"I like it here," she said. "The water suits me."

"So?"

"But I'll not be letting you get on that ship full of filthy, loud men alone."

"I'm not—"

"Yes, you are." She stepped toward me, an exasperated tone in her voice. "He's the captain of the Rose, but he's not your captain. He can't order you around."

I could have argued, but why would I? Vidar had tried to decide for me and the mere notion was infuriating. Not only that, but I felt the emptiness creeping up inside me already and I'd only lost sight of him moments ago. I stared at that dark cave and the light that gleamed from the other end where the beach was. Taupek chuckled when Ahnah moved behind me and pushed against my backside, forcing me forward.

"I'd do what the little one says," Taupek said, groaning as she stood from a bench. "She'll be angry with you otherwise."

I balled my hands into fists, my mind whirling from one idea to the next until I finally forced it to come to a stop. And where it stopped was Vidar, the bastard.

"So?" Meridan said. "What are—"

I took off running toward the beach, my eyes burning with unshed tears as the cold wind gnawed at my cheeks. When I came to the other side of the cave, the men were still there, loading a couple crates into the boat under Vidar's instruction. I wanted to rip off his head.

I slowed to a fast walk, panting as I zeroed in on him. His back was turned, but it didn't take long for him to notice his men gawking at my approach. He spun to face me.

"No," I snarled.

"No?" he said.

I grabbed the collar of his coat and shoved him into a wall of rocks near the water. He raised his hands in surrender, wide-eyed.

"I'm not staying. Perhaps I will be safe here, but out there, you will not be. I am coming with you to hunt whatever horrors come from the deep. To kill whatever men dare threaten your crew again. They are my horrors to face, too. And against all sanity and rage, I find myself aching at the thought of you sailing away from me. I won't stay. You are the captain of that ship, but you do not command me. And I will not make the mistake again of watching you leave so you can haunt me from afar for another eighteen years."

Everyone had fallen silent. The men. Vidar. Even the wind seemed to die at my words leaving only the soft whisper of gentle waves as they lapped at the gravel. I looked up at Vidar's stunned expression, daring him to refuse me. My nails ripped into the fabric of his coat as I gripped it tighter, pressing against him.

"I have many enemies," he said.

"I have more."

The corner of his mouth twitched into a smirk, his eyes roaming my face.

"Things could get very complicated with you aboard my ship."

"More complicated than the alternative?"

"What's the alternative?"

"You leave and I'll hunt you down. Perhaps take another finger or two. Even without me by your side, your dreams will never be free of me."

His head cocked at that and he nearly laughed as if questioning whether or not it was a jest.

I could hardly tell myself.

"You truly will not stay put, will you?"

I shook my head. "You'd have to kill me."

"Have I latched myself permanently to a psychopath?"

"You've latched yourself permanently to something worse. I am not peaceful. I do not sit aside when danger is about like the Maruhk are clearly accustomed to doing. I kill and I devour. I don't belong here. You know it. Save the world from me and take me into your crew."

His lips turned up again and he dropped his hands to his sides in submission before gripping my waist and pulling me against him. Our lips met and every violent bone in my body went soft beneath that kiss. He had disarmed me with his mouth alone and I quivered under the warmth of it. That emptiness in my chest suddenly swelled once more like a sponge taking on water.

When we parted, he said, "Then get on that fucking boat."

An orchestra of howls and hoots filled the air from behind us. I turned to see the few remaining crewmen smiling as they looked on and if I could blush, I would have been.

"Ahh!" Vidar grumbled, waving a hand at his men. "Get the rest of the supplies loaded, you lazy dogs."

They laughed, continuing to load up the boat as I turned back to face him. I let out a sharp, irritated sigh.

"I don't see why you had to make this so difficult. You were liable to get hurt."

"Me? It would have been much easier if I didn't care about you, love."

I warmed at the sound of that cursed word again and blinked. Vidar saw the shift in my expression and it annoyed me that he could read me so well. He lifted a hand, letting his thumb whisper across the side of my neck.

"I mean," he said softly. "If I didn't have feelings for you."

"What?"

He paused and met my eyes, squinting. "Don't make me regret saying that."

"I don't truly know what you are to me," I said. "But I know I would kill anything, man or siren, if they touched you. What should I call that?"

"Obsession."

"That's a dangerous word."

"Aye, it is, but you and I are dangerous creatures. I think I can do with you obsessing over me. As long as I get to keep all my parts and lay you in my bed every night."

"We'll discuss where you'll be laying me, captain. The bed may get boring."

I turned to get on the boat when he grabbed my wrist and forced me to face him once more. "There's nothing to discuss. I care about you, you care about me. I did it. I found the chink in your armor."

He was mocking me. I yanked my hand away only for him to grab my other arm and haul me against him.

"Fuck it," he groaned. "I am in love with a goddamn siren," he announced to his men. "And you'll all be horrified to know, she loves me back."

For a moment, the men did not seem to understand. They were silent, gaping at us like Vidar had just spoken a foreign language. But then Mullins jumped up from the boat and tossed his hands into the air.

"Better to be loved by one than be eaten by one!" he hollered. "That's what I always say."

"You've never said that," someone voiced.

"I'll start today," Mullins shrugged. He turned his eyes on Meridan, who'd been standing quietly separated from the group. "You think I could get you to love me so I have a siren of my own?"

She winced at those words, her head tilting to one side.

"Now," Vidar said, stealing my attention. "What did I tell you?"

"To get on the fucking boat," I teased. I basked in his warm stare for a moment longer and then leaned into him, savoring his intoxicating scent. "As I feared... you have found a way past my armor. I dreamed for many years to rip out your heart and eat it. Instead, you've taken mine."

He curled his hand around the back of my neck and pulled me forward as if to kiss me and said, "You'll find I'm very possessive, Dahlia. If you say your heart is mine, I'll not be giving it back until death decides he's bored of his pursuit of me."

"Then we're done with this dance of ours. I'll protect you and you'll protect me."

"Always," he muttered, his thumb grazing the length of my scar. "All the world will know you're mine."

Before I could speak another word, his mouth was pressed to mine and all the troubles that raged around us disappeared for a brief, blissful moment. The storm would come for them, and in that moment, *we* were the storm.

The end… for now.